The Sweeney Sisters

THE
Sweeney
SISTERS

A Novel

LIAN DOLAN

WILLIAM MORROW
An Imprint of HarperCollins*Publishers*

P.S.™ is a trademark of HarperCollins Publishers.

THE SWEENEY SISTERS. Copyright © 2020 by Lian Dolan. All rights reserved. Printed in the United States of America. No part of this book may be used or reproduced in any manner whatsoever without written permission except in the case of brief quotations embodied in critical articles and reviews. For information, address HarperCollins Publishers, 195 Broadway, New York, NY 10007.

HarperCollins books may be purchased for educational, business, or sales promotional use. For information, please email the Special Markets Department at SPsales@harpercollins.com.

A hardcover edition of this book was published in 2020 by William Morrow, an imprint of HarperCollins Publishers.

FIRST WILLIAM MORROW PAPERBACK EDITION PUBLISHED 2021.

Library of Congress Cataloging-in-Publication Data has been applied for.

ISBN 978-0-06-290905-3

21 22 23 24 25   LSC   10 9 8 7 6 5 4 3 2 1

For my seven siblings

The Sweeney Sisters

Chapter

1

"Does this come in teal?"

Liza looked up from her computer and tried not to make any noise that would indicate her disdain. In the decade since she'd opened the Sweeney Jones Gallery, she'd heard them all before—*Does this come in teal? Do you have this one in a larger size? Can you find me something that goes with chocolate brown?*—questions that indicated the customer had a limited knowledge of art, but quite possibly an unlimited budget for it. These two, staring at the front of the gallery, must be empty nesters with time, money, and a few blank walls, Liza guessed. She didn't want to embarrass the tan woman in the bright yellow sundress. Or her companion, the man in the golf shirt embroidered with the company logo of a local hedge fund (Olympus? Pegasus? Icarus? They were all the same). But Liza didn't have to indulge them, either; she wasn't concerned about her Yelp rating for customer service.

As the owner of the gallery, Liza had an obligation to her artists and to her own reputation. Was Liza going to discover this generation's Basquiat painting sailboats and golden labs somewhere in coastal Connecticut? Of course not. But she wasn't managing a Pier One, either.

"I can't say that we have that exact oil in teal," Liza said, rising from behind her desk and making her way over to the couple near the entrance of the gallery. "The artist is Anna Oakland. She lives in the area and much of her work involves the natural world, capturing Long Island Sound, the marshes, the wetlands, our flora and fauna. But her gift is truly abstracting the traditional landscape or still life. This piece is a study of the dogwood trees that bloom here in May, hence the pinkness of the piece. So, no, the piece doesn't come in blue because dogwoods don't come in blue. But we have more of her work in the gallery, including several paintings of Southport Harbor. They're . . . teal-ish. You might find what you're looking for upstairs. Let me show you."

"Oh, thank you. We're visiting from Jacksonville. I mean, my husband's here for work and meetings and such . . ."

"Honey, she doesn't need our whole life story," the husband said, cutting off his wife as Liza imagined he'd done a thousand times.

"I want her to know that we're visiting but adore her little town. It's like a postcard, but better. I thought a sweet little painting in our guest bathroom would be a lovely souvenir."

Southport was a postcard to the untrained eye: two- and three-hundred-year-old historic homes, most in pristine condition with expensive paint jobs; glorious landscaping and water views; built around a charming harbor, once of importance during the time of the Revolution. Its antiques shops, art galleries, a gourmet food market, a classic pharmacy, and beloved restaurants and bars had remained impervious to chain stores and financial ups and downs. Even the fire hydrants, painted like Colonial sailors in blue jackets and tricorn hats, were Insta-perfect. From the outside, the town hadn't changed since the 1700s. Inside the pre-Revolutionary saltboxes, the Greek Revivals and the Victorians, though, it was a different story altogether.

"What a lovely idea," Liza responded, as if Lady Jacksonville had single-handedly cracked the Code of Decorative Arts. In truth, about 20 percent of Liza's business was exactly this: aspirational purchases by visitors from all over the country who found themselves smitten by what this Connecticut town promised—tradition and propriety—

fiercely protected and quietly preserved. "Where New York meets New England," as the town's website declared. It was exactly why she represented artists like Anna Oakland who could take the familiar (New England) and push it slightly forward toward the edge (New York). *And a thousand-dollar sale is a thousand-dollar sale,* Liza thought, moving confidently toward the staircase. *Not bad for a Wednesday morning.*

Liza was, as a lifelong resident of Southport who had taken several years of art history courses in college (okay, the University of Vermont and she didn't technically graduate, but *still*), an expert with ten years of experience curating a collection of tasteful contemporary oils, watercolors, lithographs, and the occasional mixed media piece that hit the sweet spot where abstract art meets interior design. She had a good eye, a deep respect for her artists, and the cultured veneer her clientele trusted. Liza understood the importance of this combination of assets.

She had been raised well and married better, at least in terms of financial stability. Her business was a success and not the tax write-off her husband, Whit, expected when he gave her a lease and seed money as a Christmas gift, thanks to his particularly large bonus that year. As Whit handed her the keys to the front door, he said, "Here's a little something to keep you busy." Liza did get busy, creating a space for art that the townspeople could point to as a sign of their impeccable taste and which she could use to establish her own identity outside of her father's well-known reputation or her husband's centuries-old local heritage.

So, no, Liza didn't have to indulge her visitors, but she also understood, after ten years in sales, that you never really knew who had money and who didn't. She'd made that mistake early in her career, judging a client by his brand of shoes and letting him walk out the door, learning later that he was a newly minted billionaire. Never again would she let her unconscious bias against cheap footwear or loud clothing cloud her business practices. Just then, her cell phone rang. The screen flashed the name "Julia Ruiz," her father's house-keeper, a title that didn't even come close to describing the services and the peace of mind she'd provided over the last two decades. Julia was more like an entire home-care agency in one: housekeeper; day nurse; cook; dog groomer; plant waterer; and life coach. She had come to work for the Sweeney family when Liza's mother was sick and never left. After Maeve died, she cared for Liza's younger sisters, Maggie and Tricia, and now, for her aging father.

Liza had been Julia's point person since day one; the two of them kept the Sweeneys on track. It was unusual for Julia to call in the middle of the workday. She usually communicated via text or fridge Post-it note. "Excuse me, please," Liza said to her new best friend, who was headed to the second floor. "I have to take this. Feel free to poke around on your own upstairs. I'll meet you in a minute."

What Liza would remember when she thought back on that phone call was the pleading in Julia's voice, so unlike her usual softly accented pragmatism, as if rushing to the big house on Willow Lane could have made a difference. Liza would remember the whoosh of panic that swept through her, giving way to complete focus, allowing her some-how to explain to the Floridians that she had to close the gallery immediately due to a family emergency.

The man in the golf shirt looked concerned. "Is there anything I can do to be of service?"

Apologizing while ushering them out of the door of Sweeney Jones, Liza reassured them, "It's nothing serious, only something that needs my attention. I understand you're leaving Southport, but please, let me get your contact information. I'll have my assistant send you photos this afternoon of some paintings that would be perfect for your guest bathroom. We'll cover the shipping as a thank-you."

While the husband handed Liza a card, the wife asked if she could let them know the paint color of the gallery door, as long as she was going to be emailing them. "This is the kind of blue I'm looking for."

"It's Benjamin Moore Kensington Blue," Liza said so automatically she startled the wife.

"Well, thank you. Honey, can you put that in your phone?" She turned to Liza with her own surprise, a warm hug that Liza accepted. "I hope everyone in your family is fine. God bless you."

"God bless you" was something that Liza could never pull off saying in a million years, but coming from the petite blonde in the yellow sundress, Liza found the sentiment comforting. It allowed her to take a deep, deep breath to steady her hands so she could lock the door of the gallery. She didn't even bother with the alarm. She'd call her assistant Emily or her Sunday saleswoman Jenny once she got to Willow Lane.

But first, Elizabeth Sweeney Jones had to call her sisters.

Chapter

❀
2

Maggie poured herself another cup of coffee, wrapped her long red hair in a bun, and wondered how much longer she should let the guy in her bed sleep. It was nearly eleven. Surely it was time for Tim to go. She had errands to run and maybe even a stop at the cheap hair place near the grocery store for a cut before that thing she was supposed to go to this weekend. What was it? A summer kickoff cocktail party? Something like that. She might even paint, and Tim's being around was not conducive to painting. Today felt like a good day and she wanted to make the most of it.

Jesus, Maggie, a line cook? she thought to herself. She knew Tim was yet another poor choice, but on the hierarchy of all the poor choices she'd made since she was about sixteen, Tim was pretty low level. It was the eight-year difference in their ages that was the biggest strike against him. He was a cook at the only decent restaurant in godforsaken Mill River, a tiny town in the western part of Connecticut where she was spending a year as an artist-in-residence, with free housing, studio space, and a few public appearances to earn her keep. The age difference would have been nothing if she were the twenty-six-year-old and he were the thirty-four-year-old because she always had fancied herself sophisticated, an old soul.

But she had put a lot of distance between herself and naive Tim in the last decade: a starter marriage at twenty-three (as her sister Liza had said, "Oh my God, sleep with the bartender, don't marry him");

several failed attempts at finishing college, one ending in a hospitalization after she'd swallowed too many pills; a short stint in LA as an actress but mainly as the live-in girlfriend of a rising and controlling director; many wild nights, several Coachellas, and one Burning Man, a period of time her sisters referred to as "Maggie Sweeney: The Lost Years"; a recent pilgrimage to India and two hundred hours of yoga teacher training that she negotiated in her breakup with Darren the director; and several bouts of depression that knocked her off her feet for weeks. Tim's two years as a ski bum at Stowe didn't really add up against all of Maggie's life experience.

He was harmless, but he had to go. Like now.

"Hey, Tim!" Maggie called out, much more like a camp counselor than the exotic older woman she played last night. "Get up! You gotta go. Now."

Her phone rang. It was Liza.

Damn, Liza was going to bug her about the two paintings she was waiting for—both commissions, both nice paydays, as Liza reminded her in a text last week. Maggie never bothered to reply because, well, she didn't feel like it. Both paintings needed work and Maggie's motivation was minimal. How many more of these pleasant, easy pieces could she turn out before her creative spirit turned to stone? Maggie used to have promise, now she had paydays. Occasionally, that demoralized her.

But she couldn't tell Liza that. Not the woman who managed a career, two high-achieving children, a husband who was never home, and their difficult father with such efficiency that she even had time for tennis lessons. Liza's gallery supported Maggie's entire life, such as it was, and without that representation, Maggie's work would never see the light of day. They both knew that to be true, although neither one ever mentioned it. This whole residency happened because Liza had forced her to apply and guaranteed by letter that Maggie Sweeney would have a high-profile show at Sweeney Jones at the end of the year. ("You have to get out of LA. Come home. We'll find a soft landing, but get away from Darren. He's not good for you," Liza had said on the phone about eighteen months ago, when Maggie had called her in the middle of the night, seeking guidance, after another huge fight with Darren about one of his on-set affairs with another Next Big Thing. As Maggie had told Liza, "They keep getting younger. I can't take it.")

Liza was right about leaving Darren, leaving LA, and getting back to familiar ground, to a place where people wore black to funerals like they were supposed to. For a few months, Maggie had been on a painting jag. Her work was joyful, filled with the colors of India and highly accessible. Or, in Liza's words, "Flying off the walls at the gallery." But the last few weeks, a familiar darkness had lingered, setting Maggie's output back a bit.

As supportive as Liza was, Maggie knew she would never really understand how Maggie could spend an entire day going through the mail, puttering around the garden, and then lying in bed scrolling through Instagram accounts of artists she admired and lifestyle influencers she loathed, unable to rally to go to the store for food, never mind her studio for a productive afternoon. Liza would never let her day slip away without accomplishing a single thing.

Maggie didn't even bother trying to convey her situation to her younger sister, Tricia, who had emerged from the womb ready to conquer the world, setting and achieving goals with astonishing success: a scholarship to prep school, early admittance to Yale and then Yale Law, completing marathons. Tricia tried to be helpful, swooping in whenever contracts needed to be written or logistics organized, but empathy wasn't really her strong suit. Maggie was the one Sweeney sister who excelled at emotional intelligence and she alone connected their father with the sisters and the rest of the world. She was the glue that held the whole family together.

Maggie's phone pinged with Liza's voicemail. Maggie ignored it. She'd call her tomorrow, maybe.

"Tim, are you up? I need to leave, so you need to leave." Chances were, Maggie wasn't leaving, but Tim definitely needed to leave. The phone rang again. Again, it was Liza. Reluctantly, Maggie answered. "Hey. Sorry to miss your first call. Running in from the studio. What's up?"

When Tim did emerge from the bedroom, Maggie was on the front porch, working as hard as she could not to lose it and holding the cup of coffee she'd made for Tim. "I hope you take milk," she said.

"Are you okay?"

"I'm not okay. My father . . ." Maggie knew that if she started crying, she wouldn't stop for a while. "My sister called. My father died."

"Oh, dude. I'm so sorry." Tim, in jeans and a T-shirt that smelled like French fries, slipped into his Vans before hugging Maggie. He pulled away quickly. This wasn't what he'd bargained for last night at the bar when they flirted over darts. Still, he asked, "Do you need anything?"

"Can you watch my cat? I have to go home for a few days. The key's under the mat on the back porch."

"Sure. Text me deets." Tim climbed into his truck and gave Maggie a wave. Today, it suited them both that Tim was young and clueless.

As he pulled away, Mary Magdalene Sweeney put her head in her hands and sobbed.

Tricia had eight minutes between meetings, so she took to the stairwell. Up, down, up, down between the twenty-third and twenty-fifth floors of her midtown office building, home to the law firm of Kingsley, Maxwell & Traub. She did most of her best thinking between her office on twenty-three and the conference rooms on twenty-five. She could turn off the soundtrack of the modern workplace, the beeping and pinging of phones, computers, devices everywhere, and concentrate on the regulated reverb of her footsteps on the metal. Her daily thirty minutes of ascending and descending, stolen in eight-minute increments, was as close as Tricia would ever get to the meditation classes that had sprung up all over Manhattan.

Somedays, it was the only exercise she got. This depressed her, considering at one time she was running seventy miles a week with her college cross-country team. Now she was lucky to do the three-mile loop around the reservoir in Central Park after she got home from work at night, so to the stairwell she went when she had a few extra minutes, tracking her steps like billable hours. Tricia liked to keep track of everything in her life.

When the phone rang, she cursed. It was Liza and she knew she should take it, but the reception was sketchy in the stairwell. She owed her a call. Normally, she was a conscientious communicator, but this class action suit had taken over her life and she'd slipped into some bad habits, like blowing off friends and family, assuming that they'd all understand the life of a young lawyer. Guilt got her and she answered the call, knowing it would be impossible to carry on a conversation, and spoke before Liza could get a word in. "Hey, let me get to a place where we can talk. Hold on." Tricia sprinted up the steps two by two and slipped into the hallway on twenty-four, home to the admin staff and law library. The hallway was quiet. Breathing heavily, she asked, "Hey, can you hear me now?"

"Yes, I can hear you." Those were the last words Liza spoke that were intelligible for a few minutes. Between Liza's sobs and her strangled sentences as she choked back tears, Tricia put together the enormity of the situation. Clearly Liza had been composed until she heard Tricia's voice. Poor Liza. And poor Julia. How awful for both of them.

Tricia knew what she had to do. Liza was stretched so thin there in Southport handling the arrangements, a euphemism for all the awful details of death, that she couldn't handle any of the larger issues that needed to be handled, like informing her father's colleagues. Maggie, who was usually a minor mess, would be a complete mess for days, if not weeks. Balance and focus were always Tricia's strengths. She was the one Sweeney sister who could be both the backbone and the emotional core at this juncture and she knew she had to hold the whole operation together.

"I'll call Cap. Does he know?" A muffled "yes" came back. It didn't surprise Tricia that Liza had already called Cap, her father's friend and lawyer. It was the right thing to do. "We'll have to figure out the press piece. I'll follow up with Cap. Don't worry about that. You just do what you need to do there in terms of state procedure." The rest of the call was brief and clinical, ending with Tricia promising, "I'll get there as soon as I can. Text me if you want backup on any decisions. We got this."

Tricia took the stairs back down to her desk. It took her about seventeen minutes to make the calls she needed to make, send the emails that had to be sent, and reschedule the meetings that needed to be rescheduled. She had two brief conversations with fellow associates, imparting information with speed and accuracy. Tricia thought about all those training runs, those miserable, hot steamy miles and hills in August in the Berkshires with the team. Or the frigid early-morning speed workouts in January on the track in New Haven. All this time, she'd thought it was about running, but it was really about preparing her for the last seventeen minutes and the next few hours of pain, when she had to remain focused long enough to leave work, go to her apartment and pack a few things, and then get on the train out to Southport. This was the moment where developing all that endurance and a high pain threshold finally paid off.

"Can I see Don? It's an emergency," Tricia asked Danette, the executive assistant to the managing partner she was working for, a new hire named Don Donaldson, a name Tricia and her fellow associates at KMT had already dissected over drinks at P. J. Clarke's. (*How lazy do your parents have to be to not even bother to think up a first name different than your last name? Had they given up on parenting seconds after the birth?*) Don had been a "big hire," lured over from another firm with a giant signing bonus and immediately put on the partner track because of his impressive client list and his overall asshole behavior that seemed to be rewarded at every turn in New York City. Tricia was not a fan, but that didn't mean she hadn't worked her hardest for him over the last nine months. *Do not cry in front of this guy,* she thought to herself as he waved her into his office.

"Don, I'm going to need a few days off. I got a call. My father . . ." Tricia took a deep breath. "My father died this morning. I need to go home."

"Oh, Sweeney, I'm sorry to hear that. Are you okay?" It was the most personal question he'd ever asked her, except for the time he chest-bumped her at a Legal League softball game and then asked if her breasts were fake. "I mean, you're so skinny. How could those be real? Am I right?" Don had asked the small crowd, seeking validation for his lax bro behavior.

"It was unexpected," Tricia responded now.

Don nodded like he cared, but then it was back to business. "So, are you all covered then for your work? I mean, obviously you should be with your family, but you're covered, right?" He was referring to the class action workplace discrimination suit filed by women at one of the Big Five automakers. Kingsley, Maxwell & Traub represented the automaker. He knew Tricia's work product was invaluable to the case; plus, it didn't hurt that she was a woman. "I mean, the class just certified, this is crunch time."

Prick. "Yes, all set. I've cc'd you and Danette on several emails detailing what I was working on. Penny Caruso and Ryan Lee will take over on point on discovery. I'll keep in touch with them."

"Great. Well, good luck!" Don said it like Tricia was embarking on a slightly exotic honeymoon to Costa Rica, not a Metro-North train ride to bury her father. Maybe he sensed how cold his send-off sounded because he followed up with something more human. "What did your old man do, Sweeney? Lawyer?"

Never. "My father was a writer." There it was, the past tense. *My father was a writer.*

"Oh yeah? Did he write anything I might have heard of?"

Because that's the mark of a worthwhile career, whether or not Don Donaldson has heard of you, Tricia thought. "My father was William Sweeney."

The light dawned in his tired eyes. "*The* William Sweeney? Like *Never Not Nothing* William Sweeney? And that Vietnam book? What was it called? Um, *Bitter Fruit.* That William Sweeney?"

There was that Dartmouth education emerging from the swamp of Don Donaldson's normal workplace interaction. *Yes, Don, not only have you heard of William Sweeney, he probably blew your mind during junior year English at Hotchkiss or during Senior Seminar in Hanover. You and millions of other readers like yourself—smart, smug, know-it-all white guys who got your literary comeuppance, courtesy of a William Sweeney classic. You thought you were the hero in your own life, but thanks to William Sweeney, you discovered you were just some average schmuck, grinding out a daily existence that may or may not add up to something in the end and that enlightened you for a semester or, if you were lucky, a lifetime. You probably still have a couple of Sweeney titles on your bookshelves, Don, in your Chelsea loft that you share with your lawyer girlfriend, though you haven't read a complete novel since that old John Grisham you discovered in your rental house on Block Island two summers ago.* "Yes. That William Sweeney."

The lawyer lowered his head contritely. "I really am sorry. He was . . . brilliant. I read that piece in *The New Yorker* he wrote a few years ago about Jeter. 'The Captain.' I was a fucking mess on the 1 train."

With that, Tricia felt the tears prick behind her eyes. It was happening all over again, like when her mother died. Tricia could stay composed in public until someone said something nice, something kind, and then she felt the sadness overwhelm her. At the grocery store, the shoe department at Bloomie's, the deli buying a sandwich. One kind word from a stranger or acquaintance would sneak its way through her armor and hit an emotional bull's-eye. But not today, not in this guy's office. Don Donaldson didn't get to be the first one to see her grieve.

Tricia bit her lip to bring herself back. "Thank you. He was a brilliant writer." She had turned to leave when a thought struck. "Can I ask you to please keep this confidential? We'd like to make sure the whole family knows before it becomes public and, as you've noted, my father was a public figure, so we're establishing a protocol for releasing the information to the press."

Confidentiality was one thing lawyers understood, even DD, as Don often called himself in meetings. "Of course, Sweeney."

In reality, Tricia didn't want Don Donaldson scooping the *New York Times* with some post or tweet about how his literary hero had passed away, setting off a press frenzy. Her father deserved better, the dignity of a news alert, at least, followed by an outpouring from fans on social media.

Tricia smiled, thinking that was exactly what William Sweeney would say about some fellow writer whose career-defining death notice had been undermined by some no-name on the twenty-third floor. She could hear it in his Hamden accent: *Poor guy. His lousy lawyer blurted it out online. He didn't even get an official press release. That's no way to go out.* Her father could make a great story out of nothing. The simplest encounter became an epic. Who would tell those stories now?

"Thanks, Don." She had no doubt that this story—of keeping William Sweeney's death a secret—would become one of Don's go-to anecdotes at happy hour.

As she walked out of the office, Patricia Beckett Sweeney realized that while caring for her father for the past ten years had been no picnic, protecting his legacy would be even more complicated.

Chapter

This day feels like it's been forever, Liza thought. Everything happened so quickly, yet in slow motion. Julia, who'd been so shocked by the death of her employer that it took her hours to recover enough to drive home, had just left, after one last tearful embrace with Liza. Now Liza sat in the kitchen of her childhood home on Willow Lane, drinking a glass of white wine and eating a handful of roasted peanuts, after a long, sad day of comings and goings, the official business of death involving mountains of paperwork and quick decisions, most grim. At one point, Liza was supposed to fax all three Sweeney sisters' signatures to some state office so her father's body could be cremated. She didn't even bother trying to track down her sisters, both of whom were in transit; she signed all three names in decent forgeries, scanned the documents, and emailed them to the proper state agency. Liza knew her sisters would understand.

Her phone pinged. It was a text from Maggie saying that she was waiting at the Southport train station for Tricia. There in ten. Hang in. xoxo.

Out of habit, Liza looked around the dated kitchen and started adding up the cost of a remodel. It was something she did in almost every house she walked into, from her clients' Greek Revivals to her in-laws' early American saltbox. *Do I want this place? Is the house even worth renovating?* Her own home was a few blocks away, an easy walk that she had done a million times since she married Whit and moved into the three-story Victorian on Westway Road. The Peppermint

Ice Cream House, they'd called it as kids because it was all sorts of pink and green, but not the charming versions of those colors. When she surprised her family (and maybe even herself) by settling down at age twenty-two with local boy turned investment banker Whitney Jones III, she set her sights on the house, practically willing aged Mrs. Jennings to relocate to an assisted living facility. The house never even went on the market. Whit stepped in and made an offer and Liza set to work reviving the place. Now a traditional white on the outside, but airy and open on the inside, it was the sort of house people drove by when they wanted to impress out-of-towners. Liza loved looking out the front windows and seeing people on the sidewalk holding up their phones and taking pictures.

She'd talked to Whit only briefly today. He was in North Carolina for work when he called between meetings. "I'm sorry, hon. Do you need me to come home right away? Your sisters will be there, right? When's the funeral?" All valid questions, but she wished Whit had said he was getting on a plane that night to be with her and that he'd do anything she needed. Even though he and her father never really clicked, they tolerated each other. Whit admired William Sweeney's intellect and convictions and Liza thought her father admired Whit as a good provider and a good father—that is, when he was in town. But she never really knew for sure. The Sweeneys weren't a family that poured out their emotions unless whiskey was involved. Still, Liza thought Whit could have been more proactive in his response.

Plus, the kids were meant to leave for camp next week, but events like that rarely pierced Whit's psyche when he was in the middle of a deal. He'd barely been home the last two months. If she didn't get the two of them on that camp bus, she'd have to drive them to Maine herself. She hoped the twins, Vivi and Fitz, were coping with Whit's mother, Lolly, who had agreed to take them overnight. She hated not being there with them. They'd been very close to their grandfather, often walking down the lane to bring him dinner, or fish or swim with him off this dock. Like so many men of his generation, Bill Sweeney was a more attentive grandfather than father. This was the first time they'd been through loss of any kind—even their yellow lab, Bear, was still alive, pushing fourteen, a year older than the twins.

Lolly not only took the twins, she volunteered to drop off dinner. "You should be with your sisters."

There was Lolly's trademark attribute: graciousness. She never made a false step and always knew exactly what to say in any social circumstance, what to write in the thank-you note and what dish to bring to the book club. Lolly Jones and Bill Sweeney had gotten along like a house on fire. Lolly could tell a wicked dirty joke in private and Bill loved that Lolly had actually read his work and wasn't afraid to disagree with his essays in the cleverest terms. That was the first of many holes that Liza would identify now that her father was gone: no more family dinners with too much wine and lively discussions about all the subjects you weren't supposed to talk about in polite society, from politics to sex to religion. Or the intersection of all three, like when her father got started on the Trump administration. Liza had always made her children clear the table to shield them from the nicknames Bill Sweeney had for the Cabinet secretaries. Lolly, who held her own biases, barely blinked at such talk. Now it would just be the Jones family sitting around the table, and Whit's father, Whitney, was no substitute for her father. Frankly, neither was Whit.

Sometimes Liza wondered if she stayed with Whit because his mother was so lovely and she would hate to offend her in any way.

Finally, Liza heard car wheels on the gravel driveway. They were here, her sisters. Liza wondered, *Are you considered an orphan if you're in your thirties?* She didn't know, but tonight she felt alone in a way that she hadn't before. She called to her father's old golden, left behind and bewildered: "Let's go, Jack. It's Maggie and Tricia. The sisters. Let's go say hi."

The Sweeney Sisters were back on Willow Lane.

"IN A MILLION years, did you ever think William Sweeney would die quietly in his sleep?" Tricia asked her sisters while they were standing out at the end of the dock, the boats of Southport Harbor to the left and the open waters of Long Island Sound to the right. Liza had taken them both through all the details of the day, from Julia discovering him in his bedroom midmorning to the call from Cap informing Liza that there was a short paragraph in their father's will about scattering his ashes at high tide. The details didn't make the reality any more real. Their father being gone at age seventy-four wasn't something for which any of them was prepared.

In pairs or all together, they'd had conversations over the years about what to do about Dad, but the implication was always that they needed to work something out for the future, not next week. Nothing seemed imminent. Though no one would accuse Bill Sweeney of taking good care of himself, physically he'd cut back on drinking lately and still walked five miles a day, taking the long way to Southport Beach and back with Jack the golden retriever. His father had always walked and always had a golden. Their mother had been sick for so many years, her death at age forty-five seemed like an inevitability—but he seemed like a guy who would never fade away. And certainly not without fanfare.

"The guy who couldn't go to the post office without turning it into a piece for *Esquire* slips off this mortal coil without a word," Tricia observed.

"I wish we'd had a chance for one more conversation," Maggie said. It was the tritest of sentiments, but it was true. All the sisters fell silent, thinking about what that conversation might have been for each of them, had they known it was the last. For Liza, maybe her father would have issued an apology for taking out all his anger about Maeve's illness on her. For Maggie, a declaration of support for her work and her talent would have been the final words to carry her forward. For Tricia, a détente would have served the two of them well, allowing them both to be right for once, especially about their ongoing battles over the law versus social justice and the merits of baseball versus basketball. William Sweeney had been better in print than in person when it came to digging deep and baring his soul, usually through fictional characters. The sisters knew any imagined conversation would be more satisfying than the real thing.

"Do we know it was a heart attack?" Tricia preferred facts to speculation.

"The EMT said it looked to be a heart attack. Why?"

"I was thinking about his years of depression."

"He was fine. He wouldn't have hurt himself," Liza said.

"You know that for sure?"

"Well, I'm not a psychiatrist," Liza responded, annoyed by Tricia's implication that, somehow, she had missed signs that her father was on a downward spiral.

"I know, I'm sorry. I had to ask."

"I saw him two days ago and we talked about giving Julia some time off this summer so she could go home to Puerto Rico. He had made plans to drive up to the lodge place in Vermont where he's gone for the last fifteen years. He had reservations in August."

"I think he met a woman there," said Maggie, or as Tricia often called her, Queen of Conspiracies.

"Why would you say that?" Tricia asked.

"Because I think it's true. Remember that visiting professor from Middlebury that he had that thing with? Nadia something, the intense Russian literature teacher who came to Dad's birthday dinner a million years ago. I think they had a *Same Time, Next Year* situation happening at that Vermont lodge."

"Really?" Now Liza was intrigued, forgetting about Tricia's accusation.

"Yes. When I was living here a few months ago, he told some story about sailing on a lake with Nadia and then he clammed up like he wasn't supposed to say anything, like he'd broken the code," Maggie explained. "I'm glad he had someone."

"I don't even know what to say to that. Except, I don't think he took his own life. Is that what you really thought?"

"No. It crossed my mind for a second, only because I never thought he'd go like this. Alone."

The mosquitos emerged and the sisters headed back to their cars. Liza had decided they would spend the night at her house instead of Willow Lane. "Trust me. It feels like a crime scene. You'll sleep better at my house. And Lolly dropped off her signature boeuf bourguignon. She freezes it in bulk for such occasions. We can heat that up."

"Do you think she dropped off that really good coffee and those blueberry-chia parfaits from The Granola Bar?" Maggie asked. She and Liza's mother-in-law had a special relationship. Lolly gave her food and vintage clothing items from the seventies and Maggie painted her thank-you cards.

"I'm sure she did," Liza said and then, because she was a planner, she floated an idea she'd been thinking about for hours. "What do you say we have the wake for Dad at my house? Maybe this Sunday, sort of get out ahead of any other public services and have the send-off Dad would have wanted. You know, it's easy, I have the drill down. Carol, the caterer, knows my ovens. And she does such a great job at the school board meeting annual dinner, I'd like to give her the gig. I can have the whole thing planned by end of day tomorrow."

Maggie and Tricia waited a beat to speak, exchanging glances that Liza picked up on.

That kind of collusion between the two of them made her crazy. They had no idea how hard it was to plan a big event, from napkin color to menu to cleanup, she thought. Every Thanksgiving, they'd show up with their assigned dishes, Tricia having bought hers from some fancy shop on the Upper East Side because, apparently, roasting and mashing butternut squash was beneath her. Maggie invariably wore a silk blouse because everybody knows you can't wash the turkey pan in a silk blouse. If it weren't for Liza, Thanksgiving, their mother's favorite holiday, would consist of frozen peas, store-bought pie, and some hippie quinoa salad that Maggie conjured up. *And here they go again, mocking me because I make things happen.* Liza didn't hold back, absolutely drained from a tough day. "What? What's wrong with my house? I don't know why you need to look at each other like that. I know you think I'm a control freak. I've heard you whispering in the kitchen at family events. But someone has to think these things through."

Maggie, only eighteen months younger than Liza and her childhood sparring partner and best friend, held back. She knew that she had the least amount of leverage in this debate. The last thing she wanted was to get stuck with any percent of the catering bill or the flowers or, God knows, the bar bill if all her father's drinking buddies from the Horseshoe Lounge—called the Shoe by locals—showed up. She was flat broke and if there was any silver lining to today's news, it was that some financial relief might be coming from the estate. But she knew better than to say any of that, especially to Liza, so instead, she flashed Tricia an encouraging nod.

Tricia took the bait, like any good lawyer. Tricia would argue anything, and being the younger sister by six years had never stopped her. "Liza, there's no judgment. We appreciate everything you've done today and for the last few years. Everything. But Willow Lane is the place that meant something to Dad, to his friends, to us. It's fitting for the wake to be here. It's only right. We can do this together. And, yes, by all means hire the caterer you trust. But you don't have to take everything on. We're here now. But I do agree that now is better," Tricia continued, turning the conversation around on a dime, a tactic she used in negotiations, as if point one about location was a settled matter and she could move on to point two, timing. "If we want to be able to control who attends, we should do it sooner than later. I spoke to the head of the English department today and she said they'd certainly like to do something formal in the fall when school is back in session. And, as you mentioned, I'm sure the Pequot Library will do something in his honor. Though they'll probably want us to donate money to make it happen, but we'll get to that once Cap takes us through the will. Those will both be well-attended, choreographed functions." Tricia was winding down and looking for the emotional hook to land Liza. "But yes, we should absolutely do something personal here. This event should be for Dad. And should be fitting of Dad. For family, for his real friends and colleagues. And those guys he lets fish off the dock on Sundays. I do think that's what Dad would have wanted: a William Sweeney Wake Extravaganza. Remember the celebration we gave Mom? We can top that."

Liza crumpled at the mention of her mother. She thought of the three of them at the wake, wearing clothes they had found in their mother's closet, singing "Both Sides Now," even though Tricia was mortified to perform in front of people. The mourners openly wept. Tricia was right. Of course, the wake should be here at Willow Lane with joy and tears and song and overindulgence, the messiness of memory in its glory. Clearly, she was exhausted, not thinking straight. She was grateful to Tricia for stating the obvious and grateful to Maggie for quelling her usual overreaction and staying silent. If only Whit had come home, but he hadn't. "Yes, of course. We'll do it here. It's been a long day. We can go over the details in the morning."

They were getting into their cars when Tricia's phone pinged. She glanced at it because she always glanced at it. "Well, it's official. Here's the *New York Times* alert." Tricia read aloud to her sisters, "Acclaimed American Writer William Sweeney Dead at Seventy-Four." She'd read the rest of the obituary later, when she could focus and be alone. She wanted to savor the accolades; it was all she had to say goodbye.

Liza looked at her sisters as she helped Jack and his failing hips into the back of her Volvo. "We can get through this."

Chapter

5

"I can say without a doubt that Bill Sweeney would have loved to be here tonight." The Irish brogue of Patrick Kennerly, a chaplain at Yale Divinity, rang out. "To look out on this sea of faces, to raise a glass, to drink to the people he cherished. Yes, William Sweeney would have stayed long into the night, maybe the last to leave if he left at all. And in the morning, he would have slipped quietly out the back door and let you be with your own thoughts. Just like he did, didn't he?"

Patrick and Bill had been longtime friends, meeting first during the Greenwich Village days, sparring over philosophy and bonding over darts at McSorley's. The religion scholar and the novelist then found themselves together at Yale years later and renewed the relationship. Tonight, Patrick said goodbye to his friend. "Now, I'm going to say a prayer and you can either bow your head or you can look straight out at the sea, like Bill would do. . . ."

It was a cool, cloudy night. There would be no "red sky tonight," the promise of the old sailor's rhyme, but a salty onshore breeze; the sisters had made sure to schedule the wake for high tide. About a hundred or so family, friends, neighbors, fishing buddies, local shopkeepers, and esteemed colleagues sat in folding chairs out on the lawn of Willow Lane to "Celebrate the Life and Words of William Sweeney," as the invitations said. Unlike a traditional wake, the body of Bill Sweeney was not on the premises, but the spirit surely was. Soon, there would be singing, drinking, dancing, and toasting, but first, there would be crying.

The communal sniffling started when cousin Sean's band played "Bang the Drum Slowly." Maggie had picked all the music after talking to Sean, who was a research biologist by day and a pretty decent singer and fiddle player by night.

When Maggie landed back in Connecticut after what she referred to as "the California Experiment," she lived in her childhood bedroom for sixth months to regroup. Among her accomplishments during The Regrouping was teaching her father how to use an iPod. She created a dozen playlists for his daily walks. The Emmylou Harris song was a favorite of her father's, and even though the female lead singer was dressed more appropriately for a nineties metal night at the Seagrape than a Southport service, that girl could sing.

Maggie had chosen wisely; the mournful reworking of the classic folk song was an emotional button to Cap Richardson's moving reminiscence about his and Bill Sweeney's fifty-year friendship that started at Yale as roommates and became much more than that. Cap was her father's lawyer, confessor, fixer. Cap was able to boil Bill down to his essential elements: storytelling, laughter, curiosity, and his own brand of humanity tinged with darkness that made him skeptical of the powerful and trusting of the humble. "Not that William Sweeney was the slightest bit humble, but he valued it in others," Cap said to the laughter of the guests, then added, "The only thing that truly humbled him was fatherhood. He was in awe of his daughters."

Dear Cap, Tricia thought. *We're the closest things he has to daughters.*

Over the years, Cap had watched Bill self-destruct, thanks to booze, women, gambling, and his own mental health demons, and then somehow rebuild his life through writing and solitude. In return, Bill had never made an issue of Cap's "confirmed bachelor" status, though both of them understood that Anders Hedlund, the charming antiques dealer in town that all the women loved, was more than Cap's bridge partner. Neither Cap nor Bill ever really talked about it. They never needed to. There was a gay character in *Bitter Fruit*, Lieutenant

Madigan, that Bill had created in honor of Cap. Madigan was the hero of the story. *Cap is saying goodbye to his best friend.*

Tricia looked down the row at her sisters, sitting as they always did, in age order: Liza, then Maggie, then Tricia. *Three redheads in a row,* their father had written in *My Maeve,* his memoir of his wife's death and his subsequent two-year depression. To the outside world, the book was a brave exploration of depression, a subject few men copped to at the time. It won the National Book Award and reinvigorated his stagnating writing career about twelve years ago. To Tricia and her sisters, it was a look into their father's inner monologue about a time period they'd rather forget.

"'Suppress and deny' should be the family motto," Maggie had once commented after her father's birthday dinner when not a single sister had congratulated him on the new book, instead making conversation about current events, the ending of *Buffy the Vampire Slayer,* and the upcoming Academy Awards. None of them had ever read *My Maeve* in its entirety. But here they were today, three redheads in a row.

"A good night for a short sail. Sail on, my old friend," Cap said in his final words, his voice catching. Polished Cap Richardson had taught working-class Bill Sweeney to sail in college, the gift of a lifetime. The first few notes from Sean's fiddle were all it took for the crowd to understand that William Sweeney was truly gone.

As the song's refrain faded out, a frail David Hughes, Bill's longtime editor at Allegory Publishing stood. He hugged Liza, Maggie, and Tricia before making his way to the microphone. He told the story of reading *Never Not Nothing* for the first time, saying of the experience, "It was the greatest gift of my publishing career, to spend a weekend alone with those words before the rest of the world would discover William Sweeney, knowing it would change their lives, too." Maggie, in the middle, squeezed both her sisters' hands.

It was a perfect night and they had made that happen. Liza had out-Liza'd herself, whipping the Willow Lane house into shape with the help of Julia, who insisted on returning to work despite her own shock and grief. If Liza had another week, she probably would have managed to paint the house and re-landscape. A thorough cleaning, a carload of new towels, pillows, and cheap rugs would have to do to freshen the faded interior. Liza brought in the company who did the Christmas decorations at her house to string hundreds of white lights to camouflage the exterior. Details were her strong suit. She'd even managed to get Jack a bath and a fresh bandana for the occasion.

Tricia had contacted the guests, reaching out to all the people her father truly would have wanted there, like the mechanic who kept his old Mercedes running and the long-retired department secretary from *The New Yorker*. She excluded the people her father would have called "phony," like Millie Reeves, the head of the Southport Historical Society who denied her father a special commendation for his seventieth birthday because she didn't like the language in some of his books. There had been some loose security at the door, one big bouncer from a local bar and two assistants from Liza's gallery, to distinguish any local wake crashers from fanboy wake crashers. Locals were welcomed without a scene.

Even Maggie, who had a tendency at events to stand on the sidelines and watch rather than work, had poured her energy into making an artistic tribute to her father on the west end of the property where the lawn turned to meadow: an installation of her father's beloved sails and spinnakers, hung high on C-stands borrowed from a photographer—an old boyfriend who trucked everything in from New York, including a generator and lights.

When David Hughes ended his tribute, Liza, Maggie, and Tricia rose together and made their way to the stage. Liza had wanted Tricia to be "the official spokes-sister," claiming that Tricia would be "the least emotional" and thus able to get through the eulogy in one piece. Tricia was both flattered and wounded by the statement. It was Maggie who insisted they all speak, saying, "We're the Sweeney sisters. We're good at this. Public speaking awards, sixth grade, Mill Hill, Sweeney Sweep. Talking is our thing."

Tricia agreed. "We should each read something Dad wrote. Something that mattered to each of us."

And so that was exactly what they did. Liza, being the oldest, spoke first. She gave Vivi and Fitz a hug on her way to the stage. She stood at the microphone and breathed deeply several times. Normally a confident speaker, she made several false starts, trying to get her opening words out without crying. She looked at her sisters and settled into a quiet rhythm with a story about their father's work ethic. She told the mourners how her father would take them all through his process at the dinner table when he was working out an essay or a scene in a book. "We were his first audience for almost everything. As children, we had no idea what he was talking about most of the time, but we knew we loved listening to him tell stories."

Then she read a passage from a piece in the *Yale Review* called "Quitting Time," about his instinct for knowing when a piece of writing was done, when it was "fully finished, polished to a deep luster, but not so shiny that one doubted its authenticity." She concluded, "My father lived to the age where he attained a deep luster, but never too shiny that you didn't believe him for one minute. May we all understand our own quitting time so well."

Maggie stood next, ascending the stage with poise and hugging Liza deeply. Maggie was in a long black dress with a bright orange-and-pink scarf in her hair and silver hoop earrings. She spoke nervously at first, introducing herself with the nickname her father had given her when she was a teenager. "Some of you know me as Mad Maggie. That's what my father called me for most of my teenaged years. I have no idea why," she said, wryly.

Then she recalled the many Christmas Eves they would sit around the fire, after the tree was decorated, listening to their father read aloud the classic Truman Capote story, "A Christmas Memory." "My father described that piece as 'everything that matters in life in ten pages,'" she said. "I struggled in college, maybe some of you know that. My mother had just died, I was my usual mess. I couldn't paint, I couldn't eat. But I could certainly self-medicate in a variety of ways and lie in bed all day. I was capable of that. And this card arrives with Snoopy on the front." She held up the card her father had sent her, with the drawing of a beagle lying on top of his doghouse. There are laughs from the audience. "Inside is a twenty-dollar bill and the words, 'For your Fruitcake Fund.'" Maggie paused, collecting herself, then continued, "And as a P.S., my father added, 'This moment in time is the greatest test of your strength, my Mad Maggie. Use this pain and make your art sing.' Use this pain and make your art sing. Thank you, Dad. I did then and I will again now."

Tricia paused and let Maggie have her moment on stage. Maggie took it and then exited with a small bow and a fist-bump for her sister. Tricia wasn't the slightest bit nervous. She had worked on her material late into the night, then got up, put on her running shoes, and rehearsed it several times on her run. Tricia went to where everyone in the audience knew she must go—back to the beginning.

"Like some of you, I read *Never Not Nothing* as a teenager, because it was a coming-of-age novel intended to be read by those coming of age. Honestly, I couldn't understand all the fuss, maybe because every character in the book seemed so familiar to me. My father as the main character Ethan, of course. Aunt Frannie as the little sister. Dear Cap Richardson as the more sophisticated best friend. I like to think that my mother Maeve was Elspeth, but my mother and father hadn't met yet when he wrote the book, though I'm guessing that when my father met my mother, he knew he'd found his Elspeth. These weren't characters in a novel; these were the people in my life.

"But two summers ago, after a difficult personal situation, I found myself in a coffee shop in Greenwich Village and there was a copy of *Never Not Nothing* in their lending library, along with spy thrillers and self-help titles. I started to reread it over a latte. When I finished it hours later in one sitting, I realized that I was the same age then as my father was when he wrote it, and the book resonated with me at a whole different level.

"*Never Not Nothing* is about establishing self-identity and the impossibility of living up to standards that somebody else created. That's something you learn well past your coming-of-age years, isn't it? My father needed the distance to write the story and that's true of all of us. We need to look backward before we can move forward. But more than anything, what I missed the first time I read *Never Not Nothing* was the longing to belong—to a family, to a friend group, to another person. I already belonged to those characters on the page, or so I thought at sixteen. But by thirty, I had lost that sense of connection. After rereading the book, I understood how essential growing up a *Sweeney* was to my being. Time and distance and losses made me hunger for belonging again. I think it's why the book continues to be read and loved, because we're all a little Ethan, searching for our people, for those essential connections. And look at you all here— you were my father's people and you made his life complete, even if there were days when he wasn't completely whole himself. Thank you. Thank you so very much."

Tricia paused again, this time for her moment, and then said, "Stay for food, drink, and carousing. You know my father would have loved the carousing bit. But first, from *Never Not Nothing* . . ." Tricia looked up as she spoke the well-known final lines of the book by heart and saw that many in the audience were doing the same, like singing along at a concert. *"Ethan knew it would never be the same. The moment, that had blistered the sun, cooled, then burned out. Walk along, young man, walk along."*

As the band segued into Van Morrison's "Into the Mystic," Maggie cued the lights and the sails and spinnakers came to life. The effect was breathtaking as the glowing fabric, lit from behind, blew in the breeze in the darkening sky. The crowd clapped as the band sang, "Let your soul and spirit fly."

As LIZA AND her family led the informal procession from the boathouse to the patio, she scanned the guests. She wanted to remember who was there that day and how they fit into her life. Her father's sister, Aunt Frannie, wiped her eyes and smiled at Liza. She still lived in Hamden, taught middle school social studies, and sent her nieces birthday cards with cash inside, as a kind of wink to the fact that they were all grown-up now.

There was David Remnick from *The New Yorker*, surrounded by several other editors, as well as writers and sometimes rivals like Richard Ford, John McPhee, and Don DeLillo. Her father's publishing house, represented in person by the editorial team and the senior marketing staff, had sent flowers and a special selection of green-only M&M's, a reference from *Bitter Fruit*. And, of course, his agent Lois Hopper in a black hat and sunglasses even after dark and her longtime assistant, Robert.

Here was a crew from the Pequot Yacht Club in blue blazers and matching club ties, and the regulars from the public boat ramp, fondly called Ye Yacht Yard, in slightly less-well-cut blue blazers and ties emblazoned with buoys, both groups there to pay respects to a fellow sailor. Neighbors from up and down Willow Lane came, wives in navy or black Talbot dresses and husbands wearing sober faces because knowing Bill Sweeney had brought a special something to their suburban lives and now he was gone. Childhood friends of the sisters, the sons and daughters of Southport, showed up, the younger versions of their parents, now replenishing the gene pool with attractive children and expensively highlighted hair.

The Yale contingent turned out in full strength from tweedy

deans to fellow lecturers to dazzled grad students, who seemed over-whelmed to be at their idol's house. One tall blonde with a familiar face stood out to Liza. Was she a colleague? Or something more? Liza had seen her before, for sure. Maybe she was one of the "after coffee" women she would see slip out the side door on Willow Lane as she came in the front door to check on her father. Liza couldn't place her and didn't really feel like talking to a stranger.

Even a few actors turned up, like Ed Harris and Willem Dafoe, both of whom wanted to option the Vietnam book for a movie, which Bill declined but they all became friends anyway.

Tricia had turned out the right people, Liza thought. She'd always understood the big picture. Then she locked eyes with an unexpected face in the crowd. *Jesus, what the hell is he doing here?*

Maggie, walking behind her, noticed the same face at the same moment and whispered to Liza, "Holy shit. Is that Gray Cunning-ham? I haven't seen him in fifteen years." Maggie recovered from sobbing to man-spotting in an instant. "My God. He looks fantastic."

Of all the events over the last few days, none rocked through Liza like the appearance of Gray Cunningham. The boy who was every-thing Liza wasn't: cynical, dark, reckless. The boy who made her defy her father and disappoint her mother. The boy who broke her heart and left her for the West Coast when her mother was dying. Liza rebounded by having a whirlwind romance with steady, solid Whit Jones and walking down the aisle with him six months later, so her mother could be at her wedding. After many years, she'd managed to contain her thoughts of being with Gray to middle-of-the-night hours when her mind wandered. She hadn't even Googled him lately. Why was he here now? Was he a plus-one to one of Tricia's friends from prep school or with Maggie's small cohort of weed smokers from back in the day who had shown up uninvited, but somehow talked their way in?

Liza turned in the other direction, to look at Whit, who had waited a full forty-eight hours before getting on the plane home after her father's death. He'd avoided any confrontation by attaching himself to the twins, whose tear-streaked faces broke her heart. Good, a distraction. Liza was going to need a drink before she spoke to Gray Cunningham. She turned back to respond to Maggie, but her sister was already headed in his direction.

Of course she was.

As THE NIGHT wore on, the mood went from somber to celebratory. The guests polished off all the food and most of the drink, including her father's favorite lobster rolls, trays of roast beef sandwiches, and Garelick & Herbs jumbo cookies, plus a case or two of Jameson's whiskey, several kegs of local beer, and a keg of Guinness. The more alcohol that was consumed, the faster the barrier between locals and literati disappeared. Dancing started, followed by singing. With every song break, there was another toast or tribute to Bill Sweeney, from bawdy stories to badly recited Seamus Heaney, courtesy of the local fire captain, to a terrible version of "Danny Boy" from the drunk fishermen because there had to be at least one at any Sweeney celebration. There were tears born of sadness from a handsome Yale colleague, a librarian whose sincere admiration for William Sweeney was evident in the charming story he told about his last conversation with him the previous week, and tears born of laughter when Ed Harris did his "Bill Sweeney in a Hollywood Meeting" imitation.

Through it all, the sisters danced, laughed, and sang along with the band. Liza and Tricia made the rounds. They wandered informally through the guests, thanking all for coming, listening to their stories, accepting condolences. Maggie spent most of the night with Gray, engaged alternately in intense conversation or intense flirting. When Tricia caught up with Liza, who was taking a breather on the patio, looking down on the crowd on the temporary dance floor on the lawn, she motioned toward Maggie, who was twirling around barefoot, her black maxi dress slipping off her right shoulder. Gray was with her, breaking out a modified jig to the Irish classic "I'll Tell Me Ma." "She looks pretty broken up," commented Tricia.

"She'll be worthless tomorrow and no help on the cleanup," Liza snapped. "You know I have to get the kids on the camp bus. I can't do everything."

"Don't worry. I'll take care of her. And when has she ever helped clean anything up? Seriously." Liza relaxed and they both laughed because they knew Maggie was always the first to duck out when manual labor was required. She'd be long gone by the time they were taking the garbage out. "She really outdid herself on the sails, though."

"I know. She's talented—if she could only . . ." Tricia didn't bother to finish the sentence. She and Liza had had this same conversation for the last ten years about Maggie. Instead, she changed the subject. "Did you talk to Gray? He's back, you know. He's living in his parents' house on Harbor Road."

"That explains why that place didn't go on the market when the Cunninghams moved south," Liza responded. "I can't deal tonight. I need a few days and then maybe I can absorb everything. But not him, not tonight."

"I barely had a chance to say hello. Maggie had him sequestered. Do you want me to gather some further intelligence? I can do some digging."

"Please don't," Liza said. "I have a whole different life now."

"Where is your whole different life, anyway?" Tricia asked, looking for Whit. She felt he'd been a background figure for most of the last few days, not really rising to the occasion of losing his father-in-law. Her experience with men was mostly limited to relationships defined as *boss* or *nemesis*, thanks to her competitive streak. She saw every guy in college or law school as an academic or athletic rival. Her list of former boyfriends was very short and nothing had been very serious, except a short and inappropriate relationship with a client a few years ago that she'd blocked out for many reasons, not the least of which was her ethical breakdown. Tricia would never presume to understand marriage, especially Liza's marriage, but it had surprised Tricia that Whit wasn't more supportive of his wife or her sisters. The only one Whit seemed to have any empathy for was Jack the dog.

"He took the twins home about an hour ago," Liza answered as she took a sip of beer, then put the glass down on the stone wall. "Ugh. Don't let me drink any more of that." Liza and Tricia stood on a rise watching the dancers in silence for a while, then Liza asked, "Who is that blond girl? I noticed her before. Do we know her?"

The blonde in question was out on the dance floor, moving to the music but not dancing with anyone in particular. She was tall, thin, and fit, her body the product of equal parts genetics and athletics, with her thick blond hair clipped back off her face. She wore elegant black pants and a black silk shirt. She appeared to be about their age. She was sort of attached to the Yalies; Liza had seen her talking to some of the neighbors, too. Liza's mind was a blank.

Tricia shook her head. "I don't know. She does look sort of familiar, but I could have met her at some Yale thing. It looks like she's hearing the Grateful Dead in her head even though Sean is playing the Clancy Brothers." The sisters laughed, then Tricia turned the topic. "A few people brought plus-ones, even though it wasn't really that kind of invitation. Like, what is Gray doing here? He must have heard about it from someone, because I certainly didn't invite him."

"I know, Tricia. I didn't think you had," Liza was done talking about Gray. "Is it me or is the lead singer now barely dressed?"

The band launched into an especially lively version of "Born to Run," which got everyone out on the dance floor because nobody can resist the Boss. And the sisters knew that this was the band's signature last song. Plus, they'd played every song in their repertoire, including "Come On Eileen," which they usually only played at weddings.

Maggie abandoned Gray and danced over to grab Tricia and Liza's hands. "Last song! Tramps like us gotta dance." And for one last time at Willow Lane, the Sweeney sisters danced.

IT WAS TIME for the final toast since the last train was heading back into the city in about a half hour. Many of the guests needed to be on that train or they'd be spending the night on the rattan couches in the living room. That didn't stop Aunt Frannie from stepping up to the microphone because she wanted the last word, like any bossy big sister.

"My brother Bill was a lucky man because he had wonderful women in his life. He had me, his beloved sister." Liza laughed along with the rest of the crowd. "He had my sainted mother, Bess." Even Tricia snorted at that line, as Bess Sweeney's drunken neglect was well documented in a famous essay in *Harper's* that became a chapter in *My Maeve*. "He had Maeve, who was a better wife than he ever deserved and he knew it. And he had his daughters—beautiful Liza, mad Maggie, and clever Trish—who brought us all together for this lovely night. Bill . . ." Frannie said, looking to the heavens, then turning her gaze downward. ". . . Or maybe you're watching from down there. Wherever you are, Bill, know that the greatest thing you ever created is your girls." Frannie raised her glass, "To the Sweeney Sisters!"

Liza, Maggie, and Tricia stood side by side, three redheads in a row. Collectively, the crowd raised their glasses and their voices. "The Sweeney Sisters." Three glasses of whiskey appeared before them, courtesy of Willem Dafoe, who seemed to have been doling out his own secret stash all night. The sisters accepted the shots, clinked their glasses, and raised them up, as Liza whispered, "To us." In the distance, the sails glowed and whipped gently in the light breeze.

"May I offer you a scone? We found them on the front porch this morning, left by some real estate agents who are very sorry for our loss." Tricia offered the oversized basket of baked goods to Cap. The basket included a card from the Miller Cromwell Agency, headed by local legend Nan Miller. Nan's team included Maggie's high school drama-club nemesis Lisa Jerusalem, so the baked goods created quite a stir when they were discovered. But they provided the carbs necessary to soak up the last of the whiskey.

Cap Richardson had come by Willow Lane to discuss the will. He had waited until after the wake for the business of death. "Mourn first," he'd said to Tricia, who wanted to wrap the details up a bit sooner so she could get back to work, but Cap had been insistent. "Trust me. I've been through this many times with clients, and, of course, you're more than clients to me. Have a moment for your father and then you can move on."

But now, it was time to move on.

The sisters and Cap had seated themselves in the formal dining room, looking out across the lawn to the water. Everything about the room was familiar to Cap—the painted mural, the slipcovered chairs, the Oriental rug—but the view always delighted him. The water sparkled, hinting at summer. Maggie and Tricia had lasted less than twenty-four hours at Liza's place. The stress of watching their sister plan the wake and execute the camp packing simultaneously,

plus her tendency to play innkeeper with elaborate breakfasts and repeated instructions on how to use the shower in the guest room, was
suffocating. Maggie cornered Tricia in the hallway. "I feel like we've
been taken hostage. Let's just go back to Willow Lane. I don't care
if Dad's ghost is wandering the hallways. Liza is making me crazy."

Liza wasn't happy about her sisters abandoning her for their childhood home, but she had to make one more run to Old Navy for green
T-shirts and boxers and didn't have time to argue. "Fine, just make
sure you don't make a mess," she'd said. It was an unnecessary comment for one grown woman to make to two other grown women, but
Maggie and Tricia let it go so they could escape her oppressive regime.

The fact was that Willow Lane was already a mess. It needed a new
roof, new electrical, every room painted, and the floors redone—and
that was for starters. But the reality that Willow Lane would have to
go up for sale and that real estate agents were circling in the water
unnerved Liza. "Tricia, I don't know how you can joke about those
scones and selling this house. Doesn't it upset you that we're getting
pressured less than a week after Dad died?"

"Not really," Tricia responded. "It would upset me more if they
weren't circling, because that would mean the market is collapsing.
Right, Cap?" The two lawyers communicated on a different level. To
Liza and Maggie, Cap would always be a benevolent uncle; to Tricia,
he was a colleague and mentor.

"I had several people make offers at the wake. All cash. Good
numbers," Cap responded, selecting a blueberry scone and setting it
down next to his coffee. "I don't think they'll remember making the
offers, but I think a couple of them could actually afford the place. I
should have had them sign something."

Tricia and Maggie laughed out loud and Liza tried hard not to
smile imagining the offers Cap had fielded. She wanted to remain
slightly put out by the thought of selling her childhood home to some
drunken bidder. (They'd only gotten rid of the last of the mourners

a few hours ago, finding a couple of fishermen asleep on the leather couches in the library.) The property alone at Willow Lane was worth several million dollars. Cap hoped that once he had delivered all the news—the good and the not good—the sisters would agree that now was not the time to be sentimental. This property had the potential to be their asset and they would have to maximize its value. He hoped they were ready to hear that. "Should we go through the documents now? This may take a while."

THE THREE SISTERS let the news settle in and then Tricia spoke. She had been taking notes on a yellow pad the entire time as Cap took them through the will and then the financials. She had filled up several pages, but it really all boiled down to a few questions. "So, there's very little cash, the house is overleveraged, and the manuscript for the memoir Dad owes his publisher is somewhere, but we don't know where. Is that all correct?"

"That is correct."

"Well, at least Dad had the sense to name you his literary executor and not the bartender at the Shoe. You have a broad understanding about the options for all his intellectual property. I'm curious about the royalty income. I never knew the exact figure, but Dad had mentioned to me several times that it was solid. He said if high school teachers and college professors kept assigning his books, we'd be set for life. What's happened to that money?"

"There is some, but I think your father may have been exaggerating when he said that you were set for life. It's in the low six figures annually, very low six figures. After Lois takes her commission, you all would split less than a hundred thousand annually."

"That's a surprise. How did it happen? I mean, I know you weren't his keeper and it's not your fault, but how did he blow through a half-million-dollar book advance and why so many refinances on the house? And, please don't say he bought a lot of rounds at the bar. That's what he used to say to our mother when money was tight and we all knew it was a lie back then."

"Your father was generous with money. He bailed out his sister Frannie after her divorce and paid for Sean's education. He invested in some get-rich-quick schemes that didn't get him rich quick and made some loans to friends that were never paid back. He loaned one gentleman the money to buy a commercial fishing boat and the guy died the next year. Bill didn't have the heart to collect on the loan from his widow. But he also had a reckless streak, as you know. Some of it was gambling. It was an issue for him and he thought he'd put that behind him. But betting on sports sucked him in again. College basketball, football. I think he even placed bets on the America's Cup. He didn't tell me much about it, but he had some big losses in the last few years that ate up the advance."

"Did he use a bookie? Or go to Atlantic City?" Tricia knew enough about gambling laws to know that neither Connecticut nor New York allowed sportsbooks, but New Jersey did.

"Atlantic City. Never a bookie. He didn't want to get back into that again. But he thought he could handle a couple of trips a year to Atlantic City."

"That depresses me more than the losses, thinking of him spending a weekend in Atlantic City alone." Tricia didn't want to let her mind wander to whether he may not have been alone, but she did ask Cap, "Were there, *are there*, women he's giving money to?"

"No. He would have told me that."

"And the manuscript. You said . . ." Tricia looked down at her notes to read directly, ". . . 'it's completed but its whereabouts are unknown.' And that Dad has hidden it somewhere because he wanted to, quote, 'add a coda or do some updating and then have it published after his death,' but you don't think he got to the coda. Is that correct?"

Cap was patient, responding to Tricia carefully, "That is correct, although I wouldn't say that the manuscript is hidden. I'm sure it's in his office. Your father said he wasn't ready to turn it in yet and preferred that it be published after his death."

"Why? He usually loved the hoopla."

"He told me that in this book, he really let it all hang out. That was the phrase he used—'let it all hang out.' And that he felt too old to answer for his sins on some NPR interview show to publicize the book. He only wanted it published after his death."

"That's morbid, coming from him. He seemed to think he'd never die. What's in it?"

"I don't know. I haven't read it. I don't think anyone has. But the publisher is eager for it. At least they were last week when you father was simply fending them off with calls for more time. Now that he's gone, I'm sure now they want it even more."

"Is that why you told us to keep the boathouse locked the night of the wake?" Tricia asked, a whole new light of comprehension dawning. This was a big deal, an unforeseen issue that could damage not only the estate, but the legacy of William Sweeney. A posthumous memoir of radical honesty was valuable and potentially explosive. *Jesus, Dad.* "You didn't want those people from the publishing house poking around in there, did you?"

"I didn't. Or anyone from Lois Hopper's office. She may be his agent, but I don't think she's his advocate. We need to do this on our terms and our timeline. If you'll allow me to assist you in dealing with all these issues."

"Of course, Cap."

After Tricia's rapid-fire questions, Liza asked quietly, "Cap, did he know he was sick? This seems pretty calculated. Hiding the book until his death."

"I think he knew something. He'd made a few references lately about his heart, made a few changes to his habits." Cap was vague with the sisters. He was fairly sure that Bill Sweeney knew there were heart issues and had seen him visibly slow down in the past few months. But the girls hadn't signed off on an autopsy, so no one would ever know for sure.

Maggie finally spoke. "I don't understand what's happening. I thought selling the house would bring in millions. Do you mean we'll get nothing?" The thought had crossed both Liza's and Tricia's mind, but only Maggie was desperate enough to say it out loud. Maggie was counting on a windfall, *needed* a windfall, to stabilize her life. She didn't have a husband like Liza or a regular paycheck like Tricia. She lived a life that had been piecemealed together, funded by intermittent periods of good fortune (rich boyfriends, generous friends, occasional patrons of the arts) and periods of barely scraping by where she'd relied on the kindness of her sisters and total strangers, like the Arts Commission of Mill River, who were funding her current living situation. Even her car was a gift from her father, something a thirty-four-year-old woman should be able to buy herself. Or at the very least, lease. But when Maggie arrived home last year, Bill Sweeney took one look at her and said, "I'll buy you a car. What do you want?" He was a fan of the big gesture.

Maggie was hoping an inheritance might get her a tiny place on Martha's Vineyard or Key West, even Austin, if that's all she could afford. This was not the news she was expecting. She was torn between cursing and crying. "How is that possible?"

Tricia stepped in, like she usually did when Maggie was going over a cliff. "Listen, we'll find the manuscript and get out from under that possible litigation and financial obligation. If the advance is gone, we have to deliver that manuscript or pay back the money somehow, like using the proceeds from the house sale. Once we deliver it, we're in the clear financially, right, Cap?" He nodded. "Is this house underwater?" Cap shook his head. It wasn't. There was a lot of debt, to be sure, but they should be able to squeeze some money out of it if they got a good price.

Tricia got it. "Then we sell the house as is and we don't get greedy.

Look around. This place is a tear-down. Some captain of finance wants this property to create a compound and will pay the money to make that happen. This house isn't protected by the Historical Registry, so let's not get all emotional and look for a buyer who wants to preserve Willow Lane out of respect for Dad. Let's get out of it what we can." Tricia nodded in Liza's direction, knowing that she'd be a holdout. "And let's face it, there will be revenue from book sales and possibly other business ventures like film rights now that Dad is gone. Is everyone okay with that?"

Maggie was having a hard time controlling her tears and Liza was lost in thought. *How did we let this happen?* Whit would have a field day with this news. He was constantly harping on Liza to get her father to agree to let him take over the finances, fearing that Bill Sweeney was doing exactly this, frittering away equity and cash. Bill Sweeney's banker was a sailing buddy, not a financial whiz, who worked at the local People's Bank, known more for its charming historic building than aggressive portfolio management. *We're going to end up paying for your father one day, I know it,* Whit would say after almost every family dinner. "Why didn't Dad sell this house then if he needed the cash?"

"Your father had a lot of flaws, but he knew most of them. He knew if he sold the house, he'd spend the money. The house was part of your inheritance and he didn't want to gamble that away."

"Jesus. How fucked up is that?" Tricia asked. "His best quality was not gambling away the roof over his head. Thanks, Bill!" The four of them managed to laugh. It was true. Brilliant William Sweeney was a goddamned mess. The laughter turned to snorts. If people only knew.

When they collected themselves, Liza asked, "Is there anything for Julia in the will?"

"I'm glad you asked. You father had a decent life insurance policy through his employment at Yale. The sole beneficiary is Julia Ruiz."

"Like how much is 'decent'?" Maggie had to ask because stockpiling resentments was her lifeblood.

"Two hundred and fifty thousand dollars." This only made the sisters laugh harder, the thought of the housekeeper getting a clear inheritance, much deserved, while they had to clean up their father's mess.

Liza said that Julia would be equally shocked about the money, but also pragmatic. "Julia had told me about her cousin who had devoted twenty-five years to a Southport family of five, from the first baby's baptism to the last child's college send-off, only to be given a CVS gift card and two bags of old clothes on her last day of work. Maybe she told that story to Dad, too. I'm happy for her. She deserves this. She put up with a lot over the last fifteen years. She saw it all."

"So did we," Maggie whined. More laughter.

Their dark sense of humor serves them well, Cap thought as he prepared to drop the biggest bomb of all on the Sweeney sisters.

"As you know, your father was a man in full. He lived a life that was both rich and often complicated, the result of which could be brilliant writing but difficult personal relationships. As you come to terms with your father's death, I must add one more complication. It came to my attention about a month ago that your father had a previously unknown child outside of his marriage to your mother." Cap paused to let the last sentence sink in. *A previously unknown child outside of marriage.* "And I have an obligation to tell you about the child both legally and morally. You have a half-sister out there in the world and you should know that."

A quiet moment passed, then the sisters registered their disbelief. Maggie spoke first, straight from her bank account. "Seriously, could this day get any worse? How many more people do we have to split the money with?"

Liza muttered, "What the hell . . ."

"Who is this person? How did you come to know this?" Tricia asked.

There was a flutter of talking along the same lines by the other sisters, then Liza said, "Please don't tell us that one of his grad students has a newborn." They all cringed at the thought of their seventy-plus father impregnating one of his starry-eyed students.

Cap understood their panic. "No, the child in question is not a newborn. In fact, she is older than any of you. Your father is the biological father of Ms. Serena Tucker." Again, a pause to let the sisters absorb the name. "As you recall, the Tuckers lived next door, the blue Dutch Colonial that shares the hedge. It appears that your father and Birdie Tucker were intimate for a time and Ms. Tucker, now thirty-eight, is the result."

Tricia, the lawyer, went straight to the heart of the matter. "Does she stand to inherit any part of the estate?"

"Your father did name her as an equal heir in the real estate portion of his estate. She is to get one-quarter of the proceeds of the sale of the house."

"And the intellectual property?"

"She is not entitled to any share of the IP. The three of you are the primary heirs to any and all of your father's work, from his books to his articles to the unproduced screenplay I know he has in his desk. There is a small percentage of monies from the IP revenue granted to his sister Frannie, five percent, but she has no say in the decisions about the IP. In terms of this recently identified heir, I think having a non–family member in the role of executor will add a layer of clarity."

"Thank you for the provision, Cap. I'm sure that was your influence," Tricia said, and Cap nodded.

Liza was more focused on the name, not the law. "Wait, Serena Tucker? She was at the wake." She could barely find the words. "Tricia, she was the blonde out there dancing by herself at the end of the night. The tall skinny one."

The light bulb went off for Tricia. "The one who was doing that drunk-girl sway out on the dance floor?" Nothing about this situation was the slightest bit humorous, but Maggie snorted a bit at Tricia's brief imitation. It was spot-on. She'd seen that drunk girl out on the dance floor, too. Then, it hit Tricia. "Dad slept with Birdie Tucker? How is that possible? She was so, so . . . tan. Remember, all she did was play tennis? I don't think I ever saw her in anything but a Ralph Lauren tennis skirt."

It was true. The mention of Birdie Tucker's name took them right back to the one summer their mother signed the older girls up for tennis camp at the country club, a rite of passage for so many local children whose parents believed a reliable serve could secure a lifetime of good fortune. Maeve Sweeney was not one of these mothers, preferring the public beach, the Boys & Girls Clubs sports, and arts and crafts to the country club lifestyle, but Emmy, her friend who meant well but only saw one path to a life well lived, talked her into signing up Liza and Maggie for tennis. The sisters were constantly reminded they weren't "real members" by fellow campers, meaning their spot in the locker room hadn't been passed down by bloodline nor paid for in equity.

Liza and Maggie, then fourteen and twelve, hated every minute of it, pounding forehands during the baking afternoon sun when the club moms preferred to sit by the pool, drinking iced tea or wine spritzers. The only reason they didn't revolt entirely was the tennis pro, John Wilton, with the floppy brown hair, his Conn College T-shirts, and a maroon Saab. Liza and Maggie talked about him endlessly. Plus, there were popsicles at the end of the day.

The Tuckers were a permanent fixture at the country club courts, either playing, taking lessons, or drinking half-and-halfs on the patio. Liza could picture Serena Tucker, a few years older with tennis abilities well beyond those of the Sweeney sisters, hanging out at the tennis shack, flirting with John while he strung racquets, and her mother, Birdie Tucker, doing the same, like competitors. This was the woman their father slept with?

Now, Liza was a member of the same club, signing her kids up for the same lessons.

Maggie's voice broke a little bit as she said, "Mom was so beautiful then, so healthy. How could he do that to her? With that totally generic suburban woman?"

Liza and Tricia fell silent. The timing of the affair, if it could be called that, was hitting them. Their father was sleeping around on his young, beautiful wife—not his sick wife, or his dying wife, or even shortly after Maeve was gone, all of which might have been understandable and, if the sisters were honest with themselves, knew had occurred with various women over the years. But the possibility that their father slept around on his young, beautiful poet wife, his muse, with that uptight mom next door who was constantly yelling at the Sweeney sisters to walk on the sidewalk instead of down the middle of their dead-end street? This had never occurred to them.

Cap answered as only Cap could. "Your father was a man who moved from one experience to another, uninterested in operating in some kind of coherent direction. He wasn't a big-picture guy, except in his writing. In his life, it was often moment to moment."

"Did he tell you about Serena?" Tricia was back to business.

"No, Serena came to see me about a month ago. She had done a mail-in DNA test. When her results came back, she got an additional email about being a 99.9 percent match with a Sweeney from Southport, Connecticut."

"What idiot would do one of those tests and let everyone know your DNA information?"

"I'm the idiot," Maggie said, raising her hand. "Don't get mad at me. I had a panic about getting breast cancer like Mom and I wanted to know if I had any genetic predisposition."

"Then go to a doctor, not a mail-in kit with a public option."

Liza stepped in. "Okay, I don't think that's the point here. Let Cap tell us what we need to know."

"I understand this is upsetting, but Liza is right. Some details don't matter very much and some matter a great deal. First off, these DNA tests do hold up in court, so if you decided to contest Serena's rights vis-à-vis the will, you could stand to lose your share of the real estate holdings entirely." Cap paused to let that sink in. A legal battle wouldn't make this mess go away. Then, he continued. "Serena Tucker was born in May 1982. I was unaware of the relationship until last month when Ms. Tucker came to see me. You should know a few things about her. She is bright and thoughtful. She's single, no children, so there are no other relations to contend with. She's an experienced investigative journalist in Washington, DC. She was with the *Post*, then *Slate*, and now with the political site *Straight Up*."

"I've heard her on the *Straight Up* podcast. I listen to it all the time and she's on it occasionally. She's really smart," Tricia said that like it was a bad thing. "But I've heard *Straight Up* is in financial trouble. Their funding is drying up. Oh, this isn't good."

Liza and Maggie didn't even bother to ask how Tricia knew all about a startup political media company that they'd never heard of. Tricia absorbed information and retained names and knowledge with astonishing accuracy. It was what made her a good lawyer but a terrible conversationalist. She had a hard time not being a know-it-all.

"Why is that bad?" Maggie asked, barely tracking.

"Serena needs money or a story to sell because she could be out of work any day," Tricia announced like she was reporting the news.

Cap jumped in. "I would describe her as measured and reserved. She sat on the information for a good while and then had a conversation with her mother, who confirmed the relationship with your father. Then she came to me."

"It's creepy to think she was at the wake. That makes me uncomfortable," Maggie said, thinking more about how she'd noticed Serena at the wake because she was a knockout in the severe preppy way that Maggie herself had never been able to pull off. Maggie was too curvy; Serena was thin as a rail with what Maggie liked to call "perfect European A cups." She'd been envious of her at the wake, having no idea who she was. Now, knowing they were half-sisters, a childish jealousy was creeping into Maggie's consciousness. "I don't know who she thinks she is."

"What did she want? What does she say she wants?" Tricia asked, convinced already that an ulterior motive was at work.

Cap continued, "I didn't get the sense she wanted anything specific when we spoke other than to see your father if he was inclined to see her. She didn't mention anything monetary or otherwise."

"That's bullshit. Sorry, Cap. But the timing is uncanny," Tricia snapped. "Did she meet with our father? He must have known all along she was his. They were our neighbors for something like thirty-five years."

Liza, who'd been quiet, said, "Maybe it was a one-night stand. For all we know, Dad didn't even remember he'd ever slept with Birdie Tucker." That was entirely possible. If the stories from the wake the other night were to be believed, the main ingredient for any Willow Lane gathering in the early days was booze, lots of it. Maybe Birdie Tucker happened one boozy night.

Cap proceeded cautiously, because this part of the story did not reflect well on his old friend. "After speaking with your father about Serena, I can tell you this: he recalled the relationship; he claims he did not know the child was his; and he did not want to see Serena. I had not informed her of that last fact yet. Frankly, I was stalling, hoping that your father would change his mind. I suggested this provision in his will as a way of acknowledging her after his death. He agreed. We moved on it quickly. Then your father died and, like you, I was surprised to see her at the wake. But not entirely. She was very curious about your father, her father. And about the three of you."

The Sweeney sisters paused to consider all Cap had said. If their father was a "man of moments," not grand plans, why wouldn't he have wanted to see Serena? Wouldn't he have wanted to see what had become of a moment in 1981? Liza asked the question they all were thinking. "Why didn't he want to see her, Cap?"

Cap looked out at the three faces of the young women he cherished. "He said that seeing Serena Tucker as an adult, after having paid so little attention to her as a child, would remind him of all the ways he had failed in his life. He said talking to her now would break his heart."

NONE OF THE Sweeney sisters had the instinct to go all "Dr. Phil" as Maggie called it, rushing to meet their long-lost sister in a tearful reunion. "That may be fine for some families, but not for us," Liza said.

Tricia seconded, "I suggest we proceed with caution."

Cap suggested a formal meeting with a lawyer present as a start. The sisters agreed and Cap said he'd set it up.

By the time Cap left, it was after five, or as Maggie said while pouring herself a glass of wine, "Rosé o'clock." The sisters were drained, mentally and physically, from the last four days of grieving, planning, coping at an intense level. They'd already agreed about "next steps," as Tricia kept saying, on "the Serena situation." Tomorrow, they could figure out a game plan for finding the manuscript and getting the house on the market, but right now, they needed to absorb everything they had heard from Cap on their own time.

Tricia, normally the most rational of the sisters, was livid. Not even Cap's measured responses could calm her down and once he departed, she got all riled up again. "I can't believe this. I can't fucking believe this," Tricia said for the tenth time since they'd learned about Serena. "I am so mad at Dad for dumping this on us. 'Here, girls, here's an incredibly complicated financial situation. And, oh! Did I mention my love child? Yeah, she's in for a quarter of the house, by the way.'"

"Don't say love child. Please. Birdie Tucker is not the kind of woman who bears a love child," Liza said. "The last time I saw her, she was berating the checker at Stop & Shop for the crème fraîche shortage. She's awful. It makes me sick to think of her ever interacting with Mom."

"Me, too. I can't get past the mother to deal with the daughter. But we're going to have to." Tricia was pacing on the patio; she processed better when she moved.

"There's nothing we can do. It happened a long time ago and we have to cope," Maggie offered in her yoga teacher voice.

"Do we? It's not our problem, really. This was between Dad and Birdie Tucker. I don't really understand why we have to cope with the consequences. I have no desire for more relatives."

"That's harsh. We don't even know this girl, really."

"When Mom died, Birdie Tucker showed up at the front door the next day. I answered it because everyone else was asleep. And there she is in a warm-up suit standing there with a giant wheel of Brie and those thin crackers in the green tin."

"Bremner wafers," Liza said. "Nothing says WASP comfort food like Brie and Bremner wafers."

"I know. She handed me this cheese and this tin and she tried to bulldoze her way into the house. She hadn't done anything for us when Mom was sick, but now she that she was dead, Birdie needed to express her condolences. It was eight a.m. And why would she think Dad or any of us want Brie? I wouldn't let her in. I was fifteen and she snapped at me, something about how impudent I was. She wasn't sorry at all about Mom. Now that I know what was happening behind the scenes, I'm wondering if she was thinking that she could finally tell Dad that Serena was his," Tricia said. "It's all so awful."

"I'm with Tricia. How do I explain all this to the twins? Or to my in-laws? Or to everybody else in town? You all will leave in a few days, but I live here," Liza said. "This is going to be a real scandal. And very awkward for my family."

"But it's not Serena who is at fault," Maggie said.

The sisters fell silent. They knew Liza was right; she would bear the brunt of the social fallout. And they knew Maggie was right that their resistance might be misplaced.

"At least we get to give Julia good news." Liza said. "I'll call her and set up a time for her to come by so we can tell her together. She's been texting me ten times a day asking if I'm okay, but I think she's the one who's still in shock. I also want to put her in touch with our financial advisor so she doesn't give all that money away to her family. She's always bailing out her nephews who need new brakes or a cousin who lost a job. I want her to keep that money for herself and have a real safety net."

"Good idea. She'll listen to you," Tricia said, rising from the table. "I'm going for a run. I need to work all this out in my head."

"Sure you don't want to skip the run and have some wine instead?" Maggie asked, pouring another splash into her glass.

"Run first," Tricia answered. "But save me some."

"Oh, stop it. It's rosé, not a tequila shot. It's barely drinking."

Liza declined as well. "I'm headed back to my house. I have to fill Whit in on all this before he leaves again in the morning." She dreaded going home and facing her husband. Whit's family led an uncluttered life with clear expectations and outcomes. There were no scandals in the Jones family, no unexpected relatives arriving on the scene after an affair, and Whit liked it that way. There was no need to control the narrative because the narrative was one long, respectable story of accumulating wealth and staying out of the headlines. Everything Cap revealed today would be an issue with Whit.

Liza was only beginning to comprehend the ways in which her life might change with her father gone, the estate a mess, and this sudden sister showing up, never mind Gray Cunningham back in the neighborhood. Liza was the oldest sister. It was a role she relished, a responsibility she took seriously. In the past, she'd handled things. Now everything about that truth seemed to be unraveling. Serena was two years older than Liza. Serena was the oldest Sweeney sister now.

Her phone pinged, a text from Whit. Because she wasn't home at five like she said she would be, he was going golfing. Maybe she'd like to meet him at the country club for dinner? The memory of Birdie Tucker in her Ellesse sneakers and coral lipstick flashed through her brain. No, she texted back; she wasn't up for the club tonight. Please, feel free to eat at the bar, she told Whit, because she knew that's exactly the sort of permission he sought. They'd both be happier if she declined his invitation. Liza turned to Maggie. "You know what? I think I will have a glass of wine. I don't need to rush home."

TRICIA'S SNEAKERS POUNDED out the familiar steps. Willow to Old South to Pequot to Beachside to Burying Hill Beach and back again. She'd run this easy five-mile route hundreds of times since she started cross-country the year her mother died. At first, she ran to get out of the house, to smooth out the rough edges of anxiety she felt every day as her mother worsened. Then after, she ran to get away from the oppressive sadness, adding miles and hills and beach sprints to stay out as long as she could after school. She got faster and stronger. It was running that had taken her to prep school, along with a few strings pulled by Cap to get her in midyear, and probably some of his own money to pay the tuition. She ran competitively in college and to save her sanity in law school. *Running will get me through this,* Tricia thought, then she let the sound of the steps and the breathing work their magic. The ball of stress in her gut unraveled and her mind cleared more with every footfall. The first thought that popped into her clear mind: *I can't deal with another sister.*

"WHAT DO YOU really think?" Maggie asked Liza as soon as Tricia was out of earshot.

"I don't even know what to say to that. We have our thing, the three of us. You're you. I'm me. Tricia is Tricia. I feel no connection to this person at all. I don't see how we fit a fourth person in the band."

Liza poured out a swallow more wine and petted Jack on the head. Poor, sweet dog, lost without his owner.

"Especially one who's tall and skinny. That pisses me off. Why didn't I get the tall gene?"

"You're a much better dancer."

"That's true."

Liza looked out over the lawn, toward the water. The property had seen better days, for sure, but the memories made on Willow Lane were vivid, powerful. For all the sadness they had experienced here, the sweetness was stronger. "I hate to think of this house being torn down. That seems wrong. It's not like they're buried here, but this is where I want to come to remember them. I want to come here."

"Don't make me cry again. Or we'll finish this bottle before Tricia gets back from her run," Maggie said, pouring a smidge more wine in each of their glasses. "But you're right. This is where the memories are."

William and Maeve Sweeney had bought the property on Willow Lane in the early eighties when real estate values in Fairfield County were down and home-heating oil prices were up. No one wanted a sprawling three-acre piece of waterfront property with a damaged dock, a moldy boathouse, and a rundown, weathered gray, five-bedroom house from the 1930s that today's agents would brand "Southport Shingle Style." No one except Maeve Sweeney, a poet who saw the romantic in the mundane, and her husband, Bill Sweeney, the newest literary light in the firmament, who wanted someplace to write that was halfway between New York City and his office at Yale where he'd just accepted a teaching job. With Maeve's inheritance from her Boston aunt and Bill's advance for his second book after his coming-of-age debut novel had spent three years on the *New York Times* bestseller list, the newlyweds bought Willow Lane and made it a home and a hideout. At the end of a long drive at the end of a dead-end street, the main selling point of the Willow Lane house was privacy.

Bill's newfound fame was something that unnerved Maeve. She had wanted him to herself for a little while longer, like when they first met. She was a new MFA student at Yale, fresh from Bennington, interviewing for a teaching assistant position in the undergrad creative writing department; he was the most-talked-about professor on the faculty because of his fame, his generous laugh, and his dark Irish looks. Their intense romance surprised classmates and colleagues who assumed Bill Sweeney had a few more years of playing the field before he settled down, and underestimated the intellect of the red-haired, well-born bohemian. The two writers connected immediately and deeply. He found someone he could trust with his talent. Maeve brought out the brilliant in Bill.

It didn't take Maeve long to learn that her husband loved, loved, loved the limelight, but when he was on deadline, he needed to burrow so deep underground, no party or opening could tempt him. Willow Lane provided both of them with what they craved. Plus, his college roommate, best friend and lawyer Cap Richardson, was within walking distance, across from the Yacht Club so he could be close to his boat. Cap provided the young Sweeneys with an instant social circle and protection at the same time. He was always looking out for Bill, insulating him from his own worst behavior but, as importantly, Cap was always looking out for Maeve, who had bewitched him a tiny bit. The arrangement worked for years with few hitches.

Bill created a writing studio out of the boathouse where he would spend the next forty years crafting some of the seminal novels in the contemporary American literary canon, as well as dozens of essays for *The New Yorker*, *The Atlantic*, *Esquire*, and *The Paris Review* of equal importance. When he wasn't writing, he would spend hours in the boathouse reading, grading papers, or listening to Yankees games on the radio. Even on the weekends, you could find him napping on the rattan couches or in the attic bedroom in the boathouse that had served as a guest room for some of the greatest writers of the generation.

Almost weekly, then less so as the years went by, book and magazine editors or one of his agents, first the legendary Abe Eckstein and then after Abe's death, his protégé Lois Hopper, would make the pilgrimage by train out from the city to see Bill, trying to convince him to write a piece on this or coax him to take a look at that, then end the day with a drink while overlooking the water. Lois had cultivated a trademark fashion accessory, a bold hat for every outfit. She was a throwback, out of step with younger agents who dressed in black and had law degrees to go along with their literary sensibilities. But Bill liked Lois and her hats. Nothing about her tempted him. As he had said to Cap once, "There's no amount of alcohol that would get me to sleep with Lois."

To which Cap replied, "I think she feels the same way about you."

On other days, when he worked alone from morning through late afternoon, Bill Sweeney, drink in hand, would rig up his Laser and take a sunset sail along the coastline toward Westport. Or he'd fish off the dock for blues that he'd throw back in the Sound. The boathouse was always the boathouse, never the office, because it was so much more than that.

Maeve created a comfortable haven in the main house where all felt welcome, all invited. Mostly all. She wasn't a fan of the William Sweeney groupies, thin, well-educated young women dressed in the urban chic of black on black on navy blue, who would arrive as the plus-ones of a junior editor or a lesser writer but always seemed to have their eyes on Bill during the frequent parties in the early days of Willow Lane. But she was generous to her real friends, to her children, and to her children's friends.

But Maeve struggled to create a writing life for herself. She wrote in flashes, as if she was storing up material in her mind's eye until she had a few days of unscheduled time to get it all out. She would place a poem here or there in literary journals and even managed to publish a slim collection of poetry with a tiny press, but she was never sure if her work stood on its own merit or the reflected light of her husband's reputation. The condescending tone used by Bill's colleagues or editors when they asked about her writing chipped away at her confidence. At times, she was relieved to retreat back into motherhood and let Bill's work shine.

The Southport neighbors loved that William Sweeney brought a touch of genuine literary celebrity to their little village filled with old money, card-carrying Daughters of the American Revolution, titans of business, publishing, and media, lawyers from white-shoe firms, and bankers who played by the rules and some who didn't. But Maeve brought an unexpected touch of the suburban hippie with her long, curly red hair, flowing skirts, and poet's sensibilities. She once heard one matron at a garden party fundraiser comment, "Someone got lost on the way home from Woodstock." Maeve stopped going to garden party fundraisers.

She rode a Vespa around town in the summer, shared her homegrown tomatoes and blueberry muffins with the local firefighters in exchange for cutting rights of the magnificent hydrangeas they had cultivated outside the firehouse, and created a haunted house for Halloween that made the long walk down the driveway worth every creepy step. And while other houses in Southport, fit for the National Register of Historic Places, were stiff and formal, filled with uncomfortable but period-appropriate Early American furniture, Willow Lane was more like a year-round beach house: nothing fancy, everything could be replaced. As Maeve used to explain to guests, "Shabby and chic before Shabby Chic was chic."

In her healthy years, Maeve wrote in her own studio, a glass-roofed conservatory that capped the far wing of the house. When the breast cancer metastasized and it was clear there would be no miracle cure, the conservatory became her sanctuary, filled with plants, music, and artwork, her chemo brain too addled for books.

Life wasn't perfect on Willow Lane; no childhood ever is. There were rumors and some truth to the stories of their father's drinking and gambling, and their mother's illness hung over the family like a dark veil, but the Sweeney sisters couldn't have imagined a better place to grow up. The water, the dock, the rolling lawn, the wrap-around slate patio that served as everything from childhood playhouse to wedding dance floor when Liza married Whit. The giant trampoline that all the kids in the neighborhood used at will. The hedge of hydrangeas, the lilies of the valley tucked in along the stone wall.

For the sisters, Willow Lane would always evoke the echoes of their father's laughter, their mother's singing, the glamorous parties, and the raucous poker games. But sitting on the patio, Liza could also hear the fights in her head. The battles between the sisters over clothes or boys. The muffled fights between their parents over money or whatever else married couples argued over. Suddenly, as Liza sipped her wine, she had a thought. "Do you think that's what Mom and Dad were always fighting about—Birdie Tucker?"

"I hope not," Maggie answered. "I hope Mom never knew."

Chapter

Serena Tucker was not a good dancer. She could play the flute, hit a decent forehand, and write a strong opening paragraph, but any trip out onto the dance floor required a substantial amount of alcohol. That was certainly the case tonight. She had arrived at William Sweeney's wake filled with confidence and curiosity, determined to make a statement, but about halfway through the second eulogy, after hearing the laundry list of William Sweeney's literary awards and achievements, the praise from other writers, her bravado crumbled. By the time the toasts started and Willem Dafoe offered her a shot of whiskey, she accepted gratefully, followed by another. Then, the dancing seemed like a really solid idea, maybe the only way to get through the rest of the night, to try to blend into the wild mess instead of standing to the side observing, which was her usual habit.

Now, Serena sat at the bar at the Delamar Hotel, hoping a cranberry with seltzer would dissipate the remains of her hangover and the giant ball of stress in her gut ever since she'd arrived in Southport. The wake. The whiskey. Willem Dafoe. She was glad she made it back to the hotel, catching a ride with the mourners headed to the train station. She walked the half mile beyond the station to the hotel and promptly passed out in the four-poster bed. The luxury hotel was a splurge, an indulgence she allowed herself on occasion because that's what trust funds were for, and the high-quality sheets and steam shower had been worth the extra money. She'd spent the morning in bed, popping ibuprofen and researching everybody from the night before to make sure no embarrassing photos of her had emerged on social media. They hadn't. Apparently, no one wanted to share their night memorializing with the general public. *That's what real friends are for,* thought Serena.

After a long shower, Serena spent an hour reading all the social media tributes on #WilliamSweeney, everyone from the president, who had awarded him the Presidential Medal of Freedom, to noted writers and editors recalling their first encounter with Sweeney's work, to college kids discovering him for the first time. She had to drag herself away from the computer to get lunch in the village—a turkey sandwich, oatmeal cookie, and a Diet Coke, her usual. After a walk down to the harbor and back, Serena's head was clearer, her mind sharper. It was a strange sensation, walking through town now, past the houses of family friends—the Wyndhams, the Sills, the Vankirks—knowing that she'd grown up here with half an identity and was now whole. It mattered to her. Would it matter to anyone else?

She looked around the hotel bar for a familiar face, but Southport had changed some since her childhood. It wasn't the type of people attracted to the town who had changed—traditional, well-educated, bound to both commuting into New York City but preferring life in the suburbs—but the actual people. Many of Serena's parents' generation had sold their big waterfront homes and moved to tasteful condos or warmer climates. As Serena peered around the bar, she thought, *The faces are different, but the fashion's the same. Long live the navy-blue blazer on both men and women.* She flagged down the bartender to order a bowl of chowder. That would put her back in business, she thought. But what business exactly?

Since discovering her connection to the Sweeney family six months ago, Serena had questioned about 98 percent of the decisions she'd made in her life, including the one to redeem the DNA testing gift certificate that she'd won at the office holiday party. That night was a high point for *Straight Up*. The launch had gone well, the reviews were favorable, the money was flowing in a way that younger journalists weren't accustomed to and seasoned journalists hadn't experienced in a while. "It's like the old days, when people actually read news-papers," one veteran reporter had said, ironically toasting their good fortune to land at *Straight Up*, the next hot website, at the right time.

The journalists there were committed to speaking truth to power across the spectrum—from politics to business to sports to the cre-ative arts. They were a smart, connected bunch with edge. The site had been funded by an anonymous source, but it was an open secret that biotech golden girl Katie McFarland held the purse strings; that is, until her miracle medical testing method was proven to be a fraud, and now she was under federal indictment. Unless *Straight Up* found a buyer, the site would be gone by Labor Day and all the journalists who believed in the mission and had left their steady gigs at more established outlets would be out of work, including Serena.

But that night, at the party at the company HQ in DC's trendy Shaw neighborhood, all was right in Serena's world. The new job was a dream, the man she'd been seeing for a few months was someone she really liked and who seemed to really like her in return, even though he was in the middle of a messy divorce. Plus, she'd finally found a decent hairdresser in DC who truly understood long lay-ers, tough to find in the home of the conservative blunt cut. When she won the raffle prize, her editor Jonah, a brilliant journalist from Brooklyn who'd risen from the City College of New York to run a re-spected news organization, had joked that Serena would finally have proof she was really 100 percent WASP. Serena had laughed a bit too loud and too long, because there were mojitos involved and she'd had a crush on Jonah since they'd worked together at the *Post*.

Serena's pedigree did seem unimpeachable. She was the only child of Mitchell and Rebecca "Birdie" Tucker, formerly of Southport,

Connecticut, now of Hobe Sound, Florida. Her father, a Williams man, owned a small insurance empire that his grandfather had started at the turn of the twentieth century, and her mother, Birdie, a Vassar girl, chaired the board of the venerated Pequot Library and had won the club championships in tennis for most of the 1980s and '90s, her dominant run stopped only by a rotator cuff injury that even Tommy John surgery couldn't fix. Mitchell collected electric trains and had turned their attic into his sanctuary, constructing a massive Alpine Village, complete with tracks, Swiss chalets, and cows grazing in meadows. Birdie was more than happy to never bother him when he was playing with his trains. Mitchell and Birdie interacted when necessary and with extreme politeness, making them the perfect couple.

Serena did as she was told without much fuss. Valedictorian at Green Farms Academy, a comp lit major at Vassar, masters at Columbia School of Journalism. She played tennis and vacationed in Nantucket the first two weeks of August every summer without any pushback, even though it could be deadly boring with the same people doing the same things every year. Serena's mother always referred to her as "a serious girl," probably because she spent more time listening to NPR and watching the news than chasing down the best party or the cutest guy. She'd never be social enough for her mother, who was disappointed Serena didn't want to be a debutante, opting to do a study abroad program in Prague instead.

After grad school, Serena was primed for a life as a network morning show producer, the sort of idealized New York City rom-com career that her mother, a former associate producer at NBC News, had envisioned for herself but abandoned after marriage and motherhood. Birdie was determined that her daughter would have the career she didn't, orchestrating an entrée through a contact. Her college roommate's daughter was a producer at the *Today* show and Birdie arranged a dinner in the city for the two girls, convinced Serena would make an impression that would set her up for a life that included a tasteful Chelsea loft during the week and summer weekends in Southport. After working for a few years and securing a producer spot, Serena would be ready for a husband and child, all while maintaining a solid forehand and enviable fitness. Birdie could see her daughter's future and it was respectable.

But Serena surprised her parents by taking a less glamorous job in DC after grad school as a beat reporter. Bitten by the political bug in college and fascinated by the changing global landscape post-9/11, Serena settled in at the *Washington Post* as a national security reporter covering the Pentagon with the intent to inform and educate the American public, causing Birdie to tell anyone who asked, "She's working for that liberal rag. She won't last six months." Fifteen years later, Serena had carved out a career as a solid journalist, spending several years at the Hague bureau, reporting on international justice, before jumping to *Slate*, where she had reported on the State Department. The Washington scene suited Serena, somehow both global and clubby at the same time. She never felt out of her comfort zone.

At *Straight Up*, she focused on the intersection of diplomacy, national security, and human rights, a beat that was both professionally ambitious and personally satisfying. She'd become a regular on some political podcasts, providing a measured, well-reported point of view to counter-balance the hosts' outrage.

For Birdie, who had doubted that writing for a website was a legitimate career move, the podcast appearances sealed her impression that Serena's career had stalled mid-level. (As Birdie told her bridge club, "She used to be a journalist, but now she's what they call a blogger and a podcaster. All that education . . .") Serena's personal life had disappointed her mother almost more than her professional life.

For eight years, as she was building her career, Serena lived with another reporter named Ben Cohen in a renovated Georgetown row house near Dumbarton Oaks that she bought thanks to the trust fund her paternal grandmother had set up for her. (It was one thing to work as a journalist; it was another thing to live like one. Serena kept her private life very private from most of her colleagues, but it involved quality cashmere, French wine, and top-tier vacations, plus board positions on several charities normally out of reach for members of the press.) With Ben, it was no ring, no commitment, no kids, not even a cat, and Serena was fine with the arrangement. Ben made her laugh and didn't put any pressure on Serena to return the favor. Ben liked Serena for her integrity and her focus, not exactly the sort of qualities that might stand out in an OkCupid profile. In short, Serena felt secure with Ben. They talked about work and Washington and work again, eating takeout from neighborhood restaurants and watching CNN and *Frontline*.

Ben being Jewish wasn't exactly a big hit in the Tucker family, so it was hard to imagine a scenario that ended with a tasteful family wedding in the Tucker backyard under a green-and-white-striped tent with a Lester Lanin band playing. Still, Birdie managed to be on her best behavior the few times Ben came to Southport for the weekend, and her father, now retired, had basically checked out of any conversation that didn't involve trains, insurance, or his hero George Will, so his input was minimum. Some of the weekends felt like months.

When Ben moved out, shocking Serena by saying that it was time he found a nice Jewish girl he could marry and start a family with, she was thirty-five. She honestly thought he was kidding as he packed up his record collection, which was heavy on jazz and light on anything hummable, but a trip home to Scarsdale for his grandmother's ninetieth birthday had convinced Ben that he needed to get serious about his future with a woman who was less blond, more nurturing. "I think I need someone who is . . . more familiar with my background," Ben explained, without making eye contact once with Serena. His wedding announcement was in the *New York Times* a year later, to a woman named Tamar, twenty-seven, who was the director of fundraising at the Holocaust Memorial Museum in DC and a Duke graduate. (According to the announcement, they had met in a Jewish Singles Ski Club, which infuriated Serena because for *years* she had tried to get Ben to ski out west with her and he had always refused, saying, "My people are doctors, not skiers.")

"Well, you're a done deal now," her mother pronounced that Thanksgiving, after a few glasses of wine. She told Serena that they were selling the house in Southport and moving to Florida full time, adding, "Why stay in the Northeast if there will be no grandchildren?" It was a harsh assessment, even for her mother, who specialized in cutting rebukes. Serena's mother hadn't seemed to enjoy motherhood that much; she was surprised that Birdie wanted grandchildren at all. When Serena commented as much, Birdie responded, "It's what's expected. What else are we to do for the next ten years?"

Serena had no reply.

She was relieved, not that Ben was gone, but that her parents would be. She needed space. In the immediate aftermath of Ben's wedding announcement, she applied to and was accepted at Stanford for a Knight Journalism Fellowship. The year in Palo Alto surrounded by smart strangers who knew nothing of Ben or her parents served as the perfect palate cleanser for her personal life and a boost to her professional life. The job at *Straight Up* was a leap for her on all levels, and she took it with confidence when she returned to DC. She wasn't a done deal, she knew that.

The DNA test kit was sitting there on her mantel. It was New Year's Eve and, in the two weeks since the office party, she'd discovered that Dean, the great guy she'd met in a bar at Reagan Airport one foggy night, was actually happily married and not in the middle of a messy divorce as he'd said. Feeling down, she'd waved off every invitation from her single colleagues to attend overpriced prix fixe dinners at restaurants and all the invitations to small get-togethers hosted by her married-with-children friends who were going to ring in the New Year at nine, instead of midnight, a phenomenon Serena thought was too precious to indulge. She was leaving for an obligatory three days in Hobe Sound the next morning. The DNA kit seemed like a positive, slightly provocative way to start the new year. Maybe she'd get a story out of it, or at least, a personal essay she would submit to the *Times* or a magazine.

Six weeks later, when the email arrived in Serena's inbox about her possible genetic matches, she actually laughed at the subject line: Want to meet more Tuckers? They're out there. No thanks, she didn't want to meet any more Tuckers. Her parents were enough Tuckers in her life, she thought. When she clicked the link and spotted that she had matched with a Sweeney from Southport, she sat frozen at her desk, hoping her colleagues didn't notice. Almost paralyzed, like she'd been shot with a tranquilizer dart. As the feeling returned to her body, it spread like a warm wave of relief. Serena had felt like a fake inside her own skin for as long as she could remember. Even though she had inherited her mother's coloring and took after her father in terms of disposition, she felt disconnected from Birdie and Mitchell Tucker in a way she couldn't describe until now. She grabbed her stuff and fled the office, needing to walk off the chaos surging through her veins.

If Serena had a husband or a tight group of girlfriends, she would have texted them: WTF, William Sweeney is my father. But she had no one close enough to share her monumental secret, so she whispered it to herself as she walked in a frantic pace to the National Mall to work out the panic in her head.

The fact that she was William Sweeney's daughter and not Mitchell Tucker's daughter explained so much to her. The loneliness of her childhood, the restlessness of her college years, and the joy she found in a newsroom, being part of a team working to uncover the truth. When Serena discovered writing during high school, she felt like she'd unlocked a secret door that her parents didn't even try to understand. ("If I were you, I'd take a few accounting classes along with all the literature," Mitch Tucker had warned as they dropped her off at Vassar.) Now writing, her secret door, connected her to William Sweeney, *the* William Sweeney.

As Serena walked to the Washington Monument and back to the Lincoln Memorial, she tried to come to grips with the revelations: that her mother had had an affair, that her parents had lied to her for decades, that maybe her father had no idea that Serena wasn't his, that she had an entire family out there who didn't know she existed. And what if the results couldn't be trusted? Then again, what were the chances that her neighbor's name from Southport would pop up? Serena had only used her Washington, DC, address. The company would never have known that she'd been neighbors with the Sweeneys. Serena decided to approach this revelation like she would any story—do the research, formulate the questions, track down the key interviews, and then write the story as truthfully as possible.

For the next two months, Serena worked at *Straight Up* by day and at night at home on what she started to call Project Prodigal. Once she satisfied her skepticism that the DNA test might be bogus (it wasn't), she read everything she could by and about Bill Sweeney, including his memoir *My Maeve*, which gave her insight into what was really happening on Willow Lane during the years when the gardens went untended and the nursing care came around the clock. It was clear from the title and the text that William Sweeney had little idea about what Liza, Maggie, and Tricia were going through during and after their mother's death. She felt sorry for them, for *her sisters.*

She searched for any reference, in his fiction or memoir, to Birdie Tucker, finding only one reference in *Million Zillion*, his least successful novel, published in 1998, that a *Kirkus* review described as "a wan Wall Street satire that recycles the cynicism of *Bitter Fruit* without any of the humanity." (Bill Sweeney wouldn't write another book for seven years after the lackluster reception and sales.) In *Million Zillion*, the protagonist, a corrupt but dynamic banker who turns himself in to the FBI, is married to a character named Wren, described as "an Amazonian blonde, a slender cypher who exists on gin and tonics and vitriol and the belief that appearances must be maintained at all costs." Ultimately, Wren abandons her sexy jailbird husband for a quiet and serene life on the Maine coast remarried to an accountant. Serena recognized Wren was Birdie Tucker. Brutal. *He sounds like a jilted lover,* she thought, finding it impossible to believe that anyone of William Sweeney's stature had ever felt that way about Birdie Tucker, Club Champion.

Serena weighed whether the conversation with her mother should be in person or over the phone. The only benefit to an in-person confrontation, and she was sure it would be a confrontation, was to have the satisfaction of having the upper hand, if even for an instant, but having to make conversation with her father afterward negated any upside. Instead, she took the approach she often used with interview subjects she needed for background, an email first to set up a time including only vague information about the intention of the conversation, followed by a taped phone call on the record. Serena found this softened up potential subjects, so when she came at them with specifics, they caved quickly, not expecting the directness. She needed her mother to be honest and quick, because the last thing she wanted was details. Serena and her mother didn't have that kind of relationship and they never would.

After months of research and theories and daydreams of what her life might have been like had she known the truth for thirty-eight years instead of only the last five months, the conversation with her mother was short and simple, without apology or surprise. When the day arrived to make the call, Serena, who had interviewed dictators and drug lords, was terrified of her mother, scared to say the words out loud and make the accusation. But she found her voice: "I did a DNA test. It appears that Mitchell Tucker is not my biological father. Does that surprise you?"

It was like Birdie had been waiting for the moment; her voice was measured and calm. "I've come to believe that William Sweeney is your father. I never had any other children, so I assumed that your father couldn't. But I never knew for sure until now and I've never told anyone. Including your father. Mitchell. Dad." Then, Birdie added, "It wasn't my finest moment, Serena, and I'd appreciate it if we kept this between us. But, of course, that's up to you. I understand that you can do what you wish with the information."

Serena set up an appointment with Cap Richardson for the next week. She wanted to meet her father, although she'd seen him dozens of times in the past. He was the local celebrity. When Bill Sweeney was around, people noticed. Serena had, for sure. At the neighborhood Christmas party. Walking his dog down the lane and giving Serena a little nod and a quick word. She'd seen him at half a dozen library events, as he charmed the audience with his storytelling and humor. But she needed to talk to him in this new context. Serena wanted to meet her father, not the local celebrity.

Like any decent reporter, Serena knew she was sitting on a blockbuster story, maybe even a memoir of her own. Certainly, it was enough to get a publisher interested and that would be enough to get her out the door at *Straight Up* before it went under. She came to Southport to assess whether the truth would be worth telling to the world and what that would cost her in her life. She needed to understand what she might be losing and that involved the Sweeney sisters. Serena set to work investigating each of them. They each had a story to tell.

Serena hadn't seen them in years, since she'd graduated from college and left Southport. Watching them dance together at the wake to an ancient Boz Scaggs song, laughing and playing off each other, Serena could remember them as teenagers walking down the lane on their way home from the pharmacy in the village or sailing lessons at the yacht club. You could hear them first, either singing the Spice Girls at the top of their lungs or Liza screaming at Maggie about something she did or didn't do and Tricia pleading with them to stop fighting. Serena would look up from the big chair on the porch where she'd be reading the paper. The Sweeney girls always walked right in the middle of the road, oblivious to the few cars that might turn down their dead-end street. *The cars can wait for us*, their attitude seemed to say. To Serena, an only child who stuck to the sidewalk, the confidence of the younger girls was striking.

But it wasn't admirable to Serena's mother, who had no patience for the carefree Sweeneys. She would beep at them in her car and shoo them over to the sidewalk, remarking to her own daughter, "Those Sweeneys, they seem to think the moon and the stars revolve around them."

It's true. They did.

Serena would have expected them to have changed so much more, in their thirties having lost both their parents, to have taken up this heavy burden and wear the pain on their faces. But instead, she found herself amazed by their lightness, their collective energy. (Another reason the whiskey and the dancing had seemed like a good idea. Who could compete with these sisters?)

Liza, with her deep auburn hair and pale complexion, was petite and had matured into the classic preppy style she'd always worn. Serena had envied Liza growing up, pulling off dark blue jeans, her French striped sweaters and vintage Pappagallo espadrilles. At the wake, she was in a simple black dress, three strands of pearls, and flats for the lawn and she looked perfect. Serena was surprised to hear that she had married Whit Jones, a dull but solid guy, who predictably became his father, complete with golf tan and a receding hairline. Liza had always been surrounded by much cuter boys at regattas or cotillions. And then there was the rumor that she'd been involved with Gray Cunningham, town bad boy and the first person she'd ever known to sell prescription meds. (It must be true because Gray was here tonight and he looked fantastic, like Jake Gyllenhaal on a good night.) And yet, Liza had married Whit, raised twins, and lived in the big Victorian nearby with the decorative wreath on the front door, like a proper Southport girl. There must be something more to that story, Serena thought.

Then there was Maggie, wild Maggie, "Mad Maggie" she had heard Bill Sweeney call her once at a neighborhood Christmas party. Maggie looked so much like their mother, it was uncanny. She hadn't changed a bit with her strawberry-blond hair, tan shoulders, and wrists filled with silver bangles. She still turned heads. Serena remembered being at the market when a seventeen-year-old Maggie Sweeney had swept in to buy a Diet Coke and all the men in the store watched her in her short sundress, floppy hat, and scrunchy suede boots as she sauntered out. Serena stood at the register, mid-transaction, waiting for the clerk to recall that she was there at all. She was something then and she was something now. Taller than Liza and curvier, she looked like she'd stepped out of an Anthropologie catalogue in her black maxi dress dotted with white stars and a pink-and-orange scarf in her hair. *Who has the guts to wear that to a funeral?* she thought.

Finally, Tricia, who surprised Serena most of all, probably because she had been in braces the last time she had seen her. Now she was tall and athletic looking, like she could run a million miles before needing a drink of water. It made sense. Serena recalled that little Tricia was always running or jumping. The Sweeneys had a giant trampoline in their backyard and while Serena was upstairs in her bedroom grinding away on her homework, she could see preteen Tricia jumping up and down all afternoon. Now she was a grown woman with straight red hair in a chin-length bob, wearing an expensive sheath dress and simple diamond earrings. There was no wedding ring on her finger, so Serena guessed she had bought the diamonds herself. She knew Tricia was a lawyer and she had acted the part of family spokesperson for the last few days, speaking to the press, doing interviews laced with funny and charming stories while reminding everyone of her father's tremendous legacy.

During the wake, Serena had watched Tricia circulate through the guests like a politician, a species with which Serena was familiar, shaking hands warmly with her father's colleagues or hugging the neighbors and close friends, maintaining eye contact with everyone she encountered, working her way through all the mourners turned revelers. Tricia had a job to do and she was thorough. Serena had fled to the ladies' room inside the house when Tricia was making a beeline for the group from Yale that Serena had attached herself to. There was no way she could talk to Tricia or any of the sisters.

What had she been thinking? She was Serena Tucker, former neighbor and never really a friend to the Sweeneys. When the *New York Times* alert flashed across Serena's phone screen, she had felt compelled to return to Southport, to be a part of saying goodbye to the man she barely knew, except from his writing. She imagined there would be some gathering at the library or the yacht club she could attend. When Lucy Winthrop told her about the invite-only celebration at Willow Lane, she thought, *I have a right to mourn, to be there.*

Serena hopped aboard the Acela at Union Station in DC. She had stared out the window thinking of nothing, a rare occurrence for her busy mind, as the train made its way through Baltimore, Delaware, Philly, Newark, Penn Station, and, finally, Stamford. She rented a car at the station and drove the scenic route to Southport.

But now that she was back, she thought of what her mother Birdie had said about "those Sweeneys" and the moon and the stars. This was their universe and Serena had no business at Willow Lane.

As the bartender put down her chowder, her phone buzzed. It was a text from Cap Richardson. The sisters would like to meet. Please call me in the morning to set up a time.

"Anything else?" the bartender interrupted Serena's thoughts.

"You know what? I think I will have a glass of wine. Do you have a good red?"

Chapter

Liza, Maggie, and Tricia sat around the mahogany conference table in the law offices of Richardson & Blix waiting for last-minute instructions and gathering their courage. Serena would be walking through the door any minute and, despite their differences in careers, marital status, and degree to which they were concerned about this woman's motives, the sisters were united on one issue: Do Not Blurt Out Any Family Secrets.

Cap kept referring to the event as a "Meet and Greet," as if Serena were a potential new client and the Sweeneys were offering their services in closet organizing or home decorating. "This is the first step. You don't have to make any decisions or form any lifelong bonds today. Meet her and then decide for yourselves about how you'd like to proceed. But understand that she has legal rights here. You will have to deal with her in the future. I suggest that you be polite and positive. Don't antagonize her . . ."

"Tricia, did you hear what Cap said? No antagonizing!" Maggie said.

"I'm not the wild card here," Tricia responded, implying it was Maggie's personality, not Tricia's, that was the most unpredictable.

"Let Cap finish," Liza said.

Cap was firm, but spoke more softly when he cautioned the sisters, "Whatever anger or disappointment you might feel toward your father, try to put that aside when you speak to Serena. I know you have memories of her from years ago, when you thought of her only as a neighbor. But she is a formidable person as an adult. And now, she is a relative, so bear that in mind."

Tricia knew she could keep a lid on the situation, but was worried about Liza, who got emotional and defensive about her father and her mother, and Maggie, who, when agitated, lashed out at the agitator. Tricia wanted the meeting to feel more like a deposition than a cozy family reunion. "The key is to get Serena to talk about Serena. Ask her questions about her life, her work. Be curious about her, so she won't ask too many about us. Or Dad. I can do all the talking, if you want."

"You've told us this, like, ten times. We get it," replied Maggie, rolling her eyes like a teenager, which was probably why Tricia was treating her like one. "And I think Liza and I can handle asking a few questions ourselves. She's our half-sister, too."

"Oh, please. This isn't about sisterhood. She's a journalist and we don't know how she's going to process all of this," Tricia explained, sweeping her hands around the room to mean the legacy of the deep relationship between Cap and Bill Sweeney, and the cozy relationship that the three of them had with Cap and all the people at Richardson & Blix (except Blix, who'd been dead for decades). "She could have a story online tomorrow about her true parentage. For all we know, she's been working on something for months, so let's not get all 'Oh, she's my sister.' She's probably on the hunt for a story, not a sister."

Rose, the firm's administrative assistant and one of Tricia's classmates in elementary school, popped her head in the door. "Serena Tucker is here."

Cap stood and straightened his tie. "Please show her in, Rose."

Because of her work, Serena had walked into rooms with high-ranking diplomats and generals. She'd met with war lords, Nobel Peace Prize laureates, even Pope John Paul II as a young reporter on a pool trip to the Vatican. But nothing had quite prepared her for this moment, knowingly meeting her three sisters for the first time. She had watched tearful family reunions on daytime television for years as she'd killed time in hotel rooms before an evening press event. This was not going to be that, she knew. The sterile law office setting and the formal greeting from Cap Richardson made that clear. Even still, the emotion, the prick of tears, surprised her as she entered.

She had been so nervous about making the right impression that she had made a last-minute shopping trip to Main Street in fashionable Westport to buy something, anything that wasn't black, even if it was overpriced (which it was). She found a charcoal gray sheath dress, a Marimekko scarf, and a dark jean jacket that looked less severe than her usual uniform of black pants, black sweater or T-shirt, black leather jacket, or black Patagonia down vest. As part of the print media, she didn't have to worry about looking good on camera, so she dressed functionally, as if at any moment an international crisis might break out and she'd have to run for cover. But today, for this meeting, she wanted to put aside her reporter instincts and be in the moment. New clothes helped her do that.

She entered the conference room with false confidence, taking in the scene: Tricia, at the far end of the table, in a blue suit jacket, hair up in a messy bun, smart glasses pushed up on her forehead and lips done in deep rose lipstick, looking like a TV lawyer, sitting in front of a legal pad with notes on it already; Maggie, wearing a peasant blouse and her hair up in a scarf, could have been headed to the farmers' market; and Liza was suburban chic in one of those floral print dresses that all young mothers seemed to live in, but Serena had no idea where they could be purchased. These are my sisters. She hoped she could find her voice. "Hello, it's good to see you again. I'm Serena Tucker."

Liza and Maggie stood up to greet her. Maggie reached her first and gave her an authentic hug, enveloping her in warmth and her signature scent of orange blossoms. ("I'm a citrus," Maggie had announced when she'd returned home from California. "I had my essence analyzed and I'm a tangy sweet citrus fruit.") Serena responded in kind with a real hug. Liza stepped in with a cooler version of Maggie's embrace, but as she pulled away, she smiled, her eyes bright with emotion. "This is quite a surprise. We have a lot to catch up on."

Serena responded to Liza's light touch. She relaxed as she made her way to a seat at the far end of the table.

Tricia stood up and reached across the wide table to shake Serena's hand. "Thanks for coming in today. It's very helpful to meet face-to-face." Serena could appreciate Tricia's manner. She had used the veneer of politeness many times in her career when interviewing celebrities or well-known political leaders. Being hyper-professional helped Serena to avoid getting sucked into their charisma vortex. Tricia was using the same tactic.

"Of course," Serena replied, settling into her chair and wondering where the conversation would go from here.

But she didn't have long to process as Tricia jumped in. "So, Serena, we thought we'd start by giving you an update on everything that's happening now with the estate, covering the legal issues first. Then we're happy to answer any questions you may have. Obviously, this is an unexpected situation for us and not something we anticipated when we arrived in Southport, so feel free to jot down any thoughts on the pad in front of you and we can address them at the end."

Liza and Maggie locked eyes. This was so Tricia, managing the conversation as she had outlined in advance to her sisters. Tricia insisted on a scripted opening, while Maggie and Liza wanted a more organic interaction. "Why don't we feel the moment and see what works?" Maggie had suggested to which Tricia responded, "That's a terrible idea." Tricia won and then brought along her own yellow pads to prove it. Maggie caught Liza's eye, mouthing the words, *Here she goes.*

But Serena surprised them all by cutting off Tricia's opening statement with her own. "I hope you don't mind, but before we get to anything formal, I wanted to let you know how much I've always admired your family from afar. I know we weren't great friends and our families weren't close, but I could hear the sounds of laughter and music next door and thought of how lucky you all were to grow up in a house like that. Your mother was beautiful, a lovely person. I was sorry for her passing at such a young age. She always had something kind to say to me. I admired her spirit and loved running into her at the market or anywhere in the village. She was different, special. And your father, I admired his work so much and have read or reread almost everything he's ever written since . . ." Serena stumbled for the right phrase. ". . . since I've known. He was a brilliant writer. I really wish I'd had a chance to speak to him before his death, but we hadn't been able to set up a time. It would have meant the world to me."

None of the sisters could respond to Serena's last statement, knowing that their father never intended to acknowledge Serena publicly, or even in private, during his lifetime. They each sat quietly, avoiding her eyes. No one felt the need to tell her the truth. She took the silence as an invitation to continue.

"But my most vivid memories of him are on Halloween every year when he dressed up like King Lear with that smoking cauldron, and your mother with the eye of newt bit. I always saved your house for last because it was so magical. I know this isn't what any of you anticipated, but I hope you understand how much I admired your family and am honored to be a part of it."

Maggie dropped her head and let out a sob; Liza stared straight ahead, trying hard not to cry. The Halloween memory got them in the gut, the recollection of their father embracing the holiday, playing the part of the disillusioned king with gusto and their mother dressed as a terrible witch, stirring the cauldron and serving hot apple cider and doughnuts to the brave souls who wandered down their long, dark driveway. Amidst the sadness and sickness in the house some years, Halloween was the one day where everyone rallied. It wasn't as if Maggie and Liza had forgotten, they simply hadn't remembered the wonder of that day in years.

Tricia, on the other, kept her head, thinking to herself, *Damn, she's good.*

Serena let the revelations of the will wash over her. Cap presented the details and Tricia provided additional information when necessary. Serena had called a lawyer friend on the premise of researching a story and understood what her rights were before she walked into the conference room, but was flabbergasted that she was mentioned in the will. All she had wanted was to meet with William Sweeney. Her intention was never to go after any part of the estate. But now, her journalist's skepticism emerged. Why would Bill Sweeney refuse to meet her, but include her in his will? But her only response was, "I'm truly shocked and humbled by this. I never expected to be named an heir. I will do my best to work with all of you on this."

Serena could feel Maggie and Liza studying her, and it made her self-conscious. What could they be thinking? She didn't know them well enough to presume anything at all. Finally, a question from Tricia snapped her back to the room. "Can you tell us about your immediate plans?"

For a second, Serena struggled to understand the question, thinking that it was about lunch or what she was going to do this afternoon. Then realized it was about The Announcement: what she was going to tell the world and when. She didn't get caught in that quicksand. "I've decided to take a sabbatical from my job at *Straight Up.* I've been grinding along for fifteen years without a break from deadlines and work. I ran into Lucy Winthrop yesterday and it turns out she has a guest cottage available. She's a close friend of my mother's. It was a spur-of-the-moment opportunity and I grabbed it. I'll be here all summer figuring out what's next for me. This is the right place to do that."

"Take a sabbatical or resign?" Nothing got past Tricia when she was in the zone. *Straight Up* was on its last legs. Nobody takes "a sabbatical" from a failing business.

Serena was stalling, not wanting to clarify her intentions when Maggie, who'd been quiet since she stopped sobbing, saved her by erupting, "Oh my God, I remember that guest cottage. Ben Winthrop! Remember him, Liza? He was so cute. He went to Exeter. Remember that night after Molly Miller's deb party? That cheesy square dance thing in her barn and then we all went to the Winthrops' giant house because they had a foosball table." Maggie used air quotes around *foosball table* and what it really meant was anyone's guess, but it cracked the two of them up. "And he kept trying to rap that Jay-Z song even though he's like the whitest guy ever. His dad has been our congressman for what, like, forty years?"

"Eighteen terms," Tricia corrected Maggie.

"The congressman and his wife are one of the few Southport connections I have in DC. They invite me to things all the time, as a former constituent," Serena said, not adding that as a member of the press, there was an ulterior motive to most of the invites. Lucy Winthrop's strategy was Always Be Pitching.

"The congressman and Mrs. Winthrop were at the White House when our father was an honoree," Liza said, then immediately regretted her words. She sounded like the worst kind of entitled namedropper. It was the sort of comment she would have lectured Fitz or Vivi about on the car ride home. She quickly changed the subject. "Going back to the foosball night, Mags, you had on those purple cowboy boots and that crumpled cowboy hat. And what was that tank top?"

"I was going for Sheryl Crow, the early years. I thought I looked good."

"So did Ben Winthrop, Foosball Master."

The amount of time any Sweeney could carry on a serious conversation without a break for irreverence was limited, especially Liza and Maggie, who had shared so many misadventures. For years, Tricia had nodded along with any Liza and Maggie memory, because she was usually too young to have been included, but had heard the same stories over and over again, so at some point it became imprinted in her hippocampus like she had been there. Despite wanting to stay detached, Tricia, too, was laughing at "Ben Winthrop, Foosball Master." It had become a family catchphrase for whenever one of the sisters met a guy who was really into himself.

Maggie observed Serena's silence and apologized. "Sorry, old family joke."

The sisters settled down, taking the conversation back to the endless questions about Serena's life. Tricia asked about her job, her outside interests and volunteer work, her travels. Liza was interested in Georgetown, claiming she was thinking of opening up a branch of her gallery there. (It was true. Whit had gone to college there and Liza was smitten by the area, but Serena assumed she was bluffing in an attempt to suss out her living situation.) And Maggie asked Serena about her boyfriends, her skin care regimen, and whether she still played tennis. The conversation was light and bright with many mutual connections and common points of interest, but Serena couldn't shake the feeling of being an outsider. Would she ever?

"SHE'S A WRITER, she's going to write about this," Tricia said. The sisters stood at the window of Richardson & Blix, watching this new character in their lives get into her car, a generic rental sedan. No doubt Serena could feel six eyes on her, but she didn't look up. Tricia admired her discipline, but urged caution. "I don't like the fact that she quit her job to hang out here all summer in the foosball palace. What's that about? I'll tell you what. She's writing a book proposal."

"You're paranoid. I like her," Maggie said shrugging her shoulders and daring Tricia to challenge her assessment. "She's interesting and she's interested. She's like us but with better SAT scores."

"Hey, speak for yourself." Tricia rarely threw her superior test-taking skills and Ivy League education in her sisters' faces, but, in this instance, she made an exception. "I feel like I could take her in *Jeopardy!*"

"I liked her, too." Liza sided with Maggie on emotional issues and with Tricia on pragmatic matters. This was pure emotion.

"Like her how? What does that mean in practical terms? Sunday dinners at the house? Do we send out a Christmas card announcement with a picture of the four of us in matching sweaters that says, *Meet our new sister, Serena Tucker Sweeney*? Is that what we want?"

"I'm only saying I like her." Liza pushed back. "She's professional and she's got her act together. She's clearly not some gold digger. Did you see that trio of diamond bangles? Spectacular. I don't think she's in it for the forty-two bucks we're going to inherit. Plus, you know those Tuckers are old money. There's a bank account somewhere with Serena's name on it—the house in Georgetown, the trips to Jackson Hole she mentioned. You don't get those on a journalist's salary. But didn't she seem like one of us?"

Tricia was not backing down. "First of all, everyone's in it for the money. That may not be her motivation now, but it will become paramount. Trust me. And second, everybody we grew up with in this tiny bubble seems like one of us on the surface. We knew all the same people. We had all the same experiences. Public school, private school, prep school—it didn't matter here. We all went to the Browns' Christmas party every year. Of course there's a certain familiarity."

"I'd invite her to Thanksgiving," Maggie declared, though never in her life had she ever hosted a holiday meal. "What are you afraid of? That she might be a really lovely addition to our family? I think it's wild that she's a writer, like Dad. I mean, none of us are. Like we were afraid to compete against Mom and especially Dad in that arena. But not Serena. And that she looks so much like you, Tricia. How had we not noticed that before?"

"Because we weren't on the lookout for neighbors who looked like us. Why would we suspect that our neighbor was really our sister?

That's like a soap plot, not real life." Tricia was not softening. The fact that there was a physical resemblance only made her feel more resentful, not less.

"Well, it's our real life now," Maggie said. "All I'm saying is that I'm not opposed to, you know, welcoming her."

"Is this because you feel bad that it was your fault because you took that damn DNA test?"

"You know what, Tricia? It wasn't my fault. It was Dad's fault, okay?" Maggie was right and her tone shut Tricia up on that subject for good. "And maybe in your world, people are perfect, but not in mine. I think forgiveness and happiness go hand in hand. Letting a new person into your life may bring you immeasurable gifts. Gifts you can't imagine right now in this wood-paneled law office with the unflattering lighting. You should open yourself up to the possibility that Serena might be a gift. She may help us work through all the crap that Dad left us to handle. Maybe she's the reward. That's all." Every once in a while, all the mumbo jumbo that Maggie had internalized through meditation retreats, and self-improvement classes, and Burning Man bubbled up to the surface in a cohesive statement that impressed listeners. "Let's stay open to what our relationship with Serena might become." Liza nodded in agreement. Tricia was outnumbered.

"One thing's for sure. I'm not leaving. There's no way I can go back to work until we find this manuscript and get everything sorted out at the house," Tricia said, turning to Liza, who was surprised by the announcement.

"You don't need to do that. I can handle it," Liza said, because she was required by The Law of the Oldest Sister to sacrifice herself at every opportunity. "I mean, I need to get back to work, too. But I'm used to multitasking." Another Liza compulsion was to remind her sisters that she had a job, even though they had never diminished her work at the gallery. It was Liza who had a chip on her shoulder about what Whit called her "jobby" and her lack of a college degree.

"I love my studio manager, but she's not up to the task of mounting the summer show. It's called Still Life with Sunflowers. But there's a period after 'Still' and a period after 'Life'—get it? We have about a dozen artists showing."

Tricia held firm. "This is too much for you to do on your own. It's not fair to dump this all on you, although I have no doubt you could do it all on your own. You're completely capable, that's not the issue. Like Serena, I haven't had a break in fifteen years, either. I need one and now is the time. I'm needed here more than I'm needed at the office on some class action suit that twenty-five lawyers are already working on. There's some sort of family leave provision in my contract I can take advantage of, although no one ever does. But I can and I will. I could use a summer here in Southport, too."

It was true. Tricia had been running, literally and figuratively, since the day their mother died. High school was a dead sprint of academic and athletic achievement, slowed only by bouts of grieving for her mother and caretaking of her father. College was the same, though the grief subsided and her father recovered. After graduating from law school and passing the bar, she barely took a full weekend off, never mind a proper vacation. Even the few times she'd been wrecked mentally and physically—and there had been weeks, months of difficulty—she powered through. Yes, she'd even gone in to work on Christmas Day before hopping on the train out to Southport to open gifts. She wasn't exactly sure what the good folks at Kingsley, Maxwell & Traub would say about her summer sabbatical, but she would make it happen.

"Then I'll stay, too," Maggie volunteered, thinking of her budding relationship with Gray more than her relationship with Serena or helping her sisters. "I can talk my way out of those obligations in Mill River. Or at the very least, show up there every few weeks whenever the bus full of AARP members from White Plains shows up."

"Aren't you obligated to actually live and work there in order to get the stipend and the housing?" Liza had to ask, bearing more responsibility for Maggie's fellowship than Maggie.

"Let's be honest, the only reason I got this fellowship was because I am William Sweeney's daughter. Every time I've been forced to have a studio open house, a group of lovely women stands around watching me paint for five minutes and then asks about Dad. Or Mom. Or Mom and Dad together as if they were some sort of Jack and Jackie because they all read the Maeve book. If I tell them I need to take a break from public life because of Dad's death, it will only add to my mystique."

Liza understood. It happened at the gallery, too, mainly with the husbands who were less interested in art and more interested in discussing their literary hero.

Maggie had a brainstorm to seal the deal. "I've been thinking that doing a series of pieces of the house might be fitting. I could work out of the conservatory, like Mom did." In truth, she hadn't thought of painting anything at all until that second. It was the perfect plan to get her out of most of the work that needed to be done at Willow Lane, but still in the area to be close to Gray. Tricia was not impressed, but Liza lit up.

"Oh my gosh, yes. I would love that. I would love you to do that, Maggie. It would be so meaningful to have and to sell, and frankly"— Liza paused, then added—"pretty lucrative, I think! We could market to William Sweeney fans." There was laughter because there was always laughter, no matter how dark the subject.

Even Cap Richardson laughed as he walked back into the conference room. "Your father would be proud, Liza. He always said if anyone was going to make money exploiting Bill Sweeney, it should be Bill Sweeney. You've inherited the right. But keep it classy."

"Always, Cap. Always," Liza said. "We've decided to present a united front. Tricia and Maggie will stay here in Southport until the manuscript is found and the estate is in the black."

Cap endorsed their plan. "I think that's wise. This could drift forward for months, even years, unless you make a concerted effort to sort everything out. I look forward to working with you all."

Liza turned to her sisters. "Wait, are we really doing this? You're both staying for the summer?" Maggie and Tricia nodded. "Thank you."

Liza reached to hug Tricia, who flinched and held her off. "You know I'm not a hugger. I get that it's been a bad week, but let's not start now."

Tricia hung back as her sisters left the office. They were headed to The Grey Goose for lunch, probably to dissect every single word of what Serena had said and everything she was wearing, then back to the house to hunt for the manuscript. But she wanted a quick word with Cap. "So, what did you think?"

"Clearly, she's more like Mitchell than Birdie."

"What do you mean?"

"Mitch Tucker sold insurance to almost every person in this town. Well, at least, to every good soul that attended Trinity Church. He kept a lot of secrets about the value of people's lives, both in terms of money and in terms of prestige. The two values were not always aligned. People trusted Mitch because he was trustworthy. Birdie, on the other hand, was a terrible gossip, slipping in commentary about her neighbors, the members of the club, the board at the library. She was entertaining if you were stuck in a corner with her at a party after a few gin and tonics, but she could be vicious, sometimes downright mean. Serena takes after her father. No wonder her sources trust her, her editors." Cap poured himself another cup of coffee. "I don't know what she'll do with all of this—the information, the estate, the instant family. But I believe she will take her time in deciding. She won't do anything rash or damaging in the short term."

"Did she say that?"

"In so many words. As I walked her out, she said she's taking the summer to figure out, quote, 'all her next steps.' We have our clock."

"Good point." Tricia's phone pinged. No doubt it was a text from Maggie telling her to hurry, but she ignored it. "Oh, Cap, there was a card in my father's desk I was curious about. From an archivist at Yale." She fished through her bag and found it. "Raj Chaudhry. Is that name familiar? I'm thinking that working with an archivist may be helpful, even as I go through all the papers looking for the manuscript. We need to clean out the boathouse. It makes sense to do it in an orderly manner, but that's not really my thing. I wondered if this Raj guy could be helpful."

"Oh, I forgot all about Raj."

"Do you know him?"

"I spoke to him on the phone after your father interviewed him. Your father hired him for the summer to do exactly what you are talking about—organize his papers for the archives at Yale. He seemed like a nice young man who was thrilled to dive in. There was some sort of budget or grant for his work through Yale; Dean Payson set it all up. I haven't gotten a call from the college yet, but I'm sure they're eager to secure his papers. And poor Raj. He's probably sitting at home wondering who to call. I was drawing up some nondisclosure papers and such. But I think your father even promised him a room for the summer."

"Glad I asked. I'll set up a meeting. It occurred to me that maybe my father kept the memoir at his office at Yale. This Raj guy might even know where. I seriously doubt my father could have wiped his computer clean of all files. Someone under the age of forty must have helped him; he couldn't have done it alone. I'm headed to New Haven tomorrow to search his office. I'll try to meet with this guy."

Cap laughed and then got serious. "Your sisters are lucky to have you, Tricia. You're right to be cautious."

"Oh, another thing I'm cautious about is the royalty income. Does that seem low to you? After you mentioned the number, I did some digging. Dad's books are still taught in a lot of high schools and colleges. *Never Not Nothing* is on a lot of syllabi and so is *Bitter Fruit*. Do you think Lois's accounting is on the up-and-up when it comes to the course adoption income?"

"I don't and I was going to speak to you about that. I mentioned it to your father about two years ago after he told me that his royalties were drying up. It didn't check out to me. But he was reluctant to pursue any inquiry in that area—said it was a show of bad faith and Lois had just landed him the memoir deal."

"I'm all for a show of bad faith if we can do it discreetly. I don't think the royalty income will make us millionaires, but I also don't think Lois deserves more than her ten percent."

"I'll start to reach out to publishing people. See if the numbers sound right to them."

"Thanks, Cap." And she gave him a hug because he'd always be there for her.

DON'T LOOK BACK. *Don't look back.* Serena could feel the sisters staring down at her but she willed herself to get into the car before she let herself relax. She was exhausted, shaking. Damn it. She liked them. She liked those Sweeney sisters. It hadn't occurred to her that she might feel any connection to them. Curiosity about them? Yes. Connection to them? No.

She wanted to stay detached, to give herself time to decide what to do with the revelation that she was the daughter of William Sweeney. She walked into that conference room determined to take control of the conversation and get as much information out of the sisters as possible. She had the sense that something wasn't entirely on the up-and-up about the estate or the death. She had picked up on some murmurs at the wake about his recent foray back into gambling and later overhead a conversation between two New York–publishing types, both women in their forties who looked to be in positions of power, one of whom was bemoaning to the other, "We'll never get that memoir now. This is a huge deal for us. I'm sure that advance is long gone."

Serena added those conversations to the pile of research she'd already done on her birth father. The gambling, the drinking, the finances in shambles—that was standard operating procedure for William Sweeney, self-documented in his books and essays. But this missing memoir was a new piece of the puzzle. Could she be in it? She'd have to research the publishing announcement and see why the editor or whoever she was said it was "a huge deal." Something was up and she wanted to find out what it was.

But then, Liza, Maggie, and Tricia had disarmed her in the meeting. They were the ones asking the questions, skillfully and sincerely. With their pressure, Serena had opened up about her job, the latest boyfriend who was not exactly divorced, the ski club trips, her favorite antiques shop in Georgetown. It was like the book club she attended, but without the wine or any pretense of reading a book. Serena was flattered by the attention; she wanted in on this club.

She only had a small cadre of female friends, a few from college scattered around the country now, and some work friends collected over the years who might be posted in DC or in some foreign land. None of whom she thought of as a sister. But now she had three sisters. She had initially thought the headline coming out of the DNA reveal was that her father was William Sweeney, but, maybe, it was that she was one of the Sweeney sisters now.

She sat in the front seat of the rental car, trying to remember how the keyless ignition worked, shaking and shaken. Her decision to take a leave of absence and stay in Southport was a no-brainer. She'd made it in a snap second when Lucy Winthrop offered the guesthouse, but, in truth, she knew she was on an epic journey the moment she boarded the train in DC after hearing about the death. Yesterday, she was confident in her plan to spend the summer in Southport, getting to know her sisters and working on a book proposal. Yes, she wanted to write about this. She had a right to tell her own story, didn't she? It was a worthwhile story to tell.

But today, having sat at a table with the Sweeneys for more than an hour, sharing stories and laughs, she had to admit, she liked her half-sisters. Writing a book about them might be a betrayal. Liza was cultured and inquisitive. Maggie was earthy, warm, and a bit bawdy. And with Tricia, it was like looking in a mirror, in terms of physical appearance and personality. She appreciated that Tricia was stand-offish and skeptical. That was how Serena felt when she'd walked in the conference room. Only she'd succumbed to the Sweeney charms while Tricia remained her own person. Serena admired her.

She pulled into the parking at the Delamar. In the morning, she'd be back on the train to collect her car and her belongings for the summer. She would resign from her job before *Straight Up* closed down for good, as Tricia had suspected. She'd find a house sitter, probably that nice editorial intern who lived with four other broke college-educated interns in a two-bedroom in Hays Adams. She'd jump at the chance. Plus, she was quiet and smart, not a party girl at all. Then, she'd contact that agent, Susie Burns, from New York, who'd said to her at a party for yet another political tell-all at the National Press Club, "If you ever have a book idea, let me know. I'm interested in anything you have to say."

And maybe, just maybe, she'd return the call from her mother, who'd left a brief message yesterday, saying, "Serena, it's Mother. I hear you are in Southport. Call me. Please."

About two hours into the hunt for the manuscript, Liza, Maggie, and Tricia figured out that all the sisters searching in one small space was not going to work. The three of them bossing each other around in the boathouse had produced only the password to Bill Sweeney's computer (Sunkissed1147, the boat's name plus the Willow Lane house numbers). Tricia had spent several hours searching the hard drive with Liza looking over her shoulder, an arrangement that wasn't sustainable for either of them. Tricia was searching systematically by key words and wondering how a guy whose computer security system could be compromised by a Post-it with his password stuck to the side of the monitor could possibly have gotten rid of all digital traces of the memoir. Liza felt that reorganizing the file system on the computer would be a better place to start than with what she called "completely random word searches" that her lawyer sister was insisting upon.

Maggie, as per usual, was sitting on the couch thumbing through old magazines and texting somebody with frequency and delight, piping up every few minutes with "Need anything?" or "Let me know what I can do." When they were growing up, the only time Maggie showed leadership or initiative in a family project was if it involved boys or shopping for clothes; otherwise, she focused on what worked for Maggie.

Once they realized that the manuscript hunt wouldn't be as easy as logging on and printing it out, it took them about ten minutes to devise a plan of separate but equal distribution of work, at least on paper. Tricia would take the boathouse and its contents, including boxes and boxes of old papers that might be the perfect hiding spot for a mystery manuscript. Maggie would take the library and conservatory to do a backup manuscript search and gather any additional documents that might have migrated inside and should be included with the rest of the papers. And Liza would get the house ready to sell by cleaning out closets, drawers, and entire rooms that hadn't been touched in years, packing or donating everything in sight.

"I wish Julia was here. I bet she knows where the damn book is," Tricia said. The sisters had shared a tearful goodbye with the housekeeper. She was thrilled with the money. Clearly, she believed she had earned it but was also grateful that "Mister Bill" had come through in the end. Her plan was to sock most of the sudden windfall into a retirement account like Liza suggested, but splurge a little and spend the summer back in San Juan with her own family, including her aging parents. In the fall, she'd return to her tidy little house in Bridgeport and find a new family to care for. But she had told the sisters she would help pack up Willow Lane before leaving for Puerto Rico. "I can't let you girls do this all on your own."

"Absolutely not. You've already done too much for our family," Liza had insisted. "Go be with your own family and enjoy the summer."

They were missing Julia now, though. Tricia was right. She might know exactly where the manuscript was stashed. "I'll text her and ask," Liza offered. Julia responded immediately with the word No followed by a string of question marks. "We're on our own."

"So, we're all settled, then. Everyone knows what they need to do. Maggie?"

Maggie looked up from her phone. "Yeah, all good. Do we have enough boxes? Should I run out and get packing stuff at U-Haul?" Liza and Tricia practically did a double take at Maggie's pragmatism and offer of aid. "What? Come on, give me some credit."

"Knock yourself out," Liza said. "Go get some boxes, but not the huge ones. We need to be able to lift them. Most of this stuff is either going to Goodwill or the dump. Except the papers, which are all going to Yale."

"And some of the personal stuff. We can divvy that up later."

"No tagging any artwork until I get back," Maggie said, half joking. She didn't think her sisters would hide pieces from her, but she wasn't a hundred percent sure.

Tricia welcomed the silence in the boathouse. She had always excelled at tasks that were focused and intense, but today, she needed to be alone with her thoughts. The sudden death of her father and the unexpected arrival of this new sister had thrown her ordered world into chaos. Her strength was wrangling facts and details into order and shaping them into a narrative she could spin, but people had always given her issues, especially when they did anything out of character. That was a factor she couldn't work into her equation. Her father, a man who had spent a lifetime spinning tales, had died without a word, leaving his greatest secret unspoken.

And this secret, this Serena, looked to be a formidable person. For the last two nights, Tricia had crawled into her childhood bed with her laptop and researched Serena. She had no doubt that Serena had done the same and was months ahead of what she called, in her business, "discovery." She started by reading Serena's archived articles, including a whole series on Cambodia-Thailand relations, which was a real snooze. Then she moved on to analyzing Serena's social media, depressing in its geopolitical focus except for a clear love of *CSI*, Serena Williams, and musical theater, the latter of which seemed out of character. In the Class Notes section of the *Vassar Magazine* of spring 2014, there was mention of several journalism awards she'd won for a *Slate* piece about the Catholic Church sex-abuse scandal and the International Criminal Court's refusal to investigate, and a recent trip to Greece with her mother, Class of 1973, but no picture. Finally, Tricia dug up a Tucker family photo from the summer of 2005 in the local newspaper, of a library fundraiser, where Birdie Tucker was being honored for her twenty-five years of service and philanthropy.

There were the Tuckers in black tie, all three of them smiling for the camera. In the middle was Birdie the honoree, stick thin in a well-cut bright pink dress that made her look even tanner and her lipstick even frostier, her hair secured in the classic helmet-head pageboy that had served the local women well for decades. To the left was Mitch, stuffed into his tux with some sort of cummerbund that featured penguins drinking martinis and appeared to be needlepointed, if that was possible. Serena stood to her mother's right, tall and regal, in a gold diaphanous one-shoulder dress with simple drop earrings and her hair slicked back in a bun. Tricia's first thought was that she loved what Serena was wearing.

Then, she thought: *Of course. The library.*

Her father had been actively involved in the library from the moment he had arrived in Southport. It made sense, as he was already a well-known writer and the Pequot Library was a cultural beacon in the area, as their website said. It was a special spot, both architecturally and intellectually. It was certainly a community hub for books, theater, a dancing school, adult education classes, and afterschool programs. But Pequot had a veneer of prestige that few public libraries in small towns could match. It had extensive rare book, manuscript, and historical archive collections, assembled by notable local women in the early nineteenth century and still vibrant today. Prominent authors made it a stop on any national book tour and local authors supported the library efforts whenever possible, serving as honorary chairs of benefits, working the summer book sale, donating signed first editions or "Lunch with the Author" to auction efforts.

William Sweeney was one of those authors. He loved libraries, all libraries, having taken refuge in reading rooms during his rough childhood as a place to escape the brutality of his home life. But he particularly loved Pequot Library and his support was genuine. The question of how he and Birdie Tucker crossed paths beyond the view of their respective spouses became clearer to Tricia as she studied the photo.

Definitely, a one-night stand after some fundraiser.

LIZA WELCOMED THE silence in the kitchen. The last week had been too much—too sad, too unexpected, too stressful, too exhausting. She needed a few hours of quiet to process everything that had happened. She was happy to let Tricia take the work in the boathouse. Being in her father's office was more than she could stand emotionally. Some of her happiest memories were of hanging out in the boathouse when she was younger, doing her homework alongside her father who was pounding away at his keyboard. He was a physical writer, standing up, sitting down, hitting the keys with gusto and intention. He allowed Liza to sit at a little table and chair in the corner, plowing away at the tediousness of workbooks and flash cards while he wrote. The other sisters were too noisy (Maggie) or too young (Tricia), so Liza felt special to be allowed into the sanctuary.

When she was older and her father worked on the weekends, she'd read on the couch or do her SAT prep alongside him, not that she was very attentive to either. By then, her mother was sick and Liza was more interested in boys than books, but she loved the winter afternoons shared with her father. Now that was tainted, knowing Serena was probably sitting in her room, just on the other side of the hedgerow, reading or writing away and doing a better job than she.

Let Tricia unearth the memories, Liza thought. *I'll deal with sending the thirty-year-old couches to Goodwill.* There was nothing in the house Liza wanted or even deemed worthy of passing down to the twins—well, almost nothing. There were a few pieces of art, some books and signed first editions, her mother's fondue pot and an ancient Salton yogurt maker, maybe some of the pillows or blankets for sentimental reasons. But the furniture was heavy, worn and scratched; any china or glassware was reduced to mismatched sets of three or four; the lamps and fixtures were nothing special. Maybe there was a rug or two that was worth the effort, but Liza already had a rug-addiction issue, with several perfectly fine Turkish beauties rolled up in her attic. *I'll leave the rugs here for the staging and then Maggie can have them,* Liza thought, because her mind worked in to-do lists that extended into the abyss. *Either Maggie can use them or sell them and keep the money.* Another habit Liza couldn't break, trying to save Maggie from financial ruin, like she'd been doing since they were in college and Maggie took her housing money for the semester and bought a stupid VW Bug. Liza made up a fake student fee and told her parents she needed the money or she wouldn't be able to register. She cashed the check and sent the money to Maggie, who had moved off campus at RISD, an experiment in living and education that only lasted about six weeks after Liza bailed her out. But she owned that car for years.

And now she drives the car our father bought her, Liza thought. *Has she ever paid for her own car?*

Liza poured her fourth cup of coffee for the day and walked through the house with a pad of sticky notes and a pen. Her first order of business would be to collect the sure things for the junk man. The only helpful gesture Whit had made in the last few days was calling 1-800-JUNK-GUY and scheduling a pick-up at the end of the week. "Everything in that place needs to go. Get rid of it. Don't let anyone talk you out of that, Liza," Whit had advised while he was packing his bag last night. "Please, I don't want all that stuff ending up in my garage." Ah, Whit's real reason for the call to the hauling company: to make sure Sweeney junk didn't become Jones junk. Liza had been too drained from the conversation at Cap's office to protest. Plus, Tricia was in total agreement. "Liza, don't overthink this. We have more important issues to deal with than dining sets from the eighties. Clean house and move on."

Liza wasn't really that kind of person, though. She didn't move on quickly; she didn't let go easily. She suspected she'd never understand her father's betrayal of her mother. Yesterday's bombshell was taking hold in her psyche and she didn't see herself getting over it anytime soon.

She wasn't deluded that her father was a role model of morality; God knows there had been enough days when she'd pulled up to Willow Lane to drop off something only to run into some woman coming out the side door. And she assumed similar behavior went on during their marriage. But, like Maggie, she was surprised that a few years after the wedding her father had cheated on Maeve, and the fact that he'd conceived a child on the side made it a hundred times worse. She could feel the anger and resentment building inside and knew from previous experiences that this was not a healthy way to process negative information. At least, that's what her yoga therapist had been preaching.

She had no need for some older, smarter sister like Serena Tucker showing up and taking her place as the first-born. Liza had earned that spot over the years, leaving college to be there in her mother's waning days, caring for her father for years, hosting all those family birthday parties, organizing family Christmases. For God's sake, she married Whit to do the right thing before her mother's death and that had to count for something. Serena Tucker wasn't going to walk into their lives and take that spot away from Liza because she'd been born fourteen months earlier. No way.

Liza stopped in front of the Robert Motherwell print that hung in the front hall. It had always been her favorite piece in the house, a bold abstract in orange and blue that reminded her of those bunny ears TV antennas she'd seen in old sitcoms. This was hers. She slapped a sticky note on it that said, "Liza."

MAGGIE WELCOMED THE silence in her car. *Jesus,* she thought, *I don't know if I can take one more minute of Tricia and Liza.* The two of them tended to ignore her completely when they were facing off in the "let's do it my way" competition that had been going on for the last decade. Maggie's opinion rarely counted, which didn't really bother Maggie. Let somebody else deal with the hassle.

But she certainly didn't want to get cut out of the loop so completely that she was cut out of the money. Maggie had spent last night mindlessly scrolling through social media and formulating her strategy. She had enough awareness about her mental health to know that her father's death could affect her deeply, striking her like a lightning bolt and knocking her back off her feet for weeks, maybe months. It was a familiar pattern, one Maggie realized she shared with her father, a cycle of creativity, depression, sexual neediness. Of course, with male artists, there was a sort of "comes with the territory" acceptance that Maggie had never found herself. She knew people judged, including her sisters. As her therapist in Los Angeles had told her, "You can change your patterns, but you can't change society's perceptions. So, work on you and don't get hung up on the others."

Maggie had worked on herself and knew she needed to stay strong until the estate was settled, the manuscript found, and this Serena complication was worked out. Then she could return to her free studio space in East Nowheresville and check out for a while. In the meantime, her goal was to focus and move forward.

Still, Maggie was more intrigued than terrified of Serena Tucker and how she might infiltrate their lives. As long as Serena didn't enchant her sisters in some weird way that would relegate Maggie to second-tier status, that was, with her cool looks and her media job. Maybe her connections could help Maggie somehow; maybe Serena would like Maggie more than the others and that would drive Liza and Tricia a tiny bit crazy. Maggie considered analyzing people on the spot as one of her special skills. It was clear from the meeting

yesterday and the way Serena went on and on about the smallest details that Serena wanted a friend, a confidant. Maggie could be that
person and use the relationship to her advantage.

She pulled her car into the parking lot of the Athena Diner on the
Post Road, a classic Southport spot and the scene of some of the best
days of her life (Sunday mornings drinking terrible coffee with Liza
instead of going to math tutoring; late-night French fries with her
first real boyfriend, Drew Pearson, after they made out in his Range
Rover) and the worst days of her life (the Drew breakup; the post-ER
pancake breakfast with her father after she swallowed all those pills;
the diet plates she and Liza ate every day for two weeks after their
mother died). She pulled her Prius into a spot next to a silver BMW
sedan, and quickly checked herself in the mirror. She looked good, she
thought. The crying had made her green eyes pop and the grieving
diet brought out her cheekbones. She had grabbed one of her father's
sweaters out of his closet and tossed it on over a silk blouse, mainly
for effect, but the heather-green color worked on her. She was ready.

For one second, Maggie felt a twinge of guilt. Then she remembered
Liza babbling on about the summer show at the gallery. *Sunflowers.
How basic.* And still, she hadn't asked Maggie to participate. *I have
yellow paint. I could do something for your little show.* Liza had her own
agenda, Maggie told herself as she got out of the car. *And I have mine.*

Gray Cunningham was leaning up against his silver truck. *He looks
even better than the other night,* Maggie thought. Sobriety suited him.
His blue eyes were clear, his curly dark brown hair was longer than the
usual Southport day trader/woodworker (that's what he called himself,
anyway), and his face was tan and slightly chapped from sailing. He'd
mentioned yoga as a recovery tool the other day; that must explain
the arms. He kissed her on the cheek. "Hey, I'm so glad you could get
away. I know you must have a lot going on, but I wanted to see you
after the other night. I feel like we have more to say to one another."

She nodded. The other night. Her father's wake. Should she feel awful? Maggie didn't. "Me, too."

"Shall we?" Gray offered his arm like he was a twelve-year-old boy at a cotillion escorting her to the punch table.

Maggie, who two minutes ago was all about focus and moving forward, took it willingly. She'd had a thing for Gray Cunningham since he was Liza's secret boyfriend. All through that terrible summer as her mother got sicker, the one bright spot was Gray showing up in the shadows to pick up Liza and take her away from the misery at the house. Liza didn't want her parents to know anything about him, especially the fact that she was getting on the back of his motorcycle, so Maggie volunteered to be the go-between in order to spend a minute a day alone with him, clearing the coast for Liza or making her excuses if she couldn't escape. She was better at lying to her parents than Liza. In her brief conversations with Gray, Maggie felt like there was something there with him, but nothing ever happened between them. (Her sister would tease her that she believed every guy was hitting on her.) She had thought about him over the years, the kind of "what-if" that kept her going through rough days and long stretches away from Southport. Even though the timing was terrible, Maggie was ready to make something happen. The what-if was now. After all, Liza was married. She couldn't possibly object, could she?

Maggie smiled up at Gray. "We shall."

"HEY, I'M HOME. I got some boxes." Maggie struggled to carry a stack of boxes, unfolded and unwieldy, as she stumbled into the kitchen where her sisters were eating lunch. She'd been gone three hours. "I think I got enough, but we'll probably need more."

Tricia and Liza looked at each other before responding. Neither got up to help. They knew this was classic Maggie behavior, dodging work, offering vague excuses, if not outright lies, about where she'd been. This had been her pattern since childhood—skipping school to take the train into the city to hang out in the Village or claiming to be at a friend's house overnight when more than likely she was with a guy. After she dropped out of Rhode Island School of Design, she went to Europe for six months with her mysterious college friend "Dina" who was really a thirty-five-year-old adjunct professor of ceramics named Deon. Liza knew the truth, of course, because there were all kinds of back-channel communications about the breakup on Santorini and the lost passport and the "stolen" wallet. Liza covered for her and wired her cash to get home. It had been nearly twenty years since that European odyssey, but, in many ways, Maggie hadn't matured an ounce. Here she was with the same tropes. Liza couldn't even speak.

Finally, Tricia asked, "Where the hell have you been?"

"Did you find the manuscript? Does Julia know where it is?"

"No and no. But you've been gone for hours. I could have used the boxes to sort the papers in the boathouse." Tricia's annoyance was more pragmatic than personal. She knew Maggie's relationship with the truth was relative, but she'd never been as involved in the cover-ups as Liza had been. The six-year age gap had spared her the role of coconspirator.

"Oh, you know," Maggie responded. "I stopped at Switzer's Pharmacy and ran into Mrs. Whatshername. She lives at the top of Rose Hill in that huge Victorian with all the hydrangeas. She was mom's friend, Emmy or something?"

"Yes. Emmy Nolan. She was, like, Mom's best friend. That's who she is. The person Mom liked the most in the whole town," Liza snapped back. It was all she could do not to scream at her.

"Sorry. I haven't lived here in a while, Ms. Town Crier. Anyway, I ran into her and she cornered me for an hour in the adult diaper aisle. She wanted to know the real story about what happened and everything about you two." Red flag for Liza. She'd run into Emmy Nolan two weeks ago. Emmy, an aging role model with a trim figure and a Pond's

Cold Cream skin care regimen, had come into the gallery. She had found a thank-you note that Maeve had written to her that included a short, beautiful poem about gardens and renewal. Emmy had wanted to share it with Liza. ("Your mother had so much talent, but your father took up so much of her energy," Emmy observed.) They'd spent an hour talking and catching up. There's no way Emmy would have forgotten what Maggie and Tricia were up to in that short time. She was as sharp and engaged at seventy as she'd been at forty, which was why Maeve had bonded with her. "Then I went to Spic & Span to get a sandwich and that was a whole ordeal. Condolences, condolences. You know how this town is. The guys at Spic & Span are going to rename the tuna sandwich the Sweeney Special in Dad's honor. How great is that? Here, I brought you a few sandwiches. Have you eaten?" Maggie knew to cover her tracks. And she had seen that Emmy woman in the parking lot, so that tracked.

Tricia burst into laughter, nearly choking on her iced tea. "Dad would have loved that." Even Liza agreed. That was a touching gesture.

Maggie breathed a little easier as she watched her sisters' smiles. She was sure she'd dodged a bullet. "Anyway, here are the boxes."

Chapter

Tricia stood on the platform at the tiny Southport train station, waiting for the 9:38 to New Haven, like her father had done many Tuesdays and Thursdays for thirty years, heading to his teaching job at Yale. Her father, whose life could be so ad hoc, appreciated the ritual of commuting by rail: the waiting, the ticket taking, the names of the same small towns called out over the inaudible intercom. He rarely drove the half hour to New Haven, preferring to give himself over to the timetable of the MTA. Tricia had taken the train back and forth from New Haven during her college days, but it had been a few years since she'd stood on the platform, studying the commuters, most of whom were on the opposite platform, headed into New York. The bankers, the lawyers, the ad men were long gone, hopping on trains well before seven in the morning for their daily drudgery. The group now was mainly women, theatergoers or museum mavens headed into the city for lunch and a little culture. Only one other person stood on the New Haven side with Tricia, a high schooler with a backpack, maybe skipping school for the day or getting a late start. Tricia felt the weight of missing her father in that moment. *Don't cry, no one will understand.*

She recognized John D'Amato right away. He looked exactly like the portrait her father had painted with words in an essay about the veteran conductor. He father wrote about him for *Esquire* last year, an homage to train conductors everywhere. The essay was an insightful piece about the kind of person who works a job that is both repetitive and essential. Clearly, her father had spent years exchanging "How ya doing today, Professor?" with John D'Amato, and the essay was warm, knowing. It was longlisted for a PEN/Faulkner Award, but lost out to a piece about binge-eating that her father described as "slightly better than the diary entry essays my first-years turn in." (Amongst his many personal failings, William Sweeney hadn't come to terms with the body awareness movement.) Tricia waited for the conductor to make it to her seat, then she spoke: "Hi, Mr. D'Amato, I'm Tricia Sweeney, Bill's Sweeney's daughter. I know he was a fan of yours."

John D'Amato was taken by surprise, then he composed himself. "What a loss. What a loss. Your father was a gentleman, a good man. I was lucky to know him and happy to serve him on this train."

Tricia didn't know whether to stand or sit, so she remained seated, but pulled an envelope out of her bag. "I'm glad you're working today. I wanted you to have this," she said, handing the wiry, gray-haired conductor the white envelope with the Yale insignia. "It's the first draft of my father's essay about you. I found it in his office. You can see where he redlined it, his editing marks in his own hand. I thought you might . . ." Tricia choked up. She couldn't finish the sentence.

John took the envelope reverently. "This is an incredible gift." The conductor himself was overcome. "This is something."

"And this is for you as well." She reached into her bag for the commuter mug her father had taken back and forth to New Haven for years. He had a collection of coffee mugs from colleges all over the country, the end result of years of guest lectures and honorary degrees. He was rarely without a mug of coffee during his working hours and his mug selection became a sort of bellwether for how he was feeling, what the day might bring. The University of Iowa mug if he was literary; the Kenyon mug if he was precious, overthinking. The commuter mug was from Yale, though. He'd carried it back and forth from New Haven for years. Tricia started to explain to John why she was giving him an old coffee cup, but he knew.

"Your father had hot coffee and the *New York Times* every Tuesday and Thursday when school was in session. We'd talk about the news, the lousy politicians, the lousy Knicks. Sometimes he'd give me the name of a book I should read. And I read most of them," John D'Amato said with pride and then he made a gentle bow. "Thank you, darling."

Tricia stood and hugged the man who was a constant in her father's life. He had needed people like John D'Amato to keep him honest, in touch. To make sure he got where he was going. "Thank you, Mr. D'Amato."

"We'll miss him, won't we?"

"Yes." Tricia was beginning to understand how much.

"Hello?"

Tricia looked up from her position on the floor. She was cross-legged in her father's office, where she'd been for the last two hours, sorting through drawers and boxes in search of the memoir. It was slow going, as a few colleagues kept interrupting her, those working over the summer or finishing up department responsibilities before heading off to Maine or the Cape or any writing workshop gig at Sewanee or upstate New York. They popped in uninvited to share recollections of her father and his legendary critiques that left his students in tears. Or to retell a classic story of his ill-fated introduction of visiting writers in the Beineke lecture series or about the late nights at Mory's. Several mentioned the early morning monthly department meetings that he rarely bothered to attend. Tricia nodded and smiled. Though in a frenzy to find the manuscript, she wanted to hear these stories and remember that here on campus, her flawed father was his best self.

One professor, Abukar Abdule, a brilliant young writer who'd been born in Somalia and plucked from a refugee camp in Kenya to attend Cambridge before publishing his first literary novel at twenty-five and securing a spot at Yale a few years later, stopped by to say, "Your father and I had nothing in common, but I loved him dearly."

That about summed up her father's relationships with most of the faculty in the Creative Writing Department at Yale. He was a throwback, to the time when being a vaunted American writer meant being male, white, and heterosexual, with a drinking problem, a healthy ego, and a dark childhood. That model of the testosterone-driven man of letters was dying off, fading away like the curriculum it spawned with reading lists of Hemingway, Fitzgerald, Faulkner, Styron, Roth, Vonnegut, Cheever, Irving. The academic world was opening up to a diversity of voices and life experiences. William Sweeney, the tail end of the manliest (so they thought) generation, managed to hold on longer than most. ("What does cis mean?" he asked Tricia one day during her time at Yale when they had regular lunches together. "Students keep referring to me as cis.")

Maybe he endured because deep down inside, he knew he was a dying breed, lucky to get in on some coattails of other writers who had created the genre, letting him sneak onto the gravy train at the exact right time in literary history. Behind closed doors, when he could turn off his persona and simply be, he had enough humility about his work to make him endearing to the younger generation.

"Hello?"

Tricia looked up from her position on the floor at the handsome face in the doorway—dark hair, dark eyes, white teeth—recognizing it from the wake. The sincere librarian who told the story about having the lengthy discussions about the literary merits of *The Sopranos*, her father arguing pro-Tony and the librarian, anti-Tony. She was taken aback seeing him again so soon. He was tall and lean, in a deep blue button-down shirt with a messenger bag over one shoulder. She liked his glasses. She scrambled to stand. It was an ungainly transition from floor to feet. "Hi?"

"I'm Raj Chaudhry. We had plans to meet. You're Patricia. I was at the wake but we never had the chance to speak."

"Yes, Raj. Thank you for coming. My apologies. I lost track of time. And probably most of my mind the last few days." Tricia needed a moment to collect herself. She reached out to shake his hand. His skin was warm. "First, let me say that your recollection of my father was so typical, so perfect. I doubt my father had ever seen an entire episode of *The Sopranos*, but he was going to die on that hill, wasn't he? And please, call me Tricia." She indicated for him to come into the office and wished she had made more of an effort in her personal appearance. *I must look awful,* she thought. "Sit."

"Thank you. And thank you for the other night. He was a special man and he obviously has a special family," Raj said, never taking his eyes off Tricia. "It was a privilege to be there."

"You're welcome. We're grateful so many of his friends and colleagues could be there," Tricia said, clearing off her father's desk, so they weren't speaking over a pile of notebooks. "I'm sorry we didn't get in touch with you sooner."

"No apologies necessary," Raj said, taking a seat. "I understand, grief can be all-consuming. I was surprised to hear from you so quickly."

Tricia thought about his comment. "Did you recently lose someone?"

Raj looked at her, not connecting the dots, so Tricia explained, "You said grief can be all-consuming. Is that from personal experience?"

"Yes. A good friend," he responded, shuffling in his seat. "Some days, I'm not myself."

"I understand completely." Tricia did understand, but not for the reasons Raj assumed.

"Of course. Losing a parent is monumental."

"Losing anyone can be monumental." There was a pause in the conversation that felt more natural than awkward.

According to his biography on the Sterling Library website, which, of course, Tricia had researched before contacting him and then read aloud to her sisters, Raj Chaudhry was the associate librarian for literature in English. He did his undergraduate work at the College of William & Mary with a degree in comparative literature and his graduate work in Library Studies at UNC-Chapel Hill. (It followed that Tricia Googled "Best Ph.D. programs in Library Science" and discovered that UNC was one of them.) He was fluent in German and French and had a grasp of basic Italian and Spanish. Under "special skills," there was a laundry list of software programs, including SurveyMonkey, which, Tricia observed to Maggie and Liza, didn't really qualify as a special skill, but the guy did have his doctorate.

There hadn't been a picture next to Raj Chaudry's name, or Maggie would have commented that he looked more like an actor than a librarian, with wavy hair that hung down in his eyes and the right amount of facial hair.

Tricia collected herself. "As I said in my email, I feel like we could really use your expertise. Obviously, we'd like to get my father's papers to Yale in the best possible shape and in some kind of order. Are you still interested in working on the project even if my father won't be part of it?"

"Very much so. I feel even more responsibility to take on the work. I admire your father's writing tremendously."

"Really?"

"That surprises you?"

"A little. My father was a man of a different era."

"I learned a lot from him about life. I grew up in suburban Virginia. There wasn't a lot of guts and glory in my neighborhood. My high school was full of kids of government employees who followed the rules. I choose *Never Not Nothing* for a book report freshman year. It changed the course of my life."

"How so?"

"I was headed toward a career in computer science like my parents. Both of them are programmers who work for the military. I thought

I'd be a programmer. But then I discovered literature, like guy's literature. And that made a difference. Not that books by women can't be life-changing."

"I get it. My father's work tended to speak to males at vulnerable ages and stages. In today's parlance, a publisher would say that a coming-of-age story like *Never Not Nothing* was targeted at the adolescent male market."

"True. And guilty."

Tricia pulled a bottle of water out of the stocked mini-fridge in her father's office and handed it to Raj. "Did my father pour you a Scotch and have you watch the sunset when you came to the house?"

"Yes."

Tricia nodded. "That meant he liked you."

Raj was quiet and then, "That means something to me."

Tricia shifted topics with an all-business tone. "So how will this work? I'm not really familiar with the process of getting his papers from the boathouse to the archives here."

"For the first few weeks, it will be organizational, figuring out what is on site, what's valuable, a system of cataloguing that makes sense for your father's work. Sometimes, that's chronological, other times not. I could also catalogue by projects or genre. Then I digitize all the files on site. And then, we'll pack them up and move them to our library for further study," Raj answered. "I had planned on working with your father on additional research and annotation. That's a tremendous loss to scholarship." Then Raj backtracked. "I'm sorry. I didn't mean to imply my loss was greater than yours."

"No worries. I appreciate what you do." Tricia felt a sense of relief for the first time since Cap had read the will. Maybe her father's reputation could be salvaged after the news about the lost memoir and the secret daughter were revealed. Raj was the key to legitimacy.

"Raj, I'm sure you understand that some of the material you uncover is personal and sensitive. We had our lawyer draw up a nondisclosure agreement. There are a few . . ." Tricia searched for the right word. ". . . a few topics that may arise in your work that we as the family would like to keep private in the short term. This is a limited-time NDA. We don't intend to silence you forever. There are details about the estate we'd like to work out before anyone speaks to the press or to any other entities. I'm sure you can understand. The term of the contract is one year."

Tricia slid the five-page agreement across the desk. He didn't hesitate to pick it up and start reading it, despite Tricia saying, "Feel free to run that by a lawyer."

"No need," Raj answered. "I have a pretty good working knowledge of contract law. I interned in a law firm in college."

"That means you're pretty much a lawyer."

"You must be a lawyer?"

"I am. But I also have a library card, so I'm pretty much an archivist, too."

"I deserved that." Raj worked his way slowly through the document and then announced, "Can we make the term six months? There may be an academic paper in this work for me and I don't want to get delayed in publishing it. I'm not interested in your father's personal life, only his work." He slid the agreement back across the desk.

Tricia took a pen and found the appropriate clause. She crossed out the dates, then looked up at Raj. "Nine months."

"Seven."

"I can back out of this entire situation, you know. We're asking for privacy."

"I think you need me. Seven months. That will give me time to do the work, write it up, and find a journal interested in publishing it. I can live with seven months."

"Fine, seven months. Please don't test this." Tricia tried to keep the exhilaration out of her voice. She loved negotiating and she liked this ambitious librarian.

As soon as he signed the agreement, she was able to ask about the most pressing issue at hand. "We're looking for the manuscript of my father's memoir. But it's nowhere—not on his desktop or laptop, and we can't find a hard copy in Southport or here. Would you know anything about that?"

"Ah, hence the NDA," Raj said, eyes wide open. "Yes, yes I do. We talked about it quite a bit. It's how I got to know your father. He'd come into the library, requesting books he wanted to reference in his memoir. I'd put together stacks every month for him and we'd talk about what he was working on."

Tricia made a mental note to circle back to the content of their conversations later, but for now, she needed a straight answer. "Sorry to skip ahead here, but did you see the actual manuscript?"

"Your father asked me to put the file on a thumb drive and erase it from his hard drive. So that's what I did."

"When?"

"That day in May. The day I went to Southport to talk about the project and see his office. Before we had the Scotch and after we had talked for hours."

"Do you know where that thumb drive is?"

"No. Your father said he wanted to put it somewhere safe but I didn't ask where that was. He also had a hard copy, as I recall, in one of those manuscript boxes. I got the impression he was going to keep them together. He said to me that he wasn't quite done remembering. He wanted to sit on the manuscript for a while."

He wasn't quite done remembering. Oh, Dad. "Are you sure he didn't say anything about where he was going to hide the thumb drive?"

"No, and I wouldn't have asked, either. I didn't know him well, but he seemed very at ease that day, once I had erased the files and given him the drive. I'd gotten to know him in the library, of course, and attended some public lectures he gave, but I'd never seen him so . . . content. I think that's the right word. He was very happy that

I could help him that day and for the summer. Like he wanted to get his work in order."

Tricia looked at Raj. She could understand why her father might have relaxed in his presence. He exuded competency, reliability. And a little something extra that held her attention, so she found herself saying, "The room in the boathouse is still available, if you wanted to stay. I think that's the arrangement my father offered and I would, I mean, *we* would like to honor that. Not like Southport is a hot spot, but it's beautiful in the summer. I'll be there, too." She didn't know why she added that last statement.

"I'd like that very much. I'd like to get out of New Haven and be there. With you . . ." Raj admitted, then covered, ". . . and the papers. Plus, I've already sublet my apartment to a medical student. I have nowhere else to go."

Chapter

11

Maggie pulled the Prius into the gravel-and-oystershell driveway of Gray's house on Harbor Road. She was headed back to Mill River for a few days to make her excuses to the lovely, and hopefully understanding, members of the Art Commission, explaining that she couldn't be in residence for the summer because she had to shore up the Sweeney estate. And then she needed to pick up some fresh clothes and her cat Rufus. Tim the Line Cook had been on Rufus duty for the last week and Maggie was worried that Rufus would get attached, based on the photos Tim had been sending the last few days. Maggie had no intention of co-parenting a cat with Tim. But first, she needed to see Gray.

The Cunninghams had built one of the only modern houses on Southport Harbor on a subdivided lot back in the '70s. Its construction had been the talk of the town for years, with a substantial number of tut-tutters who frowned on the abrupt architectural detour. ("I don't understand why anyone would want to live in a big, ugly box when you could build a lovely Colonial," Millie Reeves, the head of the Historical Society, had complained to Maeve Sweeney one afternoon after a few glasses of Chablis at a luncheon. Maeve had mimicked her for years later, much to her daughters' delight, drawing out the words "lovely Colonial" for comedic effect.) But the lines of the Ulrich Franzen–designed house had held up over the decades, increasing in value as tastes changed. Finding this modern needle in a center-hall Colonial haystack would be a dream for some midcentury enthusiast or art collector.

Gray had explained at breakfast the other day that his parents had retired to Sea Island and he had offered to spend a year living in the house restoring the floors, cabinets, and the suspended teak staircase that led to the open second story overlooking the water. After spending five years in Montana, one in rehab and four in an informal apprenticeship to a master woodworker, building houses for "rich tech guys who wanted to play rancher," he had returned to town because he felt he owed his parents. Gray explained, "They sort of gave up on maintenance the last decade. It needs a little TLC before the house goes on the market. Plus, I need to make amends with about half the town of Southport, including your sister, but most of all my parents. It will probably take me at least a year to do penance."

Now, Maggie grabbed the gift from the passenger seat and checked her makeup in the mirror. She liked what she saw, so she headed to find Gray. Before she could knock, he opened the heavy wood door. "Hi."

"You startled me."

"Tulane?"

"One of my father's favorite mugs. He loved New Orleans. Lectured at Tulane any time he was invited. He had a lot of writer friends there and they'd have these wild weekends. My mom loved it, too." Maggie turned to look at the sparkling view over the water. She didn't want to cry in front of Gray, for many reasons, not the least of which was her mascara. "I thought you might appreciate it. You spent a year at Tulane, right?"

"Three semesters, two of which I had passing grades."

Recovered, she turned back to Gray. *Oh, no!* Was that shame on his face? "Too close to home?" she asked, hoping her gesture hadn't offended.

"Not at all. I had some good times in New Orleans, too. I wish I could remember more of them," he joked comfortably. "Thank you. This is something, to have Bill Sweeney's mug."

Relief. "Well, I'm off. Headed to Mill River to tie up some loose ends and get my painting supplies, so I can be here this summer." Maggie was hoping he would cut her off with some dramatic gesture or declaration of attraction, but Gray kept staring quietly, cradling the old mug in his hands. "So, do you want to come for dinner on Sunday? I'll be back and making a quinoa salad and soft-shell crabs."

"I'll put it on the calendar. Let me know if I need to bring anything."

"Do you cook?"

"No. But I make bowls," Gray said, indicating a beautiful walnut bowl on the counter filled with lemons and limes. "Will you be making salad? Do you need a bowl?"

"These are gorgeous. You made this?" Maggie picked up the bowl and ran her hands over the smooth wood. She gently placed it back down on the counter. "Like works of art. You should bring one of these. Liza may want to sell them at the gallery." As soon as the words came out of Maggie's mouth, she regretted them. She wanted to keep Gray to herself a little longer. "Maybe I could bring my quinoa and crabs over here? I don't know if Willow Lane is right for entertaining."

"Sure. Let's do that. I know Willow Lane is beautiful at sunset, but it's not too bad here, either. When you look across the harbor at the huge houses on Sasco Hill, the windows glow like gold. At least, that's what I think."

Window panes of gold. An image flashed in Maggie's mind's eye, a painting. Sometimes, when she least expected it, she returned to her art. "I'd like to see that."

He walked over and kissed her lightly, very lightly, on the lips. "See you Sunday. I gotta get back to work."

Yes, Sunday.

THE COOL BLUES and the soothing grays of Liza's living room never failed to relax her. Every time she entered the front door, she felt like she was leaving one world behind and entering another. *That's good design,* Liza thought, as she hung her jacket up in the front hall and tossed her bag on the bench nearby.

Liza had worked with a talented interior designer out of Greenwich, Rigby Mayfair, to create the look of contemporary mixed with antiques in her Victorian house. "No oak, no scrolls of any kind" was Liza's directive to her designer. "I don't want this place to look like the Haunted Mansion. Clean, clean, clean lines and colors." Rigby had delivered, creating a space that surprised and relaxed as soon as you walked in the door. Plus, it was the ultimate showroom for the art from her gallery. Liza had sold pieces right off the wall at her last committee meeting. Her friends needed to see how contemporary art could work in historic homes. Her living room did exactly that.

And for her services, Liza traded out several pieces of art to Rigby for her personal collection and agreed to split her commissions on any pieces Rigby acquired for her clients over the next two years. The two creative businesswomen enjoyed each other's company and admired each other's eye. Liza wished she had more friends in her life like Rigby—supportive but not draining. It often felt to Liza like she did all the heavy lifting, all the time in all her relationships. How did that happen?

"C'mon, Jack. You live here now, I guess."

The old golden plodded through the living room to the kitchen, where he knew there would always be something on the floor. He'd spent enough time at Liza's to feel at home, but clearly, he missed his true owner. Liza's lab Bear greeted him with enthusiasm.

"Hey," Liza called out to Whit. He'd sent her a text saying he had a change of plans and would be home for the weekend instead of working through it in North Carolina. She was excited to see him. The kids were at camp. Her sisters were living their own lives for a few days. And she was trying to put the reality of Serena out of her head until she plunged back into the organizational mountain that was Willow Lane on Monday. Whit was home. Maybe she could finally breathe. "We're home."

"In the kitchen," a male voice called back.

Whit, still in his suit, no tie, was pouring himself a Scotch and eating the men's health nut mix that Liza ordered for him from an online market that specialized in organic snacks and pantry ingredients. He looked tired, beat up, as he did a lot these days. The long hours, the travel, the stress of closing big deals had begun to take its toll on Whit.

A few years older than Liza, he'd turned forty last October and seemed to be aging rapidly. Less hair, less vigor, more back pain. Young Whit, the athletic guy who'd run up and down the AYSO soccer field doing his volunteer reffing stint even after a long week at work, was gone, replaced by the guy who'd nap on the couch on Saturdays while watching golf. Their social life had dwindled to practically zero. His work schedule was so erratic when he was in the middle of a deal, Liza couldn't even count on him to show up at an event on a Saturday night, never mind an opening reception at the gallery on a Thursday. They connected less and less frequently— at dinner, over wine, in the bedroom—and neither had the guts to mention the distance between them. The last thing Liza wanted was to become one of those wives who confided to her friends in the ladies' locker room that she only had sex once a month, but that was becoming their story more months than not.

Liza was only thirty-six; she'd had her kids young and still felt young, even though most of her Southport "mommy" friends with teenagers were a decade older. She didn't want to age any faster than she needed to, but Whit's energy loss had her worried for her own aging process. She'd be an empty nester in five years. She wanted to reinvigorate her life, but frankly, Whit was bringing her down. While she resisted, he embraced his sedentary, neatly paved future that revolved around British crimes dramas on Netflix, dinners at the club with the same few couples or his parents, and the occasional trip to the Caribbean. Only last month, after they'd managed to get themselves into Madison Square Garden to see a concert on a weeknight, Whit announced, "That's it. No more concerts for me. My ears can't take the noise." *Noise?* It was Dave Matthews!

But tonight, Liza was filled with gratitude that he was here and that they could be alone together. It had been a year since the kids were last at camp and they'd had time to themselves. "I was happy to get your text. Why the change in plans? I thought you were staying in Durham this weekend?"

"I felt like I needed to be here. Hey, Jack." Whit gave the dog a pat on the head and a belly rub. He loved that dog. "Do you want a drink?"

It was 4:30. That seemed a little early, but what the hell. It had been a week. "Sure. A vodka tonic. I'll cut some lime."

Whit made the drink with his usual care. He was good at tending bar. It was one of the things that Liza had been drawn to when they first started dating fifteen years ago, that he was an attentive host and competent bartender at gatherings. He and some college buddies had been renting a small beach house in nearby Westport for the summer, commuting back and forth from New York City. Liza had known him for years, but their age difference meant they'd never been in school together. That, and Whit was a private-school kid all the way, from Country Day to St. Paul's to Trinity for college. But in a small town, age differences fade in college and there were nights at the Shoe or house parties where they'd run into each other all the time. They connected at a Fourth of July party a few months after Gray had left, abandoned Liza, really, and she was in a vulnerable state. Her mother was dying and she wasn't going back to college.

Whit had made her a Long Island Iced Tea even though he wasn't the official party host and his composure and care struck the exact right chord in Liza. Six months later, they were married.

Liza put down the four mugs she'd chosen from her father's extensive collection, one for each of them: Wesleyan for Vivi, BC for Fitz, Trinity College Dublin for Whit, and Hamilton for her. Liza had wanted to go to Hamilton, but didn't have the grades. This mug was as close as she was going to get. She washed the lime and cut it in quarters.

"What are those?" Whit asked her, setting down the vodka tonic.

"Mugs. You know, from my father's mug collection. I thought everybody in the family should have one. Look, Trinity College Dublin for you. Close as I could get to your alma mater."

"Great. Just what we need, more crap from you father's house."

Liza was hurt. "This isn't crap. It's memories. And I don't think four mugs are going to engulf the house in clutter."

"First, it's the mugs, Liza, then it will be everything. Like it always has been with your family."

"What does that mean?"

"It means that no matter what I ask, you choose your father first. I specifically said, I didn't want all that crap here and yet, here it is."

"It's four mugs."

"And next it will be his desk. Then his favorite chair. Then all those old, dusty posters of all those dead writers."

Liza assumed Whit was talking about the beautiful hand-drawn quotes from Joyce, Beckett, and Synge that her father had collected on his many trips to Ireland. She loved those pieces. She had tagged them at Willow Lane with her personal Post-its. She thought that Fitz would like to have them one day when he went to college and realized exactly who his grandfather was. "Those are valuable. And meaningful."

"See what I mean?"

"What about Jack? Should I drop him off at the pound tomorrow? Is that the kind of crap you mean?"

"Of course not. Jack is a great dog," Whit said firmly. But then he added, "My point is that I don't really want to be surrounded by your father every minute for the rest of my life."

"What are you talking about? My father was decent to you. He . . ." She hesitated because even Liza knew *love* was the wrong word. ". . . admired you."

"He tolerated me. For fifteen years, he tolerated me. And it was clear, he felt I was never good enough for you. Or for him. I'm sorry if I prefer John Grisham to his navel-gazing literary bullshit."

"Wow. How do you really feel, Whit? I mean, maybe you could have let me know your bitterness and resentment before he died. Because now, when I'm sad and exhausted and in emotional overdrive, you've added guilt. Do you want me to feel awful that I made you suffer through all those horrible family dinners, where my father, the Presidential Medal of Freedom honoree, made you feel inadequate?"

"See what I mean?"

"My point is that he was brighter than all of us. Than me, than you, than almost everybody he interacted with. He wasn't your average dad. My God, I would think after all these years, you'd get that. We are average, maybe above average. But he wasn't. He was exceptional."

"Liza, I have watched you spend every minute of the last fifteen years worried about something—my blood pressure, our kids' standardized test scores, your sister's love life. But mainly, your father, every day. Every damn day. He's dominated our lives and I've put up with it, all of the shitshow that was Bill Sweeney. But now he's gone and I don't want his fucking mugs in my house." Whit picked up the Trinity mug like he was going to smash it against the wall, but lowered his arm when Jack began to whimper. "I'm sorry."

It wasn't clear to whom Whit was apologizing: to Liza or to Jack.

"Is that why you came home? To tell me how much you hated my father?"

"I didn't hate him. But I didn't idolize him." Whit stood in front of the corkboard wall filled with family photos and mementos. The twins at Halloween when they were toddlers dressed up as bread and butter. Tickets to the US Open at Shinnecock. Liza and Whit in Bermuda for their tenth anniversary. The big family photo from last Thanksgiving. All that mattered on one corkboard. He took another slug of his Scotch. "I've been asked to stay in Durham. To run the company, at least for one year. To be the interim CEO. And I've said yes."

Liza needed a moment to process all the words Whit said in such a rush. Durham. Year. Interim CEO. Yes. "Without talking to me?"

"You had a lot going on. And really, there was nothing to discuss. I need this, for my career and, frankly, for my sanity. I need to be away from all this for a while."

"All this? Your wife and kids?"

"Without distraction. I need to focus on work. And from what you've told me, this business with the house and the estate will take a while to settle. You'll be fully engulfed in all that drama."

"Oh, and don't forget the surprise sister that showed up. Yeah, why would you want to support me through the next few months? It'll be smooth sailing."

"I support you. But I'm not going to let this opportunity for me slip by because your family is going through its usual upheaval. I can't be a part of that drama anymore. Everything I warned you about has happened—the debt, the unfinished business, the messy relationships. I can't deal with it anymore."

"And Vivi and Fitz? Are they flotsam and jetsam?"

"Of course not. You know that. But they're at camp now and in the fall, they have school and all their activities. I barely see them because they have such busy schedules. Then they'll be off to prep school. My work will give them every opportunity in the future."

"Oh, there it is. Your standard line that your devotion to work is for everyone else's benefit."

"You've certainly benefited from my work," he snapped back, the equilibrium regained. "They can come to Durham in August and stay with me."

Her brain started to spin out of control, thinking about all the wrong things, like the club tennis championships in August the twins always played in and the annual slog to finish the summer reading before the start of school. Was Whit going to supervise that while he was in Durham, running a business and living out of a corporate apartment? Then, the flash went off. "You have someone else. This isn't a career move. You're seeing somebody."

"It's not what you think. It's nothing yet."

"Yet? Are you casually dating while we're married?" Her raised voice made the dogs slink out of the room. "That must be fun, while I'm here at home raising our children."

"Please, snippy isn't your style, Liza." Whit valued maturity.

"I can't believe it." Which was true. Liza had never suspected Whit of cheating on his marriage vows. It was the vow part Liza thought he'd uphold, not the marriage part. Whit believed in his good word more than he believed in the myth of melding two into one. He wasn't sentimental, but he was honorable. "Are we separating, then? Is this what's happening? You're using the excuse of my father's death to pause our marriage?"

"The timing is coincidental. I have an opportunity in Durham and, unfortunately, I needed to commit right away, so I did. This is for me and my career."

"And I'm supposed to hold down the fort here with the kids, my business, this house and the estate, and, oh yeah, grief?"

"Liza, I've provided a nice life for you, a very nice life. You have the resources to hire all the help you need to manage everything you think you have to manage on your own. Maybe you'll finally delegate some of the responsibilities and do the work you need to do on yourself."

"Look at you, Mr. Life Coach. Thanks for the input. Super helpful. Who'd you steal that from? The honey?"

"Don't call her that."

"What is she, then? A girlfriend? A friend with benefits? A colleague?" Whit looked up. "I see. She's a colleague. Because I never understood the importance of what you do, isn't that right?"

"I would call her someone who cares about me and listens to me."

That stung Liza more deeply than if Whit had said she was great in bed or had the perfect ass, both areas in which Liza suspected she fell short. Had Liza's emotional well-being not been so depleted from the last ten days, maybe she would have put up more of a fight, but she couldn't muster her anger. She was too tired. Now she felt old. "I see that you've clearly made a few other decisions on your own besides whether to take the job. Now, I need time. I feel like you owe me that, at least. I want to keep this arrangement between us, until I can sort a few things out and until the kids get through eighth grade and the prep school admissions process. I don't want this to tank their grades. At least not this year."

"That seems fair."

"No telling the kids or my sisters or our friends. And please, don't tell your parents. If, when we come to a permanent decision, you have to be the one to tell your mother. I can't bear to disappoint her."

Whit was contrite. "Agreed."

Liza picked up her drink and headed toward the back staircase. There was nothing in the fridge except the remains of Lolly's boeuf bourguignon. She couldn't eat that for one more night. "I made dinner reservations at the club. I thought . . ." *What?* She thought they might reconnect after everything, enjoy a civilized adult dinner where she could let her hair down a bit with her husband, after keeping up appearances for everyone else. *Oh, well.* "Never mind what I thought. We might as well change and head over there. I'll bring my calendar and we can work out the logistics of all this." Fifteen years of marriage reduced to marks on the school calendar that Liza used to organize her life.

Whit poured another Scotch and followed her upstairs. They both understood what had happened: Whit had won.

SERENA PULLED THE Range Rover onto the Winthrop property. The drive from DC had taken over six hours and she was beat. The driveway split: the guesthouse, a renovated stone carriage house, was off to the left, and the main house, an enormous waterfront gem from the early 1900s, was off to the right. She was glad you couldn't see the main house from her place. She'd be able to come and go with relative freedom. Though Lucy Winthrop was generous and charming, she was a talker. A conversation with her every day was a steep price to pay for a free summer rental. Serena had preferred to plunk down the going rate for the place, but Mrs. Winthrop, a dear friend of her mother's and someone that she saw with regularity in DC, had insisted that there was no need. However, she was required to appear at the Winthrop's Fourth of July gathering. "You'll know everybody! We always invite loads of young people. Maybe you'll meet someone. Deke's chief of staff recently got divorced. He's a catch!"

It was Mrs. Winthrop, née Davenport, who had the money, not the congressman, a fact she had announced very loudly and very publicly at one of Deke Winthrop's first rallies when a constituent asked about how he could be committed to the working man, when he himself came from money. Lucy Davenport Winthrop stood up in the front row, waved her arms, and then said, "It's my money, not his!" The line got a huge laugh, and it became her catchphrase as she spread her wealth around the Nutmeg State. An early supporter of environmental causes before it was chic, Lucy Winthrop and her money almost single-handedly saved the local wetlands, planted a million tulip bulbs at state and federal buildings, and underwrote the cleanups at local beaches. She used her wealth to fund her daughters' show-riding careers, securing a national team berth for Delaney and her horse, Topper, and a marriage to a Virginia horse family for her younger daughter, Reagan. There were Caribbean Christmases and board seats on charities in Connecticut, New York, and DC. And, of course, Lucy was one of the regulars at the Red Door, allowing her to claim she'd never gone under the knife, but the word on the street was that the regular visits to Elizabeth Arden smoke-screened her excellent plastic surgery. Lucy Winthrop was wealthy in money and influence, but not in close female friends. Birdie Tucker was the exception.

Had Birdie told Lucy the truth about Serena's father? Serena guessed no. While the two were dear friends, she suspected that they both hid secrets from each other.

Serena hadn't spoken to her mother, either, despite the voicemail from seventy-two hours ago. She had had to extricate herself from her DC life and it had taken her full attention. She was surprised how smoothly it all went. Her boss actually appreciated her resignation in advance of the mass firing. The intern was thrilled to be set up in Georgetown for the summer. And she packed up the Range Rover with the items that mattered most, her desktop computer, and her boxes of Sweeney family research. She'd been too busy to check in with her mother, but she'd make the call eventually. This week, for sure.

As she stopped the car, she noticed a gift bag on the porch. She hoped it was a bottle of white wine from the Winthrops because she could use a glass and she hadn't made it to the store as she'd planned. She picked up the bag and entered the guesthouse, flipping on the lights to reveal a well-decorated open kitchen and living room, done in blues and taupe with mainly contemporary furniture and a few choice antiques. Not her style, but warm and comfortable. The bedroom and bath were upstairs, and there was a large slate patio off the kitchen, which would be beautiful all summer.

No foosball table, Serena thought, recalling her conversation at Cap's office with her sisters. She'd have to let them know.

She opened the lime-green gift bag and was surprised to pull out a mug with the Wellesley College insignia on it and a note in beautiful penmanship. It read: *Serena, I thought you might want this mug. Our father had a large collection of them from various lectures and such that he did over the years. I guess he never spoke at Vassar, because there wasn't one of those. But Wellesley was the next closest thing, being all-women, too. You should stop by this week for a tour of the house and the boathouse, anytime. Perhaps you'd like to see it before Liza donates everything to Goodwill and Tricia shreds all remaining documents. Hahahaha. Kidding. No, seriously, come by. xo Maggie*

Serena stared at the mug, then reread the note. *Our father.* Yes, Maggie had acknowledged the truth and it touched Serena deeply. She'd already formed her own opinion about all the sisters and it didn't surprise her that Maggie was the one to reach out. She was the most open, a seeker. This was a huge gesture, and the invitation to see the house, his office, everything before it was sold was exactly the opportunity she had hoped for. The night of the wake, the office had been locked (she had tried the door) and the house itself was too filled with people to do any decent snooping. Yes, Serena would be stopping by this week.

It didn't even matter that Maggie had gotten the details wrong. Vassar hadn't been all women since 1969 and William Sweeney had, in fact, appeared there in 1972 as part of an all-male panel discussion about "the pinking" of journalism, an event protested by the Women's Union on campus. He was a male chauvinist pig, according to the enthusiastic voices of dissent of dozens of undergraduate women who blocked the entrance to his talk, according to Serena's research. Apparently, this assessment was based on a single *Esquire* article the new young columnist there had written in praise of women's legs in short skirts. He was a rookie on the New York publishing scene and his editors had sent him to Poughkeepsie as a sort of hazing ritual that he barely survived. There were photos in the Vassar newspaper of the kerfuffle and a brief mention in the *New York Times*. Serena wasn't surprised he never got a Vassar mug.

She wandered into the kitchen, flipping on the lamps in her cottage, feeling more at home and relaxed by the second. She opened the door of the sleek new refrigerator and sure enough, there was a bottle of Chardonnay, a cheese-and-fruit plate, chocolate truffles, coffee and milk for the morning, and a note from Lucy Winthrop: *So good to have you back in Southport! Cheers!*

Serena opened the Chardonnay and poured the wine into her mug. "Cheers, Dad."

Chapter

12

Over the last three days, quite a few things had shown up at Willow Lane, including but not limited to: Tim the line cook with an old minivan full of Maggie's possessions—work-in-progress paintings, paint and brushes, blank canvases; Rufus the cat; trays of sandwiches from Fortuna's Deli, and a dozen homemade cakes of all kinds from friends and neighbor; bottles of whiskey and hundreds of sympathy cards from William Sweeney fans and admirers around the world expressing condolences; the quiet presence of Raj Chaudhry, who charmed Liza and Maggie and then immediately set to work in the boathouse, much to Tricia's delight; and finally, a letter from their father's publisher, Allegory, bypassing his longtime agent, that was both polite (about how sorry they were to hear about their dear friend William Sweeney) and threatening ("But we need that memoir in thirty days or else") that spooked Liza and enraged Tricia. About the only thing that hadn't turned up was the memoir itself despite a nonstop effort to find it.

When the doorbell rang midafternoon on a Thursday, Liza assumed it was another food delivery from a well-meaning neighbor or school mom who'd missed the service because, in the words of yesterday's food deliverer, "I was out of town when I heard. Tuscany. It was glorious, but your news was tragic." (It was, after all, early summer, the official "Best Time to Go to Europe" for the locals, an annual exodus well-documented on Facebook pages with pictures of smiling families

at the Louvre or Buckingham Palace with the hashtag #familytime.)
Liza had nearly finished organizing the downstairs, everything labeled
"Dump," "Donate," or "Keep," in defiance of Whit's edict. To say the
organizing was therapeutic was an understatement. Liza worked out a
lot of anger and anxiety filling up a dumpster with old sheets and high
school term papers. She'd kept the truth about Whit to herself, sure
her sisters hadn't noticed anything amiss. She couldn't find the words
or the moment to tell them about her failure.

Liza would move upstairs tomorrow, determined to clean out her
father's closet. That was a task none of the sisters wanted to tackle,
so Liza, of course, volunteered to do it. She hoped whoever was at the
door had thought to bring coffee, too, because she could use a latte.
"Coming!" she called.

It was Serena with a tray of lattes.

"I hope I'm not intruding," Serena said, sensing that her visit was
at the very least a surprise and at most a social breach beyond comprehension, judging by the look on Liza's face. "Maggie invited me. I
texted her to let her know I'd be stopping by. Latte?"

"You read my mind. How thoughtful." *Damn it, Maggie.* Liza tried
not to look too put out by the fact that Maggie had struck up a text
relationship with Serena and invited her to Willow Lane. But she
was. Maggie had returned from Mill River inspired to paint, not to
help, and had set up a studio in the conservatory with Tim's furniture-
moving skills. Clearly, he was more than Maggie's cat sitter, but Liza
and Tricia refused to mention the obvious chemistry between the two
because they didn't want to give oxygen to yet another one of Maggie's drama-filled relationships. Instead, they treated him like a helpful Uber driver and sent him on his way when he was done.

Maggie had barely left her makeshift studio in seventy-two hours,
finishing up the pieces she had promised Liza and then starting on
another of a view across the harbor of a house on the hill with glowing
windows. Maggie was calling it *Panes of Gold* and Liza knew it could

be a highlight of her sunflower show with its striking golden tones, so she'd backed off criticizing her sister for creating more chaos than order at Willow Lane. Maggie was working at a new level, so Liza let her be and took up her duties in the manuscript search.

But here was Serena, at Maggie's request, presumably now demanding a tour of the property. Well, not demanding exactly, but still. Now, Liza supposed, she would have to spend an hour escorting Serena through the house. At least she had brought coffee.

"Come on in. Thank you for these. We have a lifetime supply of Entenmann's in the kitchen. Why don't you follow me? I'll let Maggie and Tricia know you're here."

Serena followed her from the front hall past the living room, down the wide hallway, and toward the library. There hadn't been any updating of Willow Lane, no tearing down of walls to create the open plan that was now de rigueur for any home renovation these days. Even the homes on the historic registry managed to keep their street views intact, as per the regulations, yet blew up the interior to create one big twenty-first-century entertaining room from many small nineteenth-century rooms. That wouldn't have suited Bill Sweeney, who liked to have his own space when he wanted his own space.

At Willow Lane, each well-proportioned room was separated by doors and entryways. Despite Maggie's warning to get there before Liza gave everything away, Serena had waited a few days to follow up. She didn't want to seem too eager for information. As a result, the rooms did have a "just about to move" look with tagged furniture and boxes in the corners.

As they moved past the library, Liza stopped, reversed course, and opened the pocket doors, and went in, offering up the first insight into the house as a home. This handsome room featured three walls of built-in bookshelves painted a striking dark blue that Serena suspected Liza had chosen. The fourth wall was all windows facing out to the sea. There was no desk; instead, there was a faded red velvet couch and two wingback chairs upholstered in a handsome striped fabric. There was a ragged Oriental rug on the floor and the room was lit by brass floor lamps. Prints of what looked to be hand-drawn quotes from writers hung on the few feet of wall not covered in shelves.

"I love this room," Liza said. "My father's work papers are going to Yale, but all of these books from his personal library are going to the Pequot Library. I'm not sure they need more copies of John Updike and Robert Ludlum; you'd think they already have enough. But Pierce Crane was insistent that they get the complete library, even the airport paperbacks."

Serena noticed that Liza didn't say "our father" like Maggie had in her note. She tried not to let it bother her and took a lighter tone. "Maybe they plan on re-creating this room there, like Julia Child's kitchen at the Smithsonian. You should give them the couch and the chairs for the reading room. That would add a mystique to the library." As soon as she said it, she regretted it. She didn't have enough of a relationship with Liza to suggest such a thing. Plus, she wanted the wingback chairs for herself, if offered.

But Liza surprised her. "That's a fantastic idea, Serena. None of us want these things, but I bet Pequot would. They could attach small plaques that say, 'William Sweeney Sat Here.' Actually, it wasn't until after my mother died that my father spent much time in here at all. He preferred reading out in the boathouse when we were little. It was quieter." There was a pause, and the two women, the two sisters, took in the moment.

"It's a lovely room," Serena said, still holding the tray of coffees.

"Kitchen's this way."

TRICIA LOOKED DOWN at her phone. Liza's text said that Serena was in the kitchen and wanted a tour. Oh, and she had brought lattes for all. Then she had added several emojis of the panicked cat face imitating *The Scream*, presumably to indicate her personal panic, but Tricia knew that she would welcome Serena graciously. Liza had grown into politeness, any rebelliousness worn down after years of Jones family training and her own position in town as a business owner and arbiter of taste. Liza could no more be unwelcoming to Serena than she could to those tourists who wandered into the gallery, more interested in the whereabouts of a public bathroom than a watercolor.

Tricia felt the need to oversee any touring about the property. Though the pressure was mounting to find that memoir, she was more worried about what Serena might write than what her father did write. She'd successfully pushed thoughts of Serena out of her head for a few days, but now she was back, standing in the kitchen and demanding a tour.

She looked over at Raj, who was carefully flipping through *Dispatches*, a book on the Vietnam War that her father had used to research *Bitter Fruit*. Even as a writer, her father had never felt like the physical books were sacred items, meant to be kept pristine and perfect. Bill Sweeney commandeered books, underlining, writing in the margins, tearing out pages if necessary. "I own it," he used to say by way of explanation. "It's mine." *Dispatches* was one of those books and Raj was taking photos of certain pages that looked particularly hard-worn. Someday, a doctoral student in literature would use the notes William Sweeney wrote in the margins as the basis of a doctoral thesis about major novels on the Vietnam War, including *Bitter Fruit*. Raj had told Tricia that his job was to make sure all the pieces were in place for that to happen.

"I'm headed to the house for a bit. Do you need anything?" Raj had settled into the boathouse with a few belongings, his computers and gear and his bike. In a few short days, Raj and Tricia had established an easy working rhythm. Like two diligent high school students working together on a research project, they were shy with each other, trying to keep the focus on the work at hand and ignoring the obvious mutual attraction. They worked side by side for about five or six hours a day, mainly Raj asking questions and Tricia guiding him through the contents of the office. Then she'd go for a long run and spend the evening wondering what Raj was doing in the boathouse loft and if he was only laughing at her jokes or catching her eye at various times throughout the day because she was Bill Sweeney's daughter. Or was it because he felt like she felt? Like something was happening between them.

Tricia felt foolish; there were so many other pressing issues at hand and she was distracted by some guy. She knew in a few days she'd be done searching every possible nook and cranny for the thumb drive and would have to move her efforts into the house—the attic, her father's bedroom, the library. But she wasn't ready to leave Raj yet. His presence was something she couldn't describe, at once familiar and exotic. She wasn't used to being off-kilter around a man.

In fact, in the previous relationships she'd had—including the college boyfriend, the guy in law school, and the ill-advised fling with the client—the major draw was that she was exactly on kilter, comfortable to a fault. "Wow, that sounds sexy," Maggie had once said when Tricia described her relationship with Steve, the guy from law school, "like dating a good fleece jacket."

Even with Blair Wynan, her client and a man she should not have been seeing, the tenor of the relationship hadn't been the frantic forbidden love portrayed on TV dramas where the female lawyers wore lace bras under their silk blouses, ready for action in the middle of a depo. Despite the twenty-year age difference, she and Blair shared similar academic credentials, athletic backgrounds, even lived on the same Upper East Side block. Had he not been a client, had Tricia not gotten pregnant, the two of them might have moved toward marriage. The second for him, of course. But when she discovered she was pregnant, thanks to his vasectomy failure, a gulf opened up between them.

Tricia, who was meticulous about birth control, was furious at his cavalier attitude about the pregnancy and equally disappointed in his lack of compassion over the miscarriage. Even though she was terrified of the professional repercussions of a child so early in her career, a fact she was later ashamed of, she expected some sort of understanding from Blair. He was relieved, thrilled actually, when she lost the baby at nine weeks. ("Phew. Dodged a bullet!" were his exact words when she called him from the gynecologist's office.) When Tricia ended the relationship, he thanked her for her sacrifice with a straight face.

Tricia hadn't been involved with anyone in the years since or even mentioned the miscarriage, except to her doctor. She wanted to power through on her own and she thought she'd handled it well, having no idea that Liza and Maggie's back-channel communications often revolved around Tricia's verbal shortness and exasperated tone of voice.

But now, in the wake of tremendous loss and upheaval, Tricia found herself attracted to this accidental officemate and she was thrown.

"Hey, Raj . . ." Tricia said again because she loved saying his name. "Did you hear me?"

"I didn't."

"I'm headed up to the house to talk to a . . . journalist." That seemed like the safest description. As she had learned from the hundreds of hours listening to true crime podcasts while walking to work, when you're lying, it's best to stick as close to the truth as you can. "Can I get you anything?"

"No, thank you. I'll make some tea here in a bit. Where's he from?"

"The journalist? It's a she," Tricia corrected. "She's from nowhere. Freelance, fishing around for a story."

"Ah, my mistake. Is there one?"

"One what?"

"A story to tell. Beyond the missing memoir."

"I think there might be. But I'm not sure who the protagonist is yet."

IMMEDIATELY, TRICIA WAS struck by the familiarity of the scene: two sisters, sitting across the kitchen table drinking coffee and eating Entenmann's while the sun streamed through the big picture windows. The Sweeney sisters had spent hundreds of hours at the old butcher block table tucked in the cozy corner of the kitchen playing games, doing homework, drinking coffee, drinking tea, and eventually drinking wine. Talking, laughing, crying, complaining about their parents, their boyfriends, their schoolwork, and their bosses. The night their mother died, Julia fixed them all hot chocolate while they sat, dazed and devasted. Maggie even fell asleep at the table that night, simply putting her head down and closing her eyes. It felt like their whole life had unfolded at that kitchen table and now, Serena sat with Liza, sharing a moment.

"Welcome to Willow Lane." Tricia had decided to emulate her big sisters and be as warm to Serena as she could muster. Kill with kindness was her new motto, and by *kill*, she meant kill any possible tell-all that Serena might be planning. As Tricia had discussed with Cap, she was frustrated about splitting the estate with another person mainly because there wasn't much of an estate to cash in on. But, in truth, Not Much Left divided by four Sweeney sisters wasn't significantly less money than Not Much Left divided by three Sweeney sisters. Still, it wasn't easy for her to be warm. "Oh, that's right, you were here at the wake. And Halloween. Well, welcome back. And technically, you do own a quarter of it now, so you should have a look at the place."

"You know, I don't think about my piece of the estate like that. This is your home, not mine." Serena was determined not to let the Sweeneys get the upper hand as they had at Cap's office. She was going to stand her ground. She wanted them to know she wasn't as taken with them as she had appeared. "This always was a very special house. I remember your mother hosting those May Day celebrations. Didn't she have all the neighbor girls over and we danced around the maypole in crowns made of flowers? She taught us some Irish songs, too. I recall being here for several of those. Not that many people celebrate May Day. It was memorable."

With only a few words, Liza was taken back to her childhood.

Maeve had celebrated the day with a nod toward her Celtic heritage, and Serena was right. There was dancing, singing, lots of little girls in party dresses with flowers in their hair. Her mother would dress as the May Queen with all sorts of hippie-inspired flourishes and recite poetry with great flair while the other mothers in town, clutching their wine spritzers and Nantucket straw bags, looked on in bemused confusion. Liza imagined that Birdie Tucker had plenty to say at the next Ladies' Day at the club about "that crazy pagan poet Maeve Sweeney." The celebrations had only gone on for a few years, while Tricia was still very young. Then their mother was diagnosed with cancer and the May Day parties stopped. Liza hadn't thought about them in years. They had been wonderful. "Do you remember those, Tricia?"

"I don't remember the parties, but I remember that photo of Mom. She looked like a character out of *A Midsummer Night's Dream* with some sort of bird's nest in her hair and she was wearing a toga. She was not really Southport material."

"We should find that one. It must be here somewhere."

After Maeve died, the photos of her that had been all over the house slowly disappeared. Every time the girls came back from school or a trip, one or two more had been tucked away, as if their father couldn't bear to witness her image. There was one photo left in the boathouse and the sisters each had photos in their own homes, but here at Willow Lane, Maeve was a memory. Liza turned to Serena. "What did your mother make of those parties, Serena?"

"My mother stood in harsh judgment of most events that involved genuine joy and spontaneity. Frivolity wasn't her thing."

"Huh," Tricia said. "Then how did your mother end up sleeping with my father?"

Liza snapped, "Tricia!"

"I'm sorry. It's the obvious question. We all want to know, so let's not pretend we don't." So much for killing with kindness, but Serena had opened the door by characterizing Birdie Tucker as a woman who was neither passionate nor spontaneous, two essential elements for a one-night stand or any sort of illicit affair between married coconspirators. "You're a journalist, you must have asked her. What happened between the two of them? When? Where?" Tricia wanted to ask why, but that seemed over the top.

Serena was about to answer when Maggie burst through the swinging door into the kitchen. She was wearing a white utility jumpsuit covered in paint splatter and her magnificent red hair was tied up in a scarf. She was glowing in the way a person might after they'd encountered a secret crush. Her work was going well and her spirit reflected it. Seeing Serena seated at the kitchen table with Liza and Tricia was a shocking sort of throwback to the best and worst days in the Sweeney family history. Maggie made a beeline to hug Serena. "Hey, you're here. I'm so happy!" Then Maggie took a breath and noticed the cool temperature of the room. "So, what'd I miss?"

There was dead silence. Then Tricia spoke up. "I asked how her mother and our father happened to sleep together."

"I can't believe you," Maggie said, always comfortable taking the underdog's side as a sign of her superior empathy. In this room, Serena was definitely the underdog. "I'm so sorry. My invitation was not an ambush. *Jesus,* Tricia."

"Please, I feel like the least we should be with each other is honest. This isn't an ideal situation. And we're here because the adults in our lives were less than honorable. So, everybody should hop off those high horses."

"I didn't ask," Serena insisted. "I never asked my mother how or why."

"How is that possible?" Tricia wouldn't let it go.

Serena didn't back down. "I need more information before I seek an explanation. That's how I work, Tricia. I research first, ask questions later, if possible. I would rather go to my mother with a folder full of facts for her to confirm than sit in front of her with a blank notebook and have her tell me a story that may or may not be true.

This is my training." The four of them sat at the table drinking the lattes and feeling each other out. Liza, uncomfortable with the content of the conversation, organized a plate of lemon cookies to go with the marble loaf cake. Nobody ate anything, but at least the exercise of plating the cookies gave her an excuse to avoid eye contact with Serena. Maggie, on the other hand, was completely engaged, nodding along to indicate her solidarity with Serena.

"I understand that you all want to know about their relationship before you can move on with our relationship . . ." Serena waved her hand around, indicating the four of them. "So do I. But my mother isn't like I imagine your mother was, open and articulate about life and emotions. My mother and I don't hold each other in confidence. Someday soon, my mother and I will sit down and have a conversation about this. But first, I need to understand more about William Sweeney and what's at stake."

"I don't get that at all. It's the first question I'd ask," Tricia said.

"Me, too," Maggie agreed. "I'd want the details."

"Not me," Liza said.

For a moment, there was a communal understanding of the strangeness of the situation. How did they all get here? And, really, what questions did they want answered?

Maggie saw an opportunity to be the great defender. "Are you satisfied, Tricia? This isn't a trial. Can we give Serena a tour now?"

"Yes, of course. I apologize, Serena. The last few weeks have been filled with change and information, some of which, frankly, has been startling. You've had a chance to sit with these . . . revelations for several months. For us, it's been a lot to take in. I ask questions first, put it all together later. That's *my* training." Tricia's phone rang and she popped up to answer it. "It's work. So much for my sabbatical. This could take a couple of hours. Excuse me."

Liza was relieved that Tricia had left the kitchen. "Why don't we show you the boathouse first?"

Chapter

Liza walked Serena across the lawn, making conversation. "How's the guesthouse at the Winthrops'? I think she's done some work on it recently. She used Mike Costello as the general contractor. He was working for me at the same time doing some upgrades at the gallery, a new mini-kitchen for openings, but Lucy Winthrop had Mike wrapped around her finger, tied up every day. I had to personally appeal to Mrs. Winthrop to let Mike finish up my job before a big opening. She gets wants she wants, Lucy Winthrop." Liza was desperate to change the subject. "Here we are. Did Tricia mention that there is an archivist here from Yale sorting out the papers? Knock, knock."

Liza was relieved to hear Raj's voice from within: "Come in."

"Hi, Raj. Sorry to bother you. We have a visitor who wanted to see my father's office before everything goes off to New Haven. This is Serena Tucker."

"Nice to meet you. I'm Raj Chaudhry. Tricia said you were a journalist, but she didn't mention you were a relative."

"She is a journalist," Liza said, irrationally, hoping to throw off the flow of conversation.

"Pardon?" Serena said.

"Well, you must be a cousin. You look exactly like Tricia with blond hair."

"Yes," Liza said. "Something like that."

Standing in the boathouse, taking in the literary importance of the space, Serena was emotional. This was William Sweeney's office. This was her father's office.

She wished the contents hadn't been organized, boxed, and labeled. She wished that her father had agreed to meet with her as she had requested. She wished she had had a single moment with him during his lifetime where the two of them could have acknowledged the truth, forgiven the past, and talked about the present, about writing and life. Serena was bitter about her mother withholding the truth, but she was more bitter that she didn't get any time with her "birth father"—a term she hated because it made no sense. He wasn't there for her birth and he'd never been a father to her.

Serena knew in her heart that Mitch Tucker was a decent man, stable to a fault and probably responsible for her steady emotional state. He was and had been a fine father. But William Sweeney was an extraordinary talent, a genius, even. Standing in his office was not enough, but it was something. And that something made her weepy.

Raj shot Liza an alarmed look. Liza said quietly, "We'll give you some time here, Serena. Raj, can I speak with you on the dock?"

Serena was grateful for the time alone. And, she realized, Liza trusted her enough to leave her alone in the boathouse. She was also grateful for that. She watched Liza and Raj walk toward the water, both without looking back. *Liza is handling this well,* Serena thought. *Like someone who's old enough to withhold judgment.* Serena wandered around the office. The mementos were few, a couple of photos from talks, an official portrait with former president Clinton, a photo of Maeve in what looked to be a wedding dress, no veil, only a spray of roses and baby's breath woven into her hair. There were various medals of honor and honorary degrees in a pile. A framed *New Yorker* cover signed by the artist. Serena noticed there were only a couple of family photos. One was of Liza's beautiful children, whom she had seen at the wake. In this picture, the twins were tan and happy, on a sailboat. *My niece and nephew,* thought Serena for the first time, surprised that she hadn't connected the family dots beyond the three sisters. *I have a niece and nephew and a brother-in-law.* As an unmarried only child, those kinds of relationships hadn't even occurred to Serena. Now, she had an extended family. She studied the photo. The boat's name was *Sunkissed*, and that's exactly the way the children looked: sunkissed.

The other photo was the sort of family shot that was mandatory in all holiday cards these days: posed and perfect. Serena wasn't sure when these sorts of cards had become mandatory holiday missives; she didn't recall the onslaught occurring in her childhood. Certainly, the Tucker family didn't make the posed portrait an annual event. Maybe at her deb ball there was a photo card, or something from that one perfect ski vacation in Sun Valley, but Birdie Tucker favored cards from the Metropolitan Museum of Art that she had engraved and then personalized with a short note. These days, Serena got dozens of cards every year from classmates and colleagues who wanted to advertise their excellent gene pool and tout accomplishments (*Starting pre-K at Sidwell! MVP of the soccer squad! Youngest girl on the Robotics Team!*). Serena tossed them all in a silver bowl by the front door for a few weeks and then tossed them out on January 2. Serena was sure Liza sent out these trophy cards on expensive stock with gold engraving. Maybe she'd get one next Christmas.

But this Sweeney formal family picture seemed out of character for free-range Maeve and her daughters. Liza and Maggie were tweens and Tricia was about six. All the Sweeney women posed on the lawn of Willow Lane, as if a picnic were about to break out, snuggled close to each other, hugging and laughing. Maeve was in a white sundress with silver bangles on her arm, her hair up in a loose bun, gold sandals on her feet. *God, she was gorgeous.* The three sisters were in coordinated blue-and-white flowered dresses, all with their long red hair neatly combed and held back in headbands with tiny purple flowers. Serena did the math and thought about those May Day celebrations. This photo was probably Maeve's last good year, before the diagnosis and the years of treatment, remission, recurrence, and more treatment. The photographer took the photo from above and all their lovely faces were tilted toward the sun.

I was probably sitting in my room, five hundred feet away, listening to the laughter, Serena thought. She looked out the window of the boathouse and saw her childhood home. *I was there the whole time.*

Enough melancholy. Raj and Liza were at the end of the dock, talking about her, she presumed. Tricia had said she could be on that work call all afternoon. And Maggie had wandered back to the studio, instructing Liza to swing by after the boathouse tour. Serena guessed she had at least a few more minutes.

She went to the six-drawer file cabinet behind the desk, assuming that's where the personal papers might be held and opened it. She didn't know quite what she was looking for, but she was sure she'd know it if she saw it. Her mother had given her one tiny clue in their only conversation: William Sweeney had called her mother Rebecca, her given name. Maybe somewhere in the office there was a file titled "Rebecca," which held the answer to the only question Serena really had: Did Bill Sweeney know that he was her father all along?

LIZA AND RAJ walked the length of the dock in silence. The weather was warming up. It would be hot and sticky by the Fourth of July in a few days and then the summer would start in earnest, with American flags flying on every house, lobsters and cocktails on the beach, and fireworks up and down the Connecticut shoreline. If it was a normal year, Liza would be organizing a party at the club for "their crowd," meaning the couples that passed the test: Does he talk about anything other than work and golf? Does she talk about anything other than the kids? From this bottom line, Liza and Whit had built a group of regulars at parties that included a mix of old Southport, new money art collectors, and a few fun gay couples who summered in town. But not this year. She'd taken the event off her list when her father died, sending out a short email to participants about her decision. With Whit's departure, Liza realized she might never host another "Festive Fourth," as floral designer Anthony had called it every year in his beautifully handwritten thank-you note.

Liza watched a fleet of junior sailors in Bluejays, heading out the mouth of the harbor for a sailing lesson, laughing and shouting boat to boat as their sails picked up more wind in the open water. She imagined Vivi and Fitz at camp, sailing on the pond in Maine. Vivi loved sailing on a lake but was too scared of sharks and sea monsters to sail on the Long Island Sound, like Liza had been when she was young. But the kids out on the boats today had no such fears. Their enthusiasm made Liza smile. *Freedom.*

It was Tricia who had been the sailor in the Sweeney family, attracted to the rigor and discipline of the sport. Liza and Maggie were interested in sailing *instructors*, but not sailing. When they were teenagers, they would sit on the end of the dock in their bikinis and wait for the cute sailing instructors, from Brown or Hobart, to motor by in their Boston Whalers. *We wasted a lot of time on boys,* Liza thought as she and Raj reached the end of the dock. *We should have learned to sail.*

"I know this is none of my business, but that woman had a very strong reaction to your father's office. Is that normal?"

"Do you know who that is? Serena Tucker. Is that name familiar?"

"The name's not familiar. Should I know her?"

"She's a journalist. *Washington Post. Slate. Straight Up.*"

"Tricia said that, but she didn't say 'cousin.' Did they have a falling out?"

"You signed that NDA, right?"

"I did."

"Well, then, here you go." Liza made the split-second decision to tell Raj. "Yes, she's a journalist, but not our cousin. Here comes the NDA bit: we recently learned that she's our half-sister and Tricia is freaked out by it all."

That felt so good. Liza had been on the verge of exploding since

Whit had packed his bags and headed back to North Carolina with everything he could jam into the back of the Cayenne, from his golf clubs to the top-of-the-line one-touch espresso maker. Telling Raj about Serena put her back in balance. One secret was enough to keep. Two was killing her.

Raj was the perfect confessor—a sensible neutral party new to the neighborhood, slightly in awe of her father's legacy and silenced by a nondisclosure agreement. Given enough time and wine, Liza might tell him every secret she's ever held, from her one truly wild night with the lead singer of the Goo Goo Dolls in 2002 to the time last New Year's Eve when she and Whit stole a bottle of champagne off a room service tray on Necker Island. Liza, who felt like she'd been hiding in her own life for a decade, was now having trouble staying quiet.

She needed to confide in someone about something, and Raj was standing right next to her, legally barred from repeating anything she said. The perfect stranger. "Our father had an affair in the early 1980s and Serena is the product of that affair. The affair was with the mom next door, which is . . . disappointing. So, Serena grew up across the street from us, but we didn't know her well because she's slightly older than me and her parents were super snobby. I'm sure my mother wasn't good enough for them and I have no doubt that Mr. Tucker thought my father was a drunk, no-talent communist from the way he waved from his driveway but never once attempted conversation with our family. But we learned the truth last week. There is a fourth Sweeney sister."

"Whoa." It was all Raj could think to say, having very little experience being on the receiving end of such confidences. He had friends who were female, but they were usually other people's girlfriends or wives, secondary acquaintances who might blurt out a few things in the kitchen after a long night of Scrabble and drinking. But he didn't usually get the good stuff. An illegitimate daughter living next door? This might have huge implications on the interpretation of Sweeney's work, he thought, then realized that was a purely academic reaction to a very personal revelation. He added, "That's a lot of information for the three of you to take in during such a difficult time."

"Thank you, Raj. It is. And I'm telling you not to burden you but so that you're informed about everything concerning my father. You may come across something in your work that would be helpful to us in terms of understanding our father's actions. If you do, we'd appreciate you passing that on."

Raj noticed that Liza and Tricia had the same affect of using the word "we" instead of "I" when speaking about anything Sweeney related, as if they represented an organization or a foundation more than a family. "I hope this doesn't come off wrong, but having an affair and then a child outside of marriage is kind of on-brand for William Sweeney."

The comment made Liza laugh. "That is one way to think about it."

"Do you understand that this information has value in terms of your father's work? This is the kind of personal detail that may inspire new interpretations of classic pieces."

"We do." She tried not to sound exasperated with Raj. "It's all Tricia talks about. We get it and it's why we'd like to get to know Serena better before we announce it to the world."

"And why you are so desperate to find that memoir."

"Do we seem desperate?"

"Yes." They both laughed. "Does Serena know about the memoir? There could be some true surprises in the book if your father reveals the truth about her."

"She hasn't said anything about the memoir. But she must know. She's a journalist and Tricia's convinced that she's been researching her own book for the last six months since she accidentally discovered the genetic link. *Deep background*, Tricia keeps saying. Making ominous predictions about how what Serena has told us is only the tip of the iceberg about what she knows."

"Why wouldn't Tricia tell me this?" Raj wondered if Tricia was ashamed of her father. Or jealous of Serena. Or both.

Liza started to explain, "Tricia's a lawyer. She has trust issues." Then she noticed the disappointment in Raj's face. *He likes her.* Liza knew she needed to soften the blow, but that wasn't easy. Tricia's preferred state of being was firm, bordering on rigid, when it came to opinions, regimens, romance. "She's protective of my father's legacy in every way. From the literary interpretations that you mentioned to his personal reputation here in Southport. She sees every issue from every angle. That can make her cautious."

"Every collection I've ever worked on is filled with unexpected truths."

"What do you mean?"

"Case in point, five years ago, I was the primary archivist for the Celia Longley collection that had been donated to Johns Hopkins. Do you know her work?"

It occurred to Liza to lie, covering up for what she perceived to be a gap in her education, but what was the point, really? She knew art, Raj knew books. They weren't in competition. "Never heard of her."

"She was a contemporary of Emily Dickinson's. In fact, they were correspondents, exchanging letters and poetry and some pretty hot passages, if you know what I mean. Like Dickinson, Longley didn't publish much in her lifetime, but her work was discovered afterward by an ardent Dickinson scholar who unearthed the poems while studying Dickinson's letters."

"Where's this going, Raj? Doesn't everyone know Dickinson liked the ladies?"

"It's a disputed theory. But it was Longley's personal papers that hid a mountain of really unpleasant information. Sure, she was into Emily and many other married Amherst women, but that's not career-ending these days. In fact, her work was gaining popularity in LGBTQ academia. But digging into her papers, I discovered that Celia was an anti-Semite, vocally anti-immigrant, and a big believer in castration or sterilization for the disabled and mentally ill. Plus, she practiced the dark arts in her basement, and that included animal sacrifices. The truth about who she was as a person really made people rethink her charming poems about peonies. Her work was dropped by a lot of anthologies and curriculums just as it was starting to be recognized at the same level as Dickinson's. You never know what lurks in people's papers."

"My father was no saint, but I don't see him engaging in animal sacrifice."

"Probably not. But this happens all the time, new revelations after death. Writers are real people and their lives are messy. But that informs the work."

"Any advice?"

"You will survive the truth."

You will survive the truth. That was exactly what Liza needed to hear. "Thank you, Raj. Let's go back before Serena figures out that my father's password is the name of his boat. Which will probably take her about twenty seconds."

SERENA LOOKED UP and saw Liza and Raj heading back to the boathouse. She quickly closed the bottom drawer of the file cabinet. What was she thinking? That William Sweeney would keep a big file titled "Rebecca" in his office? Or that Tricia—thorough, methodical Tricia—wouldn't have already found it? She felt foolish about her actions.

The door opened and, to Serena's surprise, it was Tricia. "You're finished here." It came out as a command, not a question. "Maggie has requested that I deliver you to her studio. She's working on a few things she wants to show you. Which never happens—neither the frantic work nor the sharing—so maybe you're some kind of muse to her now."

Was that jealousy in Tricia's voice? Serena thought so. She grabbed her bag and took a last look around. Maybe if she could get Tricia to trust her, she'd be allowed to come back to the boathouse on her own. To soak it all in.

Chapter

14

Maggie looked out across the lawn from the conservatory where she had set up her studio in record time. She saw Serena walking with Liza and Tricia and the two old dogs, Jack and Bear, plodding along beside them. She felt victorious. *I am doing a good thing. I'm bringing people together.*

Ever since her return from California by way of the ashram in India, Maggie had struggled to find her place amongst the sisters. There was Liza, so successful, so organized, and goddamn if she still didn't have that same killer body after two kids. She would always be the gold standard for the Sweeney sisters, even if she wasn't quite as book smart as Tricia. And Tricia would never know how beautiful she was because she insisted on wearing gender-neutering navy-blue suits and a perennial blunt cut. She could handle anything, despite being the youngest sister. Liza and Tricia were two above-average bookends in the family; Maggie felt like the gooey middle with not much to show for it except a longer list of exes and the best hair.

Even this artist-in-residence stint was more make-believe than substantive, better on paper than in real life. But here she was, back at Willow Lane, and despite the shock of her father's death, she was holding it together personally and beyond. The art installation at the wake. Her willingness to meet Serena beyond halfway. The new energy with which she was painting. Like her father had said, use the pain and make her art sing.

And then there was Gray.

Maggie knew, she *knew*, that the whole relationship was what Tricia would call "ill-advised." Yes, pursuing the boy who broke her sister's heart was ill-advised, but that had been a long time ago, and look at Liza's life now. Big house, solid husband, perfect kids, a creative and money-making career. Maggie didn't have any of those assets; how could Liza begrudge her Gray?

Dinner the other night at Gray's had been one long tease, like some sort of foreplay marathon with an open-ended conclusion. Gray had been charming, funny, generous with his laughter. He'd given her some lingering looks and praised her soft-shelled crabs. Maggie had felt the spread of warmth at the end of the night she usually associated with the right amount of red wine and candlelight, except there had been no wine because of Gray's sobriety and Maggie did what she always did with men, acquire their eating and drinking habits. (When she was with the starter husband, she became a fussy cocktail and red meat fan. When she was with Darren, the controlling film director, it was all about plant-based proteins, green drinks, and vodka, the lowest-carb booze. The only exception was Roger, the ballet dancer. He didn't drink caffeine, so Maggie tried to give up coffee but that wasn't sustainable and neither was Roger.)

Maggie thought the evening was perfect; even the few minutes she broke down about her father didn't faze Gray. Maggie thought everything with Gray seemed right on track for something more to happen. But nothing did. Another light kiss on the lips, another lingering look, and she was sent back to Willow Lane alone.

Maybe it was for the best. Maggie knew this wasn't an ideal time for a new relationship, but that was usually when she plunged in anyway.

When Tim showed up with the van full of easels and paints and brushes the next day, Maggie knew exactly what to do with all her extra energy: use this pain and make her art sing. Maggie loved seeing the look of disbelief on Tricia and Liza's faces when Tim started unloading the U-Haul like Maggie told him to do.

"Really, Mags, a dishwasher?" Liza said as the three sisters studied Tim.

"He's a chef."

"No, he's not."

"Okay, he's a line cook. But a very, very talented line cook."

Maggie had poured herself into finishing the two paintings she owed Liza and starting *Panes of Gold*. She knew Liza would want the new work for her Sunflower opening even though there wasn't one damn sunflower in the piece. She loved these tiny victories over her sisters.

It was one of the reasons she saw Serena as an ally. Maggie knew that neither Liza nor Tricia was ready to embrace Serena, but that made it all the more appealing to Maggie. The invitation, the texts, the big hello and the hugs. If there was to be a fourth Sweeney sister, Maggie wanted her on Team Maggie. Growing up, it was Liza and Maggie who were inseparably paired, the twosome who got into trouble and had each other's back. But more and more lately, as Tricia matured, accepted more responsibility, and acquired skills like contract law that made her contribution to the family invaluable, it was Maggie who felt like the third wheel, the one the other two sisters talked about behind her back.

Serena was a chance to even the sides. Maggie needed her.

"You made it! This is the studio. Welcome!" Maggie waved the three of them in. Liza and Tricia stepped aside at the doorway, letting Serena enter first so she could soak in the atmosphere on her own. Then, they followed her in, standing to either side of the door, observing Serena's reaction.

"This is an amazing room. Maggie, these paintings are beautiful." Serena wandered around the glass-enclosed conservatory, taking in the explosion of color and texture. The two commissioned works were finished and leaned up against the end of a wooden picnic table covered in paint and brushes. Both were abstract landscapes, one rich with blues, greens, and purples, the other the warmer tones of fall. The new piece was on the easel, big and bold, a shift in tone from the other paintings. "I had no idea that you were so talented, Maggie."

"Thank you. I've had a good couple of days," Maggie answered, stroking Rufus the cat. "Maybe grief is good for me. Do you find you write in bursts, depending upon what's going on in your life?"

"No. I started as a beat reporter and I will always be that in terms of work output, getting it done every day whether I'm inspired or not!" Serena laughed and all three of the Sweeney sisters joined in.

"That's what our father always said when he walked out to the boathouse. 'Time to punch the clock.' You're like him," Maggie offered to Serena like a gift. "I'm more like our mother, fits and starts. All in or all out. My mother would write nothing for months, then lock herself in here for a few days and turn out an entire collection of poems. She wrote *Winterland* during the one week in 1996 when we got all that snow. We had the whole week off from school and it was a free-for-all. Peanut butter and jelly for all three meals because she was writing."

"*Winterland*?" Serena asked, although from her research into all things Sweeney, she knew it was the title of Maeve's only published collection. Serena had even picked up a copy on Ebay for twenty-five bucks. She knew nothing about poetry, except what she had studied in high school English. But Serena had liked the poems, found them accessible and easy to read. Plus, every physical description took her back to Southport.

"That was the one poetry collection she published. I think the print run was about five hundred copies. It's a beautiful little collection. I wish she'd had the chance . . ." Maggie's voice fell off.

"Our mother didn't write much after that. She sort of gave up. Too much going on here with us and my father. Then her health became her primary focus," Liza explained when Maggie couldn't.

"That's a shame," Serena said. "The world needs more poetry."

Tricia rescued the conversation from the maudlin turn it had taken. "I remember that storm. We made those tunnels in the snowbanks. The whole street was out there for days, building and sledding. Mrs. Beamon brought us hot chocolate."

"I remember going to school until the first of July because we had so many snow days that year. It was endless," Liza added, realizing at that moment that she never really had loved school. "Serena, where were you that winter?"

"Here, I guess." The room fell quiet. Serena had been right next door all along, but never a part of their world.

Maggie backtracked. "As I said, like my mother, I'm all in or all out. But to Liza's relief, I'm all in this week."

Serena nodded. "Whatever your process, your work is beautiful."

Of course, Serena had seen Maggie's work before, on a surreptitious visit to Liza's gallery when Liza wasn't there. And in her deep Pinterest and Instagram research, finding the occasional Maggie Sweeney popping up on a board or a feed. But better to let Maggie think that this was her first interaction with her art. Serena had already figured out that Maggie was playing a bit of one-upmanship with her sisters and she was happy to be a part of the game. "Tell me about this room."

Liza jumped in, as the unofficial Willow Lane docent. "This was original to the house, believe it or not. Apparently, the first owners of Willow Lane were world travelers and the wife wanted a giant greenhouse where she could grow exotic plants and tomatoes in the winter. The glass ceiling and the black-and-white-checkered marble floor were her touches. My mother told us the room was little more than a storage unit when they moved in. Subsequent owners didn't want to pay the enormous cost of heating the conservatory in the winter for a few tomatoes. My mother turned it into her studio, writing her poetry here, growing a few herbs, sewing us some truly unflattering dirndls in the late eighties. She would hang tapestries on the windows to warm it up in the cold months. We loved being in here with her. She had a craft table in the corner for us."

"Well, only those two loved crafts. I hated them," Tricia said. "I liked to read in the enormous chair, covered in blankets." The chair was still there, tucked into a cozy corner, clearly reupholstered in the recent past in blue-and-gold-striped fabric. The sisters all smiled at the recollection and Serena felt that flash of longing she'd experienced in the kitchen.

Liza continued, "Julia and I did a massive clean-out a few years ago. My twins Vivi and Fitz spend . . . spent a lot of time here and this was their magic spot. For some reason they thought it looked like the Ravenclaw Common room in Harry Potter, so I recovered a few things, bought some rugs, and had them paint their own faux crests. I think they'll miss this place."

The thought hadn't really occurred to Liza before, that this place wasn't only part of her childhood, it was part of Vivi and Fitz's childhood, too. *Please don't let me cry*, thought Liza. "Sorry. That got to me."

Maggie stepped closer to Liza and rubbed her back while the others stood in silence. After a moment, Maggie spoke, "Now, it's my studio. At least temporarily."

"This is shaping up, Mags," Tricia said, looking at *Panes of Gold*. "This is the view across the harbor, right, to the big houses on Sasco? Where is this vantage point?"

"From Perry Green." Maggie lied so quickly she surprised herself. "I'm hoping to have this done for you, Liza, if you want it for the opening next week."

"Will the paint be dry?"

"Just about," Maggie said. "Have you told Serena about your next show? Sunflowers. Opens next week. Big Saturday night opening, but I think we can get you in."

"I'd love to go."

Tricia noticed Liza's strained face. "Honestly, Liza, I can't believe you're taking that on after . . . everything."

"It was on the calendar. My artists depend on me. Right, Maggie? I can't let them down."

Liza was giving herself a pep talk as much as answering Tricia's question. It was obvious that her usual authentic enthusiasm was absent. Obvious to Tricia and Maggie anyway, so when Serena offered to help, it was particularly awkward. "If you need any help, I'm available. I'm finding that being unemployed really frees up my time. I can pitch in."

Tricia cringed. She knew comments like that got under Liza's skin, the implication that mounting a show in a gallery was akin to volunteering at a school bake sale. Tricia had witnessed interactions like this before when she was out in Southport with her big sister— random encounters at the market, on the sidelines of one of Fitz's games—and Liza's friends would offer their unsolicited advice to her about publicity or which wine to serve at an opening. Some volunteered, as Serena had, to work an event if their husband was out of town and they had "a free night," as if selling art was easy-peasy and they could do Liza's job with little or no training. It made Liza crazy. Tricia almost felt sorry for Serena in that moment.

But Liza remembered what Raj had said about surviving the truth. Liza's life today looked so different than Liza's life last month. The truth was she had no father, no husband, and now this new sister. Could forming a relationship with Serena be the key to survival? "That is so kind of you. Why don't you put your number in my phone? I'll be in touch. I'm trying to wrap my head around everything that needs to get done in the next day or two."

It wasn't accurate to say that Tricia gasped, but she did emit a strange sound as she watched Liza hand over her phone to Serena. *What was happening here?*

Maggie, also sensing a significant shift in attitude from Liza, chimed in, "As long as you're adding things to your calendar, put the Fourth down." She turned to Liza and Tricia. "I'm thinking we should have one last big blowout here at Willow Lane. Have a bunch of people over for a barbecue, watch the fireworks from the dock or maybe light off a few of our own. I feel like we owe that to the house. We can't let Dad's wake be the last party. That's maudlin."

It was on the tip of Tricia's tongue to object. She had had several calls this week with Cap about the threatening emails and calls from the publisher in search of the memoir; even Lois was getting antsy about the situation. Tricia knew time was better spent on memoir recovery than entertaining. And she felt like she was losing ground in keeping Serena at bay. Clearly, Liza and Maggie were growing more comfortable with the idea of Serena as a permanent fixture. She understood Maggie's desire for a relationship. Serena was a shiny new toy and Maggie was never one to look away from those. But Liza? Liza had been in a fog these past few days, so uncharacteristic of her usual rapid-fire existence, and she'd been complaining about exhaustion and lack of sleep. Tricia didn't think there was any rush to embrace Serena, but clearly her sisters did.

Still, a Fourth of July barbecue was the perfect excuse to invite Raj to something after dark. She'd been trying to give him his space in the evenings, but a party in the backyard on the Fourth was an automatic invite, right? "I'm in," she said. "You know, I was forced to take a cooking class at some bogus firm retreat last fall, but at least I know how to make potato salad now. Not the mayonnaise kind. The fancy kind."

"Liza, is that okay with you? I know you usually go to the club."

"Not this year. I don't have the energy. And Whit is flying straight to Maine from Durham to see the kids at camp." Liza tucked that detail in so smoothly, no one questioned her about why he would go alone. "One thing, I'm happy to be a guest at your party as long as you do everything. Or anything, really. Do not commit to this and invite all these people, then disappear."

Maggie was delighted with Liza ceding control. "I got it covered."

"Do you do a lot of barbecuing now? I don't really think of that as your thing," asked Tricia. As far as any of them knew, Maggie had not grilled a single thing in her entire life. Then she added because she couldn't resist, "Maybe we can ask Tim to come back and do some cheffing. Oh, I'm sorry, line cooking."

"Stop it. I'm sure he's very busy," Maggie fired back, though it wasn't a bad idea. "And I barbecue. Darren and I grilled all the time in LA. Well, Darren did. I'm sure I can figure this out. Invite whoever you want. I'll take care of the details. Serena, we hope you can make it."

Serena was dying to ask about Tim and Darren, but didn't feel like she'd earned that intimacy yet. She was quietly thrilled to be on this guest list. "I have to make an appearance at the Winthrop party, but I'll come after. I don't cook, either," Serena said, turning to Tricia, "but sangria is a specialty of mine."

"Bring lots! Now, everybody has to leave because if I don't get to work, the gallery owner is going to kill me. She has no mercy when it comes to missing deadlines." Maggie hugged Serena once again, a public demonstration of her enviable open heart. "I'm so glad you came over. Text me. Let's make a coffee date."

Tricia had a sinking feeling, as if her sisters weren't even trying to keep some distance from this relative stranger. Serena was the new puppy that everyone in the family wanted to play with except Tricia because she was prone to hives. She needed some fresh air. "I need to get back to work, too, so I'll say goodbye here. Looks like we'll see you in a few days," Tricia said, bowing formally and heading back to the boathouse.

Liza and Maggie looked at each other and then Serena. "That's Tricia on a good day," Maggie explained. "So warm and fuzzy."

The more time Serena spent with the sisters, the more dissimilar she found them to be. Same parents, different personalities. As an only child, she had this fantasy that sisters were multiple versions of the same person, sharing clothes and makeup. As an adult, she'd met enough sets of sisters to know that wasn't true. Somehow, she was going to try to figure out these Sweeneys one sister at a time.

LIZA WALKED SERENA out to her car. There were a million things she was tempted to say. Like, *I've never had a big sister before.* Or, *My husband is never coming home.* And, *I miss my parents so much even though I'm a grown-ass woman.* But not yet. It wasn't time yet. Maybe, one day soon. Instead, she said, "I've been thinking. I could use an extra pair of hands and a few extra brain cells next week. I do feel a little overwhelmed. I haven't gotten to editing the artists' statements and getting out some press releases. My regular PR person is on maternity leave. I know a press release is way below your usual assignments, but if you are truly interested, I would so appreciate your help."

Serena guessed it was one of the few times in Liza's adult life that she had asked for help. "Whatever you need."

"Thank you. I'll call you." Serena closed the car door and Liza tapped on the window. It came down. "I'm glad you came by today. Come by anytime."

TRICIA BURST INTO the boathouse. "Hey, want to go sailing?" She needed to clear her head after what she had witnessed in the studio. An afternoon sail was the ticket.

Raj stood up from the desk and folded his arms over his chest. "That journalist is your sister."

Tricia didn't expect to be challenged, but she liked it. "Half-sister."

"Why didn't you tell me?"

"Because I don't really know you." It hurt Tricia to say that, but it was true. She'd thought about telling him a dozen times over the last few days, but couldn't find the opening sentence. "It's not the most natural thing in the world to bring up."

"But you had me sign an NDA, in any case."

"We would have had you sign that regardless."

Raj unfolded his arms and looked at her. "Did you think I'd judge you and your family?"

"One day, I lost my father and the next, this girl across the street shows up and she's my sister. It's disorienting to have the fabric of your family change overnight," Tricia said by way of explanation. Raj moved closer to Tricia. She thought he might reach for her, but he stopped short of touching her. She panicked. "But I see that Liza had no issues with filling you in."

Stepping back, Raj said, "She blurted it out after I noticed the physical resemblance between you and Serena. I think that's her name."

"Yes, that's her name. I'll tell you what I know, but not today, not now. I need a break." Was Raj bewitched by Serena, too? She was on the verge of furious, but trying not to show her frustration. "Do you want to go sailing or not?"

"I don't know how to sail."

She loved it when men admitted to not knowing something. "I do. It's a beautiful afternoon." Tricia wanted to be alone with him. "Please come."

Raj looked around at the mess in the boathouse, but the afternoon was beautiful. And so was Tricia. "All right, let's play hooky."

Yes, let's play hooky, Tricia thought.

"You have a life preserver, right?"

"They're called PFDs. Personal Flotation Devices. And yes, of course we have them. It's the law," Tricia said. "You do know how to swim, though?"

"I swim. But I also embrace flotation devices when available," Raj answered. "Do I need special shoes?"

"No. Those Converse I've seen you in are fine."

Raj noted that Tricia had noted his footwear. That must mean something. "Okay. I guess I can let you take me sailing in William Sweeney's boat. It's sort of like research."

"Does everything have to be research with you?"

"Pretty much. But you're the same."

"I was the same. But maybe not anymore."

MAGGIE PICKED UP her phone and texted Gray: Big party here on the Fourth! Bring sparklers.

Chapter

15

The late afternoon sun was warm and the Winthrop pool was warmer, heated year-round because that's how much money the Winthrops had. The congressman had been a swimmer at Princeton nearly fifty years ago, and Lucy claimed anytime someone from the press was nearby that her husband swam every day of the year, even in the dead of winter. "He's a polar bear!" she would exclaim, leaving out the bit about the pool being heated to eighty-five degrees. "That hearty New England stock."

Serena was more of a floater than a swimmer and since settling into the guesthouse, she'd availed herself of the warm water every day. The pool was located on the lawn between the main house and the private beach. On a day like today, it was luxurious to float around in the deep end, staring at clouds with the sound of waves lapping in the background. *This is going pretty well,* Serena thought. The house tour today. The party next week. A possible connection with Liza. Serena felt sure she would have some idea after the Fourth of July where she stood with the sisters. The question in Serena's mind was whether her story would be a warm-hearted memoir or painful exposé.

"Hello, my dear. Iced tea?" Lucy was fast approaching, in some sort of vintage Lilly Pulitzer beach cover-up and floppy hat, carrying a tray with two glasses and a sense of urgency. Something was up. Serena braced for impact. Lucy had been fishing around all week for information on exactly what Serena was doing in the guesthouse and what her sabbatical entailed. It wasn't impossible that DC sources could have informed her about the *Straight Up* resignation. Lucy lived in Southport most of the time, attending to her philanthropic interests and maintaining her award-winning garden, but she spent enough time in the capital to keep her contacts current.

"I'd love some. Thank you." Serena paddled over to the side of the pool and hopped out. Lucy studied her as she toweled off, like an art lover might study a Rodin bronze. Serena grew self-conscious, slipping into a cover-up she'd picked up at the hotel shop in Antigua during her last getaway with Ben.

"Hmm. Now I see it," Lucy said, as she settled into the lounge chair next to Serena. "I just got off the phone with your mother. I know."

Serena's heart rate spiked. It was out, her secret was out there. In the hands of the most well-connected woman in town who could, if she wanted, weaponize the information, or at the very least, scoop Serena's book pitch. *Don't panic.* Early in her career, Serena had made mistakes with sources who opened conversations like Lucy did, announcing they knew the details. In several early interviews, Serena ended up giving her subjects more information than they gave her, simply by filling in the blanks for them with previously unknown information. "Know what, Lucy?"

"About William Sweeney."

Okay, that was major. "What about him?"

"Really, Serena. Are we going to do this? You know what about William Sweeney! That he's your real father," Lucy declared. Then, softening her tone, "It must have been quite a shock, my dear."

"Yes and no."

"What does that mean? Your mother said it was one of the gimmicky DNA tests they advertise everywhere."

"Yes. It was a lark. A gift certificate that I redeemed in a low moment."

"What was it like the minute you figured it out?"

Nobody had asked Serena that yet. "Like winning Powerball, I imagine. Not the luck part, the disbelief. I kept refreshing my computer and my mind was racing but my body was paralyzed. I looked in the mirror and my face looked different. I couldn't tell where I had come from. I needed to keep checking the results, as if they were going to disappear and everything was going to be normal again."

"But it won't be."

"No. It's changed everything in ways I couldn't imagine," Serena said, feeling comfortable talking to Lucy in a way she would never talk to her own mother. "Did you know about the affair? Did you suspect?"

"No, I didn't know and I didn't suspect. I know your mother liked to flirt with the men in town to be noticed and have some fun. No disrespect, but Mitch isn't exactly a live wire and, in any marriage, you need a little fire once in a while. But she never told me until this afternoon about Bill Sweeney." Lucy paused for a moment. "Everybody has secrets, Serena."

The rumor around DC was that Congressman Winthrop had an unusually close relationship with his chief of staff, Tom Whiteside, the one who had gotten divorced, whom Lucy described as "quite a catch." Serena had always assumed it was pure speculation, but maybe it wasn't. Lucy continued, "Your mother is more complex than people give her credit for. Let's face it, every mother is more complex than society gives her credit for."

Serena breathed deeply. She was relieved. Lucy might be the perfect confidant after all. "I'm so angry at her for not telling me when I could have had the chance to sit with him and talk to him. I didn't have that chance."

"That's true. He had his demons, but he also had his gifts."

"I'm so angry that she hid this from me, I can't get past that to even talk to her, ask her the most basic questions. And I don't know how to be angry like this. It's not in my DNA."

"Or so you thought! Maybe you should get your Irish up."

The women laughed. They sat in silence for a bit, finishing their iced teas, side by side. Then Lucy said, "Your mother desperately wants to talk to you. She's ready now. It's why she called me, so that I could talk to you. Your mother is willing to answer your questions."

"I get it. And I'm getting there. It's funny, the one question the Sweeneys want answered is how did this happen. How did my normal mother lure their famous father away from ethereal Maeve Sweeney? They want the details that I don't."

Lucy let out a laugh. "That is funny. It says to me those girls let go of assuming the best about their father a long time ago. That's the luxury that men have. They can be awful and beloved. Women don't get that kind of leeway. Plus, your mother isn't normal. She's sharp. She needed a career. That would have helped her immensely, given her a place for her intellectual gifts. But, she went the motherhood route."

"And I think we can both agree, motherhood didn't highlight her skill set."

Lucy nodded. "Probably true. Though she is an awfully good tennis player. And a bridge whiz. I think it's time for a cocktail, don't you? I'll text Sadie and she'll bring out something." The Winthrops had a house full of staff for all kinds of tasks, but everything went through Sadie, an Irishwoman who'd been with them for years. Within minutes, a tray with gin and tonics arrived with a small silver bowl of nuts. "So, let's talk about the sisters. What do the Sweeney girls think of you? And what do you think of them?"

Serena got emotional, much to her surprise. She hadn't had to articulate her feelings to anyone, so she hadn't realized how Liza, Maggie, and Tricia had gotten under her skin. "I have to say, they have something. Individually and as a unit." Serena thought about the moment in the conservatory, when Liza faltered and Maggie went to her immediately, without a word. "It's a connection to each other like I've never seen."

"Some sisters have that. I wish my girls had a stronger connection, but they had too good an upbringing. They didn't go through what the Sweeney girls did—their poor mother. She was no match for her husband. His career swallowed her whole and then the cancer finished her off. I always thought it was strange that Bill Sweeney was a mess after her death. He seemed like a one-man band when she was alive, but I guess not. Were you aware of that?"

"Yeah, I read the book."

"Of course you did. How did they react to you?"

"True to form, I'm guessing. Liza was warm. Maggie was truly welcoming. And Tricia was and is cautious around me. We are strangers, really, just getting to know each other."

"And is that what you want, to be the fourth Sweeney sister?"

"I'm not sure yet."

"I heard Whit Jones moved out."

"What?"

"That's what I heard from Janey Masters. She heard it from her daughter-in-law who went to Georgetown with Whit and ran into him at the airport in some city in North Carolina. Durham? I think that's it. Well, she said Whit told her he was relocating there permanently, but his family wasn't moving down because he and his wife were splitting."

"Poor Liza. Obviously, no one's told me anything that personal."

"Well, from what I hear, there's a lot brewing in that family in terms of finances and such. I mean, *your* family," Lucy said, suddenly delighted by the idea. "It's really something to get a whole new family halfway through your life. You are writing something, aren't you? Please tell me this is going to be a *Vanity Fair* blockbuster piece with all the salacious details."

Serena filed the information about the Sweeney family financial difficulties away for further research, responding, "Lucy! I thought you were my mother's friend!"

"I am. But, let's face it, this is a pretty sexy story. Bill Sweeney and the mom next door. It has it all: literary genius, family secrets, broken hearts. You owe this to the world."

"What about my father? What do I owe him? I think about that."

"I think for the answer to that question, you should talk to a therapist, a lawyer, and Mitch Tucker, in that order."

"Oh, I've been to a therapist. And lurked in online groups for NPEs. That's what we're called, Not Parent Expected, a bastardization of a genealogy term. It means people who didn't quite get the DNA results they thought they were going to get. We're a growing cohort. I'm not sure it's my cohort."

"All I know is that I've reached an age where I wish I had my own story to tell."

"I'm not sure I believe you. I'm pretty sure you have your own vault of sexy secrets under lock and key." The older woman shrugged innocently, drink to lips. "Wait, broken hearts? Whose broken heart?"

"That is your mother's tale to tell. You should call her, Serena."

The two women looked out across Long Island Sound to the pink sky. The paddleboarders and sea kayakers were headed back to shore as the light faded. Serena finished her drink, imagining the stories that hadn't been told all up and down the Gold Coast.

Chapter

16

It was late, but Liza hadn't wanted to go home, so she stopped at the gallery to catch up on paperwork and write up her master to-do list for the next week. A part of her wanted to cancel the whole show. She had overheard Maggie tell Tricia, "Sunflowers is a lame concept, designed to please the lowest common denominator of art buyers who would be wandering through the gallery over the summer season."

Maybe Maggie was right. But a few months ago, Liza had walked into the studio of one of her most reliable artists and a dear old friend, Kat Ryan, a true local whose mother, Cordelia, had also been a beloved painter and art advocate in the area. (Both had educated and inspired Liza to start her gallery; there was no value Liza could put on their friendship and support.) Kat's new work blew Liza away. Kat had spent the previous fall in Provence and had committed her recent work to pay tribute to van Gogh. When Liza saw her glorious oils of fields of sunflowers saturated in Provencal light and colors, she said, "We could make a fortune on these. How many will you have by July?"

"Six big ones and a dozen guest-bathroom sizes." The old friends laughed.

Cha-ching. They committed to the show right there. The summer crowds liked beautiful. They liked pleasing. And Kat's sunflowers were both, but with enough technique and depth to attract more sophisticated collectors who needed something for their new sunrooms or she-sheds. With a few other artists on board using sunflowers as a

literal or metaphoric theme, the show was shaping up to be the biggest and potentially the most lucrative in Sweeney Jones history. Still,
Liza wished it would all go away.

Truth was, she did need Serena if she was going to pull this off.
She hadn't realized how behind she'd let things get while looking for
the memoir. She sent a quick text, asking Serena to report for public
relations duty in the morning.

There was a knock on the gallery door. Liza, startled, looked up from
her computer screen. Bear, sitting at her feet, barked at the man in the
window. It was Gray. He waved at her and motioned to her to unlock
the door. She did as he asked, unlocked the door and then turned her
back on him, returning to her desk. She needed some sort of physical
barrier between herself and this man, her present and her past.

"I didn't mean to scare you," Gray called out to her back.

"Surprised more than scared."

"I was driving home and saw you through the window," Gray said
as if that was enough of a reason to interrupt her life after fifteen
years. He held out a beautiful wooden bowl, clearly hand-turned and
high quality. Was it black walnut? Liza wasn't sure, but it reminded
her of the coveted Andrew Pearce bowls from Vermont. "I wanted to
show you this."

She took her place behind the desk. "A big bowl. Did you make this?"

"I did. I do woodworking now and someone suggested that you
might be interested in carrying these in the gallery." Gray's blue eyes
had not dimmed one bit in all these years. If anything, they were
brighter, deeper. Liza forced herself to be unreceptive. *Of course Gray
has such extreme self-confidence that he walks into my gallery after more
than a decade of no contact to try to get me to rep his fucking bowls.* "I
don't sell housewares," she said flatly, knowing she could probably
sell ten a week, easy.

Silence. "I'm sorry, Liza."

"About which part, Gray? Abandoning me? Never reaching out to me? My dad? Showing up here with your salad bowl after fifteen years and expecting me to go into business with you?"

"All of that. And a lot more. I feel like you are one of the people in my life that I hurt the most and one of the people that will be on my apology list for life."

"I'm good, Gray. I'm not that twenty-one-year-old girl anymore. You don't need to keep me on any list." Liza turned her back on him, pretending to file some papers. She didn't want to hold eye contact. It was too hard.

"I am very sorry about your father."

She turned back to face him. "He never liked you."

"That was clear. And I don't blame him. I was a colossal asshole who treated his daughter like crap. But I know he liked you. And you liked him, so I'm sorry for your loss."

"Is that why you showed up uninvited to the wake? Did you think I'd be so overcome with emotion that I'd welcome you back like a long-lost friend?"

"I've been back in town for a few months, hoping every day to run into you. But never did. I heard about the wake from some guys in town and wanted to see you. That's all. It was clear that you didn't feel the same."

"Apparently, hostility is a sign of grief. Did you know that? The funeral home sent us a handy-dandy pamphlet today on what we can expect over the next year—exhaustion, sleeplessness, headaches, anxiety, anger, and hostility. It's a winner list. That's what I felt when I looked up and saw you at the wake: hostility."

"I understand."

"Do you? Do you really? I was in love with you, Gray. My mother was dying. I had to drop out of college to care for her. And still, I covered for you in every possible way, with your parents, the law, everyone I knew who said you were trouble. I did crazy things for you. And you got on your motorcycle one day and left. And I never heard from you again."

"I heard you married Whit."

"I married Whit to get over you." Those were words Liza had never said aloud. She was tired. She shouldn't be having this conversation.

Gray looked genuinely remorseful. "I didn't know that. I was so into myself, my addiction, I barely registered anyone else. That was wrong."

Liza softened. "Maggie told me that you're sober and healthy and restoring your parents' house. I'm happy for you, Gray, in the sense that I'm happy for anyone who can take back control of their own lives. Please know that. But I've moved on in so many ways since you left Southport. I know that sounds stupid because I live three blocks from the house I grew up in. But, believe me, I have moved on."

"Liza, I understand. I'm not expecting you to welcome me back into your life, like nothing's happened. Honestly, I wanted to say I'm sorry. And I thought you might like the bowls."

"The bowls are lovely. But not for the gallery."

"Keep this one, then, for you. A gift. From an old friend."

Never once had Liza thought of Gray as an old friend. "Thank you."

"Well, maybe I'll see you around."

Liza shrugged. "It's a small town."

As soon as the door shut behind Gray, Liza picked up the bowl and ran her hands over the smooth dark cherry wood. She felt something taped to the bottom of the bowl. It was Gray's card. She slipped it into her pocket.

THE HOUSE FELT enormous and empty. Even the sound of Bear barking for his dinner couldn't fill the void that the kids and Whit left. There were days when the twins were little that Liza would dream about a moment like this: alone in her own house for weeks. She would have settled for a few hours. But between Whit's nonstop travel, the constant coming and going of the kids and their playmates, the breakneck activity schedule, the household help in and out, and the ever-present contractors or painters or drywallers, Liza barely managed a few hours alone, never mind weeks. But this was not how she thought it would feel when she daydreamed. She thought she would feel satisfied, at ease. Instead, she was exhausted, anxious, lonely, and, yes, hostile. She was the entire Signs of Grief list in one human being. "Come on, Bear. Let's get you supper."

Please don't die, Bear, Liza thought, looking at the sweet old boy. *That would be the end of me.*

Gray Cunningham. Goddamn Gray Cunningham. He had ripped her confidence to shreds at twenty-one. It seemed so stupid now that she put so much time and energy into a guy who used her and treated her like an accessory, helpful to have around to deflect trouble but easily forgotten if he wanted to get high with his buddies, none of whom were really his buddies, just guys in it for Gray's stash. It blew Liza's mind to think that she was only five years older than Vivi when she had fallen for Gray one night at that old bar Sidetracks, the only place where her fake ID fooled the guy at the door. Or maybe it was the extra-big smile she'd employ. She'd spotted Gray throwing darts in the corner, surrounded by people laughing at his jokes, and that was it. Long before, they'd seen each other at tennis tournaments or country club dances, but Gray, a few years older, had headed to prep school, failing from one to another, and disappeared from the proper Southport social scenes.

That night, Gray had told Liza that he was "between educational institutions" and Liza thought it was the funniest line she'd ever heard. Over the next four years of a volatile romance, Gray used that line a hundred times on different people, mainly his clientele and the occasional mother. Somehow, he got a laugh every time.

But not from William Sweeney. Her father had never fallen for Gray, never shared a beer and a joke with him. Liza flashed back to the scene at three in the morning in the driveway at Willow Lane, the worst night of her life. Liza and Gray pulling up on his motorcycle and her father storming out of the house with a baseball bat. Gray didn't yield at all to Bill Sweeney and that enraged her father. Both men had had too much to drink. Both men had enormous egos. And both men felt they had a claim on Liza. It was lucky no one got hurt or worse. The sight of Maeve, so sick and thin she could barely walk, standing in the doorway in her nightgown, pleading for them to stop fighting was the image Liza still couldn't get out of her head. She'd never gotten over the guilt.

Maeve had stopped Bill Sweeney from killing Gray Cunningham. Such an old-fashioned territorial and pointless scene, father versus boyfriend, but it sent Gray packing. And Liza married Whit for what? Penance?

Liza poured herself a glass of white wine and rummaged through the fridge for some food. She grabbed some olives, cheese, and prosciutto that still looked edible. She sliced some apples and made herself a plate. She always joked with Whit that she really wasn't an entrée person, preferring three square meals a day of hors d'oeuvres. But Whit liked a plate of meat and potatoes, so that's what she had cooked for years. *Well, now I can eat olives all day long,* she thought. One upside to being alone.

She thought of something else, too. *I could sleep with Gray if I wanted. Nothing's stopping me.* Whit had all but asked for permission on his end; why should the rules be any different for her?

It was too quiet here. Liza picked up her phone and sent a text.

Chapter

17

"You're up late."

Tricia looked up from her laptop as Maggie, covered in paint, came into the kitchen and grabbed a beer. "So are you."

"Where's the hot librarian? I saw you two headed off for a sail. The old 'trapped in a boat' scenario. Very clever. I thought for sure you'd be in the boathouse doing some late-night archiving." Maggie was delighted with herself.

"Just stop. He'd never sailed before and tonight I realized how much I miss it. It's relaxing, being out on the water. That's all it was." That wasn't all it was, but Tricia wanted to keep the details to herself for a while longer. Raj's nervousness that turned to laughter and joy. Her own confidence with the tiller in hand. Catching Raj staring at her while she washed the salt off the sails and the rudder after putting the boat away. Then Raj asking her to dinner tomorrow night at her favorite place and nodding seriously when she said yes and then saying, "Good. Very good. Tomorrow night, then." Maggie didn't deserve those details quite yet, so Tricia repeated to Maggie, "A short sail. That's all it was."

"That is not true. I've seen him look at you. He's very handsome. I'm just saying, you could stand to cut loose a little."

"I'm not you, Mags. Cutting loose is not my thing."

"One day, you're going to discover the joy of not being so goal-oriented. At the party on the Fourth, I'm going to dress you up in one of my sundresses and you'll be halfway there. Loose, flowing, sending out those good vibes to Raj."

Tricia laughed. "I wish it was that simple. Put on a magic dress, change your personality."

"It works for me!" Maggie handed Tricia a beer. "You had it rough, Trish."

They weren't talking about boys and boats now. "I'm not even over missing Mom. And now I have to add in missing Dad, too?"

"I was thinking about Mom all day. Being in her studio, it's like her ghost is there inspiring me. I know you don't believe in all that woo-woo stuff, but I feel like she had all these things to say still and didn't get the chance."

"I believe that Mom sacrificed her career for us. It's the ghosts I don't really believe in."

"She was so amazing and we never appreciated it. Why were we so awful to her? Remember that time Mom told us she was taking us to a surprise concert and we were so excited because we thought it was the Spice World tour and it turned out to be an acoustic Ani DiFranco show and we were such assholes the entire night?"

"You and Liza were assholes. I was ten. I was happy to be included in the big night out. I had no idea what was happening at the concert."

Maggie took a sip of beer. "Why do you think he did it, Tricia?"

"What, hide the manuscript or die suddenly?"

"Sleep with Birdie Tucker. I can't stop thinking about the why. I mean, I know why, but *why*?"

"Ego. Both his enormous public ego and his fragile private ego. He spent his whole life answering to both those extremes."

"Maybe. I've been wondering if it was something else. Like a sticking-it-to-the-Man kinda thing. And by the Man, I mean those WASPs. I've been rereading *Never Not Nothing* and Dad did not like those super-preppy types. Those were not his people. Other than Cap, there's a lot of hostility toward the ruling class from the poor

Irish kid from Hamden. Maybe Birdie Tucker was some sort of revenge relationship."

"Wow! You have a theory and literary supporting evidence. You're halfway to a master's."

"That's what I need, a career change and student debt. Are you mocking me?"

"No. I assumed it was all about wanting something that minute and not being willing to wait. But you have a point. Sometimes I would see that underlying mistrust when he talked to Whit. It was more than a personal issue. It was about class and background. You know, like how he liked Whit, but didn't trust him."

"I don't trust Whit."

"What do you mean?"

"Don't you think it's weird that he's spending the entire summer in North Carolina? No wife, no kids, no Bear. Leaving Liza alone weeks after her dad dies. Now he's going to Maine for the Fourth by himself? I don't feel good about it. To me, Whit has classic narcissistic personality disorder."

"Did they teach you about that at yoga school?"

"That's not what yoga teacher training is about. I took an online psychology course at UCLA when I was with Darren because I wanted to know why he cheated on me all the time. Why he thought an open relationship was a super idea for him, but not for me. And it's because he's a narcissist. Lack of empathy, needs attention, above the rules, exaggerating talents. Doesn't that sound like Whit?"

"Not at all. It totally sounds like Darren, but not Whit. Whit is a pretty straight shooter. Isn't that kind of the problem? Super predictable. He didn't even like his name in the local paper. Liza told me he stopped coming to art openings because he didn't like the publicity. He may not be the guy for you, Maggie, but he was decent to Dad, he loves his kids, and he and Liza have made their relationship work."

"I don't know. I have a feeling. Something's up with him." Maggie got up and started pulling eggs and cheese out of the fridge. "Want a fried egg sandwich?"

"Yes, please." Tricia refreshed her screen. Four new emails since Maggie had walked in the kitchen, all from the law offices of Kingsley, Maxwell & Traub except one forward from Richardson & Blix. "I'm so tired and I have work to do. This family-leave thing is not really the holiday I imagined. The new team in charge at the firm has a lot of questions. And there are a bunch of emails from Cap. We need to find that manuscript. The wolves are closing in."

"What do you mean?"

"There have been some overtly threatening letters from the publisher and some mildly threatening emails from Dad's agent who is supposed to be on our side. Et tu, Lois?"

"I never liked her. Very suspicious." Once Maggie latched onto a new idea, she did not let go. But, as much as Tricia hated to admit it, Maggie did have a good radar when it came to the duplicitous. Maybe it took one to know one.

So Tricia fished around. "Another case of narcissistic personality disorder? Or something else?"

"Lois has some sort of secret life. Or a scalp disease. I'm sure of it. It's the hats. The hats aren't normal." Maggie put a grilled cheese, egg, tomato, and pesto sandwich next to Tricia. "I'm headed back to the studio. One more hour. Get some sleep, Trishie."

"Thanks, Mags."

Tricia looked out to the boathouse. The light in the upstairs window was on.

"I THOUGHT YOU might be thirsty." Tricia stood in the doorway of the boathouse, holding two beers and a blanket. It was the first seriously humid night of the summer and the wind had died down to nothing. She was in a camisole and cropped jeans, flip-flops on her feet. She'd put a swipe of lipstick on in the twenty seconds between "Don't be an idiot" and "I should do this." She'd practically sprinted across the lawn so she wouldn't lose her courage. A light sheen of sweat appeared around her neck and across her chest. She was slightly out of breath. "I, I . . ."

Raj didn't need to hear the whole sentence. He pulled her toward him and kissed her softly, first on the mouth, then down her salty neck, and back to her mouth, this time harder. His glasses bumped her and they both laughed.

"You can take those off."

"That's a good idea. Come in. Please come in."

Too many ghosts. Maybe I do believe in them. She shook her head. "Let's go down to the rowboat. You know the one under the dock, on the little beach."

"Is that where you took all the boys in high school?"

"There were no boys in high school."

"I don't believe that."

"It's true. Too skinny."

"Too intimidating."

"Maybe that, too. But it is where I fantasized about taking all the boys." Tricia pulled his hand and started toward the well-worn path in the rocks to the beach. Raj hesitated. "I don't have . . ."

"I do. I have everything. Come on."

The rowboat, beached under the dock for twenty years, was definitely not seaworthy. Tricia had spent many afternoons there as a kid, hiding out reading. As a teenager, she did more daydreaming, imagining just such a night. The fantasies had started again after Raj arrived at Willow Lane. She dug the beer bottles into the wet sand at the edge of the water to keep them cold. Then, she spread the blanket out over the wooden slats as he watched. She turned to Raj and touched his chest like she'd been thinking about for days, letting her hands slide all over him. His T-shirt was a soft cotton, but underneath the fabric, she could feel his taut muscles. He closed his eyes and leaned his head back as she took in his whole body with her touch—his arms, his shoulders, the back of his thighs and around to his abdominals. She reached under the T-shirt and felt the soft hair on his belly, then slipped her fingers under his waistband. "Let's get in the boat," she whispered to Raj. "Do you want a PFD? Would you feel better with a flotation device on?"

She picked a couple of orange PFDs off their hooks on the wall on the boathouse and tossed them in the boat for pillows.

"Very funny." Raj opened his eyes and grabbed her. She let him. He let his fingers run across her collarbone and slowly down to her breasts, tracing them once, twice over the tight material. Then he used his lips to arouse her, but he wanted more. "I do think we should remove this, though. I wouldn't want it to get waterlogged and drag you under should the ship go down."

"That's a good idea." Tricia pulled the camisole off, then her jeans while Raj watched. She tossed them on the sand. She had nothing on but a pair of hot-pink boy shorts. Raj admired her standing there in the dark, lit only by moonlight. "I didn't figure you for a pink lingerie kind of girl."

She climbed into the boat and lay back against the blanket. "Good. Then there will be a lot more surprises for you." He took off his glasses, folded them, and placed them carefully on a nearby rock. Then he peeled off his own shirt while she watched and climbed into the boat.

"Careful there, landlubber. You're never supposed to stand up in a rowboat," Tricia said. He dropped to his knees and melted into her body.

Chapter

18

It was Maggie who found the hidden memoir by accident. She was looking in the attic for a vintage Fourth of July patchwork skirt that her mother used to wear. She thought it might be in the old camp trunk with the other dress-up clothes from childhood. When she opened the trunk, it was filled with all the photos of Maeve that had disappeared from all over the house, random awards for various literary accomplishments, and a stack of old magazines, but right on top was a manuscript box with the words *Snap: A Memoir by William Sweeney* in her father's loopy lefty handwriting. Maggie grabbed the box. Inside was a thumb drive—no note, no explanation, just a thumb drive. *Snap: A Memoir.*

The title gave her chills.

It took everything she could muster not to run downstairs screaming, "I found it! I found it!" She knew it would be a huge relief to both Liza and Tricia, whose behavior had become increasingly frantic over the last few days as the legal threats had increased. But they would also find it galling that she had found the golden manuscript after spending about forty-seven seconds total searching for it while they had spent weeks combing through everything from junk drawers to laundry baskets to boxes of old tax returns. Maggie wanted her moment of glory. But she had a better idea, a bigger idea, so she slipped the thumb drive into her pocket.

Now, I want to find that skirt.

By the time the guests arrived on the Fourth, Maggie was practically bursting out of her skin. She wanted this to be one of those nights they talked about in Sweeney family history forever. She'd managed to organize dinner, decorations, even find the skirt and pair it with a simple tank top for a perfect throwback look and salute to previous Fourths that their mother had hosted. On top of that, the two commissioned paintings had shipped to their new homes, and her work for the show was done and she knew it was something next-level. Maggie, attuned to the universe, believed her mother was guiding her these days. She could feel her spirit in the conservatory when she was painting. Even the inspiration to search the camp trunk came from her, Maggie was sure of it. Her mother wanted to clear the air, free the past before the house was sold and all the bits and pieces that had constituted a family were packed away or given to charity. Maggie needed to honor her intuition. She wanted tonight to be as inspired as she felt.

Serena was set to show up and Maggie encouraged her to bring along any refugees from the Winthrops' more civilized party who wanted an escape to a more casual event. That nice couple from Brooklyn—Connor the architect and David the shoe designer, whom Liza had invited to stay at her house for the entire month of July at the last minute—offered to bring lobsters, which was a relief because Maggie couldn't afford them. (She'd put the meat and the gourmet brownies on her father's house charge at Spic & Span, hoping her sisters wouldn't ask, wouldn't notice, or wouldn't mind once they saw the bill.) At Maggie's insistence, Raj invited two colleagues from Yale, newlyweds Nina and Devon, who happened to be staying in a rental in town, because she wanted a few more witnesses and because it was clear that Raj and Tricia had something going on. Maggie was all for it and wanted Raj to feel like one of the family. Tim was coming because he'd been fired for stealing twenty pounds of frozen shrimp and a bottle of Scotch from his restaurant job and she really did need someone to grill the tri-tip. ("It was a barbecue for everyone from work. I thought they wouldn't mind," Tim explained to Maggie, who could totally see his side of the story.)

Maggie knew she was making some mischief by inviting Gray and not telling Liza, but that was the point of the whole evening: unexpected fireworks. Cap was set to swing by for drinks with Anders. They were a maybe for dinner, but Maggie was certain that once they saw the lobsters and Tim on the grill, the two gentlemen would stay and be there for her announcement.

Maggie cranked up the music, and it blasted through the house as she started to set the table with her mother's silver that she had also unearthed in the attic. Whatever her father was trying to hide, Maggie was determined to set free.

"WHAT THE HELL, Maggie?"

Liza had pulled her into the library, away from the ears of the other guests who were mingling on the patio. About a dozen people in various shades of red, white, and blue sipped sangria and ate the complicated cucumber-and-crabmeat canapés courtesy of Connor and David, who had taken over Liza's kitchen while she was at the gallery doing last-minute prep for the show opening the next day. She'd stopped at home and changed into a white halter jumpsuit she'd bought on a whim, getting a toast of approval from her houseguests ("Here's to our own Julianne Moore!"). Liza was thrilled David and Connor's summer rental in Westport had fallen through at the last minute, thanks to a burst pipe and a flooded basement. They jumped at the chance to spend a few weeks in Southport, unsuspecting of the true reason for Liza's invitation: diverting conversation and chaperones. With the two of them around, she wouldn't slip up and beg Whit to come home or Gray to come over.

Liza arrived at Willow Lane in a decent mood, determined to enjoy a relaxing night with family and friends, one that she didn't have to plan, a tiny miracle. Then Gray showed up, in jeans and a blue shirt, undeterred by their conversation the other day at the gallery. He walked straight over to Liza, giving her a kiss on the cheek while the others watched. "You look beautiful," he whispered.

Liza was not amused and was ready to blame Maggie for her sudden turn of mood. "Why did you invite Gray?"

"Because, because he had nothing to do."

"Why is that our problem? He's a grown man. He can entertain himself. Honestly, Mags, it's hard enough on the Fourth without the kids and Whit. And Dad. The stress of the show tomorrow. I'm down already. I can't deal with Gray. Why are you even in touch with him?"

"He's an old friend and he's lonely."

Liza didn't believe that was the only reason. She sensed that Maggie was interested in Gray herself because he was exactly the sort of man Maggie attracted: handsome, damaged, and selfish. Throw in "involved with another woman" and that sweetened the pot for her. In this case, the involvement was years ago, but still, it was textbook Maggie. Her attention to detail, from her outfit to the place cards on the table, made it clear that she had something up her sleeve.

Liza also believed that Serena was a factor. Maggie's Open-Heart Policy, as Tricia had been calling it behind her back, was taking off in unexpected directions. It was Liza and Serena who had spent nearly all of the last forty-eight hours together, getting the gallery ready for the show, writing the press releases and artist statements, finalizing the guests, and reaching out to a whole new list of people who Serena suggested. Liza had welcomed her help and found that as she got to know Serena, her admiration, maybe even affection, for her had deepened.

It was Serena whom she told about Whit, the separation, his affair or whatever he might call it with his colleague. She confessed about the moment she nearly texted Gray, but instead texted Connor and David to come to Connecticut for the month to act as her minders. She had confided all this to Serena, not Maggie, not Tricia. Serena seemed like a clean slate, somehow, who had a connection to her, but not any baggage. Had Maggie noticed? Was she jealous? Was that really why she had invited Gray?

"Are you interested in Gray? Or is this some type of payback?"

"Payback? No. And why would I have Tim here if I was interested in Gray?" Maggie lied.

"I don't understand why you would do this to me. Gray hurt me. And that pain changed my life. Is that clear? He's not some cute guy I used to make out with in the old rowboat and now that memory has faded into 'great to see you at the reunion' status. Gray nearly destroyed me. I'm not happy to see him for old times' sake. Please stop with the 'healing.'" Liza even used Maggie's signature air quotes. "This is not something I want healed."

Liza was wrong. Maggie had done some growing up. If she hadn't, the conversation in the library would have become a confrontation with yelling, stomping, and a fuselage of accusations and grievances from the past. But not tonight. Maggie was in control and wanted to stay that way. "My mistake. I didn't realize it was still that raw for you. I get that now."

"Thank you."

"Can I ask you to make it through one night with Gray so I don't have to throw him out like Dad did? I'll be your best friend." Maggie resorted to a childhood phrase to evoke Liza's cooperation.

Liza shook her head. "You make me crazy, Mags."

"You could use some crazy." The two sisters headed back to the party, temporary truce in place. "Oh my God, did you see Tricia's potato salad? It looks disgusting."

SERENA WANDERED AROUND through the crowd refilling sangria glasses and introducing herself to new faces as "the former neighbor." She hadn't been in Connecticut in quite a while for the Fourth and she had forgotten how the town embraced the holiday. Fourth of July was

Southport's Super Bowl. The day had been a picture-perfect Fourth, warm and humid with cotton-ball clouds in the sky and a breeze all day, so the shoreline teemed with sea kayaks, paddleboarders, wind-surfers, and small fishing boats. Sailboats, big and small, streamed out and back into the harbor after a day of regattas. The annual bike pa-rade through the Village to the library featured well-groomed children in red, white and blue madras shorts or sundresses riding scooters or bicycles decorated with streamers and balloons. Dogs wore star-spangled bandanas. There were flags on every flagpole, even patriotic bunting on a number of houses. The first of the hydrangeas and roses were in bloom. There was a decorative wreath on every door. Fathers were organizing the legal fireworks they'd bought from stands along the Post Road and the illegal ones they purchased in Chinatown on their way out of the city. Inside the houses, the matrons of Southport were preparing the Fourth of July feasts with blueberry muffins and a haul of steamed lobsters that would be carted to the beach or the boat, complete with tablecloths, centerpieces, and citronella votives, in anticipation of fireworks later that night.

Standing on the patio, Serena could hear the band from the coun-try club across the water playing a classic Stones song and the shouts of children on the beach in an organized Capture the Flag game. It brought back vivid memories of her own childhood, memories that didn't involve the Sweeneys at all.

For the past few weeks, Serena had been focused on the parallel lives she and the sisters had led and what she had missed out on. So much so that she'd almost forgotten the best moments of her own upbringing, like the long, sweet, salty Fourths when she'd spend all day at the country club, playing in the family tennis tournament, competing in the pool games like Greased Watermelon, and then changing into her blue-and-white sundress for dinner on the beach, fireworks, and maybe a game of hide-and-seek in the lockers with Pierce Janssen or that cute Teague Palmer. She wondered if she would ever be able to square the fact that she was both Serena Tucker and Serena Sweeney.

Over the past few days, Serena experienced what it was like to have sisters, to be a sister. Helping Liza at the gallery became two days of intense bonding. No one was more surprised than Serena when Liza confirmed what Lucy Winthrop had said. Liza and Whit were separated and prospects were very hazy, if not grim. "He waited fifteen years to tell me he didn't like my family. I wanted to scream that sometimes I don't like them, either. But I was too tired to argue," Liza told her.

"I'm sorry." Serena had focused on listening to Liza rather than advising her. What advice did she have to give, after all? Liza had been holding the truth in for years—about her feelings for Whit, about the burden of caregiving for Bill Sweeney, about the pressure to keep up in a town where keeping up was important, about pushing Vivi and Fitz to be high performers, about proving her worth through work. Liza had a lot to unload and Serena had learned over the years through her work that when someone wants to talk, you let them. Listen, ask questions that help them tell their story, and wait for the good stuff.

"I married Whit for the wrong reasons and I thought I was stuck. But Whit unstuck us; he walked away. I didn't think he had it in him. I didn't."

"Now what will you do?"

"What I want, I guess. I've done what other people wanted for such a long time. Be there for the kids, run the gallery which I love. Move to a smaller house, maybe, and not care so much about stains on the couch and dog hair on the rugs. Hide from society for a little bit after this opening because I'm embarrassed that it looks like I couldn't even hold onto Whit Jones. I'll be fine."

Serena saw a lot of herself in Liza, especially the benefits of being the oldest girl in a family. And the burden of expectations. Serena had shed those expectations the minute she headed to DC instead of the *Today* show, but Liza had managed to live up to most of them. No wonder she was exhausted, drawn, in her own words, "depleted." For Serena, the role as confidante was new, at least in her personal life.

Even Tricia was starting to come around. They had met up on a run one morning by accident and now it had become a daily ritual, heading out for four miles after coffee. With Tricia, there was no soul-baring, no emotional truth telling. They talked about work. Clearly Tricia was a news junkie, well informed, and had done her own research into Serena's history, which Serena found flattering. Tricia peppered Serena with questions about articles she'd written, reporters she'd worked with, interviews she'd done with the likes of Malala and Madonna on the subject of human rights. Serena did the same, interested in Tricia's work life, how she'd settled on commercial litigation, what life was like inside a big New York City law firm. They'd swapped stories on bias and barriers, both real and imagined. Serena saw the same focus and diligence in Tricia that she had. They were both grinders—talented grinders, but grinders nonetheless.

Maggie was a texter, the emoji queen, the type to send a link to a Lady Gaga video or a goofy GIF in the middle of the day and caption it "thinking of you" or simply "LOL." It would be easy to dismiss Maggie as the crazy sister, truly a "mad Maggie" who amused herself with boy toys and sound baths and made her way in the world by sheer luck, not design. But Maggie's artistic talent was undeniable. She had inherited the creativity gene, either from her father or mother, or maybe both. If only she'd had Tricia's work discipline or Liza's organizational skills, Maggie might be a household name. Instead, she floated along, sometimes on top of the current, sometimes below, and occasionally she needed a life preserver.

In a few weeks' time, Serena began to see the role she might play in this sisterhood. A loyal friend to Liza. A workplace sounding board to Tricia. A source of support to Maggie. *There is a place for me here,* Serena thought, looking around the patio at the small crowd of attractive people, chatting, drinking, and laughing, comfortable in each other's company, a family by birth and by choice. *I can be one of them.*

"I WANTED TO say a few words before we finish our beautiful meal and the fireworks start," Maggie said, standing at the head of the table and tapping the side of her glass of rosé for attention. The lively dinner conversation ceased, all eyes on her. Liza, at one end of the long table, and Tricia, at the other, exchanged glances and then they both looked at Cap, who shook his head. This was an unannounced Maggie Sweeney performance.

"Thank you all for being here tonight. We all have our own memories of Willow Lane and what it means to us. Some have deep memories and some are relatively new. Cheers to Raj and Nina and Devon. We're so glad you're here." All raised a glass to the trio of academics, delighted to be anywhere with a sea breeze and very good wine.

Maggie continued, "This is a special place and it's our pleasure to share it with you for one last Fourth of July. A big thanks to Tim for the fantastic job on the grill." Maggie winked at poor Tim, who was in over his head conversationally with the Ph.D.s but had really nailed the perfect medium rare on the tri-tip. "And to Connor and David for the lobsters and the crabmeat. Can you come back on Labor Day?" There was general laughter and some light applause. It had been a delicious dinner.

"As you know, Liza, Tricia, and I recently lost our father. He was a man of many words and many, many stories, but there is one story he never told us in his lifetime, so I thought I'd tell it tonight." Maggie stepped away from the head of the table, freeing herself from any constraints. Tricia looked at Liza in a panic and mouthed, *Please, no.*

"Tonight, I would like to introduce you all to a new family member that we've gained. Turns out the girl who lived next door was not only a neighbor, she's our sister. Our half-sister, to be precise, because I know Tricia loves precision, but our sister nonetheless. That, of course, is Serena Tucker. Serena, please stand. We welcome Serena to the family."

The moment could not have been more awkward. The last thing Serena Tucker wanted to do was stand and hug Maggie in this choreographed announcement, but she did so because Maggie was lifting her out of her seat with strong arms and hope on her face. There was stunned silence and then low murmuring amongst the guests, until Tim the Line Cook blurted out what everyone was thinking: "Wait, what?"

Tricia stood up, because it seemed the thing to do, explaining in the most saccharine voice she could manage, "Thanks to the magic of over-the-counter DNA tests, we've recently discovered that there is a fourth Sweeney sister. It's been a delight to get to know Serena. If you've ever been to a party here at Willow Lane, you know that 'the more the merrier' is a philosophy our family embraces. And we thank you for your discretion in this matter in terms of sharing this information. When we are ready to share this news with the world, we will."

"Well, you won't have to wait long! Look what I found!" Maggie reached under the table that was serving as the bar. She pulled out several handled bags, hidden behind the blue tablecloth. Tucked inside the bags were what looked like reams of paper. It was the memoir. "I was searching the attic looking for this fabulous patchwork skirt my mother used to wear on the Fourth. I thought it might be in the attic, in a trunk where we kept our dress-up clothes. When I opened the trunk, there was the memoir right on top. Oh, and I found the skirt in the cedar closet with the mothballs. We can all read the full story here."

Cap leapt up to intercept what he imagined would be the distribution of the manuscript like gift bags at a gala. That could not happen.

"Maggie, I have to step in here. As your father's lawyer, a reminder that we do not own the rights to the book; the publisher does. We would be in breach of contract if it was distributed to the public.

Why don't you let me take a look at this first and then all these lovely people can pay full price a year from now when it's published?" Cap deftly collected the bags of paper and carried them into the house. Anders put his arm around Maggie's shoulders, in part comfort, in part restraint, and led her back to her seat. Then he deflected the conversation. It all happened so quickly that Maggie couldn't protest. "Tell us more about the attic, Maggie."

As Maggie rolled into her material on finding the skirt in an antique chest of drawers tucked under an eave, Liza and Tricia followed Cap into the house. Serena was the only person left standing as the fireworks started from the beach club across the water. She turned to the guests, a table filled with complete strangers, and said, "Should we go watch the fireworks from the dock?"

Connor leaned over and whispered to David, "I think we already did."

"WHAT THE HELL was she thinking? She knows better than to hand out copies of the manuscript. She's not that clueless," Liza asked out loud to Cap and Tricia as they stood in the library, fireworks booming in the background. "She literally has no sense of propriety at all. Did you see Serena's face?"

"Poor Serena. Welcome to the family! Now she knows what it's really like to have Maggie as a sister. She may want to go back to being an only child," Tricia said.

"That is terrible," Liza scolded, but she had been thinking the exact same thing. Being Maggie's sister was a lifelong roller-coaster ride. One day, dancing in bare feet and a flower crown in the VIP section of Coachella; the next day, having to bail her out of credit card debt so she could charge her airplane ticket home. And the whole time, everything that went right was her doing and everything that went wrong was someone else's fault.

Cap agreed, "Serena's been so discreet with this information for months. To her credit."

Tricia nodded. "And then Maggie gets ahold of a few specialty cocktails and announces it to the world."

"Only David and Connor seemed to be enjoying the moment because they appreciate family drama," Liza said. "I hope they don't call the dozen journalists they know with the scoop. I'll talk to them."

"At least she found the memoir," Tricia said, flipping through a copy to make sure it was genuine. "How many copies did she make?"

Cap did a quick count. "Ten."

Liza and Tricia started to laugh. None of this was funny, but it was a relief. "She was going to hand them out like candy, consequences be damned. Let's hope that Nina or Devon haven't already tweeted this out on literary Twitter, despite Cap's plea."

"Yes, I was going to hand them out." Maggie appeared at the door. "I don't understand why this has to be some big secret."

"Did you even read the book?" Tricia asked, pretty sure of the answer. "Do you have any idea of what's even in it?"

"I didn't have time. I was finishing my painting and planning this party. And anyway, the news is full of reunited children and sperm donors. These stories happen every day now. Seriously. Let's tell ours. Why not?"

Cap stepped in. "Maggie, dear, in this case, we really don't have the right. Or, should I say, rights. This book belongs to Allegory Publishing. The estate owes them this manuscript. Of course, you can tell anyone you'd like about Serena, but I do think it's wise to consider the timing for all involved. And, of course, you should consider Serena's wishes. She has many people in her life affected by this admission."

"I'm sure she's relieved for it to be out there."

"I'm sure she's not," Liza said. "I've gotten to know her over the last few days and I can tell you that she is a private person." No one could make Maggie feel more regretful than Liza. She could pare down all of Maggie's big ideas to tiny whims.

Cap came to Maggie's rescue. "You've made these copies and the people in this room should read the memoir before handing it over to Allegory. We should all know what's in the book for many reasons, but certainly so that we can anticipate any repercussions. I believe that's the best course of action. And, Maggie, thank you for finding this. You did a wonderful job at that."

Cap had a way with Maggie; he was the Crazy Whisperer. "I guess. But I do think Serena should get a chance to read the book along with us."

"Oh, so now you're really concerned about Serena, after you outed her as a Sweeney," Liza said. "She deserved consideration, Maggie."

"So, let her decide what happens next with the book," Maggie suggested, having a limited grasp on the importance of the memoir.

"No." Tricia couldn't hold back. "Serena is not one of us. She has no say in this."

Just then the dogs came bounding into the room. Everyone turned and saw Serena standing in the doorway, face fallen. She announced, "The dogs seemed upset by the fireworks. They wanted to come in. I didn't mean to interrupt."

"Serena . . ."

Serena wasn't having it. "No need to explain, Tricia. I get it. I'm not one of you—that's for sure. I don't laugh easily. I don't have the same memories. I don't tell stories like you all do. For the past few weeks, I've tried to understand where I might fit into your lives, but never once have any of you asked about where you might fit into my life."

Maggie started to protest but Serena was not done. "I've had a rough few months, too. My whole world has flipped upside down and inside out, but here on Willow Lane, you seem mainly concerned about how this all looks for you, for your family and your father, without a single expressed concern for me. I have a professional reputation to protect, too. I sit on the boards of several charities. I have a father in Florida right now and he has no idea about what's coming—that one of those lovely party guests may blow his whole world apart tonight!"

Then Liza tried to jump in, but Serena was angry and in no mood to listen. "You have your lives and each other and your magical iconic parents. Now that you've found the manuscript, the legal and financial troubles will fade away. Yes, I figured out that the advance is gone, the house sale will barely cover the tax bill, and there is no grand William Sweeney Estate. But don't worry, because once this book comes out, Bill Sweeney will be a hero again and you will always be his daughters. I have none of that. So, you're right. I'm not a Sweeney sister." With that, she exited the library and bolted down the hall toward the front door.

"Nice, Tricia," Liza sneered. "Serena, wait." Liza bent down to grab one of the manuscript bags and headed out the door to catch her. The dogs went with her.

Maggie piled on. "Way to go, Tricia."

"I meant legally, Maggie. Serena has no say in anything to do with Dad's intellectual property *legally*, either the memoir or anything else he's ever written. Sure, we can be cordial and let her read it ahead of publication, but she doesn't get to, quote, decide what happens with *Snap*," Tricia tried to explain. "I know consequences aren't really your thing, Mags, but there are a lot of question marks about this manuscript. For starters, it could be badly written, a crappy half-effort to fulfill the contract. Or damaging beyond belief to Dad or to Mom. Have you thought about that? There is a scenario by which we don't hand over the manuscript to the publisher and instead we pay back the advance from the sale of the house to protect Dad and the family. That would be a decision you, me, and Liza make. Not Serena. That is all I meant."

"It didn't sound that way. Not to me and obviously not to Serena. It sounded truly bitchy."

"Stop it, Maggie. This is all you. *You* created this scene tonight. Your sense of drama wanted a production, when a normal person would have kept this news inside the family. What's the rush to let the world know what a lousy father and husband William Sweeney was? His flaws are known to the world—the drinking, the gambling, all the things that male artists get away with because that's part of the package. But screwing the neighbor and then abandoning the child you fathered isn't at all charming. I'm not advocating white-washing the truth, but I, for one, would like to know what the truth is before flaunting our flaws to Tim the Line Cook."

"Serena's right. You don't care about her at all."

"Yes. You're right. I'm the thoughtless one." Tricia knew what she really wanted to say but held back, because there were some words and phrases the sisters never used with each other, as if crossing that line was the gateway to permanent disharmony.

"Let's all take a deep breath," Cap advised. "The good news is that we have a manuscript we can evaluate. We should all read it and then decide the best way forward. Agreed?"

"Yes."

"Fine."

Cap continued, "And now we have to do damage control with your guests. This secret won't stay secret for long now. This is an irresistible truth and it will get out."

"That was my goal all along," Maggie said as she sashayed out of the room.

Cap looked at Tricia. "This will work out."

"I'm not trying to make a saint out of him, Cap. But I don't want him to be trashed. Or our mother."

"I understand. And Serena?"

"I know we have an obligation to her, but we don't owe her our entire past. Maybe my father did or her mother, but it's not up to me, Maggie, and Liza to provide context to her life. It's possible there's a future that includes Serena, but she has no right to our past."

"I'm going to speak to the guests again." Cap picked up one of the bags with the manuscript inside. "A little beach reading. Should we

meet Monday morning with our notes and plan our next steps? I'll
have coffee at the office."

"Thanks. I'll be there."

Later, Tricia sat in the library alone, listening to the nonstop booms
of the grand finale. She knew that she had lied to Maggie. Sure, the
law was on her mind, but not entirely. Serena wasn't one of them.

LIZA CAUGHT SERENA in the driveway, about to throw her car in gear
and pull out of Willow Lane. The fireworks boomed in the distance,
only partially visible over the roof of the house. Serena lowered her
window to talk. "Please, Liza, don't even try to apologize."

"I can't. You're right. We haven't spent a minute thinking about
your life. We've been self-absorbed brats. We need to do better."

"I think it's best if I take a few days for myself."

Liza knew Serena was right, but still, she had an agenda. "Take
the book. Read it and call me. Tricia doesn't speak for all of us," Liza
said, leaning into the window and tossing the bag in the back of the
Range Rover. "Please come to the gallery opening tomorrow night.
If you decide you'd like to really go public with this information, you
can announce it to the crowd."

"I wouldn't count on it."

"Please, Serena." Liza meant it.

Serena's phone buzzed and out of habit she looked at it, despite
the heaviness of the moment. "My God, no."

"What?"

Serena looked at Liza with familiar eyes. "My mother's here. She's
at the Winthrops'."

"Hey."

"Hey."

Raj walked straight to Tricia and opened his arms. The pair were the same height, so Tricia nuzzled her head into Raj's neck. He ran his hand down her back, pulling her in tighter. Tonight she'd worn this long blue dress, soft and flowing with a slit up the front because Maggie had insisted she "get out of those sad white jeans." Raj couldn't take his eyes off her and her strong, slim shoulders, her tan legs. They had been together for five nights now, but it felt like five years.

They followed their night in the rowboat with dinner at the waterfront place in Westport, sharing their life stories with each other. Tricia told Raj about her mother, why she started running and what kept her running, and her doomed relationship with Blair and losing the baby. Raj told stories about his two sisters, his brother, and his million "cousins" in their extended Indian family in Maryland. The lines blurred between when the talking stopped and the touching began. The last three days, they had done everything together but archive.

Raj was in love. He had felt a strong attraction since their first meeting and debated the ethics of it in his mind for weeks before Tricia knocked on the door of the boathouse. She wasn't a colleague or a client. He wasn't her boss, nor she his. She was simply somebody's daughter, and that shouldn't pose a professional problem, he decided. Once he had settled the question in his mind, he moved forward in the only way he knew how, by connecting intellectually. He admired Tricia's strategic mind, her confidence, and her dry sense of humor. And the long curve of her back, the way her small gold hoops looked in her earlobes, the scent of her skin after a sail. It had only been five days, but Raj didn't want to let Tricia go.

Tricia felt the same way, but her emotions were complicated. Was this part of the grieving process? Or was this the relationship she'd been waiting to find her whole life? It seemed too good to be true and in Tricia's limited romantic experience, if that was the case, heartbreak was around the corner. Raj was thoughtful, well-read, and comfortable in his own beautiful skin. He was competent on all fronts, from his professional tasks to ordering in restaurants to tracing her cheekbones in exactly the right way. Tricia saw competency as an aphrodisiac. She hoped whatever this was with Raj wasn't a product of heightened emotions, but the real deal. She had to think that her father had a hand in this, befriending Raj at the library, bringing him to Willow Lane, offering the boathouse to him for the summer. Her father had never been that generous with any research assistant or grad student before. But Tricia wanted to believe Raj was for her.

Raj let go of her. "Quite an after-dinner speech. That was unexpected."

Tricia shook her head. "Poor Nina and Devon. They got the full Sweeney Show. Are your friends appalled or thrilled?"

"Both. But mainly they are terrified, because Cap told us in the most gentlemanly way possible that he would sue us to kingdom come if we told a soul about Serena. I thought he was going to throw our phones into the Long Island Sound. He's a very good lawyer. I'm not sure we should even be keeping company."

"Oh, is that what we're doing?"

They kissed, because they couldn't get enough of each other. Tricia wanted the entire mess to go away—the book, the estate, Serena—and escape with Raj to some sort of seaside bungalow in Maine or the

Cape where they could have sex, do the *New York Times* crossword puzzle together, and sit on a porch overlooking the water in the evening, drinking wine and fantasizing about going to bed early. But it was because of the mess that she'd found Raj, so she knew she had to stay. She kissed him deeper and then whispered, "Lock the door."

"Are you sure?"

"One hundred percent. This night needs some kind of spectacular nightcap."

LIZA HEADED TOWARD the kitchen. She was always on the cleanup crew at every event, and Willow Lane was where she learned to finish the job. Somebody would have to do the dishes tonight and her guess was that Maggie had already ditched the party with Tim. Or Gray. But she heard talking, laughing, and dishwasher loading happening down the hall. She peeked through the door to see Maggie was organizing leftovers, David and Connor were busing dishes and making jokes, and Devon and Nina were washing pots and pans. For once, it was good not to be needed. Liza took the dogs outside through the French doors onto the slate patio.

Gray was there, straightening up the porch furniture. "There you are."

"Here I am." Liza looked at Gray because he was something to look at. She had watched him all night long, sipping sparkling water as he talked to David about design and Nina and Devon about their program in comparative literature, genuinely interested in their stories. He wandered over and helped Tim with the grill and pulled out the chair for Liza when she went to sit down at the table. The Gray who broke her heart never put others first. This new Gray was humble.

He reached down to pet Jack, then smiled at Liza as he said, "Is it true? What Maggie said."

"As far as we know. DNA tests and all."

"How did that happen?"

It was such an obvious question, it made Liza laugh. "Believe it or not, we don't really know. I mean, beyond the birds and the bees bit. Serena wasn't ready to get the specifics from her mother yet, and we only found out a few days after my father's death about Serena. It's all new to us. Maybe the memoir will tell us."

"Are you okay with it?"

"I don't have a choice," Liza answered, then changed her mind. "Actually, I do have a choice and I'm fine with it. I'm letting go of a lot of things these days and perfection is one of them. Could be a messy family tree isn't the worst thing in the world. Could be it's the way life goes."

Gray took a step closer, until he was face-to-face with Liza. "And is that a new Liza thing?"

"Could be." Liza wasn't stepping away. She could feel the linen of Gray's shirt against her arm. She had to admit, it had been a long time since she'd felt electric physical attraction. Years, in fact. She and Whit had regular physical contact, but it wouldn't fall into the hot-and-bothered category. Liza knew a spark was missing and in the middle of the night, when she lay awake thinking about Whit's leaving, she rationalized that it was 90 percent about sex and 10 percent about emotion. Feeling this, feeling something like what she felt right now, was intoxicating. She lifted up her chin to Gray.

Gray kissed her. It wasn't the careless kiss of her teenaged years that she remembered. It was deeper, stronger, more mature by all measures. Gray's rough hands slipped down Liza's bare back as she leaned into his body. He still made her feel reckless. She wanted to be ready for this, but she wasn't. Slowly, she pulled away. "I'm sorry."

"No need for that." Gray smoothed her hair, letting his fingers linger on her neck. "I know it's probably too soon after Whit leaving and all."

"What?"

"Too soon. Rebounds are never a great idea. I should have waited."

"How did you know about Whit?"

Gray shrugged. "Ran into a couple of his squash buddies at the gym. They mentioned that you two had split."

Liza paused and breathed deeply. Whit had lied to her. He had planned this and told his pals at the Racket Club it was happening. And they told their pals. The man who thought photos of art openings in the local paper was too much publicity was wandering all over town announcing to people that his marriage was over. Liza ran through the timeline in her mind. He must have told these people before he had informed his own wife. Liza could hear Tricia's voice in her head, "Control the flow of information and you control the situation."

Liza had lost and she was humiliated. "I wasn't aware that our separation was public knowledge. This is news to me. I need a minute."

"Oh. Now, I'm sorry. Liza, I didn't know that you didn't know."

"How could you? Not your job to know about me. I don't know what I was thinking out here. I am a mess. Please, excuse me." She called to the dogs and went inside. She needed to wrap her head around the fact that her failure was out there in the world for all to see. She thought about all the familiar faces who'd be at the gallery tomorrow night, people that she and Whit had known their whole lives. Neighbors. Classmates. His parents. Whit had hightailed it out of town and she was stuck holding the truth.

She heard more laughter from the kitchen and stopped short. She couldn't face the people in that room right now; she couldn't face anyone. David and Connor could find their own way home. She went to open the library door to get her copy of the manuscript. She'd already decided she wasn't going to pick it up until after the opening. Now, after a double whammy of disappointments by the men in her life, Liza wasn't sure she wanted to read it at all. For some reason, the library door was locked. Probably Tricia hunkered down and halfway through the book by now, determined to beat Serena to the end, Liza thought. Fine, let her be the first to read it.

Like her father had so many times, Liza slipped out without a proper goodbye, taking the dogs and a flashlight. She'd walk home alone.

"I'M PRETTY DRUNK. Can I crash here?" Tim slurred in Maggie's general direction as she wandered through the living room looking for the last dirty dishes to collect. He was propped up against a wingback chair in the corner, barely standing. "Your friends brought all that expensive beer. I guess I had too many."

Maggie looked at Tim, who was listing to the left. "Ya think?"

"C'mon, Mags. I did a good job with the tri-tip." He started to lurch toward her like he was making a move.

Liza was right. He is a child. "You are definitely not driving, so yes, you can crash here. There is a small guest room down the hall. It's perfect for bed spins. You can touch both walls from the mattress," Maggie spoke with authority. She'd spent some nights in the guest room back in the day. "Head that way—I'll bring you a gallon of water and something for your hangover."

"Is that all you're going to bring me?" Tim said hopefully, tripping over an ottoman.

"Yes." Of that, Maggie was sure.

Tim saluted her and stumbled down the hallway toward the guest room at the far end of the house. Maggie went off to get the water and aspirin when movement on the porch caught her eye. It was Liza and Gray, kissing. She froze. She felt guilty and furious at the same time.

Maggie had invited Gray to the party to tweak Liza a little bit and she'd spent the night flirting with Tim to tweak Gray a little bit. Apparently, neither had noticed her efforts at all.

Just then Tim called from down the hall, "Hey, is there any lobster left?"

"Shut up," Maggie yelled in reply and shuffled upstairs to her childhood bedroom alone, forgetting all about Tim's water and aspirin.

Chapter

"Do you want some coffee?" Serena asked her mother, pouring a second cup into the Wellesley mug, a subversive act that boosted her courage.

"No, thank you. I've had enough."

Last night, when Serena returned from the gut punch that was the Sweeney's Fourth of July party, she found her mother and Lucy Winthrop sitting in the living room enjoying a final glass of wine while the congressman polished off a brandy. Her mother looked defiant, in navy blue and white with a sparkling red cardinal on her lapel, one of the many bird pins that Birdie Tucker had collected over the years. She greeted Serena with a pretentious double cheek kiss and then quickly suggested they catch up in the morning, clearly not wanting a scene in front of Lucy and Deke, or anyone, really. There would be no scenes in front of anyone ever, if Birdie Tucker had her way.

But after what had transpired at Willow Lane, Serena was done with civility over truth. She was done with discretion and she was done with deferring to those around her. Instead of shuffling off to bed and waiting her turn, Serena asked, "I assume the fact that you're here alone means you told Dad that William Sweeney was my biological father. Did you?"

Deke Winthrop whipped his head back and forth from Serena to Birdie to Lucy, while Lucy Winthrop put her finger to her lips to keep her clueless husband quiet. "Serena, dear, let your mother settle in.

You can discuss everything in the morning. When you're both rested. Isn't that right, *Birdie*?"

Clearly, this two-on-one strategy had been discussed in advance. Her mother didn't lose a beat. "Yes, of course. Thank you, Lucy. That's a wonderful idea. Don't you think so, Serena?"

"Nothing about the last six months has been wonderful," Serena said, pouring herself a brandy. "But sure, we can put off discussing the fact that you slept with the man next door and then left me in the dark for thirty-eight years. Please come to the guest house at nine." And with that, she walked out the side door with the crystal brandy snifter and her head held high.

I'm going to write that book, Serena thought as she headed toward the carriage house, knowing for the first time in six months the best course of action.

Her mother, though, didn't appear as confident in the morning light. She was in a Ralph Lauren navy track suit that could have been from this season or 1994, so impressive was Birdie's clothing-preservation program. (Serena referred to her mother's closet as "a Ralph Lauren Museum.") She was wearing Tretorns and her highlighted blond hair was a little flatter than last night, the top pulled back in tortoiseshell clips. Birdie had discovered sunscreen early enough to prevent the full leather face that other tennis players of her generation experienced, but her sixty-something décolletage had paid the price for all those sets in the sun. She was makeup free except for a swipe of lip gloss. She could have used some mascara.

Serena herself was exhausted. She'd had a terrible night's sleep and it was all she could do not to turn the light on and start in on *Snap*. But, before she read Bill Sweeney's interpretation of events, she wanted to hear her mother's story. She felt like she owed her mother that.

"Let's go sit in the living room. You can tell me how Dad reacted." As Serena walked over to the couch, she flipped on the recording device on her phone. She would need it for her book.

"I'm recording this."

"Oh, am I a suspect now?"

"I'm not the law, Mom. I'm a journalist. It's for my records."

"Whatever you say. You've certainly been treating me like some kind of criminal, cutting me out of your life."

Serena's patience with her mother was done. "What are you here to say?"

Birdie sat up straighter in her chair, as if she thought she were on camera. "As you suspected, my presence here does mean that I informed your father about your DNA test."

"That's a roundabout way to say it, Mom. Isn't this about your infidelity, not my DNA test?"

"Oh, stop it, Serena. Don't get precious with me." Birdie Tucker never liked being corrected, especially by her daughter. She had used the same tone when Serena was a teenager and started pushing back during dinner table discussions about politics or science or history when her mother was careless with the facts to prove a point or Serena had a different opinion than her parents. While Birdie and Mitch Tucker were happy to pay for their daughter's excellent education, actually using it at the dinner table was discouraged. "Yes, I told your father that I had a relationship with William Sweeney and that William Sweeney is your biological father. I did as you asked."

"Again, this is not about me. Mom. It's about your behavior. What did Dad say?"

"Some of that is private."

"I think it's your turn not to be precious, Mom."

Birdie's edge was slipping away. This was a conversation Serena had run in her head for months. She was ready. "Your father was not entirely surprised. He said he had always wondered why I only got pregnant once after many years of trying to have other children, both before you were born and after. And he said that he needed some time to work out his feelings for me, but it didn't change his feelings for you." There was a catch in Birdie's voice. "He is honored to be your father."

The last line hit Serena hard. Mitch Tucker was a decent man, even if he wasn't the most demonstrative or dynamic man. Serena had no doubt that he meant what he said. "And how did you leave it with him?"

"Your father and I will be fine. We've been married long enough to know neither of us is perfect. As for you, your father said that you should call him after we talk. He expressed his sympathy to you and his anger at me, for upending your life like this. He said that it must be particularly hard for someone like you whose life's work was to uncover the truth."

Unlike her mother, her father had admired Serena's career and felt like she was fighting the good fight, as long as she didn't come down too hard on the Bushes or bring up the scandals of the Reagan administration. Serena appreciated that her father understood what no one else had expressed. "I'll call him."

"So, now, what do you want to know?"

"I want to know what happened between you and Bill Sweeney. And how it happened." Serena realized she was ready for this story now.

"I met William Sweeney when I was a senior at Vassar. I was an editor of the paper and I was helping to organize a panel discussion about women in journalism. We had two journalists from the *New York Times* and a columnist from *Esquire* scheduled, but at the last minute, the columnist canceled, so *Esquire* sent William Sweeney instead. He had just written a controversial article about the glory of miniskirts or something like that and they knew they were sending him into the lion's den."

"Like hazing."

"Exactly—our editor in chief was set to moderate and she was a radical feminist, you know, the whole hairy-armpit, no-bra thing that was happening in the seventies. It wasn't my thing, but it was hers. I marched down Fifth Avenue. I wore an ERA button. But I shaved my legs. She, on the other hand, was ready to make an example of Bill Sweeney. Her name was Lorna, Lorna . . . Feldman. I think what Lorna really wanted was to work at the *New York Times* and she hoped her insightful critique and dismantling of his work would get her noticed.

"Anyhow, they asked me to be his campus escort. I had to pick him up at the Poughkeepsie train station, get him to the pre-panel wine-and-cheese event, and then make sure he attended the post-event dinner at the president's house. When I picked him up at the train station, I remember thinking that he looked like Paul Newman, a young, tall Paul Newman. I was entranced by his intellect, his humor. I had never met a man like him. We immediately went to have a drink, bypassing the official reception, the mandatory rehearsal. Everything I was supposed to do, I didn't. I was twenty-one and he was twenty-six, but he seemed to have the world on a string. I warned him about the protests, the questions that would be coming at him. By the time we got to campus, he was fully prepped and slightly inebriated. He relished his role as a Male Chauvinist Pig, wore it proudly, and wore down the poor moderator. It enraged the student protestors even more.

"After the panel, we escaped through the back door and headed straight for the guesthouse on campus where he was staying for the night. He whisked me upstairs and I was sunk."

A picture of young Birdie Tucker flashed through Serena's mind. Tall, thin, blond, in a suede maxi skirt, Frye boots, and white beret, the product of Northern European genes, a Darien, Connecticut, up-bringing, and a rigorous tennis-training schedule. Throw in a top-notch education and a healthy sense of entitlement and it was easy to see why the college senior was such an attractive mark to the young Bill Sweeney who, until he landed a scholarship to Yale, had none of the advantages that she had enjoyed. A theory was beginning to de-velop in Serena's mind, but she let her mother continue.

"For the next three years, my life revolved around Bill Sweeney. After graduation, I moved to Manhattan and got a job at NBC News, but really, my life consisted of our interactions. He was writing *Never Not Nothing* at the time we met and by the time he left me, he was an international literary sensation. He lived in the Village, which was so exciting, and I lived in Murray Hill, safe but boring. I'd wait in my apartment every night to see if he was going to call and ask me to his place. Sometimes, I'd see him every night for two weeks straight and then he'd disappear into his work for a month. We'd go out in the Village, but never with other people. He said he wanted to keep me for himself, but I think he was a little embarrassed by me. I wasn't edgy, I wasn't the next big thing. I was an associate producer at NBC News primarily because I checked the female box and my father knew the president of NBC News at the time. They were members of the same club in Manhattan. Mainly, I got coffee and made copies and picked up dry cleaning for the men in the office. I was no Jessica Savitch. I suppose you'll think poorly of me, but I wasn't looking to change the face of journalism. I wanted a husband, a family, stability. I knew I would never marry Bill because he was a Catholic and, you know, Mimi and Granddad never would have approved of that."

Serena thought about her mother's opposition to her ex-boyfriend Ben because he was Jewish. "I know how that goes."

"What does that mean?"

"Nothing," she said, not wanting to derail the story. "Go on."

"Bill Sweeney was a dynamic man. I couldn't walk away. I didn't have to, though. He walked away from me. I wasn't what Bill Sweeney wanted."

"What did he want?" Serena asked drily.

"Someone flashier. When he left me for good, I was devasted, really lost. I wasn't the independent woman I pretended to be. I didn't want to be on my own, stay in the city and love my job and sleep around like everybody else in the seventies. Six months after Bill dumped me in a restaurant in Chinatown for Dyan Cannon, I met your father at the wedding of a college friend and we were married within a year. It was time."

"Dyan Cannon? The actress."

"Yes, the actress. Once the book came out, he was the hottest thing in town. Writers became celebrities in the seventies and everybody wanted Bill Sweeney at their party. And he wanted to be at every party, not that he would take me. Then Hollywood noticed and directors flew him out to LA, trying to persuade him to sell the movie rights to *Never Not Nothing*. He wouldn't, of course. People thought it was because he had integrity, but actually he just wanted to keep getting those trips to LA. But on one trip, he met a beautiful actress and that was it for me. I don't think it lasted long with Dyan Cannon, but I couldn't compete with that or any of the other Dyan Cannons to come."

"Why did he live next door? Was that intentional?"

"No! Of course not! It was a complete coincidence. We hadn't been in touch since that night at the Chinese restaurant. I'd followed his career and his picture was everywhere, but no one was more stunned than me when I learned that the new neighbors were William Sweeney and his lovely new wife, Maeve. I hadn't even told your father about him. How could I? By then, he was so well-known, I didn't want to make your father self-conscious."

Serena was on her third cup of coffee. She brought two cans of seltzer over to the living room and her mother gave her a look, so she stood back up to get a glass. "You never told Dad about your relationship with Bill Sweeney? Ever?"

"I know you think I'm rigid, but I have some soft spots. Your father is a good man, but he couldn't compete with William Sweeney on any level. What was the point? I was happy enough. I willingly walked away from a career to be a wife and mother. We had money, a nice house, good vacations. Your father provided all of that and more. I am embarrassed by what happened."

"What did happen?"

"A very selfish affair. The last flicker of a relationship that meant everything to me and, I think, meant something to Bill. But it was short-lived the second time around and the details are rather seedy. I'm not going to tell you any more than that, because I'm entitled to my own life. But we both knew it was wrong and it wouldn't last. It ended and a few weeks later, after five years of trying to get pregnant, I learned I was pregnant. Your father was thrilled, I was thrilled. It was the eighties; we didn't ask a lot of questions then. Soul-searching wasn't required. I went on and Bill Sweeney went on. We had very little contact after that. I would see him at the library at official events and occasionally run into him on Willow Lane. We spoke after Maeve died, but our connection burned out."

"Did he know?"

"That he was the father?"

Serena nodded.

"I didn't know he was the father. Not for sure. Which is another aspect to this story I'm not proud of. But, honestly, I think he was too busy being William Sweeney to notice my pregnancy. After our relationship ended, I wasn't exactly lingering at the end of the driveway after picking up the morning paper hoping to see him walk by with his dog. I avoided him and he was easily avoided. Our worlds didn't intersect that much. I was a Southport housewife. Bill was reaping the rewards of his second literary masterpiece, *Bitter Fruit.* And, in public, he was the devoted husband of Maeve, an esteemed faculty member at Yale, a new father of one, two, then three girls. He chose not to know and I chose not to tell him."

"Were you and Maeve friends?" Serena asked that more for Liza, Maggie, and Tricia than herself.

"Friendly, but not friends. I was curious about her, of course, and, I admit, not kind to her behind her back. I was jealous. She was a decent person but very naive. I think Bill must have had two different lives: one on Willow Lane and one when he was out in the rest of the world. I did understand more than most what he was like when he was working on something. I was there through *Never Not Nothing.* One day, he was on top of the world; the next, wanting to burn the entire manuscript. He threw money away. I wished I could have explained that to Maeve, that we had that in common, but she was vulnerable. And then sick for so long. When she died, I brought over a cheese platter and that youngest daughter wouldn't even let me in the door."

"Tricia. Her name is Tricia. I look exactly like her, except with your coloring. How could you not notice that?"

"Everyone always said that you looked like me."

There was silence for a bit. Her mother had filled in the missing pieces, most anyway. The story had such a bittersweet veneer that Serena didn't end up thinking less her mother, but more. She understood the affair. Serena couldn't judge her mother for that. She thought about Dean, the guy from the airport. She'd slept with a married man, too. She hadn't known it at the time, but if she'd gotten pregnant after finding out he was married, would she have told Dean about that baby? Serena couldn't honestly say that she would have. It seemed like the most complicated solution, to involve a whole other person, a whole other family. Birdie simplified the situation with her choices, or so she must have thought. At the very least, Serena could understand that instinct.

Over the course of Serena's lifetime, it seemed like families were allowed to be more complicated, less cookie-cutter versions of the one mom, one dad, loving siblings version of previous generations. There were endless combinations and formations of families now, sending out holiday photos like everyone else. Serena had seen that in the NPE social media groups where she lurked. These DNA kit discoveries had led to some pretty complicated family trees. Certainly Birdie Tucker, with her family tree of straight and blue blood branches, could never have come clean about Serena's true parentage without social repercussions. Her mother chose a path that many women had before her, the path of least resistance. Serena saw her more as a coward than a liar.

Birdie poured the seltzer into the glass and found a coaster so she could set it on the side table next to the couch. She was tired of disclosing. She didn't know how the younger generation did it, dumping so much personal information onto the world at large. She took a sip of the seltzer and waited for Serena's next question.

"Do you regret not telling him?"

Birdie didn't hesitate. "Not for one second. Bill Sweeney was a not a reliable person. He drank too much, he was narcissistic. Don't idolize the father he might have been. Just ask his daughters."

"Do you regret not telling me?"

"I do today," Birdie said and the two women shared a laugh. "Now, can I ask you a question?"

"Yes."

"If you had found out that your father was some sperm donor or the tennis pro, would you have cared this much? Would you want to pursue a relationship with a sperm donor's children? Or is it because your DNA matches William Sweeney's that you care?"

"Oh my God, did you sleep with the tennis pro?" Because Serena had and that was something she didn't want to share with her mother. One night in college after a few too many shots at the Shoe, she and John Wilton had consummated her high school crush in the back of his Saab. It was a disappointment.

"Of course not. His mother and I played bridge together," Birdie said, her outrage real. "But I feel like I'm being punished because your biological father was famous, not because I didn't tell you, so which is it?"

"Both." It wasn't like Serena hadn't asked herself this question many times over the last six months, and she was ready with the answer. "I'm angry that you thought you could keep this huge piece of information to yourself, and that would be true if the test had revealed a donor, a tennis pro, or a literary genius. But it especially hurts because my real father was a writer. Like I am. Didn't it occur to you when I pursued English and journalism in college that maybe that interest came from him? I have been working away in a field that has lost resources and prestige over the last decade. I could have really used one parent who understood what it's like to face a blank page and think, 'Well, this is all I know how to do, so I have to keep doing it.' You've acted like my career has been a hobby, something to do while I waited to get married. But writing is more than what I do, it's who I am. So, yes, it matters more to me that my real father was a great writer. I never got the chance to talk to him about that. And you must have known and you didn't care."

"For the record, your father and I are both very proud of your work."

The conversation had taken a lot out of Serena. Birdie, too. They both needed a break, some fresh air. Still, Serena continued with one more question, pursuing the theory that she'd been formulating.

"Mom, are you Elspeth? From *Never Not Nothing*?"

"'She moved with the confidence of privilege . . .'" Birdie quoted from the book. "Yes, I believe I am."

Chapter

21

"Holy shit. Birdie Tucker is Elspeth. He doesn't name her. Her calls her Rebecca in *Snap* like he did in real life according to Serena, but it's Birdie Tucker, for sure."

"Wait, how'd you get ahead of me?"

Tricia and Raj were holed up in the boathouse reading *Snap*, each taking up a corner of the ancient couch, a light blanket over their feet despite the fact that it was a warm summer day. Of all the things that convinced Tricia that Raj was predestined, his tendency to have cold feet was the one that hit home. She had cold feet, too. And there was nowhere that Tricia would rather be than in the boathouse reading with Raj.

"You're a slow reader."

"I'm a careful reader. Don't say any more. Let me get to the end of the chapter."

Tricia valued his opinion. It was worth getting his impression of the book as a piece of writing and for its value to scholarship, an evaluation William Sweeney's daughters and his best friend wouldn't be able to make. The two of them were reading the book together chapter by chapter with a discussion in the breaks.

Bill Sweeney had organized the book in ten sections, each inspired by a snapshot from his life. A childhood photo. A shot from his Yale days. A picture of his writing pals at the 21 Club in New York. The chapter titles were one word: Home, Wine, Women, Money, Time, Work, Love, Play, Death. Except the last chapter, which was called What I Got Wrong.

The device surprised Tricia. "I don't think of my father as being visual at all. I don't remember him ever going to a museum or commenting on a piece of art. Isn't this weird?"

"It's a bit of a gimmick, but it's working. The chapter on his childhood was new material, not recycled from his essays or from *My Maeve*. I liked the update on his sister Frannie and the bit about visiting the cemetery where their parents are buried. Some very powerful passages on the abuse he endured as a child. New information is good for scholarship and for sales. The Yale chapter, too. I thought I'd heard every Yale story, but there are some new ones. And he's very honest about his teaching there, suffering from jealousy over his talented students and bias against certain stories."

"Yeah, like stories from women, people of color, and the entire LGBTQ community. I feel like we should definitely push to have the Yale ceremony in his honor before this book comes out."

"Your father was no different from other professors there. They all have biases; they're just different biases. Plus, despite his shortcomings, he managed to get a lot of his students published. Ultimately, that matters more than anything that might have been in his heart."

"That lapsed Catholic guilt is good for something."

The two went silent as they read the fourth chapter titled Women, an assessment of the influence of the female sex on his life, his work, his humanity. Somehow, this chapter managed to be more about manhood. Bill Sweeney ran through a list of former girlfriends, lovers, bosses, and female writers who got under his skin, thanking them for being agents of change, making him a better human being. There was a surprise appearance by Dyan Cannon as his perfect Hollywood Moment and, of course, an apologia to his wife for his many failings as a provider, subjecting her to the feast-or-famine school of family finances but ultimately letting himself off the hook because that's the "writer's life."

Tricia thought his excuse was a bit cavalier, the sort of explanation that a man who was contrite, but not truly sorry, would make. It verged on the solicitous language she'd heard a half dozen male lawyers use when accepting their Partner of the Year award, explaining that they'd "married up" and thanking their beautiful wives for "making it all possible" and "being my much better half," instead of simply saying thank you and moving on. Tricia witnessed one partner hold up his engraved Tiffany glass bowl and declare, "We made it, baby," as if they'd achieved a meaningful lifelong dream instead of a hokey award for working a hundred hours a week and barely seeing your wife and kids. The sentiment made her teeth hurt. She looked around for other horrified audience members who felt as sorry for the wife as she did, but instead, saw that some people, men and women, had tears in their eyes. Audiences loved men who claimed to love their wives.

Tricia was taken aback that her father had fallen for that trope.

But primarily, the chapter was about Birdie Tucker, as a girlfriend, archetype of the One That Got Away. There was a photo of a stunning young woman in a wrap dress with long tanned legs and platform shoes sitting on a stoop in Greenwich Village. She stared right into the camera, her knees together, her long, straight, golden hair framing her face. Underneath the photo were the words *Rebecca on the Block 1975*. Tricia recognized the pre-helmet-head, pre-tennis-elbow Birdie immediately. She was so young and carefree, no sign of the tight lips and the disapproval that would mark her later years, the memory Tricia held of the mother next door. This Birdie was something else.

Tricia had no idea that their relationship started that early. At Vassar! In 1972! How was that possible? By the time she had finished the chapter, two truths had emerged: William Sweeney was mesmerized by Birdie Tucker and Birdie Tucker was Elspeth.

"I think you're right," Raj said as he put down the last page of Chapter 4. "He uses the same language to describe Birdie as he used in *Never Not Nothing* to describe Elspeth: patrician, poised, and of course 'the confidence of privilege' is a direct quote from *Never*. This is important. He never confirmed that Elspeth was based on a real girl, a real person, before." Raj noticed Tricia's strained face. "Does this upset you?"

"I assumed Serena was the product of some drunken flirtation at a library fundraiser that went too far. Straight-up suburban boredom," Tricia said, getting up off the couch and moving toward the big window that looked to the east, toward the Tuckers' old house. "It never occurred to me that there was a relationship, a real relationship. She was actually the product of something meaningful and, I can't believe I'm saying this, but poor Serena. Her biological parents made her feel like her parentage didn't matter, was inconsequential. And then I piled on that."

"Does this make it harder to compartmentalize Serena?" If this question had come from Liza, or Maggie, Tricia would have lashed out, reacting to the notion that she could neatly separate her life or her work from her emotional needs, a tired accusation her sisters had tossed at her over time. But Raj had made it clear that he admired her clear-eyed approach to finding the manuscript, settling the estate, and processing the complications that came in the form of Serena Tucker, so she heard his question as a call for more information, and not an accusation.

"It does," Tricia said. "I guess I felt like she hadn't truly earned the distinction of being a Sweeney simply because Bill Sweeney was the sperm donor. Big deal, he was your biological father, but he wasn't your dad. Now, it's like Serena's in our club. Birdie Tucker meant something and still my father was unwilling to acknowledge Serena in real life. It's the same level of disappointment that we all felt in my father at some point. From small stuff, like missing out on our games or our plays because he was too involved in his writing or too absorbed in self-promotion to care about anyone but himself. Or watching him move about the kitchen with the heavy head of a hangover, barely able to make coffee. To the big stuff, like his inability to cope on any level after my mother's death and his hubris at thinking that he was the only one who missed her. I got so angry reading the first chapter of *My Maeve* at prep school, I literally threw it in a bonfire one night. When I met Serena, with her normal, stable, *living* parents, I felt like she hadn't earned the status."

Raj stood behind her and massaged her shoulders. Tricia had gotten used to his comfort with intimate gestures. "You're allowed to work through this however you need, Tricia. At whatever speed. There's no road map for this."

She turned around to face Raj, running her own hands over his shoulders. "Thank you. I don't always like being the uptight sister, you know."

"I like uptight girls." He kissed her. He tasted like blueberries.

She pulled away slowly. "Thank you. Do you think less of him reading this book?"

"No, but I'm not reading this book to form an opinion of who William Sweeney is. I knew your dad and I liked him. He was smart, curious. He made me laugh. Plus, now I know he slept with Dyan Cannon. That's pretty cool."

"That will be the headline in the *Esquire* review, won't it?"

Raj nodded. "Yes, it will. And I predict a photo will emerge and it will be unbelievable. But I'm reading it to understand how he came to be and what mattered along the way. He's not my father, Tricia."

"You never know. Have you done an over-the-counter DNA test?"

"That's creepy."

"As creepy as the mom next door being the muse for Elspeth? That's stunning to me."

"It's a blockbuster piece of information. Elspeth is such an iconic character. I mean, every man who ever read *Never Not Nothing* was in love with her. But knowing what we know about a later relationship and an unintended pregnancy, your father didn't exactly come clean. Nor did he mention that she lived next door for decades. He pulled his punches. I thought you said he was going to let it all hang out in this book."

"Cap said he was hoping to update the manuscript, add a coda. Maybe he was going to own up to it. He does write they 'tried again,' but that their moment had passed," Tricia said, still staring out the window. "That's quite a euphemism. Not exactly the full story, huh?"

"No, but *Never* fanboys will go crazy. It answers the question of why there was never a sequel."

"We have six more chapters to go. Should we skip ahead and search for Serena's name? Or mine?" Tricia was impatient now. So far, the memoir was better that she had expected. Funny, sharp, filled with memories new to her, insights about his process. There was a certain attitude about the pages, like he was letting the world in on some Bill Sweeney secrets. The next chapter started with a photo of her father with Reggie Jackson. It would be about baseball or gambling or both. She was afraid to read how much money Bill Sweeney actually had lost.

"No, let's read it the way your father meant us to read it, one page at a time. What time is the opening at the gallery?" Raj asked.

Liza had been adamant that it was all hands on deck. She had texted early in the morning that the book and the rain and the hangovers were no excuse. She needed backup. Her text had read: You all owe me. Think of all the Thanksgivings. Be there at 6. Doors open at 6:30.

"We have at least three more hours before we have to be at the gallery, but I want to make a stop beforehand." Tricia's phone pinged. It was a text from Maggie. "It's Maggie. She's trying to smooth things over."

"What do you mean?"

"Tim is making tacos with the extra tri-tip. Wants to know if we want to join them for lunch. That's her way of saying 'I'm sorry for last night.'"

"Works for me. You know, I like Tim. He has a lot of thoughts on craft beer."

"DOES HE MENTION us at all?" Maggie asked, handing Tricia a plate of three carne asada tacos. The two sisters were sitting at the kitchen table while Tim and Raj plated the food. There had been no conversation about the previous night and both women were on board with that strategy.

Tricia knew she meant the book. "Not yet. But it's good. Revealing to a point. There are some classic passages with his signature biting humor laced with humanity. He had some good writing days with this one. You're never going to read it, are you?"

Maggie swooped her loose hair up into a scrunchie. "Probably not. Maybe bits and pieces. Let me know the good parts."

"I suggest Chapter Four."

"What happens in Chapter Four? CliffsNotes version."

Tricia paused, then said, "In Which We Discover That Birdie Tucker Is Elspeth and All Our Romantic Notions About Our Mother and Father Die."

"Oh, don't tell me that. Now I'm never going to read it. That will kill me." Maggie used to say dramatic things like that all the time when she was in high school and the family reacted with mockery. Her father called her Sarah Bernhardt and went on about the vapors. They'd all laugh until Maeve insisted they stop, patting Maggie's hand and telling her to breathe. But after the family got the call from the hospital in Providence informing them of her overdose, they stopped accusing her of being overly dramatic. Though it had been a long time and Maggie was more stable now than at age twenty, Liza and Tricia listened more than they laughed.

"If that's the way you feel, don't read it. I give you permission to pass on it."

"I know I'm supposed to be comfortable with the idea of Dad as a flawed human being, but I prefer to think of him as Dad, you know?"

"He did date Dyan Cannon."

"I knew that. He told me once after Mom died. I didn't know who she was, so I looked her up. He was very proud of that."

"Oh, and you were right about the Russian professor! They did have an annual weekend together. A long-running affair."

"How long running?"

"He's vague, of course, about the number of years to shield his marital status, but he writes that it continued after she was married. In the book, he calls her Ludmilla, not Nadia, which I'm guessing is some kind of inside joke because, you know Dad, he liked feminine names for his female characters. He writes that it 'fed his intellect,' which is some sort of bullshit justification."

"Classic Dad. Feminist scholars will have a field day with this book," Maggie said, taking a bite of her taco. Then she said, "Birdie as Elspeth. That's a disappointment. Now you must feel really bad about Serena."

"Thanks. I do." They laughed liked they always did when something hit too close to home emotionally.

Maggie's phone buzzed and she looked down. It was a text from Liza. "Well, I guess she's forgiven me for last night, because now she needs a favor."

"Neither of us have forgiven you, Maggie. But you know what Mom would say: 'Let's not dwell . . .' What does Liza need? Can I help?"

"Nope, she needs Tim," Maggie said, then raised her voice a bit. "Tim, do you want to bartend tonight at the gallery opening? Liza's in a jam. Twenty-five bucks an hour."

"Do I actually have to know how to bartend or is it a white wine thing? Because, like, I don't know how to make a Singapore Sling or anything."

"You don't really need to know how to bartend."

"I'm in," Tim said, shaking his long hair like a happy golden retriever. Maggie responded to Liza with the good news and added a few beverage emojis for fun.

Tricia nodded toward Tim. "How is it he's even upright? I think he drank all the beers last night."

"He's twenty-six, that's how."

Tim turned around. "That's not how. Age has nothing to do with it. It's the patented Tim Yablonski Hangover Cure. Get up early, drink two cups of coffee, run five miles, take a cold shower, and then eat a meat product that's heavily salted, followed by electrolyte water. Today, after the run, I dove into the sound and then took a cold shower. Well, we took a cold shower. That was killer. I feel great."

Maggie studied the handsome guy standing at the stove who had been kinder to her in the last few weeks then any man in recent memory. "Your last name is Yablonski?"

"You know it, baby." Tim did a little dance at the stove.

Maggie laughed. "Is that the Yablonski shuffle?" Maggie turned to Tricia, resuming their conversation. "I feel terrible for Serena. She should have had a chance to talk to Dad. And he wouldn't see her. He was never going to see her. I don't think she should ever know that."

"I agree."

"IT'S TRICIA SWEENEY. Here to see Serena Tucker."

The gate opened slowly at the Winthrops' estate. Tricia had only been on the property a few times, once to interview the congressman for her high school paper, another time to receive a Daughters of the American Revolution scholarship from DAR member Lucy Winthrop, and a third time to attend a fundraiser for the wetlands with her father. She had no idea how they ended up at a charity event for a cause neither of them cared about, but she remembered the food was mediocre and the white wine was warm, a sure sign that Lucy Winthrop didn't want the party-goers to linger. Today, Tricia was hoping to get in and out without seeing either the congressman or his wife. She drove down the long driveway toward the main house, as directed by the male voice coming out of the intercom.

Lucy Winthrop was standing under the portico, waving her left hand slightly. Apparently, there was to be an audience with the queen before Tricia was permitted to see Serena. Tricia rolled down her window, hoping to keep it short.

But Lucy Winthrop wanted more. "Hello, Tricia dear. Why don't you park here? We'll have some iced tea in the solarium and then you can go visit Serena. Ten minutes is all I need."

Tricia acquiesced, somewhat curious about what Mrs. Winthrop had to say, even though the cool summer day was better suited to coffee than iced tea. "Sounds lovely."

Once inside, seated in the wicker chairs, Lucy started in. "First, let me say how very sorry I am about your father. I have spoken to Deke and he's going to propose some sort of official commendation the next time Congress is in session. Your father was a favorite constituent and a great talent. He'll be missed here in Southport and around the world. I hope that gives you comfort," the congressman's wife said, using her "I speak for him" tone of voice. She was sitting in a heavy wicker chair upholstered in a muted coral fabric, the kind of indoor/outdoor furniture you would never put outside. The sunroom was filled with antique touches like French cachepots, framed Audubon prints, and a stunning Oriental rug. A half dozen large orchids and standing planters of ferns gave the room an exotic feel. Lucy Winthrop looked comfortable and in control as she prepared to serve Tricia.

"Thank you for the wonderful gesture. That will be meaningful." Tricia imagined hanging the framed commendation up in her office.

The partners would like it, Don Donaldson especially. Maybe she'd even go to DC to watch the moment in person, she thought, realizing that after a lifetime of being present at ceremonies and galas in her father's honor that there would be only a handful of such obligations left.

Lucy poured out two tall glasses of iced tea and added a sliver of lemon with silver tongs. "By the looks of you, you don't take sugar. You're very thin, my dear. Here you are." Tricia accepted the drink while Lucy continued, "I assume you got my condolence card. I haven't received anything in return but there's no rush."

The custom of forcing grieving families to send thank-you cards for sympathy cards was something Tricia would never understand. But fortunately, Liza did, so she was sure an appropriate acknowledgment would be forthcoming. "You're very kind to think of us. It was all so sudden, but I know that Liza is working through the thank-yous. She's very conscientious. We've all had tasks to do since my father's death." There was only so far Tricia would go to placate Lucy Winthrop.

"Liza's a good girl. She is a wonderful asset to our community. I don't know what Whit is thinking. But that's a conversation for another time."

It would have to be because Tricia had no idea how to respond. Was Maggie right again that something was up with Whit and Liza? Tricia went for a vague response. "Yes. We're all focused on the art opening tonight and then making a joyful homecoming for Vivi and Fitz when camp ends. That's what sisters are for."

"Aren't you a great support system? I hope my girls can rally together if they ever face a real challenge," Lucy said, implying that the lives of her daughters, Delaney and Reagan Winthrop, had been a breeze up until now, even though Tricia suspected the elder had an eating disorder and the younger married for status rather than love and spent more time with her horses than her husband. At least that's what her Southport friends implied when they got together over the holidays to catch up. "Speaking of sisters, I know the truth about Serena. From Serena's lips and from Birdie's. She's here now."

"Serena?"

"Well, yes, Serena is here but I meant Birdie. She arrived yesterday to talk with Serena." Lucy Winthrop's voice had the tone of a woman feigning sympathy and dying to dish with one tiny push from Tricia.

"I see. About what, I wonder?" Tricia knew what was happening. She proceeded with caution.

"About the whole . . . you know. They talked all morning and through lunch. According to Birdie, it was emotional and exhausting. Birdie is lying down and I imagine Serena is doing the same."

"Sounds like it was a difficult conversation." Tricia had heard enough, from Lucy Winthrop anyway. She wasn't giving the world-class gossip any more encouragement.

"Aren't you curious about the details?"

"Curious is the wrong word. I'm interested because it involves my family as well, but I'll let Serena decide when and if she wants to tell us about the conversation. It's really her decision, her life."

"I can see why Cap admires you so much. You've always had a good head on your shoulders, even as a teenager. You went through a lot with great reserve. So, I ask you this, please consider all the people in this story before you make any announcements. As a congress-man's wife, I understand what it's like to put public perception first. I've lived with that restriction for decades. There are real people to consider and, of course, the reputation of the town. Be thoughtful."

In a flash, Tricia felt the generational chasm open. There were no heroes in this story. Both William Sweeney and Birdie Tucker had served their own needs first and foremost, hiding the truth from each other, their spouses, and their daughter. Tricia heard Maggie's voice in her head questioning why everything needed to be a secret. Now, Lucy Winthrop was suggesting that the next generation play along, so nobody, including "the town," got damaged. What a crock.

"Mrs. Winthrop, I believe that everybody has a right to tell their own truth. Or not. You forget, my sisters and I are the daughters of two storytellers—one in prose; one in poetry. We revere stories. And Serena does have a tale to tell."

As soon as Tricia said it out loud, she knew she believed it. Her father's memoir. Maggie's speech last night. The book she was sure Serena was working on. Everyone had a truth. "I'm going to knock on Serena's door now. Thank you for the iced tea. Perhaps we'll see you at the gallery opening tonight. My sister Maggie will be debuting a stunning piece painted right here in Southport. The show is called Still Life with Sunflowers. There's a period after 'Still' and 'Life.' Get it?" Tricia said as she stood up.

Oh, Lucy Winthrop got it. The conversation was over. Lucy Winthrop, used to dining with presidents and billionaires and celebrity environmental activists, would surely turn down the invitation. She wasn't playing second fiddle to a bunch of sunflowers.

Lucy Winthrop watched Tricia walk away like she had watched Serena walk away last night. How had she never noticed the resemblance? *Two peas in a pod.*

"What I said at the house was petty. I was speaking about legal standing, but I understand that it didn't sound that way. I'm sorry. I apologize for the hurt I caused," Tricia declared, standing at the door of the carriage house, using the words she tried out with Raj. She was good with straightforward, but stymied by emotional depth. She felt like she walked the line with her apology, sincere and heartfelt. She noticed Serena looked foggy. "Did I wake you?"

"Yes."

"I'm sorry for that, too." Serena was wearing the sort of lounge pajamas people wore in TV shows, a bit dressy for a midday nap, Tricia thought.

"I needed to get up."

"Are you coming to the opening? Liza will kill me if you're not there. She said she couldn't have gotten the show up and the word out without you. She would love to have you there. Plus, you could just wear those fancy PJs."

"My mother gave them to me. A silk peace offering after four decades of deception." The two women laughed. Then Serena asked, "Is that why you're here? To get me to the gallery opening?"

"Not entirely. I read our father's book this morning."

Our father. Tricia had said it, finally. Serena waved her into the living room. "I'm going to make a coffee. Do you want an espresso?"

"Yes!" Tricia nodded. "I make one every afternoon at the office."

"I do, too." Serena moved into the open kitchen and fired up the espresso maker. "This is about the only thing I know how to make."

"I have no kitchen skills, either. It's why I'm assigned wine at every family event. Liza used to try to make me cook squash and I couldn't handle it."

"Maybe after-dinner coffee will be my assignment," Serena said, setting down a steaming cup in front of Tricia.

"Yes." Tricia took a sip. "So, should we talk about what your mother told you and what my father's book told me?"

"I think we should."

"Did you know your mother was Elspeth?"

Serena swallowed the espresso. "I found out this morning in my conversation with her. How did you know?"

"I found out this morning after reading it in our father's memoir."

"It's in there?"

Tricia nodded. "His side of the story anyway. You can read it and see if it matches hers. It looks like it was a real love story."

"That's how my mother described it. At least when they first met. The second time around, not so much."

"That's good to know. My father doesn't say much about the second time around. So, I'm going to carry that with me to help me work out my feelings of anger on behalf of my mother. But now you can name the book you're not writing *Elspeth's Daughter*."

"That's a pretty good title."

"I agree." Tricia laughed.

"I thought my mother was privileged to have been immortalized in *Million Zillion*, but inspiring two William Sweeney characters is quite an honor."

"Elspeth and Wren." Serena seemed surprised that Tricia understood the reference. No one was going to beat Tricia at Bill Sweeney *Jeopardy!* "I've been doing my research, too."

"I'm sure you have."

"Serena, this situation is a mess. Our father's death didn't make it any simpler. Raj said to me today that there is no road map for this. I have to work through a lot of stuff right now. You're part of that stuff. As my sisters will tell you, I'm sure I'll underwhelm you with my emotional intelligence. But I'm trying to say that I'll try to be a part of your life if that's what you want and I'm hoping you'll let me."

"My mother asked me today if I would have cared the same if I found out my father was a random sperm donor. I said I would have cared either way, but I don't know if that's entirely true. My motives may not have been pure. Being William Sweeney's daughter has a certain glamour to it that being donor #4798's daughter doesn't have. I need to work through my stunted emotional intelligence, too."

"Fair enough. We don't have to figure this all out today," Tricia said.

"That's true."

"But what I do know is that I respect your right to do whatever you wish with your story. You don't owe us anything, Serena, except maybe a heads-up when the book you're not writing comes out. And Maggie will insist on a very flattering photo of her on the book jacket, so you'll have to shell out for her hair and makeup at the shoot."

Serena studied Tricia. "When I came to the wake, I was looking for something, some connection to your family. I assumed it would be through your father, but seeing you all together again reminded me of the envy I felt when we were kids and you'd walk down the lane together laughing and singing. You were the same twenty years later. I see what you do for each other—you cover for each other. I haven't had that in my life. I've been out there on my own. No one to provide coverage. It's a new concept to me."

"I guess you're right. I never thought of it like that, but that's what ends up happening. One of us is always having a crap year or decade and the others step in. You might want to take some time to decide whether you want to be part of that in perpetuity." Tricia looked at her watch. She had to get moving. "I have to go. Liza needs our help at the gallery. I do hope you swing by. It would mean a lot to Liza and so it would mean a lot to me."

"I'll see."

"Oh, I asked your landlord, Lucy Winthrop, too. I think she was appalled to get a verbal invitation and not a handwritten note on Tiffany stationery. Good to have the old guard still around to keep us in our places, right?"

Serena almost made a joke about her mother being ready to pass judgment at the drop of a hat, but realized that might be premature. Finding a spot for Serena in the Sweeney family was one thing. Finding a spot for Birdie and Mitch Tucker might be a bridge too far.

"I have five minutes and I need to tell you something," Liza said to her sisters in the back office of Sweeney Jones. The gallery doors were set to open in about a half hour, but the mood at the gallery was calm, like the staff had been through this drill dozens of time. Emily, Liza's longtime assistant gallery manager, and Jenny, her Sunday salesperson and social media whiz, were both in black and moving about the space, seeing to last-minute details. After a brief thunderstorm, the evening sun was streaming through the clouds and the humidity was at what Liza called "Optimum Balmy" in terms of going out at night without a sweater. There would be a good crowd, Liza was sure. Tricia and Maggie had arrived separately, but on time, a family trait, and they were ready to do their part to make the night a success.

Liza looked lovely in a slinky black dress, strappy sandals, and a fresh blowout. She was confident about the show, but that wasn't what she needed to talk to her sisters about. "Whit and I are separated. It happened a few weeks ago and I didn't tell you because we agreed not to say anything to anyone over the summer. We wanted to be sure where we were headed. But, apparently, he doesn't view it as a trial separation. It's come to my attention that other people in town know, so you might hear someone say something tonight. I didn't want you to be blindsided. I'm sorry I didn't say anything, but I couldn't deal . . ." Her voice trailed off, thick with emotion.

"You don't have to be sorry. We're sorry, Liza," Maggie said. She was dying to blurt out that she'd known something was up and that she'd spotted Liza and Gray making out, which she felt better about now that she knew Whit and Liza were separated, but still not entirely happy about. But Maggie kept her mouth shut. She wanted to sell that painting tonight. "You're amazing to be standing here after everything that's happened in the last month."

"Do you need anything from us tonight?" Tricia asked, although she had about eight million other questions, especially about whether Liza had signed a prenup or contacted a lawyer.

"Do me a favor—don't say anything unkind about Whit to anyone. Not tonight, not ever. Let's rise above this for the twins' sake. And don't say anything to his parents, if they are here. I don't know if they even know. Everything will reflect back on Vivi and Fitz, so acknowledge the truth but move on. Got it?"

Both sisters nodded, but Tricia was struggling with the timeline and with Whit. "I don't understand. How could he tell you one thing and tell everybody else another?"

"I don't know. Whit is done with me, apparently."

"What a bastard." The old Maggie was back. "You've always been too good for him. Too pretty, too smart. Much more fun than him. Much more. You totally improved that Jones family gene pool. I mean, Fitz and Vivi are gorgeous because of you, not chinless Whit."

Tricia tried to silence Maggie. "Okay, no more rosé for you."

"It's true," Maggie said, holding on to her glass.

"But it's exactly what she doesn't want us to say."

Liza agreed. "I need to get through this and then I can give you the full story later, but not tonight. Maggie, this night should be about you and your beautiful piece. And the fact that we're all here together." Again, Liza choked up. "You know, Dad rarely came to these openings because, as he said, I don't serve real booze. But I think it was actually in deference to me. He wanted me to have my own moment. He knew he was a distraction. Maggie, I'm sure he would have been here for you tonight." All three sisters had tears in their eyes.

"Oh, sisters!" Maggie joked after they collected themselves. "Group hug?"

"It's too sticky to touch," Tricia said, fending off Maggie who was coming in, arms outstretched.

"Let's never change," Liza said. "Mags, are you ready to be the star? I think you're going to sell that painting tonight. Did you see the price I put on it?"

"No!"

"Go look."

Maggie dashed out of the office, leaving Liza and Tricia. Now that Maggie was gone, the two sensible sisters could go a little deeper. The oldest and the youngest sisters connected in a different way when the middle sister wasn't around to hijack the conversation. Tricia waited a beat, then asked, "I have one question. Did you call a divorce attorney yet?"

"Yes." Liza was no fool. She had called the day after that dinner at the club with Whit, already feeling like she was too late. Sometimes, it was good to live in the same small town forever because she knew exactly who to call, an old school friend, Michelle Esposito. Michelle was a partner in a family law firm in Stamford now. Liza was always a little scared of Michelle growing up. She had four brothers and the mouth to prove it. "Michelle Esposito. Remember her? She was that tough girl on my softball team in seventh grade, that one year I played? The one who cussed at the ref and got thrown out for hurling her bat at the opposing pitcher? I hired her. She's mean, in a good way."

"Perfect attribute for a divorce lawyer," Tricia replied. "And is that why you invited Connor and David for the month? So you wouldn't be lonely?"

"No, so I wouldn't be weak and send pathetic texts to Whit."

"Or Gray? I noticed him noticing you last night."

"Yeah, longer story there. Do me a favor, if he's here tonight, keep him away from me. He makes me do stupid things."

"Will do. And I should tell you this, I apologized to Serena. I think she'll show tonight, but I can't guarantee it. Her mother arrived last night and I guess they had a tough conversation."

"I can't imagine." Liza shook her head as if she were really trying to picture the scene in her head. "I can't stop thinking about what we would have said to Dad about all of this, if he hadn't died. I get furious thinking about it."

"Me, too. I do a lot of yelling at him on my runs. I call him selfish, indulgent, accuse him of hubris in the highest degree. Then I feel terrible for Serena that he didn't want to see her. What a coward."

"I hate to think of him that way. Honestly, I don't want to read the book," Liza confessed.

"Then don't. You've already done so much for him, for us. I'm reading it so you and Maggie don't have to."

"Thank you."

In that moment, Liza looked more vulnerable than Tricia had ever seen her big sister, so she switched the topic to something they could rally around. "You don't think we have to be nice to Birdie Tucker, do you? I mean, she's not family, right?"

"Oh, no. She's not family. We don't have to be nice to her." The sisters were united on this. Their definition of family would extend only so far.

"Good. One more thing. I was forced to have a conversation with Lucy Winthrop today and I should tell you that she knows about you and Whit."

Liza's head jerked up. "What did she say?"

"Something about you being an asset to the community and Whit was a fool."

"Well, if that's the best sentiment I can get out of this mess, I'll take it. But seriously, how did she know?"

"I don't know." But the Sweeney sisters knew: it was a small town with long tentacles. Not only did everybody know everybody, everybody knew everybody's prep school roommates, college friends, or summer camp bunkmates. Everybody knew everybody's debutante escorts, bridesmaids, and birth class pals. They all shared a common acquaintance from some study abroad program in high school or law school class. Amongst a certain stratum in Connecticut, the six degrees of separation was reduced to two: you and the nearest person in boat shoes.

"I can deal with that later. Now, I have to deal with this," Liza said, pointing out into the gallery, convincing herself more than anyone. "Did Maggie buy Tim all new clothes for tonight? He actually has on pants."

"She did. FYI, she put it on your credit card."

THE GALLERY SPARKLED and buzzed. The sparkle came from the gleaming faces of the patrons, in full summer regalia with freshly showered skin after their day on the beach or the golf course, renewed tans and pink attire on the men with their whale-embroidered khaki shorts and the women in their sensible sheath dresses. Sweeney Jones had attracted the locals and their weekend guests en route to dinner. The locals were eager to show off the sophistication of their little village and the visitors were charmed by the art, which was, in the words of one Manhattanite, "Not terrible. Really pretty good."

The buzz came from Bill Sweeney, as it often did. Even though he was gone, his name was on every art lover's lips. *You know, the owner is the daughter of William Sweeney. The neighbors told me Bill Sweeney's wake went on till all hours. Such pretty girls; they must miss their father. The artist who painted* Panes of Gold *is Mary Magdalene Sweeney; she dedicated the piece to her father.*

Liza was pleased at the size of the crowd, but even more pleased about the genuine collectors who had shown up on a holiday weekend to see the collection of Kat Ryan's sunflowers that she had featured on the postcard. There were already three red dots next to Kat's vibrant oils in the first half hour. Kat was beaming and she was a wonderful salesperson of her own work. When you met Kat, not only did you want to buy her painting, you wanted to be her best friend. She talked about her work in an earthy, pragmatic way that even neophytes could appreciate. Connor and David had been entranced by the work and the artist and were the first to buy, then the red dots accumulated. Liza loved getting her gut instinct validated. There may be other gallery owners with better credentials, but not better instincts.

Other artists in the show were present as well. Vincent Williams from Chatham on the Cape had three abstracts in the show, heavily influenced by warm shades and organic lines, lovely paintings for the risk averse. His work was very strong and so was his jawline. He wore a blue linen shirt and black jeans to every event and women never failed to notice that his eyes matched his shirt.

Maxie Chow, a Brooklyn artist whom Liza had stumbled upon at a street fair in Red Hook one Sunday when she and Vivi were having a girls' weekend in the city, stood next to her lithographs in neon-orange overalls and a black bra, inspiring more than a few furtive glances from the men in the gallery. Maxie's work was firmly rooted in Pop Art, but the half dozen pieces that Liza had shown previously sold quickly to more adventurous collectors. Her saturated portraits of animals with still life elements brought an urban energy to the gallery. As Maxie explained to Liza, "Imagine if Warhol had liked dogs and rabbits and guinea pigs as much as he liked Marilyn Monroe." Though the subject matter was quotidian, Maxie was a skilled printmaker and Liza knew she would be big someday.

But the star of the night was Maggie's piece, *Panes of Gold*. All night long, there was a steady murmur around the painting. The locals responded because it was an unexpected, ethereal view of Southport Harbor, a familiar subject usually painted in crisp tones of red, white, and blue, but not in Maggie's version. The collectors responded because William Sweeney's daughter, in the weeks after his death, had created a painting that seemed to shimmer on the wall. Maggie, in a long green dress and an oversized silver sunflower necklace, never moved more than five feet from the painting all night.

"My father once told me to use my pain and make my work sing and that's exactly what I did," Liza overheard Maggie telling her story to an attractive couple from Tribeca who started the interior design firm Meeks & Beauregard, named after their corgis. (Liza could never remember the actual names of the men when they wandered into the gallery, so she thought of the short one as Meeks and the tall one as Beauregard.) She watched Meeks snap several photos and send them off, presumably to a client who was in the Hamptons or Watch Hill or Kennebunkport for the holiday. That's when she knew she had priced the work right. Expensive enough to get extra attention, but modest enough to get sold. The price tag was a big leap up for Maggie. *I hope she can keep producing,* Liza thought, *and doesn't do another disappearing act.*

That's when Liza heard Beauregard ask the million-dollar question of Maggie, "Are you working on anything else? We'd love to come by your studio."

"I have a million ideas. Let's set up a time for a studio tour." Sometimes, it was an asset that Maggie could lie like a champion.

TRICIA WAVED CAP over. He was good to put up with a Sweeney event two nights in a row. Tall and trim in his white button-down and Nantucket reds, Cap made his way through the crowd, speaking to several familiar faces briefly before reaching Tricia. "Hello, my dear."

"I didn't expect to see you tonight. I thought last night's chaos would be enough for one weekend." The two kissed cheeks.

"Only here for ten minutes. I wanted to see Maggie's painting. It's something."

"Yes, if only she could sustain the effort."

"She'll find her way," Cap said for the hundredth time about Maggie. "Did you have a chance to read any of the memoir?"

"Through Chapter Four, then I had to take a break after that bombshell. You?"

"I scanned the whole thing."

"Did you know about Birdie?"

"I didn't know that much about Birdie," Cap said. "There's a lot more to come in the book, Tricia. A warning."

His grave tone surprised her. He wasn't prone to drama. "I don't think Liza and Maggie are even going to crack it open."

"Good," Cap said. "That's wise. At least for now."

"I'll finish it by Monday when we meet."

The two lawyers understood each other. The task was no longer personal, it was business. A similar thought occurred to Tricia about the Liza situation. "You should know, Liza and Whit are separated. Liza thought it was temporary, a trial separation, but it appears Whit has made some moves to indicate that it's permanent."

"Oh, dear. I'm not surprised. Whit seemed to tolerate your father, but that was a wedge, for sure. The timing is cruel. That seems beneath him. His mother will be appalled. She's very fond of Liza; I'd say fonder of her than him. Lolly Jones will not be happy with her son. Liza has a lawyer?"

"Michelle Esposito."

"She's good." Cap looked across the crowd to where Liza stood, speaking animatedly to a couple interested in the Vincent Williams abstracts. Liza's warmth reminded Cap of Maeve. He wished the girls had gotten to know their mother better, the Maeve before the cancer and the long slow march of treatment and pain. The Maeve who could stand in the corner of one of Bill Sweeney's book events and draw the crowd to her even though Bill had the bigger personality. "I'll reach out to Liza next week and connect with Michelle Esposito if she needs me to. There may be questions about your father's estate that she needs answered. I enjoyed getting to talk to Raj last night. He seems like a fine young man."

"Yes, he is." Raj had positioned himself as Tim's barback, restocking the wine and the beer while Tim poured for the thirsty crowd intent on shaking off their Fourth of July overindulgence with more indulgence. Cap and Tricia stood quietly, taking in the scene. Both knew there would be a letdown for Maggie and Liza, the end of a period of intense emotions and effort that started with their father's death and ended tonight. Tricia had a sudden thought. "I'm glad I took the summer off. I don't know if I can go back."

Cap was about to respond when a familiar voice interrupted, "There they are! The brain trust, huddled in the corner as usual."

It was Lois Hopper, William Sweeney's agent. She was wearing her signature black hat. She was the last person either one wanted to see at that moment. With Tricia's approval, Cap had hired a forensic accountant to dig into whether Lois had been skimming off the top of the royalties. They'd get an answer soon, but neither wanted to tip off Lois that they were investigating her accounting. Her presence here was alarming.

"Kisses, kisses," Lois said, waving her hands in the general direction of Cap and Tricia. She wasn't getting anywhere near their faces. "So . . . how is it?" she asked. She could only be referring to the memoir.

Tricia and Cap played dumb while mentally going through the exercise of who could have been the leaker. Tricia guessed an accidental leak from Nina or Devon who told someone at Yale who told someone in publishing in New York who knew someone spending the weekend at Lois's house in Westport. Cap assumed it was David or Connor who texted a friend in Montauk after one last glass of late-night wine who mentioned it on the beach the next day to a former editor at Allegory whose niece was an intern in Lois's agency. Either way, she knew something was up.

"The show is great, isn't it? What a surprise to see you here. I don't think of you as a visual arts connoisseur, Lois." Tricia remained unruffled and Cap remained silent.

"Not the show, dolly, the book! My sources tell me you have the memoir in hand. That's great news for all of us," Lois said, as if it was a given they were all on the same team, despite her threatening emails and terse voicemails over the last month. "The situation was starting to get very tense with Allegory."

The situation in the gallery was starting to get tense for Tricia. Of all the characters who hung around Willow Lane as detritus of William Sweeney Inc., Lois Hopper stood out to Tricia as the least genuine, the most in it for the money and not for love of the written word. Maybe it was the stupid hat. Or maybe she did have a secret life, like Maggie suggested. "Oh, I wouldn't say we found the memoir. That's a stretch. We found some pages that we're taking a look at. We'll let you know next week if there's anything there. They could simply be nonsense, an aborted effort. You know how my father wrote, Lois, tossing out thousands of words before settling in on a final draft. That may be the case here."

"We have a William Sweeney scholar from Yale evaluating the material. Raj Chaudhry. Very bright guy," Cap added, playing off Tricia expertly. Tricia looked up at that moment to see Raj mingling amongst the crowd refilling glasses of Chablis and chatting with her Aunt Frannie.

Lois was not appeased. "I have stuck my neck out time and time again for your father. Now that he's gone, I'm not inclined to get my head chopped off. William Sweeney would have faded into obscurity without me. I made him relevant again. I have a reputation to protect. I hope you both understand me. Whatever those pages are, whatever that guy from Yale says, we need to turn something in to Allegory by the end of the month or they will file suit. Then they'll want to see all your father's papers, everything, so unless those pages are grocery lists, I suggest you release them to the publisher without these lousy stall tactics."

Tricia took a deep breath. She had been right all along about Lois being insincere, not a genuine believer. The meal ticket was dead and she was done. That gave Tricia immense satisfaction and courage. "Thank you for letting us know where you stand, Lois. Tonight is my sisters' night and we're done talking to you about my late father's legacy. Rest assured, by the end of the month, this will all be settled. Believe me, you won't be required to stick your neck out any longer for one of the great writers of his generation. You can go back to repping celebrity cookbooks and all those exercise guides from reality TV stars. Now, if you'll excuse, my aunt is here. I'm going to say hello."

Tricia walked away thinking, *I can be mean in a good way, too.*

Cap bowed, signaling the end of the conversation. "Good night, Lois. We'll be in touch."

MAGGIE CAUGHT HER breath when she saw Serena and Gray come through the door together. *Oh my God, this is getting complicated.* But then she spotted Lucy Winthrop attempting a grand entrance behind Serena, pausing in the doorway, raising her chin and giving a little wave as if she were walking the step-and-repeat at a gala. No one noticed Lucy's entrance but Maggie, much to Lucy's chagrin, who looked right through Maggie and covered her embarrassment with some manufactured waves to imaginary friends in the back of the room. *Please don't let me become like that in my old age,* thought Maggie.

Maggie motioned to Serena, who worked her way through the thinning crowd, Gray by her side. She was still suspicious of the two of them together, but she tried to let it go and gave Serena a quick hug. "I'm so glad you're here."

"Me, too. What a crowd. Oh, Maggie. It looks amazing now that it's completed. Really lovely."

"It's special, Mags." Gray gave her a warm embrace, a warm brotherly embrace. Maggie knew right then that last night with Liza was real and whatever happened with her was not. "I'm going to take partial credit."

"Why would you take partial credit, Gray dear?" Lucy Winthrop joined the circle, focusing her attention on Gray and ignoring Maggie again. "Oh, look, it's the Dumbarton place." Lucy moved in for a closer look and to inspect Maggie's technique. Even she had to admit, the painting was evocative.

"Yes, you recognize it. Maggie captured the view from my parents' house at sunset, Mrs. Winthrop," Gray explained just as Liza arrived in the vicinity. She'd come to welcome Serena and hadn't noticed Gray standing there. Now she was trapped.

"Of course. Your parents hosted so many gathering for Deke, I recognized it right away. It's what you see from your porch looking across the harbor to the houses on Sasco Hill. *Panes of Gold.* Yes, you captured it," Lucy Winthrop said, reading the information and then looking Maggie up and down, not sure what to make of her tangle of hair and necklaces. "Hello, Liza dear. What a charming little event."

"Thank you. It's an honor for you to make time for Sweeney Jones." Liza nodded to her guest, who clearly felt she was distinguished. Then she looked at Maggie for confirmation. "I thought you said this was the view from Perry Park?"

"Close to that." Maggie tried to brush it off. "Look, Serena's here."

"Yes, I see." Liza reached out and gave her hand a squeeze, but stayed on task. "The Cunningham house isn't close to Perry Park. It's a half mile down Harbor Road."

"Well . . ." Maggie said, as a way of explaining nothing. She was always at her worst when she was backed into a corner; lashing out was her exit strategy. "It's a harbor view. Why does it matter exactly which vantage point? I was having dinner at Gray's and the sun was setting and the windows lit up like panes of gold. And I painted it."

"I see. Good to have the full story," Liza responded coolly, looking from Maggie to Gray and back to Maggie again. "Maybe the two of you can split the payday. Meeks & Beauregard bought the painting for a client. *Panes of Gold* will find a happy home in East Hampton. The new owners said they'd love to have you out to the house for the installation. Congratulations, Maggie." There was little joy in Liza's voice. "I'll break out the champagne. Excuse me."

Gray followed Liza, leaving Serena and Lucy to wonder what they had witnessed, although they had a pretty solid idea. Lucy, back on top of her game, remarked, "There's nothing like a sister to really make you feel special."

"WHAT IS WRONG with you? You come back to town and it's not enough to romance one Sweeney sister, you have to go for the majority of Sweeney sisters?" Gray had followed Liza into her office to explain. There was no escaping the hum of the party, but at least no one could see Liza's face. She was struggling to pull this whole charade off: the dead father, the missing husband, the random sister. She could not handle one more complication. "Please leave me alone."

"Nothing serious happened between me and Maggie. A kiss or two."

"Oh, a kiss or two? That's not nothing to me." Liza leaned back against her desk, crossing her arms. She wanted to seem as unreceptive as possible.

"There was a moment when I thought something might happen between Maggie and me. I felt conflicted, so I asked her to leave. She's the one who suggested you might be interested in my bowls. She's why I came in here that night. Then you and I had a conversation and I knew it wasn't Maggie I was interested in. It's you, Liza."

"Then why would she lie to me about the painting?"

Gray shrugged. "You know Maggie better than I do."

It was true. She did know Maggie. And, if Liza was honest with herself, she would admit that what Maggie and Gray did was none of her business. They were single, she was the married one. She was the one with obligations. "Gray, I need a lot of space right now. Like years of space. There's nothing between us except some sexual residue. I can't act on that now or ever. I have too much going on in my life."

"I get it. But I wish it wasn't true. I thought with Whit gone, I might have a chance."

"And that's why you came to the Fourth of July party? For me and not for Maggie?"

"Yes, for you," Gray said, moving closer to Liza. Liza froze, unsure of whether to close the gap between the two of them or turn away. She couldn't get the way she felt with him last night out of her head. She wanted more of that in her life. She took a step.

There was a knock on the door. It was Tricia who popped her head in, like Liza had asked her to do. "Hey, Liza, you're needed out here."

Gray understood, nodded at Liza, and walked past Tricia. "Don't worry. I'm leaving."

"You okay?" Tricia asked.

"Give me five. Thanks for the backup."

"I wasn't lying. You are needed. Your in-laws are here."

LOLLY JONES STOOD straight and tall, in a beautiful Escada silk tunic and white pants, an ensemble that Liza had seen her mother-in-law wear at many events over the years, as she was a believer in the Spending Money on Statement Pieces school of dressing. It always looked lovely on her. She was reaching out to Maggie, one hand on her sister's arm, clearly expressing admiration for her painting. Whitney Jones Sr. stood holding two glasses of wine, waiting patiently to give one to his wife. As Liza made her way through the crowd, Lolly looked up and smiled at her, then lowered her chin and shook her head slowly. She had heard, through the grapevine or from her son himself. In a way, Liza was relieved.

But there would be nothing negative tonight. "It's a triumph!

You've done it again!" Lolly said, switching back to party mode and giving Liza a quick hug. "Isn't that right, Whit?"

Her husband, always good at taking direction from his wife of forty-two years, lifted up both cups of wine in an awkward toast and said, "Brava to you both." He once went to see *Tosca* at the Met and liked to prove it by tossing Italian phrases into his conversation.

Maggie used the moment to make her excuses without making eye contact with Liza, directing all her energy at Lolly. "I think I see an interested buyer I have to charm. Excuse me, all. See you soon, I hope!" She headed off to the bar, leaving Liza alone with her in-laws.

It was Lolly, of course, who stepped into the void and said what needed to be said. "You've done a wonderful job with this gallery and with Fitz and Vivi. You've made us very proud. Work, children, family—you'll have that as a foundation so you can move forward. We know you'll be fine." Unlike so many of Liza's friends whose mothers-in-law aimed their arrows of disapproval at them, with stinging comments about the nanny raising their grandchildren, Lolly had always been supportive of Liza's work. On several occasions when stopping by to chat with Liza at the gallery, she'd expressed her own regrets that she'd not had the opportunity for a career. Now, in the middle of a crowded room, Lolly was making it clear that she would remain a loyal Liza supporter and that this gallery may be her salvation.

"Thank you."

Just then the event photographer swung by and asked to take their picture for the paper. Liza hesitated but Lolly agreed and instructed Whit to keep the wine glasses down out of the picture, so his clients didn't think he had a drinking problem. They all smiled for the camera and the photographer got what she came for. Liza knew when all of Southport saw the photo, they'd know whose side Lolly was on . . . which was exactly what Lolly intended.

"Let's have lunch soon and we'll really talk. Now, Whitney, what do you think about that painting over there? It's a Kat Ryan. I'm thinking of replacing those tired nineteenth-century prints of sail-boats in the front hall with something punchier, more fun. That piece is front hall material, isn't it, Liza?"

"Brilliant, bold. For sure, front hall material."

BY NINE O'CLOCK, the last patrons had filtered out of Sweeney Jones. The wine was gone and the door was locked. Only a handful of people—Tricia, Raj, Connor, David, Tim, Maggie, Kat, and Serena—remained to clean up, rehash, and wait for Liza to bring out the champagne from the back. Serena had been set to leave earlier, but Liza insisted she stay and celebrate at the afterparty. "You were a part of this," Liza told her, squeezing her arm. "Thank you." Serena busied herself like the others, feeling grateful to be included.

Emily, in charge of sales for the evening, was running the final numbers at the desk. "Fantastic night, Liza. Congratulations, Kat and Maggie. This was our biggest summer show ever."

"Don't forget the commissions, too!" Jenny added, tapping away on her tablet, posting the party pictures on social media.

Tricia, who hadn't eaten all night, positioned herself next to the remains of the oversized cheese board, once abundant with cheeses, meats, fruit, and nuts and now a sad skeleton of the dried apricots no one ever ate and the intimidating blue-veined cheese. She ate the crackers and the decorative grapes that had collected around the edges and thought about the encounter with Lois. Regardless of what the forensic accountant discovered, she and Cap had agreed that Lois had to go. She watched Serena move around the room, comfortable in the company of family and friends, and that gave Tricia a sense of purpose. She was formulating a plan.

"Cheers," David said, emerging from the back with a couple of bottles of champagne. Connor followed with clean glasses. Raj found some folding chairs and arranged them in the front window of the gallery. One by one, the exhausted team took a seat, chattering about what a night it had been, how great all the work looked on the walls, all except Liza, who scurried around the gallery, clearing the last of the wine glasses and cocktail napkins.

Maggie knew Liza was working out her anger with the frantic cleaning. Liza had always used housework as therapy, mopping the floors or folding laundry with vitriol whenever she got punished for something that Maggie had initiated. Staying out past curfew or skipping school to take the train into the city—when the punishment went down, Liza got to cleaning. Twenty years later, she was still doing it.

Serena watched her for a minute, then whispered to Maggie, "What's the deal with Liza?"

Maggie whispered back, "Cleaning as coping. She's mad at me and at Gray, so she's taking it out on those used cocktail napkins."

"Liza, honey, come sit. We'll get all that mess in a bit. You must be exhausted. Have some champers and we'll fix you a charcuterie plate, but sit down," Connor insisted, trying his best to usher Liza to a chair. "I stashed some prosciutto in the office so we'd have some to share now. I didn't want those freeloaders eating it all."

For a second, Liza protested, then to everyone's shock, she dropped the wineglass in her hands, shards of glass flying across the hardwood floors. Then she started sobbing, choking out the words, "I can't do this anymore."

"Don't move!" Tricia warned, while dashing into the office to grab a broom to sweep up the shattered glass.

Liza froze in place, her head in her hands. "I'm so sorry. I'm so sorry," she said over and over like she was trying to self-soothe. Tricia swept up the glass around her while Serena moved in to comfort her, stepping over the shards to get to Liza. She was inconsolable. "I'm so tired, so *fucking* tired of holding it all together while the men in my life do exactly what they want. Dad. Whit. Gray. Just once, I would like to do what I want." Liza collapsed in Serena's embrace. The two women stood together in the center of the studio, Liza crying softly and Serena assuring her, "You have nothing to be sorry about. It's okay."

The men gathered around the bar, desperate to find something to do so they didn't have to stare at Liza and Serena. They started putting away the chairs in the front of the gallery. Liza noticed them and immediately felt awful. "Oh, not you. You're not the men I'm talking about. The other men in my life."

Tricia finished sweeping the glass carefully while Serena walked Liza back to her office so she could have some privacy in her pain. Maggie stood in the background and watched the scene unfold, like it was a play and she was an audience member.

"WHAT THE HELL happened?" Later, in the kitchen on Willow Lane, Tricia grilled Maggie after taking Bear for a walk. She had to clear her head after the opening and walking Bear, who was clearly lonely and confused, was her best option. Poor dog. She ran into Maggie in the kitchen, making herself a cup of tea. "What went on between you and Liza?"

"What do you mean?" Maggie responded, resorting to evasion, as if Tricia were going to fall for that.

"Mags."

"I told her that my painting was a view from Perry Park when it was actually from Gray's front porch," Maggie spit out as if she were the put-upon party.

"Oh."

"Nothing happened between me and Gray. It was dinner. At sunset. I swear, nothing happened. I mean, I totally would have let something happen, but it didn't."

"Why would you do that?"

"Because he's cute and I've had a crush on him since I was nineteen."

"Do you understand why she was mad?"

"Not really. I think she needs some meds. Maybe some Xanax."

"She's lost her father and her marriage in the last six weeks. She is being forced to sell her family home, find a divorce lawyer, and maintain her business because she's going to need that income stream. I think she needs understanding, not a diagnosis."

"She was making out with Gray last night."

"She was?" Tricia was shocked.

"Yes. I know everyone thinks Liza is perfect and I'm a mess. But . . . not true."

"But, generally true."

"Gray and I did make out a little bit on the night of Dad's wake."

"You can never tell Liza that. Ever."

"I know. Even I'm sorry for that. The whiskey."

"You know you should stay away from him, right?" Tricia used her nice voice so Maggie wouldn't shut down. "Please."

"I know. I will."

Chapter

23

In 1997, William Sweeney was named the Grand Marshal of the St. Patrick's Day Parade in New York City. He was thrilled at the prospect of walking up Fifth Avenue, with a grand orange, white, and green sash, one of a hundred thousand marchers in the parade but in his mind, the most important one. He relished the chance to celebrate his heritage and be cheered by the spectators who lined the streets for thirty-plus blocks. He insisted that Maeve and the girls march beside him, the four fiery redheads in their green wool coats as a testament to their Irishness. Maeve was reluctant; she didn't want the girls on display to the inebriated crowd, but she acquiesced to her husband's wishes as she often did and March 17, 1997, went down as one of the worst days in Sweeney family history.

The story of How Dad Abandoned Us at the St. Patrick's Day Parade and We Got Lost and Then Had to Take the Train Home and We All Cried and Mom Yelled became a family favorite. In the sisters' version, the parting of ways was accidental. The end of the parade was chaos and Bill Sweeney went one way, toward the bars on Second Avenue, and Maeve and the girls went the other way, toward the car that the parade organizers had promised would be waiting a few blocks away to take them back to Connecticut. The crowd closed in, separating the family and, in the primitive days before mass cell phone ownership, the mother and the father had no way to communicate with each other. The fact that there was no waiting town car became a laugh line in the storytelling with the girls describing the four of them cold, hungry, and exhausted standing on the corner of 80th and Fifth hoping for a miracle. Maeve had tried to use the phone in a coffee shop to call somebody, anybody, but without luck. The schlep back down to Grand Central was when Tricia, then seven, started to melt down and Maeve started to yell, an uncharacteristic reaction by their even-keeled mother. By the time the Sweeney girls jammed themselves on the standing-room-only train headed back to Southport, Maggie and Liza were crying from the stress of the day.

Maggie, who had insisted on wearing her new Ugg boots, complained that her feet hurt and her mother fired back, "I told you those were a terrible choice. What do you expect with no arch support?"

Liza, who previously could tune out almost any conflict, had recently started her period and was a hormonal mess. "Please stop crying," she kept saying between tears.

In the dinner table version, the Sweeney sisters practically crawled the mile home from the train station, no taxi in sight. Little Tricia, who slept on the floor of the train, caught a second wind and ran home ahead of her sisters, a precursor of athletic achievement to come. When the Sweeneys arrived at Willow Lane, cold and dark, Maeve slammed a box of cereal and a quart of milk on the kitchen table, saying, "Eat this!" and took to her bed. The denouement of the tale was that Bill Sweeney arrived home twenty-four hours later, no explanation, and Maeve made him sleep in the boathouse for a week.

Over the years, the girls told the story to Cap and Aunt Frannie and random dinner guests and new boyfriends and college roommates. When Maeve was alive, she would stay silent in the retelling and roll her eyes when Maggie got to the part about their father staying in the boathouse.

They always put a glossy veneer over a grim story until one day, Liza, then a wife and mother of four-year-old twins, said to her sisters while they were doing the dishes after a family dinner, "You know, it was pretty shitty of Dad not to make sure we got to that town car. I mean, he knew where we were supposed to meet the car and he never showed up. I know the car didn't show up, either, but he could have gotten us a cab to Grand Central at least if he wanted to stay and drink. Whit would never abandon me and the twins like that. Tricia was so little."

The sisters must have known that to be true the many times they'd entertained with the parade story. After Liza's comments, they stopped joking about the St. Patrick's Day Parade. But it wasn't until Tricia read the final chapter of her father's memoir, the chapter titled What I Got Wrong, that she truly understood what Liza really meant. The St. Patrick's Day Parade story was one extended metaphor about what William Sweeney got wrong. In his own summation, he got fatherhood totally wrong.

"Did he hate us?"

"Of course not."

"Well, it sounds like he hated us," Tricia said to Cap in his office Monday morning. She had finished the memoir the previous night, promptly thrown up, fallen asleep curled up in the fetal position next to Raj around three a.m., gone for a run at dawn, and was now trying to make sense of what she'd read. Cap had been right. When he said there was difficult material at the end of the book, Tricia had assumed it was about her father, not about her and her sisters. Even Maeve got one last devastating swipe from the grave. Reading it, she felt like she'd gotten hit by a truck. "He definitely uses us in the book."

"I understand it's hard for you not to take this material personally, but remember, your father was a writer. He sought meaning in the banal. He's heaping a lot of importance onto this one day and using it as an extended metaphor for his shortcomings. It's a literary device."

"Yes, I went to Yale, too. I understand literary devices," Tricia said, unusually snippy with Cap. "I'm sorry. That was childish. But the attacks get very personal. I'm too focused, too ambitious. I won't color outside the lines and I run to run away from my problems. Damn straight, because the house was so depressing after Mom died, I ran as fast as I could away from the place and I'm still running. I'm not going to apologize for using a coping mechanism to gain control over my life."

"I know . . ."

"And Liza, who literally married a guy she wasn't all that crazy about to please her parents, is going to love being called a slut in high school and repressed as an adult. Thanks, Dad."

"It's not that stark, but, yes, your father was uncomfortable with Liza's burgeoning sexuality and he admits that. A double standard for sure, but relatable for many fathers. Although he was not too complimentary about her marriage choice."

"Maggie can never read this. He flat-out calls her untalented."

"He blames himself for not cultivating her talent in a broader fashion, going too easy on her discipline-wise, so that she never fully developed her craft. He believed she was gifted, but he also believed she did not work to her highest potential."

"At least he didn't mention her overdose in college. That would have been unforgivable."

"I was relieved about that, too."

"I like that he identifies all our issues but then fans himself with a mea culpa to let himself off the hook."

"He writes, let me see here . . ." Cap searched for the passage. "'I wasn't generous enough to be a good father. I couldn't put anything ahead of the work. I take all the blame.'"

"Really, Cap? The work? That was the problem? How about the drink? The women? His giant ego? He found a convenient and time-honored excuse."

"I warned you it was harsh."

"I think about everything I've been through, like my mother's death, my father's depression, my miscarriage two years ago . . ."

"Oh, my dear, I'm so sorry."

"Thank you. It's not something I've told a lot of people about—you're the third and Raj is the second. I'm saying that the tough stuff we've all been through was not caused by our father nor were we rescued by our father. He takes this bizarre credit for our downfalls but gives us no accolades for our resilience."

"I can see your point about a lack of self-awareness," Cap said, loyal to his old friend but torn by what he had read, too.

"And dangling the fact that he has another daughter out there, but doesn't name her or explain the circumstances of her birth, I mean, come on, you have to be disappointed in that, Cap."

Cap shook his head. "As a lawyer, I'm relieved he didn't name Serena. She may not want that. It could have been the basis of a lawsuit."

"Here's the thing, unless you're me, Liza, Maggie, or the mystery sister, this is going to look like a brave statement on male inadequacy. That's what Raj said, and I think he's right. William Sweeney opening up and admitting his failure as a father and the consequences to his daughters of his inability to connect with them on a meaningful level because he was too focused on great literature. A cautionary tale sort of, because no one will ever believe that William Sweeney, the man who wrote *My Maeve* and created Elspeth, didn't worship women. No wonder he wanted to be dead when this came out."

"Take a breath. Do you need water, coffee?" Tricia nodded. Cap called out to his assistant, "Rose, can you bring us a carafe of coffee and some water, please."

"The only one who comes out looking good is Julia. At least he gives her credit for imparting some wisdom and humanity to us, saving us from ourselves. Again, a little pat on the back to himself for hiring Julia in our darkest hour." Tricia didn't need more stimulants but she accepted the coffee with milk that Rose prepared. Rose looked at Tricia with understanding eyes as she handed her the cup and saucer.

When Rose left the room, Tricia moaned, "Oh my God. That's the look we're all going to get for the rest of our lives once this book comes out. The look Rose just gave me with the sad eyes and the 'poor you' face. 'Oh, those Sweeney sisters. They're all a mess.' I won't be able to take that, Cap. I know I have issues. But I own them. That one day in New York in a green wool coat being dragged up Fifth Avenue, then down Madison Avenue didn't determine the rest of my life."

"We could always delete the last chapter. No one knows."

"Except the tech at Copy World where Maggie took the thumb drive. I have no doubt Maggie blurted out the truth about what she was copying as she stood there. Somewhere out there is a file with the complete manuscript. It will all come out at publication and then we'll look like spoiled women who couldn't face the truth when it emerges."

Cap had to agree.

"The real tragedy here is that Liza, Maggie, and I were fine with who he was. Sure, we knew he was no picnic, but our mother taught us to give him a wide berth. I thought we'd had fun together. We'd sail. We'd listen to the Yankees games on the radio down at the dock. He'd show up at my cross-country meets at Yale, wearing his floppy tennis hat. Why would he do this, Cap? You knew him as a person. I guess we really didn't."

"Your father was a complicated man. He had his own complicated childhood and he was always looking for answers to questions. I have to guess that Serena's appearance had something to do with this essay, one last meditation on fatherhood, a subject he really didn't write too much about. He struggled with the truth on this one."

"You know, even I'm starting to think William Sweeney wasn't a very good father. And he was a terrible, terrible husband. What he did to Mom, to her work. How could he do that?"

"I was horrified as well. I had no idea. I thought he respected your mother's work, even if he didn't exactly show it. He could have been so much more helpful to her. Instead, she was more helpful to him, managing his life so he could write."

"But to burn her poems after her death because she was more talented? Out of spite? Couldn't he have saved them for us, even if he didn't get them published? It's killing me."

"It was a tremendous disappointment to read that in the book."

"I don't know how I'm going to tell Liza. How do you explain away behavior like that?"

"Like I said, he was a complicated man."

"Complicated? Or selfish? Because he always seemed to do right by William Sweeney."

WHAT AN ASSHOLE, Serena thought as she flipped over the last page of William Sweeney's memoir and sat back on the couch with her cup of tea to absorb what she had read. *Brilliant, but an asshole.* She was not surprised that she was mentioned, in so much as one could count "a daughter born outside of marriage" as a mention, but she was surprised it was a single line of prose without any exposition. Reading the chapter made her think of the conversation she'd had with her father, the man who raised her, Mitch Tucker. It was short without a lot of exposition, too.

"So, I know what happened. Mom told me."

"She told me, too. Serena, it changes nothing for me."

"Me, either."

"Being your father is a . . . a great privilege. It didn't seem like we would ever have children. And then we had you. It doesn't matter to me how that happened."

"Really? It doesn't matter?"

"Not in the way you think. And not now after all these years. I sold insurance for a long time. I know everyone thinks that's a deadly boring career, but it meant I could see inside people's lives. And I have to tell you, some of those lives were pretty complicated, if I interpreted those surprise beneficiaries correctly. I also watched a lot of fine families get torn up over claims and money and valuables. I don't want that to happen to us."

"Me, either."

"You're my daughter. Nothing will change that. And Birdie is my wife. For better or worse, right?" Her father's dry sense of humor came through over the phone.

"That's one way to think about it."

"Come see us soon."

"I will."

And that was it. Mitch Tucker, acknowledging that without Bill Sweeney, he would have no daughter, so he was letting the circumstances of her conception go. It was generous, the sort of generosity that William Sweeney acknowledged he didn't possess.

Serena felt like she got off lucky in the book. She felt like the momentum of the memoir was building toward some sort of confessional and she had guessed what it might be when she saw the chapter title, What I Got Wrong. First, the bombshell about Maeve's poems. Then, the dismissal of his own daughters. She didn't anticipate that Liza, Maggie, and Tricia would be collateral damage.

As a writer, Serena found it unnecessary to drag innocent bystanders down into one's truth.

As a sister, Serena wanted a chance to correct the record.

She thought about the conversation with Tricia the other day, before the gallery opened. About the coverage the sisters gave each other. Even in moments that tested their family bonds, they let the hurt slide. An idea hit Serena, as she sat there drinking her tea, reflecting on the memoir and planning her next steps. She realized she could provide coverage, too.

Chapter

24

Willow Lane was nearly cleared out a week after the gallery opening. Most of the boxes had been distributed either to Goodwill, the Pequot, or the Yale Library. Maggie and Tim managed the last details of the main house. Tim, as it turned out, could really pack a moving box. He had no sentimental attachment to anything in the house, except the signed Aerosmith poster, a relic of some charity auction. Tim thought it was "awesome," so Maggie promised it to him and he worked efficiently to earn it.

Tim was growing on Maggie. The one-night tri-tip grilling gig had morphed into ten days of Tim and she wasn't sick of him yet. He was the opposite of Gray, uncomplicated and open and that suited her. Plus, he wasn't hung up on her sister, so that was a major bonus. She was sure that if not for Tim, she might have crashed after the opening, exhilarated from the sale and guilty from her deception. But his energy, his insistence that they walk to the beach every day for a half hour of vitamin D, his willingness to join in on her sun salutations on the dock, and his nonstop singing of anything by Chris Stapleton kept her on track. Every time she asked him a question, he responded by singing the chorus to "Fire Away," completely misinterpreting the song. Plus, he really liked her cat.

Tricia and Raj took control of the boathouse, watching the official van from Yale haul the years of work away under Raj's watchful eye. The school took William Sweeney's desk and chair, too. "Apparently, donations have come in in his name, so the school will rename a reading room in the library after him," said Raj. Tricia suspected that Cap had rallied the class of '68 to pledge the gift. It would please her to see the room during the campus memorial in the fall. Raj was back in New Haven for a few days to oversee the acquisition.

Tricia had thought she would feel deflated, almost like watching a burial rite, as her father's papers were carried away, but none of the sadness came. After the last few weeks and the revelations in the book, Tricia was relieved that William Sweeney's work would be stashed away in the sterile, safe archives of a university. Academics could pursue their theories while she absorbed the reality.

She wanted the boathouse for herself for the rest of the summer; well, her and Raj when he had time to get away from his work in New Haven. She felt confident that they were serving her father's literary legacy in the best manner possible. The personal legacy was another story. "Working on my own timeline," Tricia responded when Raj would check in with her emotional state.

The sisters decided to leave most of the furniture in the main house in place until the house went on the market in a month or so. Not that any of it was any good, but they needed somewhere to sit. Their realtor Nan Miller was practically begging them to put it on in August because, as she said, "Young families want to be in place before school starts in September." But the sisters knew it wouldn't be a young couple with noisy children moving into the house. It would be a developer buying up the place and tearing it down to build a Twenty-first Century Rich Guy Compound. Maggie and Tricia tried not to talk about it and Liza couldn't even think about it.

Tricia had moved most of her things, including her laptop with dual monitors, into the boathouse so she could work in private. There were details about the estate that she wanted to deal with on her own before informing her sisters. The boathouse offered her the space she needed, both physically and emotionally. Without the clutter of her father's books and ephemera, the main floor was bright and open, bigger than her Manhattan apartment. *I'd paint it a pale blue if I stayed here,* Tricia thought.

There was a knock, immediately followed by Maggie bursting through the door. "You'll never guess what I found in the attic. In that old chest where I found Mom's skirt. I hadn't gone through all the drawers, but look! Mom's notebooks! Six of them. Filled with poems!" She held up notebooks triumphantly. "Tim and I started emptying the attic and there was the chest with a few classic Laura Ashley sundresses and her glorious poetry!"

"Let me see those." Tricia grabbed the aged black-and-white composition books out of Maggie's hands. She had to feel it, hold her mother's work in her hands. "I can't, I can't . . ." All the composure that Tricia had willed since the day she'd taken the call from Liza in the stairwell dissolved. She handed the notebooks back to Maggie and started sobbing.

"Trishie?" Maggie had never seen her sister like this. She had no idea what to do. "What's going on? Do you need water? Deep breathing?"

Tricia held up a finger. She needed a minute to collect herself. "In the last chapter of the memoir . . ." Another deep breath. ". . . Dad admits that he was jealous of Mom's talent, her gift. And resentful that she could write with such ease, without needing alcohol or angst. That she could sit down and write for hours on end and create little jewels, that's what he called her poems. 'Little jewels.' She gave him a folder of her favorite poems right before she died, asking him to get them published. But in *Snap,* he admits to getting really drunk and really angry. So angry, in fact, that he burned the poems instead."

"What a fucking child. He lit her poetry on fire instead of using his influence to publish it after her death?"

"He claims that's what triggered the depression. The guilt, not the grief. I can't believe you found Mom's poems, Maggie. She must have stashed her original notebooks in that chest and given Dad copies."

"We're all going to need a lot of therapy to unpack that. Group sessions."

"I know. This revelation has been doing a number on me since I read it. I was terrified to tell you both."

"It would have pushed Liza right over the edge," Maggie agreed. "I always thought Mom had stopped writing, but she hadn't. She kept writing and we never gave her credit."

Tricia shook her head. "Why would he do it? Did he think burning the poems made him look like some kind of literary badass?"

Maggie knew. It was the same sort of professional jealousy that had engulfed her in the past. She'd bad-mouthed other artists, acted blasé when she'd really been blown away by someone else's work. Once in college, she hid the piece of another student, not destroying it, but making sure it wasn't on the wall next to hers in a show. It was found weeks later in a closet in the English department. She could understand wanting to burn the competition, to literally light another's work on fire. Maggie did her best work on that edge and she guessed her father did, too. But she didn't say any of that to her sister, who had played by the rules for her entire life. "You know Dad, he liked the grand gesture. For all we know, he thought it would make a great short story one day. Or he was just really hammered. After Mom died, that was a bad period. For all of us."

"This is a miracle, Maggie! I feel like I can breathe again," Tricia admitted while paging through one of the notebooks. "But I still think we're going to need the group therapy."

"I don't think you should tell Liza. You know how she worships him despite everything."

"I know. I'm deleting that section from the memoir before turning it over to Allegory. I don't care if it compromises the integrity of the work. What he did, it's fucked up. And Liza can never know."

"Make sure Serena knows that Liza can never know."

"I will," Tricia said, thinking about how Serena would appreciate the need for discretion. And maybe a tiny bit honored to be taken into the Sweeney circle of confidence. "Cap will be so relieved. He felt worse than I did, I think. And I felt awful."

"He always had a thing for Mom. In his way," Maggie said, picking up one of the notebooks. "Can I keep these? I'll make copies for everyone. But I feel like I owe something to Mom, to make up for not understanding her. There may be something in these poems I can use. Plus, I found them."

Maggie resorting to the "finders keepers" legal argument made Tricia smile. "How about we not turn these over to Copies R Us like *Snap*? When Raj returns, he can scan them properly for posterity. You can have them after, okay? These are special."

Tricia rubbed her hands gently over the cover of one of the notebooks. It triggered a memory of her mother during the last year of her life, sitting in bed, writing in these familiar black-and-white notebooks, a rose-colored pashmina around her thin shoulders. Why hadn't any of them recalled that detail about their mother? "Remember the day Dad died and I said that I wished we could all have one more conversation with him? Well, here's the conversation we all deserved to have with him: 'What the hell, Dad?'"

"Amen to that."

"I need to sit a second and read some of this. Like Stop, Drop, and Read," Maggie said, recalling the game they used to play as children with their mother on rainy days. In the middle of picking up the house or a fight between the sisters, Maeve would call out, "Stop, drop, and read." The sisters would scramble to find the nearest book or magazine and for the next ten minutes, the house would be quiet.

Moving toward the little galley kitchen that she had recently stocked, Tricia said, "A little tea with your poetry?"

"Oh, yes."

Tricia opened the cabinet and took out two of the college mugs, Oberlin and Evergreen, and placed them on a tray she'd swiped from the main house. She dropped in apple cinnamon tea bags and poured over the hot water. While the tea steeped, she fixed a plate of gingersnaps. She carried the full tray over to the couch and set it down on the well-worn pine table. *I'd get all new furniture, too,* she thought. *Clean, classic.* The two sisters took opposite sides of the couch, each opening a notebook to read the words their mother had written years ago, but now with a deeper sense of compassion, like maybe this was the way the story was meant to unfold after all.

LIZA HAD LITERALLY spent the week in bed after her breakdown at the gallery. She'd sent all who witnessed her collapse a dozen texts, explaining her exhaustion, thanking them for their support. The group texted back dozens of kissy face emojis in a show of solidarity. Individually, they reached out with more personal notes. Kat Ryan dropped by several times to talk and bring gazpacho from her garden tomatoes. Connor the architect returned to the city for the workweek, but David the shoe designer stayed in Southport and played the role of support staff, cooking, fetching tea, and watching Netflix while Liza physically recovered her strength. "*Sweet Home Alabama* is healing," David insisted, as he fixed Liza a plate of scones and berries.

The pamphlet from the funeral home had mentioned that exhaustion was a side effect of grief, but Liza had no idea it would be this overwhelming, the kind of tired she experienced when she was pregnant with the twins. Like can't-keep-your-eyes-open tired. She was grateful that Emily and Jenny from the gallery could handle the follow-up to the opening like pros. *I'll give them a bonus at the end of the summer,* Liza thought.

The word about Liza and Whit had started to trickle out and the texts came pinging in. Her old Southport friends, the mothers from school and sports, even her hairdresser voiced support and offered help. Liza felt like she'd been in a blackout for the last six weeks since her father's death and the supportive messages reminded her that she was, in Lucy Winthrop's words, "an asset to the community." Liza knew the next year would be one of tremendous transition. For her, for the twins, for the relationships in her life that were Whit-dependent, like with her mother-in-law. Soon, her sisters would be gone, returned to their daily lives in different cities and towns, the contact reduced to texts and calls and the occasional weekend visit. Even Serena would return to DC and resume her career. When the summer ended, it would be this circle of support that she had cultivated over the years outside of her family that would get her up and get her going.

She returned every supportive text with a message that ended: I appreciate your discretion in this situation. The twins are still at camp for a few weeks. We'd like to tell them in person and not have them find out via stray conversation. Thank you.

If Liza had bottomed out last Saturday, she was feeling stronger by the following Friday. She called her mother-in-law to let her know that she'd be coming by next week to install the new painting that they'd bought at the opening. Lolly suggested she stay for lunch afterward so they could, as Lolly put it, "have a good talk about the future." Liza agreed. The two women were in sync. Then, Liza put in a call to Whit that she needed to talk to him as soon as possible.

Then her phone pinged again. It was Tricia and she was calling a family meeting. She needed to talk to her sisters.

THE THREE SWEENEY sisters sat on the patio looking out over the lawn, past the boathouse and the dock to the water. It was the first time since the death of their father that they wrestled with a long list of action items. For the most part, they'd completed what they needed to do: plan the wake, find the memoir, empty the house, and hold it together at all costs. The original list hadn't even included "deal with Serena," but they felt like, individually and collectively, they had done that, too. But that didn't mean there wasn't more to discuss. Tricia brought legal pads for all; hers was filled with notes. She distributed the pens to her sisters.

Liza and Maggie waited for Tricia to talk. It was her meeting, after all. The sisters understood their individual strengths and weaknesses and this seemed like a Tricia moment, as it pertained to legalities. Had it been about holiday planning or home renovation, that would have been Liza's. Maggie had never called a meeting but she was good at snacks and beverages. There was a basket of pretzels on the table and a fresh pitcher of iced tea provided by Maggie.

"I wanted to give you all a couple of updates and then get your thoughts on a few options in terms of the estate. Please feel free to ask questions at any time," said Tricia as she straightened her legal pad and pen to her standards.

Maggie and Liza knew better. In a million years, they would never interrupt Tricia when she was on a roll. She was not a believer in the adage "There are no bad questions." She absolutely believed there were bad questions. They knew to tread lightly. "I'll write mine down for later," Maggie said.

"Fine, here we go. In terms of *Snap*, I have read it in its entirety. It's well done. Dad told Cap that he had let it all hang out, and while that's not exactly true, he lets a lot of it hang out. Not only will it sell, there are sections of the book that will be excerpted and debated, everywhere from Reddit to *Vanity Fair* to academic journals.

"In terms of our portrayal, the material is difficult. Our father had some issues with being a father and the three of us get a pretty rough edit in the last chapter of the book. Serena gets a mention, but is not named. You don't have to read it, but you should be aware that it may have a ripple effect on your lives when the book comes out. More on that later. Cap and I turned the manuscript over to the publisher. We did a few minor edits that we felt were warranted, but other than that, this is the book our father wrote."

"Thank you, Tricia," Maggie said quickly, preempting Liza from asking about what was in the edited passages. "I'm sure your judgment was impeccable." Maggie would have skipped over the edits altogether, had she been in her sister's place, but not Tricia. She couldn't quite bring herself to outright lie.

"Are you ready to move on?" Liza and Maggie nodded. "We fired Lois."

"Yes! Farewell, Sad Hat Lady!" Maggie cheered.

"We terminated Lois's agreement, but first, we had to threaten a lawsuit. Turns out, Sad Hat Lady been skimming a substantial percentage of Dad's royalties over the last five years. Instead of her fifteen percent, she was taking more than thirty percent. It's why the revenue had dropped sharply. She caved immediately when we brought her the evidence we had collected. She's on a payment plan to reimburse us the money, but I don't know if that will ever happen. Apparently, Maggie, she did have a secret life. As a terrible agent. Dad was one of her few clients left and she needed to milk him for all she could to pay for the apartment and the country house and the plastic surgery."

"That's awful, but I knew it! See, sixth sense. So how much are we talking about? I mean, not to be greedy, but what can we expect?"

"Split three ways minus taxes, legal fees, and Frannie's cut, I would say enough to pay an annual mortgage on a modest house in lesser Litchfield County, if you wanted to consider buying a place near Mill River. At least for the next five years or so until they change the curriculums of high school and college-level literature classes."

"Oh my God. I could get a place with a yoga studio."

"Tricia said a modest house, Mags," Liza reminded her.

"Cap and I will handle anything that needs to be handled from here on out. Cap will be the literary executor making decisions about the IP and any future deals with regards to Dad's work. I'll assist him on the legal side. It's a cozy relationship, but you know we have Dad's best interests at heart. Any questions on that?"

Liza and Maggie shook their heads. Both were relieved that Tricia was so on top of matters like this. Liza couldn't possibly manage one more legal strategy and Maggie wouldn't even know where to start.

"To that end, I've been doing a little lawyering this week in my free time. I called a classmate from law school, Chip Darnell, who's an agent now at a boutique firm in LA, and had a long talk about possible interest in terms of film and TV rights. He assured me there would be some from producers and actors and to strike while the iron was hot."

"Is that a euphemism for 'famous author recently dead?'" Maggie asked.

"Yes, you could say that. Upon my request, Chip called around to various production companies about the memoir and, really, any other property that belongs to William Sweeney, from articles to *Bitter Fruit*. Nothing is set yet, but the response was good. You know how Dad always swore he would never 'go Hollywood,' but Cap said he'd had a change of heart recently. He'd asked Cap to look around for somebody to make his life story."

"Was Cap telling the truth or paving the way for us so we didn't feel guilty?" Liza knew what was up.

"A little of both. A caveat—there aren't zillions to be made in this, but something. And the works get to live and breathe again. Plus, it's Leo who's interested in the memoir."

"Leonardo DiCaprio? As our dad?" Maggie was ecstatic.

"Maybe as an actor, but definitely as a producer. He has an advanced copy now."

Liza was more skeptical. "I'm fine with most of this, but I don't ever want to see *My Maeve* as a six-episode series starring Jessica Chastain as Mom, even though I love Jessica Chastain. That whole book was Dad writing his way out of the guilt he was feeling over the way he treated Mom with a glamorized version of his spousal devotion. I couldn't stand to see that myth portrayed on screen. Not now."

"Fair enough," Tricia said, jotting down notes on her legal pad.

"If we get stipulations, I stipulate that Darren never gets to direct anything associated with Dad. I couldn't stand that, either. Imagine him on the press tour talking about our relationship. It would be a nightmare." Liza and Tricia were both pretty sure that Maggie would actually enjoy the drama of her former boyfriend talking about her to the national press, but they said nothing.

"So noted."

"How did you do all this?"

"Cap. People have been calling Cap for years with offers, queries about the rights. He kept a list for when, he said, the time was right. Now is that time. Allegory said the memoir may be as soon as December. They're going to crash the book." The sisters knew enough about publishing to know that "crash" meant to rush the process for the soonest publication date. *My Maeve* had been a crash. "So, my question is, are you comfortable with me moving on these sorts of revenue streams? Any objections, other than the ones you've stated? And speak frankly, we don't want this to be an issue going forward, and we all have an equal stake in this."

"How bad is the book? I mean, about us?" Liza asked.

"Yeah. CliffsNotes version," Maggie added.

"It's one bad paragraph."

"Go on . . ."

"In a nutshell," Tricia started, then hesitated. ". . . I'm a frigid control freak. Maggie, you're an undisciplined dilettante, and Liza, you were a hussy but now you're too uptight to party."

And the moment Tricia said the words out loud, the sisters started howling. It was like a spell was broken. Then Maggie said, "As if we didn't know that! Nailed it!"

"Did he say anything nice about us?"

"He thought we all had really good hair. He wheeled out that St. Patrick's Day Parade story and made it all about himself, of course. He had disappointed himself by getting swept up in the buoyant atmosphere of New York. I think that's the word he used, *buoyant*, instead of public drunkenness run amok. And he claimed if he had dragged us down Madison Avenue to Grand Central instead of Mom that we would have made it in good spirits. It would have been the adventure of a lifetime and he deprived us of that to satisfy his own *thirsts*—that was the word he used to describe his desires. That kind of bullshit. But he did mention how our hair shone in the harsh spring sunlight."

"Ironically, we got our hair from Mom," Maggie said.

"Given that we will have to live with the consequences of the book, I say we sell out. Do we get to fly to the coast and meet with Leo?" Liza asked.

"Please don't talk like that," Maggie advised. Her five years in Los Angeles might actually prove to be useful. "You know who I'd be interested in meeting with? Any member of the *Buffy* cast."

"Or Alexander Skarsgård."

The sisters were slightly giddy. Tricia, true to form, brought the dose of reality. "I think we should be aware that these things can take time and we may only make significant money if something goes into production. Residual books sales would also benefit the estate. We're seeing that already. Since Dad died, his sales have spiked. He would have liked that. But yes, we should totally meet with Alexander Skarsgård."

"Do you think Dad would be mad at us?" Liza asked, still seeking to please.

"No. I don't. I feel like it's a trade-off for this memoir and a way for us to come to terms with a few legacy issues. And, if we're involved in some way, we can use our judgment on who would best serve the material and we can always bail. Change our minds. I think that Dad's work may get pushed to the side unless we make him relevant again."

"Listen to you, 'best serve the material.' Is that what your friend, the agent, said?" Maggie asked.

"Yes, I am quoting. Honestly, I think that's why Dad wrote the memoir he did. It's sexy, it's honest, it's new material, and it's meant to be provocative. And then he specified that it not be released until after his death. He wanted to stay in the public eye even after he was gone. Movies, film, television—that's one way to keep William Sweeney up front and center, where he liked to march. I think we'll be honoring his wishes, in a weird way."

"We trust you, Tricia," Liza said. "Are you sure you want to take this on? I don't know anything about these kinds of deals and I know the next year for me will be rough."

"I'm more than willing to do it. I feel like it's my duty."

"I can help if you need me," Maggie said. Tricia and Liza looked at each other, trying to hide their bemusement over what "help" from Maggie might look like in negotiating film rights. She caught them biting their tongues. "Again, I'm the only one who's actually lived in Hollywood."

"Thanks. That's a good point, Maggie. If we need juice bar recommendations, you're our first call."

"Very funny. Hilarious," Maggie said, not amused.

"Seriously, though, when it's appropriate, I will go through all the options with both of you. I want you both to feel comfortable with the decisions we make. The worst thing in the world would be to get into one sister suing another. Let's try to stay on the same page on this."

"Could I sue you for money?" Maggie asked.

"No. For control. Which has no monetary value unless exercised correctly," Tricia answered.

"Forget it, then."

"Okay, there's one more big agenda item," Tricia said, then pulled out her phone to send a quick text. "Serena has some news she wants to share."

"Oh, can I go first? I've been thinking about the real estate piece of all this," Liza announced, surprising her sisters.

"Are you going to turn your house into a B and B so you can instruct different people every week on how to use the shower?" Maggie said while Tricia snorted.

"Stop it."

"You deserve that."

"I don't want to sell Willow Lane. I want to sell my house and move into Willow Lane," Liza said, confidently.

"Really?" Maggie and Tricia said at the same time. They were shocked. Liza's house was perfect in every way, historic and updated, a showplace. "Are you sure?"

"I can't stand to think about this place being torn down for some ginormous faux mansion with a screening room and heated toilet seats. I can't let that happen. Not because of Dad, more because of Mom. She made this a happy place for us and now we know how difficult that task truly was. This place is special. Look around. I know you and Cap said we shouldn't get emotional, that this is our prime asset. But I can't let this go."

"Now that we turned in the manuscript, some of the financial pressure is off us. It's still a lot to take on, Liza. And I thought you loved your house on Westway?"

"I loved what that house represented. How much is that worth now? I spoke to Whit yesterday. With the permission of my attorney, so don't freak out, Tricia. We're starting to move toward a dissolution of our marriage and dividing the assets. Whit admitted that he had no intention of coming back to Southport permanently, but he was too chickenshit to tell his own parents. So he told a few friends figuring it would leak out, and it did. The trial separation was a ruse to buy himself time. He was hoping his mother would find out by rumor. This was all about saving face with his mother, not about me and the kids. He was more concerned about his mother's feelings than mine—which says it all, doesn't it?"

"I didn't think that of Whit," Tricia said, shaking her head.

"Me, either. But his guilt may come in handy. My lawyer is ready to pounce to capitalize on that for the settlement in terms. Whit seemed relieved that I wanted to sell the big house. And, when I told him that I didn't want the kids to go to prep school, that I wanted them to be closer to home in high school so they wouldn't turn to self-medicating by abusing ADHD drugs or cutting to deal with the turmoil of their parents' divorce, he agreed. Mr. St. Paul's even said he would entertain the idea of the kids going to Fairfield High School. Public school!"

"Sounds like Whit wants to lower his expenses now that he's on the hook for two households," Tricia said, more cynical about the new populist Whit than Liza.

"I need to talk to Vivi and Fitz, of course. But I think they would love living here. It would be an adventure. And, I'm going to try to be more relaxed about everything. Maybe I'll even let them eat on the couches in my presence. I don't know how a deal would be structured, but I can buy you out of your shares, not both at once, but over time. And I'll have to work something out with Serena, too. Maybe you can help me structure a deal, Trish."

"That brings up some very interesting opportunities, for us and Serena. I'll think that through. But you don't have to buy me out of my share," Tricia said. "I've been thinking about the boathouse, about how much I'd like a little place like that out here. And how impossible that would be to find—a small, cozy place on the water with a dock and beach access under a million dollars. I'll stay in as co-owner, if I can have the boathouse. Does that sound reasonable?"

"That would be great. I would love to have you here more. Is this permanent? Or weekends only?"

"Weekends after Labor Day. I mean, I have to go back to work at some point. But, you know, it's a good halfway spot between Manhattan and New Haven." Tricia looked at Maggie, who was squealing like a tenth grader. "Do not make those noises."

"It would be great for me and the twins," Liza said. "Plus, that might leave me some money to do a little renovation, not much! Update the bathrooms, paint. I'm not spending one dime in the kitchen." Tricia and Maggie didn't buy that last line at all.

"Okay, well, I'm going to take the money," Maggie announced to no one's surprise. "As long as I can still use a guest room."

The sisters discussed the necessary steps—an appraisal, determining the debt load, assessing equity, buying out Maggie's interest—which prompted Maggie to add, "I don't know what any of those words mean. All I ask is that you don't swindle me."

"Hello, all." It was Serena, pushing through the screen door. She was in a short dress and sandals, her long legs tanned. Her movements were comfortable, confident, a world away from her body language at the first meeting in Cap's office. She had a bottle of wine in her hands and she'd grabbed four glasses from the bar area. "How's everybody?"

"Were you hiding in the kitchen or something? How did you get here so fast?"

"I was waiting in my car for Tricia's text. It's a quick drive over."

Liza looked between Tricia and Serena. "We're going to have to watch you two."

"Wait until you hear Serena's news," Tricia said, then turning to Serena, she teased, "And, we have a proposition for you."

Serena twisted off the cap and poured the wine into the four glasses. Each sister took one and they raised their glasses to a toast. Maggie found the right words. "To us."

THANKSGIVING
Four Months Later

Liza was up early, because she wanted to get a few tasks done before her guests arrived at Willow Lane. In years past, her goal would have been to accomplish nearly one hundred percent of the to-do list prior to the turkey coming out of the oven, so that her family could be both impressed and a little bit demoralized by her style and efficiency. This year, everything about Thanksgiving felt different. The setting, the food, the dress code, and the collection of faces around the table.

Thanksgiving 2.0 was what Liza had been calling it in her emails to guests, not nearly as detailed or demanding as in years past. *This Thanksgiving is the start of new traditions,* Liza thought, *but it's still Thanksgiving. I'm not letting the whole operation sink to paper napkins and takeout turkey from Whole Foods.*

Vivi and Fitz were still asleep upstairs, or at least in their rooms under the covers, scrolling through social media on their phones. After Liza and Whit told the twins about the split, they took them to the Apple store so they could each get new phones. It was an emotionally cheap way to soften the blow that their parents were divorcing, but Liza had come to accept that a certain percentage of modern parenting was transactional. She felt like she'd done a pretty fine job with the nontransactional portion of the fallout. She had really been there for Vivi and Fitz in a way she wasn't before. Not having a husband or a father to care for had freed up Liza's time and her mind. Not that single parenthood was a picnic, but she thought back to Whit's accusation about her nonstop worrying for fifteen years. She had expended enormous energy caring for other people and shaping other people's perceptions. Since moving to Willow Lane, she limited her care to Vivi, Fitz, and herself. The "other people" in her life could manage themselves.

Now, there was more cooking in the house, more hanging out in the kitchen with the kids, more Monopoly after dinner, and less of the "resume-building" activities that had clogged their family schedule in the past. Signs of rebellion had popped up lately. Vivi announced she was a vegan, which Liza thought of as the most palatable form of self-harm, and Fitz made it clear that getting him a car at sixteen would go a long way toward making up for the divorce. Liza and Whit agreed. Fitz's math grades had dipped and Vivi was making a half-effort in Spanish, but instead of rushing in with high-priced tutors, Liza left the extra help to the study center at school. One mother expressed concern that Liza's kids weren't attending PSAT prep class on Saturday mornings like the rest of the class, telling Liza, "Those tests don't take themselves. I hope Vivi and Fitz don't get shut out of the top-tier prep schools. Or colleges. No one wants to pay that money for second tier."

Liza thought of Vivi and Fitz, who'd been schooled by their grandfather during those afternoon sails on how to read carefully and connect the dots between literature and life, how to tell a story with a beginning, middle, and punchline. Liza said, "I know my children will be fine, no matter where they end up."

The house on Westway sold quickly in a bidding war. Her agent had priced the house well to attract multiple offers. The new owners, transplants from Southern California, even offered to buy the furniture and artwork, explaining, "All our mid-century modern furniture is wrong for this part of the world." It made the move seamless and less sad somehow, like a new family would be stepping in to inhabit the house that Liza had worked so hard to make a home.

Liza positioned the move to Willow Lane as an adventure and Vivi, in particular, had loved picking out the paint colors for her new room, tagging along with her to buy a few fill-in furnishings, picking out cheap fun lamps for the dining room. Liza told Vivi all about Maeve's "shabby and chic before Shabby Chic was chic" aesthetic and Vivi embraced the idea of the grandmother she'd never met. One day, when Lolly, who in fact had chosen Liza and the twins in the divorce over her own son with whom she was "tremendously disappointed," came by to drop off apple butter and muffins, Liza heard Vivi tell her, "My grandmother Maeve had all these things called slipcovers. We're getting some for our couches."

Fitz was too busy growing to care about a lot more than his next meal. He'd hit his growth spurt, shooting up five inches over the summer, a sprint so fast he had stretch marks on his back. He was eating four to five meals a day and resisting showers, but Liza tried to give him space. He missed his father, for sure, and she knew repercussions might come along down the line, but for now, she tried Big Love over Big Worry. Her personal mantra had become "Stop Nagging." She felt like the bulk of her conversation with her children for the last ten years was nagging about doing homework, getting to tutoring or dance class on time, and clearing their dishes. She wanted to get away from the all-nag, all-the-time lifestyle; at least, that's what her therapist suggested. It killed her to keep quiet, but Liza was trying. So far, Vivi and Fitz were coping.

It helped that Julia Ruiz had returned to Willow Lane, working three days a week to keep the family on track and keep an eye on the twins while Liza was at the gallery. She had never really wanted to find another employment situation—too much effort to get to know a whole new household, a whole new set of "crazy white people," as she told her own sons. She was happy to be back with the Sweeneys.

Her presence was like a weighted blanket to Liza, calming and stress-reducing. Lolly had picked up Julia's extra two days during the week, even though there was rarely a pillow out of place at her home. She felt like it was the least she could do to make up for her son's behavior. For her part, Julia enjoyed spending quiet afternoons at Miss Lolly's ironing sheets and napkins or running to Stop & Shop for skim milk.

Whit was flying back home two weekends a month. Before Liza and the kids moved to Willow Lane, he was staying in the guest room at the house on Westway, the two adults interacting with extreme accommodation, putting their best faces forward for family and friends. Liza wanted nothing more than a good divorce, but she knew normalized relations with Whit would have to wait until after the papers were signed, as they were still negotiating the custody agreement. She spent most of the weekends working at the gallery while Whit shuttled the children to sports or dance or birthday parties. But when Liza and the kids moved to Willow Lane, a smaller house where Whit had never felt comfortable, he rented a modest condo nearby instead of occupying the guest room. The kids had no interest in ever sleeping at the condo, but it saved Whit from having to bunk in with his parents.

Liza finished setting the table in the dining room. Her one indulgence in the move to Willow Lane was a beautiful new extended dining room table in blackened oak that would seat twelve on the matching benches. She ran her hands along the smooth wood. She'd decorated it with a rustic flax-colored runner, replaced the polished silver of years past with everyday flatware, and the linen napkins were pumpkin, instead of traditional white. Lolly had dropped off several beautiful low arrangements of bittersweet in pewter vases and a bag of pressed and shellacked fall leaves for Liza to scatter on the table. The result pleased Liza.

She was about to set the place cards around the table when she stopped herself. Someone else could put the place cards around the table this year.

"HELLO, WE'RE HERE."

"You're early."

"Tim wanted to make sure the grill was all good to go and he had plenty of time to cook the turkey. You look gorgeous. What's happening with your hair? I like it." Maggie's arms were full of pie and cider but she gave Liza a hug. She handed Fitz the pie, saying, "This is my first attempt at apple pie from scratch. I'm counting on you to like it, Fitz."

"I will, Aunt Maggie. Can I have a piece now? I'm starving."

Maggie looked to Liza. To her surprise, Liza okayed the pie. "Sure, but don't eat the whole pie. Have some milk, too. That will hold you over."

"Vivi, I made this for you. I'm taking a jewelry-making workshop at the Arts Collective in Mill River. The teacher is this super-talented designer who moved to town from Brooklyn. Is this rubbish? Or would you wear it?" She handed her niece, who was a Liza Mini-Me in her skinny jeans and navy-blue V-neck sweater, a silver wire cuff bracelet with tiny tourmaline beads. It was small enough to fit on Vivi's slender wrists, but made a statement.

"I love it, Aunt Maggie. You could sell a million of these at my school art fair."

"That's because you have sophisticated friends who can afford semiprecious stones," Maggie said, looking at Liza. "So, she's staying at the fancy private school?"

"Probably, but no boarding school for either. Fitz wants outta there. He wants to go someplace with a, quote, real football team."

"So, Jesuit."

"If he gets in."

"Fitzy! Vivi! Come here, Bear. Where's Jack at?" Tim had taken to yelling upon arrival at Willow Lane. He'd become a favorite with the twins, somewhere between a cool older brother and the fun uncle. The dogs loved him. Even Liza had to admit to Maggie that Tim brightened every event, softening up some of the harsh edges of "right" and "proper" that had developed in the Sweeney family over the years. His commitment to grilling everything had expanded their holiday menu planning. This year, the bird was going on the grill. "Happy Thanksgiving, Liza." He gave her a quick hug and dropped a case of beer in the bar area. "I'll put that on ice in a bit. Okay, you guys, I need help unloading the truck and getting the grill going. Who's with me?" The twins, who on a normal day complained about pouring milk in their cereal, leapt up to help Tim.

Maggie waited for them to leave. "So, I saw the new table arrived in time for Thanksgiving. Was it a special delivery?"

"Stop it."

"Gray did a beautiful job."

"He did."

"And?"

"It's too soon for anything serious. And this town is too small."

"Still, you have seen him, right?"

"A couple of times."

"Am I correct in assuming that now you'll deign to sell housewares in your gallery?"

"Did he tell you about that?"

"Oh yeah." Maggie was enjoying the memory.

"Let's not relive your relationship with . . ." Liza paused, not sure how to describe the role Gray was playing in her life now. Once the summer ended and the kids were back in school, Liza found that her mind wandered to Gray every spare second. She wondered if it was because she was overwhelmed at the thought of starting over with someone new and he was close and familiar. But after running into him at the movies one night and going for coffee afterward, she knew it wasn't lack of imagination on her part that made Gray so attractive. It was him. He was full of energy: intellectual, physical, emotional. He could be there for her on every level now if that's what she wanted. She felt like she regained years of her life every time he wandered into the gallery at the end of the day or opened the door for her at his house. She felt adventurous, thrilled. "Let's call him Gray for now."

"Not your boyfriend?"

"In five years, when the twins will go to college, I can date. Whatever that means, in this day and age. But until then, I'd like to keep everything very low-key." Liza was holding Whit to a similar standard. She didn't want Savannah, his "work colleague," to start showing up when Whit had the kids over for vacation, heading off to the master bedroom at the end of the day. Liza thought that would be unpleasant for teenagers and she had to stick to the same standard herself. As her lawyer Michelle had insisted during negotiations, "No overnight guests in the mix until the twins are eighteen." While Whit seemed fine with that constraint, Liza was pretty sure Savannah, who looked to be about thirty-two from her LinkedIn profile, might not be so thrilled to wait as her biological clock ticked away.

"Five years! Why would you waste what you have left of your thirties?"

Liza thought about last Saturday night with Gray at his house. The twins were both at sleepovers, so she and Gray had twelve hours to themselves. She thought back to the attention he paid to every part of her body. *I am not wasting my thirties*, Liza thought. But, she knew part of the physical excitement came from the fact that their relationship was not for public consumption. The secrecy was intoxicating. "You're not getting any more details out of me."

"Is he coming today?"

"No, no. It will be a long while before we go public. If ever." Liza and Maggie made their way toward the kitchen. "Don't you think it's going to be weird enough today?"

"It's going to be smashing. We're creating the new normal. We're breaking the constructs of modern society and creating our own infrastructure of love and family," Maggie said, her voice layered with cynicism.

"I hope you're right—that our sociology experiment pays off."

"We have nothing to lose," Maggie declared, even though Tricia had warned them all that they definitely did have something to lose if this rollout didn't create the buzz they expected. "Oh, I brought the two commissions with me and the four 'guest bathroom' oils you wanted."

"Four! Ambitious. Those will sell this weekend. Seriously. I think of them as Southport Stocking Stuffers. Perfect Christmas gifts. You've been busy, Mags."

"And I brought some of the sketches I've been working on for the poetry project. You can take a look at them after dinner."

Maggie and Liza had hatched a plan to publish their mother's found poetry in a limited-edition book along with paintings created by Maggie. The poems were rooted in domestic life with references to simple objects like coffee cups and blow-dryers and plenty of commentary on mothers, sisters, and daughters. But the language was vivid, filled with imagery of color and natural elements like water and earth. Maggie was inspired. Liza was excited to oversee the project along with a high-end art press. It would be called *Willow Lane*. There would also be a less expensive version printed so that Maeve Sweeney's poems would be available to all. The proceeds would go to fund poetry workshops at local schools and a poet-in-residence program at the library.

Maggie wasn't too keen on the charity aspect at first, but Liza convinced her by explaining how the value of her original artwork would increase due to the book. Liza finished the guilt trip by adding, "It's what Mom would have wanted." Maggie agreed, even though charity was her least favorite activity.

Liza, checking her watch, started to move around the kitchen with purpose. Liza could only feign easy-breezy for so long. She had work to do. There would be time later to dive into Maggie's art. "I can't wait to see what you've brought. It's great to see you so happy and productive."

The sisters began to organize the kitchen in synchronicity. "I can't believe I'm saying this, but life has been good. I'm happy there in Mill River. I admit, I had a bad attitude in the beginning. But after being here this summer, as great as it was to spend so much time together, I needed someplace with less history, more possibility. And Tim and his brothers think they'll have the brewpub open by New Year's Eve. It's all coming together."

Tim's grandmother, the sausage queen of Western Connecticut and Southern Massachusetts, had died twenty years ago and created a trust fund for the four Yablonski brothers—now a banker, a lawyer, a contractor, and a cook/beer enthusiast. After two decades, the brothers gained access to the money and promptly bought an old grain storage facility in a historic district with all kinds of development incentives. Mill River Brewing Company was born, with Tim and older brother Teddy the contractor running the day-to-day operations. Tim was naming the IPA after Maggie. Mad Maggie IPA. There would be Tim's Taco Tuesday, of course. Liza commented when she heard the news, "I didn't know people named Yablonski had trust funds."

"Why is Tricia late? She's not working, is she?"

"No. She and Raj are running the Turkey Trot."

"Poor Raj." The annual 5K race had been going on for forty years in Southport, a Thanksgiving tradition. Tricia had reached the podium five times over the years in various age groups, starting at age twelve. She was in it to win it, not burn calories in order to eat more pie.

"I know. He has no idea."

Maggie made herself a cup of tea, like she had a thousand times. "Are you sad? First Thanksgiving without Dad?"

"Yes. The holiday makes me think of both of them, Mom and Dad." In the days when Maeve was healthy, Thanksgivings were epic affairs with family, friends, and grad students showing up with potluck items and touch-football aspirations. There was lots of wine, of course. After dinner, there was a talent show with everything from terrible magic to poetry recitals. It took all weekend to clean up the mess.

"Me, too." Maggie watched Liza move around the kitchen, the dated maple cabinets and brown countertops newly turned to white-on-white in what Liza referred to as "a touch-up, not a renovation." She pulled the serving dishes out and lined them up, ready to be filled with whatever side dishes arrived. Maggie would have waited until five minutes before dinner to organize serving platters, but not Liza. She needed to start paying more attention to the kinds of small details that Liza paid attention to. "So, guess what? I'm pregnant."

"VICTORY!" TRICIA CAME into the kitchen with her arms raised. Raj followed behind humming the Olympic fanfare. He was proud of his girl. "First place, Women Thirty to Thirty-eight. After a five-year drought, I'm back on top. It's good to be the youngest in a whole new age group."

"Is that the real reason you moved back here? To win the Turkey Trot?" Maggie asked.

"One hundred percent. Who needs to be a partner in a big New York law firm? I am a three-time Turkey Trot champion."

"I can confirm that she has been secretly training. I think my excellent pacesetting made a difference, at least for the first five hundred feet until she dropped me." Raj let the cat out of the bag and Tricia pretended to be mad. So far, the closest Tricia and Raj had come to a genuine row was a disagreement over the finest Dr. Who. They seemed to be in a couple bubble that disharmony couldn't penetrate.

Maybe it was because Tricia looked and felt like a different person than six months ago when she took the phone call from Liza in the stairwell of her office in Manhattan. After Labor Day, Tricia had gone back to Kingsley, Maxwell & Traub for two weeks and felt the joy drain out of her body, hour by hour. She was snapping at strangers, short with her sisters on the phone and her summer tan faded back into a color that could only be described as Midtown Mud. The moment Cap offered her the opportunity to replace him at Richardson & Blix, now Richardson, Sweeney & Blix, Tricia knew it was the right move. The money would be less and the high-profile clients would be fewer, although Cap had a few surprising boldface names amongst his clientele. It was the pace and the location that lured her back to Southport. She was unwilling to live a life in Manhattan without regular sailing, running, and, of course, Raj. She never would have guessed she'd be so satisfied at a small firm in her hometown, doing everything from wills and trusts to real estate law. The boathouse was the icing on the cake.

When Tricia took in the scene, two sisters at the kitchen table, it was clear something deep was happening. "Raj, do you want to see if Tim needs any help?"

"Ah, yes. My cue. See you anon," Raj said formally as he made a slight bow and exited through the new French doors Liza had added to the kitchen, to "open it up a bit." The view of the backyard to the water did, indeed, open up the space.

"What's up?"

As soon as Raj was out of earshot, Maggie announced, "I'm having a baby. With Tim."

"That's so great. I'm so happy for you both." Tricia gave Maggie a deep hug, then retracted. "Are you happy for you both?"

"Yes. Absolutely. It was planned! I planned this."

"Really?" Tricia had to ask because, as usual, Maggie's timing was backward.

"Yes, we did. After spending the summer here, I realized that it was time to create my own family. I liked being part of all this again. I'd been away for so long, I'd forgotten how special this could be. Being here when the twins came home from camp, fixing up the house for Liza. I liked being part of that and so did Tim. We're nervous, but we're happy, very happy."

August had been like family camp on Willow Lane. Once it was a done deal that Liza would be moving back to their childhood home, fix-up began. Tim was employed as a handyman/house painter/grill master working on small tasks like replacing the doors that had been stuck for twenty years and making various tacos a few nights a week for dinner. Maggie painted canvases and walls, both under Liza's encouragement. Tricia, still on sabbatical from her real job, went full press on finding a home for *Snap* in Hollywood and impressing Leo when he insisted on coming to see them, instead of vice versa, because he wanted to see where William Sweeney wrote. Serena came over most afternoons, after writing all day, to swim and have dinner. Lolly had taken to dropping by a few mornings a week to walk the dogs with Liza or play Scrabble with her grandchildren at the kitchen table.

The twins spent long days at the house, Liza having given up entirely on micromanaging their summer schedules. There were no mandatory tennis tournaments or math-refresher classes. They sailed with Tricia and did their summer reading with Serena, who downloaded audio versions of the books, much to the twins' delight. The three of them would listen as they played on the beach. Fitz hung out with Tim, learning to hammer a nail, use a level, and rewire a lamp. Vivi spent hours in the studio with Maggie, working on a collection of macramé plant holders that had a surprisingly sophisticated vibe. "I'm going to take a few of these for the gallery and we'll see how they sell," Liza said, alluding to her new interest in housewares. It had renewed the sisters' faith in family, maybe Maggie most of all.

Liza and Tricia did their job as sisters and asked all the right questions about her health ("No nausea, but tired and craving red meat"), how far along (nine weeks), and the sex of the baby ("Tim doesn't want to find out. He said it's like watching the last ten minutes of the movie first. I'm okay with that."). Then, Tricia asked, because she had to, "And can you still take your antidepressant safely?"

"Yes, and I will. I have a good therapist in Mill River and I'm eating well and not drinking. I'm back to yoga, which has been an important piece of my wellness plan. I feel good, all the way around. I want to be a good mother."

"You will be."

"Is Tim ready to be a father? He's young."

"He turned twenty-seven. Not that young. And he's from a big family with lots of nieces and nephews. He's ready." Maggie knew her sisters wanted some sort of explanation or assurance that Tim and the baby were all for the best. In the past, she might have dug in and defended her actions instead of explaining them. But the past year had changed Maggie. "Tim's very kind to me. He works with his hands. He's very physical. He takes care of what needs to be taken care of. I've spent my life with men who have complicated internal lives and no follow-through. That's not Tim. Not that he's not smart, but he's not wrapped up in analyzing everything all the time. It's a relief. It means I don't second-guess myself all the time."

"And his mother? Is she on board?" Liza asked because she understood the importance of getting the mother-in-law on the right side.

"Nancy Yablonski wants us to get married before the baby, which we're not so sure about. And she thinks I'm only thirty. But other than that, I'm pretty sure she likes me. She told me my artwork was 'very colorful.'" Air quotes employed.

"You know when Dad's book comes out, your true age will be revealed, right?"

"She has no idea who Dad is. She loves a Nora Roberts book and that's all right with me."

"*Are* you going to get married before the baby is born?" Liza had to ask, her mind racing ahead to how beautiful a small Christmas wedding could be at Willow Lane, a good distraction for her as the kids would be skiing in Vermont with their father.

"I'm not so sure. If we do, it will be a city hall quickie. Any party will be after the brewpub is open and the baby is born. Tim wants to have a big blowout there. Maybe over Fourth of July."

"That's one way to top last year's debacle."

"Make sure to invite Nina and Devon. Because they weren't traumatized enough by the big Serena reveal, followed by Cap's legal threats," Tricia said, thinking of the quiet academic couple who could barely look her in the eye when she ran into them in New Haven with Raj.

"Maybe we'll spare Nina and Devon, but we're definitely inviting Connor and David so they can pay for lobster."

"I'm happy for you," Tricia said without an ounce of jealousy and only slight concern, relieved that Maggie had used the buyout money from Willow Lane to put in an offer on a small house with a studio in Mill River. The deal would close after the first of the year. It needed work, but it was hers. Stability was the key for Maggie. And it would be for the baby.

"Me, too," Liza echoed, glad that Maggie would be on this side of the country as a new mother, so she could keep an eye on her and be the best auntie for the baby.

"Thank you. It's about time Vivi and Fitz have a cousin. You can get in the game," Maggie said, looking at Tricia. "We could be pregnant together."

"I wouldn't do that to you. You'd hate sharing a baby shower."

"That's true."

"If I can't give you a wedding, please let me give you a shower."

"Free gifts! Yes, I'll take one of those. Can we do it before I get huge? I mean, look at these things," Maggie said, pointing to her breasts. "If they are a harbinger of things to come, I may be in trouble."

"You look fantastic," Liza said, adding, "but my advice is to stay active and don't eat for two, eat for one and a half." It was the same piece of advice that Liza had given a dozen friends over the years when they asked her how she got back into shape so quickly after the twins. She thought it was a diplomatic way of saying, *Don't stuff your face for nine months.*

In the lull before the party prep whipped into high gear, the three sisters sat around the kitchen table. Liza was peeling potatoes, Maggie was flipping through *Traditional Home*, and Tricia was reading the *New York Times*. Tricia looked up from the paper. "Is everybody ready for Tuesday? Should we talk about that now or wait for Serena?"

"Let's wait for Serena." Liza stood up to toss the potatoes in the boiling water. She basted the backup turkey in the oven because she didn't trust the grilling method completely. She was willing to give in to the curried cauliflower that Raj was bringing and the vegan stuffing that Vivi insisted upon, but she wasn't fooling around with the bird. "She texted me this morning when she left DC. She's picking her parents up at LaGuardia at two. They should be here by three."

"You know what? You're totally right," Maggie said, referring to Liza's earlier comment. "This is going to be really weird. Now I'm sorry I can't drink."

"MAGGIE AND TIM are having a baby." Tricia stepped out of the shower as Raj stepped in. The boathouse bathroom left something to be desired in terms of size, but the water pressure was magnificent.

"Does Tim know?"

Tricia laughed. "Of course."

"Well, he only seems to care about his hops-to-wheat ratio and the new hard cider they pressed last week." Raj and Tim had formed a bond over the last few months that centered on beverages and a mutual love of the Bourne films. It seemed to be enough to sustain conversation for hours.

"I think he'll be a great dad."

"Yes. He will. And your sister will be fine, don't worry." Tricia didn't answer, so Raj asked, "Did you ever tell your sisters about your miscarriage?"

"No. I never found an opening that felt right this summer. And now, it's past time. I don't want to jinx Maggie. I'm okay."

"You're a champion. Remember that."

"Do you think your mother will like me?" Tricia blurted out, worried about their Christmas visit, her first time to meet the Chaudhrys. "Even though I'm not Indian?"

"Where did this come from?"

"Liza was talking about her mother-in-law and Maggie mentioned Tim's mother. It got me thinking about your mother."

"She will love you, even though you're not Indian. You did go to Yale and Yale Law. That will go a long way with her."

Tricia leaned into the streaming water and kissed Raj. "I'd like to have a baby someday."

"So would I. With you."

LIZA SNAPPED A photo of the table and typed a message to Gray: Next year, place for you? Then second-guessed herself, erased the message, and texted instead, Happy Thanksgiving. See you Saturday night.

She was in no rush.

MAGGIE FOUND TIM outside, stoking the charcoal, getting ready to put the twenty-pound spatchcocked turkey on the grill. Vivi and Fitz were bouncing on the new trampoline, their interest in grilling exhausted. Maggie pulled her purple cashmere wrap tighter around her shoulders. The temperature was dropping. It might snow like the news predicted. Maggie thought that she and Tim could stay at Willow Lane if they needed to. She had packed an extra bag for both of them just in case.

Tim drew Maggie toward him with his barbecue tongs and kissed her. "How'd it go?"

"I don't know why I was so worried. They couldn't have been more supportive," Maggie admitted. She'd expected Liza and Tricia to lecture, to go heavy on the reprisals and light on the acceptance. But they seemed to genuinely believe that Maggie could pull off motherhood. "I'm so relieved."

"I think it's me. I'm the glue holding this whole operation together." Tim used his tongs as a scepter, pointing to the house, the grill, Maggie's belly, which hadn't quite popped yet but would any day. He wrapped his arms around her. "Just think, next year at this time, little Sweeney Yablonski is going to be about the same size as this turkey."

Team Sweeney was assembled and ready to go by half past two. Liza, Maggie, and Tricia were dressed in what Liza called "casual harvest chic" and fortified for battle, thanks to several helpings of the classic pâté that Cap and Anders always brought to winter season gatherings at Willow Lane. Anders volunteered to do the wine service throughout the day, a job Liza normally assigned to Whit. Cap was ready to play peacemaker and buffer between guests should any tensions break out. Tim was on turkey duty and maintaining the fire in the living room. Raj was tasked with carving the backup turkey and providing entertaining bits of academic and literary trivia. Vivi and Fitz, briefed on the situation, which made them feel very grown-up, were prepared to read their "What I'm Thankful For" essays if conversation dried up.

"We're all going to be fine," Tricia told everyone for the tenth time that day as Serena's Range Rover pulled into the driveway. "We're all going to be fine."

LIZA OPENED THE front door and welcomed the Tucker family with her patented graciousness. "We're so glad you're here to celebrate with us. Please come in."

Mitch and Birdie Tucker were first through the door. Mitch looked exactly the same as he had in 1993, in a stiff blazer and with thinning hair, holding a bottle of French wine. Birdie was overdressed in a tweed suit and high heels, carrying a cheese plate with Brie and

Bremner wafers as a hostess gift. After spotting the Brie, Maggie and Tricia struggled not to make eye contact with each other. Serena followed her parents into the front hall, after she paused to give Liza a hug. "Here we are. And I brought my assigned decaf coffee!"

Liza took the Shaw's bag from Serena, then whispered in her ear, "If this starts to go south, don't worry. I have a lot of wine."

Serena had barely eaten on the drive up, drinking too much caffeine and worrying about this entire plan for most of the six hours on the road: the meeting of the two families; the publication of Serena's piece, "Elspeth's Daughter and Her Sisters," about her personal journey over the last year in *Vanity Fair* on Monday; the television appearance on *CBS This Morning* the next day with Liza, Maggie, and Tricia; and the blitz of publicity that would follow, thanks to the publication of *Snap* on the same day as their television appearance. By Wednesday, Serena Tucker would become Serena Sweeney in the minds of many people and she felt ready for that, thanks to the many hours she'd spent with her sisters over the past few months, and her therapist.

Serena and Tricia had worked out the response over the summer after the memoir had been found, read, and digested. As Tricia suspected, Serena wanted to tell her story to the world, of discovering that she was Not Parent Expected and everything that followed after that moment. Tricia encouraged her to not only write her story, but to tie it to the publication of *Snap*, so both the article and the book would benefit from the media attention, an idea that Serena would never have had the guts to suggest, though it had crossed her mind as well. Serena's literary agent had secured the magazine piece in *Vanity Fair*, as Lucy Winthrop had predicted, and would be fielding any subsequent book or film offers that Serena's piece might generate. Cap would carry on in his role as managing William Sweeney's intellectual property and news like this would fire up that market. As these pieces were falling into place, Serena and Tricia told Liza and Maggie about the strategy to present a united front, to support Serena, and, in turn, she would provide an alternative narrative about the sisters to the world, different than the one presented in *Snap*. It was Serena who had assured Liza, Maggie, and Tricia that she wasn't out to trash them. "I've come to value all of you."

The sisters agreed to cooperate with a candid portrait of themselves through Serena's eyes. "Let's get this out there publicly so we can move forward privately," Tricia said. Maggie wanted to know if they would be on the cover of the magazine and Liza insisted they mention the gallery in the article, adding, "We want our fifteen minutes to mean something." Serena had headed back to DC after Labor Day to write the piece, but promised Liza, Maggie, and Tricia they could read it first. "No hatchet job. I envisioned that this piece would be about searching for William Sweeney. But now, I think it will be about finding you all. I am going to have to take a hard look at Maggie's big Fourth of July announcement because that was not cool."

Serena agreed to trade her share of the house for limited use of their father's intellectual property in her work. She knew she wanted to use chunks of *Never Not Nothing* and *Snap* in her writing, which she now admitted was a memoir. Tricia knew if Serena had the rights to use the excerpts, the publication of her memoir would be more valuable, splashier. They worked out the deal on a cocktail napkin. One pink-hued summer afternoon on the patio of Willow Lane over a toast, the four sisters had taken their first steps forward together in unison.

The only hurdle left was Mitch and Birdie Tucker. Serena wanted her father's blessing. She knew she had to write about her childhood and her feelings of disconnect, the DNA test and its revelations, her failure to talk to her birth father before his death, and the subsequent building of the relationship with her sisters. Serena, the writer, needed to put the events of last year down on paper to make any sense of it, but she wanted to avoid dragging her father through her truth. Serena was less concerned about her mother. Frankly, she was certain that Birdie would enjoy the notoriety. It would set her slightly above and to the left of the other members of the Hobe Sound Beach & Tennis Club. For Birdie Tucker, that was her preferred perch.

She flew to Florida to talk with her father in person. To Serena's relief, her insurance-selling father, after a lifetime of high-level discretion with his clients and low-level deception from his wife, agreed to the entire plan, but with one caveat. He insisted that he and Birdie could reconnect with the Sweeney sisters and establish some kind of relationship before the media push began. "We want to get to know your sisters," Mitch said so plainly to Serena that it broke her heart.

Serena had approached Liza, Maggie, and Tricia with the request, apologizing in advance for any anger it might trigger. "I hate to even ask, and in no way do I want to be disrespectful to your mother, but it seems to be important to my father to meet you all and reach détente," Serena said one fall weekend in Southport when they gathered to do the photo shoot for the *Vanity Fair* piece. It was Maggie who answered for all the sisters when she threw up her hands and said, "What the hell? Why not?"

They all laughed.

"It's not a terrible idea," Tricia had said at the photo shoot, always thinking strategically before emotionally. "I know your parents have said that they'll do no interviews or make any statements, but your mother and father will be the subject of a lot of attention, whether they want it or not. I think it will go a long way if we can extend an olive branch."

And so it was that Birdie Tucker, the mom next door, the real Elspeth, and her understanding husband, Mitchell Tucker, model train collector, came to be standing in the front hall of Willow Lane to have Thanksgiving with the Sweeney sisters.

"What do you need me to do?" Serena asked as she entered the kitchen. After an hour of chitchat and crudités, the guests in the living room had settled into polite conversation verging on genuinely warm. Mitch found a kindred spirit in Anders, who also loved trains, and Cap, who focused on mutual friends and the latest news from the Yacht Club. Tricia and Raj organized the touch-football game, which included Tim, the twins, and both dogs in fresh bandanas. Liza passed hors d'oeuvres and continuously checked the oven to avoid getting stuck talking to the Tuckers for any length of time, thinking of Serena's parents as faux in-laws, the awful kind, not the stalwarts that Lolly and Whit Senior had become. Plus, Birdie would always be the calculating "slender cypher" from *Million Zillion* to Liza, even though she'd never admit that to Serena.

But Maggie, who found Birdie to be a worthy adversary, rose to the occasion by exaggerating her position as artist-in-residence in Mill River and describing Tim's brewpub like it was a Michelin-starred restaurant. "Bringing the Sweeney swagger," Maggie whispered to Liza on one of her sweeps with the vegan stuffed mushrooms.

Looking around the room watching her old family and her new family engage, Serena relaxed for the first time in months.

But now, it was go time. The fifteen minutes prior to sitting at the table together that could make or break Thanksgiving. No one could manage the clock like Liza. While she had tried "inclusion" as a theme this year, allowing guests to bring the random food they wanted to eat, she wasn't going to serve lukewarm mashed potatoes or underdone turkey to Birdie Tucker or anyone else. While Tim carved the grilled turkey and Raj carved the roasted turkey side by side in the dining room, Liza executed her serving plan.

In the kitchen, the three sisters were veterans of dozens of successful Thanksgivings together, where the side dishes made it to the table piping hot and the cranberry sauce was perfectly tart. Liza was pulling casserole dishes out of the oven and handing them off to Vivi and Fitz to run to the buffet table. Maggie, never one for taxing herself or diving into manual labor, was assigning the proper serving utensils to the dishes as they went out the door. Tricia was at the sink, loading up the dishwasher with first course plates and leftover pots and pans. She'd run the load during dinner then unload it after, so she could execute the same process again. She was a master dishwasher.

The three sisters moved with the kind of choreography that was the result of years of being in the kitchen together, putting out meals big and small. Serena stood in the middle of the organized bustle and asked again, "What do you need me to do?"

Liza, the general, was holding a baking dish of mashed sweet potatoes, hot out of the oven. She looked around the kitchen for a task for Serena. She spotted the shaved Brussels sprouts salad and pomegranate vinaigrette that Anders had contributed. "How are you at tossing salad?"

"Fairly competent," Serena said, not sure what the standards were in the Sweeney household.

"We've never served salad before at Thanksgiving. We've always been root vegetable people. So, new frontier for us. Can you handle that?"

Liza pointed Serena in the direction of the wooden salad bowl in the cabinet.

Maggie handed her the silver tongs.

And Tricia said, "Don't overdress it."

Serena was assembling the salad when Liza had another thought. "When you're done with that, can you put the place cards around the table? They're on the end of the buffet, next to the candlesticks. That can be your job from now on."

From now on. "Got it."

Acknowledgments

One of the great delights of writing this book was the opportunity to work with my editor, Rachel Kahan. I'm honored to be part of the William Morrow imprint and I appreciate the support of Gena Lanzi, Alivia Lopez, Jennifer Hart, and Tavia Kowalchuk.

More thanks and gratitude to my agent, Yfat Reiss Gendell, who provides equal parts encouragement and tough love. Her team at Foundry Literary + Media is topnotch.

Writing is a solitary business which is why you need all the help you can get to get it done. I'm lucky to have circles of support. Thank you to the following:

My writing teacher and top-tier reader Erika Mailman for her honesty and her enthusiasm and writer Allison Singh Gee for pep talks, coffee, and commentary. You both made a difference.

My Southport Squad, Lucinda Sill Morrison, and Sheila Lahey Duffy, for being old friends, early readers and advocates.

My legal team, aka, my sister-in-law Mary McGuire Dolan, Esq. and my niece Meghan Dolan Saporita, Esq. for their contract law advice and Fairfield County shopping knowledge, and my niece Katherine Dolan Nordenson for her encouragement. Also, Devon Palma of Campolo, Middleton & McCormick for her estate law expertise.

My fellow Roger Ludlow Flying Tigers and longtime friends, Alyssa Burger Isreal, and Elizabeth Csapo Greene, for driving me around Connecticut and for making the best playlists. My Tuesday Night Mahjong Crew of Robbie Ross Finnegan, Ryan Newman, and

Peggy Flynn who provided emotional support and snacks. My Satellite Sister and the original Sweeney sister, Sarah Sweeney, for loaning me her last name.

My first writing home, Prospect Park Books in Pasadena, especially Colleen Dunn Bates, publisher/friend/neighbor for a decade of support. Cheers to the women of PPB, including Patty O'Sullivan, Dorie Bailey, and Caitlin Ek. My spiritual home, Vroman's Bookstore in Pasadena, for being the best indie bookstore on the block. I'm grateful for booksellers like Allison Hill and the entire Vroman's staff. My writing retreat hosts, Writing Between The Vines, founder Marcy Gordon and the folks at Horse & Plow Vineyard in Sonoma County for providing solitude and wine at a critical time in the book's creation.

My bookish Satellite Sisterhood—the readers, the listeners, the book clubs, the service organizations and all the women who stopped me in the produce section of the grocery store to ask me when my next book was coming out—for keeping me at the keyboard.

My four sisters, three brothers and their families, I promise all the names have been changed. Remember, no free copies.

Finally, my husband, Berick Treidler, and my sons, Brookes and Colin. Thank you for everything. Every. Little. Thing.

About the author

About the book

Insights,
Interviews
& More . . .

Read on

Meet Lian Dolan

Brookes Treidler

LIAN DOLAN is a writer and podcaster. She is the host of *Satellite Sisters*, an award-winning podcast she created with her four real-life sisters. She is the author of two bestselling novels, *Helen of Pasadena* and *Elizabeth the First Wife*, and the coauthor of two collections of essays, *Satellite Sisters' UnCommon Senses* and *You're the Best: A Celebration of Friendship*. She has written columns for *O, The Oprah Magazine* and *Working Mother* and is currently a columnist for *Pasadena* magazine. A graduate of Pomona College, she lives in Pasadena, California, with her husband, two sons, and a big German shepherd. ⌒

Behind the Book

I am a professional sister. I didn't start out this way. In my early years, I was simply "the baby sister," as the youngest of eight children, the fifth of five Dolan girls. We grew up in a well-regulated Irish Catholic household in Connecticut where family dinners and daily mass during Lent were requirements. You learn a lot of invaluable life lessons growing up in a big family, mainly that you're not the center of the universe. In a big family, you're never alone, both literally and figuratively. There is always some sibling that has got your back or can provide cover if you go off track for a night—or a few years.

My career as a professional sister began twenty years ago, when my four sisters and I cocreated a radio show—now a podcast—called *Satellite Sisters*. Our tagline: *We have the same parents, but very different lives.* We wanted to represent the idea that women could have a full range of interests and emotions, could disagree with respect, and wrap the conversation in empathy and humor. From the very first show, we fielded questions about relationships between sisters. So many of the questions focused on sisters who didn't get along, sisters with issues, or, on the flip side, women who have always wanted a ▶

sister. People are fascinated, curious, and sometimes envious of the sister-relationship.

It was a simple post on our Satellite Sisters Facebook group that inspired my new book, *The Sweeney Sisters.* We have a closed group of thousands; people share all sorts of things, from recipes to graduation photos to thoughtful inquiries about how to handle a parent with dementia. One day, a listener posted a photo of herself, her brother, and her "new sister"—a woman in her fifties that she had just discovered through an over-the-counter DNA test. Of course, I 'liked' the post and wrote a cheery comment: *How great!*

But then I got to thinking, *Is it great?* Would it really be *great* if some random person just showed up one day and announced that she, too, was a Dolan sister? My sisters and I are a well-oiled machine. A sister showing up now would throw everything off—the birth order, the dynamics, who brings what to Thanksgiving. Not to mention the mandatory rethinking of everything you thought you knew about your parents, your past, and your place in the world.

The Sweeney Sisters was conceived to examine those questions of family, belonging, and, of course, sisterhood. I set the book in my hometown of Southport, Connecticut, a charming seaside village about an hour from Manhattan, where Yankee values of propriety and discretion still reign. Towns like Southport have picture-perfect historic homes from the outside, but inside, you'll find complicated relationships and truths that may be unflattering. Setting the book in Southport gave me a chance to revisit the places and events of my childhood, from readings at the Pequot Library to middle school dances at the yacht club to the dingy bar where every kid in town had their first legal drink (and for many locals, their last).

In *The Sweeney Sisters* there are secrets, scandals, and social satire, but ultimately the book is about sisterhood and what that looks like from the inside, both in terms of being a sister and having a sister. ❧

Reading Group Guide

1. Proper and socially graceful Liza, bohemian Maggie, razor-sharp corporate success story Tricia: which of Bill Sweeney's daughters do you most resemble? Do you have sisters—biological or otherwise—who fit into or defy those molds?

2. Early in the novel it's revealed that despite her lack of professional success and personal stability, Maggie "was the glue that held the whole family together." Does that ring true to you? By the end of the novel, has each sister contributed her own unique talents to holding the family together?

3. When Bill was alive, Maggie said: "Suppress and deny should be the family motto." She was talking about their father, but were the sisters also guilty of suppressing and denying things in their own lives?

4. Bill never spoke to Serena or revealed that he was her father because, according to his best friend, "seeing [her] as an adult, after having paid so little attention to her as a child, would remind

him of all the ways he had failed in his life. . . . Talking to her now would break his heart." Was that the right decision? What do you think Bill should have said to Serena if he'd had the courage to speak to her?

5. "None of the Sweeney sisters had the instinct to go all 'Dr. Phil' as Maggie called it, rushing to meet their long-lost sister in a tearful reunion." How would you have reacted?

6. Is *The Sweeney Sisters* a cautionary tale about taking DNA tests? Have you or someone you know had surprising results when they took one?

7. What did you make of the revelation that Bill had burned his wife Maeve's poems instead of having them published? How did you view Bill as a person at the start of the novel versus at the end of the novel, after there were so many revelations about his actions?

8. Liza says, "Could be a messy family tree isn't the worst thing in the world." Was learning the truth ultimately a positive experience for the Sweeneys? ▶

Reading Group Guide *(continued)*

9. What do you think becomes of each Sweeney sister in the years after this book ends? What do you think their lives will be like? ∽

Also by Lian Dolan

Elizabeth the First Wife by Lian Dolan
Published by Prospect Park Books
(May 2013)

Elizabeth Lancaster is completely content with her dull but perfectly orchestrated life. She's an English professor at Pasadena City College where she teaches Shakespeare through humor and passion to her classes. She's inherited a stunning Early California hacienda from her grandmother with a garden that brings her joy and a kitchen that has its quirks. Her life is practically complete.

So why does her family of accomplished academics and doctors keep telling her she needs a more prestigious job, upgraded countertops, and, most of all, a better man than her famous ex-husband, movie star FX Fahey? Elizabeth silences her family and surprises herself when she accepts a job at the Oregon Shakespeare Festival from none other than FX. She's imagining a magical summer in Ashland producing a cutting-edge version of *A Midsummer Night's Dream*, but summers can be filled with surprises.

The production doesn't go quite as planned, the director's undermining ▶

Also by Lian Dolan *(continued)*

her at every turn, and she can't seem to get the handsome house sitter she hired to look after her home out of her head. Over the course of a summer like no other, Elizabeth discovers that men can change, politics can be sexy, dogs rule, and she can learn a thing or two about modern relationships from William Shakespeare.

Praise for
Elizabeth the First Wife

"A charmingly funny and effortless read. . . . [A] wonderfully developed cast of characters."
—*Library Journal* (starred review)

"Whip-smart. . . . *Elizabeth the First Wife* tackles reinvention, love, and finding yourself—all with a delicious soupçon of Shakespeare."
—Caroline Leavitt, *New York Times* bestselling author of *Pictures of You*

"Brings humor and warmth to a contemporary story about a woman coping with family, career, and romance."
—*Tampa Bay Times*

"A joyous and delightful tale."
—Shelf Awareness

Helen of Pasadena by Lian Dolan
Published by Prospect Park Books
(October 2015)

Helen Fairchild is leading a seemingly
perfect life of privilege in sunny
Pasadena: she's married to a pillar
of the community, her son is a star
water-polo player destined for the most
prestigious high school, and she spends
her free time as a volunteer on the most
fashionable committees. The daughter
of Oregon fiber artists, she only rarely
misses her old existence as a struggling
Ph.D. student in ancient history, the
rigid rules of high society in Pasadena
appealing to Helen much more.

And then comes along a Rose Parade
float, destroying her world and killing
her two-timing husband. In a flash,
Helen is broke, forced out of her perfect
home, and scrambling to salvage her
enviable existence. Enter Dr. Patrick
O'Neill, noted archaeologist, excavator
of Troy, and wearer of adorable nubby
sweaters. A job as Dr. O'Neill's research
assistant is the lifeline Helen needs
to reinvent herself professionally,
personally, and romantically. Helen's
world widens to include a Hollywood
star, a local gossip columnist, an old
college nemesis, a high-powered benefit
chair, an unforgiving admissions
director, the best real estate agent in
the biz, and, of course, the intriguing ▶

Also by Lian Dolan (*continued*)

Patrick O'Neill. While uncovering secrets about ancient Troy alongside Dr. O'Neill, Helen discovers something much more: a new sense of self and a new love.

With its keen observations on society and whip-smart humor, *Helen of Pasadena* is the ultimate tale of reinvention.

Praise for
Helen of Pasadena

"A compelling narrative and a memorable cast."
—*Publishers Weekly*

"Lian is known for her humorous take on day-to-day issues facing women everywhere."
—Oprah.com

"A send-up of a fortysomething mom who finds herself suddenly widowed, broke, and forced to reinvent herself. . . . Opinionated, energetic, and sassy."
—Mandalit del Barco, NPR

"A knockout debut. It mixes up the classics and class structure in a deliciously witty romp."
—Caroline Leavitt, *New York Times* bestselling author of *Cruel Beautiful World* and *Pictures of You*

"Every reader will see something of herself in Dolan's likable heroine, Helen of Pasadena. Offering up every woman's worst fear, Dolan pulls the rug out from under Helen, and we get to watch as she recovers and reinvents herself with wit, charm, and smarts."
—Sally Bjornsen, author of
A Single Girl's Guide to Marrying a Man, His Kids, and His Ex-Wife ❧